The
BARBARIAN

The Herod Chronicles

Wanda Ann Thomas

The Barbarian

by
Wanda Ann Thomas

ISBN: 978-1503023758
ALL RIGHTS RESERVED
Cover Art by Dar Albert of Wicked Smart Designs
Formatting by Nina@NinaPierce.com

~ *Dedication* ~

For Darcy, Katie, and Michael
My pride, my joy, my heart

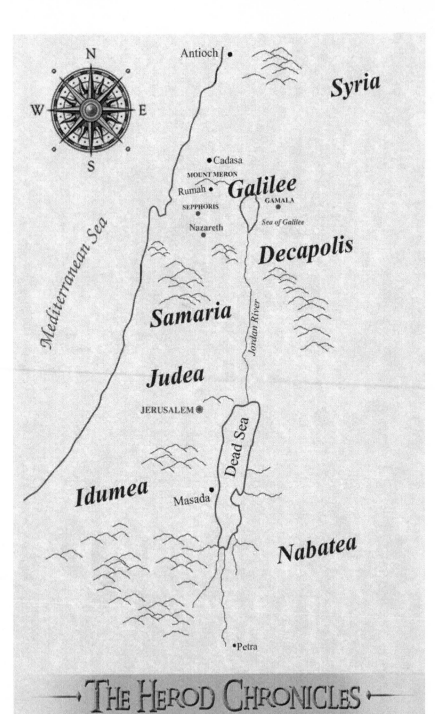

Jerusalem

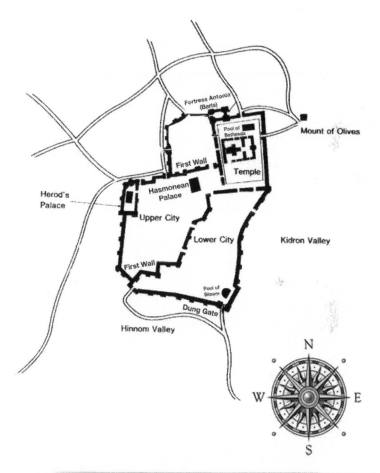

Fortress Antonia
(Baris)

Mount of Olives

Pool of
Bethesda

First Wall

Temple

Herod's
Palace

Hasmonean
Palace

Upper City

Kidron Valley

Lower City

First Wall

Pool of
Siloam

Dung Gate

Hinnom Valley

N

W   E

S

THE HEROD CHRONICLES

~ *Acknowledgements* ~

I'm fascinated by the longstanding, working relationship between writers and editors. No matter how talented the writer, they have always collaborated with an editor to enhance and improve the quality of the story they've created. Thank you to Faith Freewoman for helping me to put my best foot forward. My book is better for the time and talent Faith poured into it. It's been a pleasure and a privilege for this writer to work with a pro-of -an-editor.

I want to give special thanks to my critique partner Megan Macijauskas. Her beautiful writing and vivid voice are an inspiration. I'd be happy to write prose half as lovely as hers. My heroes are more heroic and my scenes are more vibrant because of Meg's keen eye for character and setting. What makes our partnership invaluable though, is our agreement to always be honest in our appraisals, to tell it like it is, both good and bad. Thank you, Meg, for pushing me to dig deeper, for challenging me to take my writing to the next level, for encouraging me not to settle for mediocre. I count our teaming up together one of the biggest steps forward on my exhilarating, frightening, unpredictable writing adventure.

Many thanks to Kimberly Budd for making suggestions for a specific type of wound I needed my hero to suffer and for lending her medical expertise on the blood and guts portion. I also want to thank Kim for her enthusiastic support and praise of the first book of the series. As a debut author it was very heartening to have someone love the story and characters as much as I did.

Warm thanks to beta-readers Marti Chabot and Wendy Thomas for pointing out typos, mistakes, and inconsistencies. My beautiful cover and cool maps were created by the talented Dar Albert of Wicked Smart Designs. Her incredible patience in the face of my indecision and second guessing myself was most welcomed. Thank you to Nina Pierce for formatting my book for digital and print and for her continuing guidance with my writing career. And hugs to Nina for generously sharing of her expertise, time, and talents whenever I e-mail or call to say "Help!".

Love and hugs to my wonderful husband and children for laughing with me, and encouraging me, and for making life beautiful. Bountifully blessed, I count you as the most precious gift of the many blessings the Lord God has graciously bestowed.

Chapter 1

Alexandria, Egypt - *47 BC*

Kadar the Northman grimaced as he wiped grit from his wind-chapped face. He stepped onto the first rung of a ladder he'd "borrowed" from a nearby construction site, touched his hand to the hammer-shaped amulet hanging around his neck, and stared up at Lydia Onias's bedchamber window.

Lydia Onias.

Six months ago he helped rescue the highborn Jewess from a band of religious zealots. He'd carried her out of the rebel camp, tended to her while they journeyed to her father's home, and lost a piece of his heart to her. He had assumed she'd quickly forget him, if she even remembered anything of those first days. If only he could have done the same. But thoughts of her had lingered, haunting his dreams and occupying too many of his waking hours.

Still, this breakneck journey from Egypt to Jerusalem to rescue her was pure foolishness. But it had been impossible to ignore her plea.

His hand went to the note tucked inside a worn leather pouch. She hadn't forgotten after all.

I have need of you. The words were burned into his mind. And not just because he'd taken the letter to a scribe and paid the man a great deal to read and reread every word until Kadar could repeat them in his sleep.

Greetings and peace to you, kind and gentle guardian. Though I have no right to ask anything of you, I must. I have need of you. I am desperate to escape my uncle's house and go into hiding. I can offer you no reward for your help. Know,

7

whether you come to Egypt or not, my thoughts toward you will always be kind. You have my grateful thanks for your goodness to me, Lydia Onias.

I have need of you. The declaration had sparked a glimmer of hope. Perhaps. Maybe. If the gods were merciful, Lydia would confess she wanted to be his woman, even though he was a pagan barbarian.

After arriving in the crowded, jostling city at midmorning, Kadar had first located Lydia's uncle's sprawling, two-story villa, guarded by a row of spindly palms. Then he scouted through the three large Jewish quarters, searching for escape routes and bribing a household slave to deliver a message to Lydia, telling her to expect him that night.

A loud crash came from nearby. He spun away from the ladder, pressed his back against the house's warm foundation stones, and peered down a long, narrow alley littered with empty crates, heaps of broken pottery, and other household refuse.

A gray and white striped cat emerged from the dark. Kadar stepped out of the shadows. The feral feline arched its back and hissed.

He chuckled, picked up a pebble, and tossed it onto the dirt at the cat's paws. "Off with you, feisty beast."

The tiger cat dashed for cover.

A cloud crossed in front of the moon. Sobering, Kadar scaled the rungs to a green-shuttered window. He knocked on the wood panel and held his breath. No response. Another rap, this one louder.

"Kadar?" a soft, steady voice asked. His heart thumped harder. Lydia's composure heartened him. She'd been silent, passive, and unresponsive after he rescued her from the zealots.

"It's Kadar. Open the shutter and step back, and I'll come to you."

"Be careful. It's a long drop to the floor."

If someone caught him sneaking into her room he'd have

more problems than a few broken bones. "Don't worry about me. I have experience getting in and out of tight spots." He crawled through the window and jumped down beside her.

Moonlight illuminated the sleek lines of her jaw and graceful neck. She leaned closer, sending her long, silky hair cascading over her shoulders. "You came. I hardly dared to hope."

"I'm glad you called on me."

She reached out and briefly touched his arm with a small, warm hand. "I'm sorry to ask so much of you."

She quickly stepped back and tucked the hair behind the delicate shell of her ear. She smelled of warm blankets and white jasmine. His chest tightened.

A baby's soft mew intruded, and Lydia hurried over to a narrow bed set against the opposite wall.

Kadar shook his head clear. Ah, yes, the baby. A child fathered by the insane leader of the rebel band, who had taken Lydia as his "wife" and subjected her to who knew what other evils. Kadar's hands fisted. He wished Judas the Zealot was alive so he could rip the fiend apart.

Lydia lit a small oil lamp. Light shimmered over her rose-dusted cheeks.

He'd feared she would never fully recover from the harsh ordeal, but everything about her spoke of health and strength. Her spirit wasn't broken—her brash bid to escape a distasteful arranged marriage proved her mettle.

Coins slipped into the hands of slaves from nearby homes had provided Kadar with the details. Lydia had given birth to a baby boy two months ago. Her heartless father planned to marry her to his brother, a potbellied father of eight, who already had a wife. Kadar hated the man, sight unseen.

Lydia picked up the child, still just a tiny bundle, cradled him against her chest, and crossed the room. Rocking the babe, she smiled. "Meet my son. I named him James, after my brother."

The baby calmed.

Kadar stroked his knuckle over the infant's soft cheek,

and chuckled when its tiny mouth puckered. "I hope the little fellow proves better-natured than your brother." Lydia's eyes and face lit with the most beautiful smile Kadar had ever seen. "James is a good baby."

His blood heated. He wanted to taste her mouth and run his hands over her luminous skin. Pregnant, mother, betrothed—it didn't matter—this woman turned him inside out.

But it wasn't why she had called him here. He backed away. "We need to leave."

"Take James while I change clothes."

He nearly choked. "I've never held a baby."

Lydia set the child in his arms. "Hold him as carefully as you would your woman."

He eyed the child warily, but it remained calm. "I don't have a woman."

"Why not? You are a strong, able man."

A heaviness filled him. The same dark weight that pulled at him every time he thought of his family, his people, and the Northland. He had cheated the gods, and escaped death, but at a painful cost. An outcast for close to two years now, he could never go home. "Soldiers who make their living as mercenaries don't marry."

"Why don't you take up another trade?"

"Me? I was born with a sword in my hand."

She laughed. "You'd think I'd asked you to kiss a crocodile."

Her lively openness came as a surprise. The few days he'd spent in her company, she had been so quiet, so reserved. Her fragile state had called out to him, impelled him to act as her protector. He understood at a soul-deep level how devastating and disorienting it was to be torn away from all you'd known. The strain could have easily have broken her. But the courage and determination in her eyes reminded him of the Northland maidens who rode to battle beside their men, fiercely and gloriously wielding their swords on behalf of their loved ones and their people. Here was a young goddess of a woman, one to make the gods and men beg. The heavens knew he'd kneel at her feet right now if she asked.

"Turn around while I change," Lydia said. Though not the request he'd hoped to hear, he obeyed.

The whisper of silk slipping over skin told him she'd slipped out of her gown. He glanced over his shoulder. Her straight brown hair danced over slim hips and skimmed her bare bottom. Her olive skin glowed invitingly. His loins tightened. She turned her head. Her large doe eyes widened. He arched a brow. She'd get no apology from him. He was a scoundrel. If she hadn't realized it before, she certainly did now.

The baby fussed. "Finish dressing," Kadar said, returning his attention to the small bundle in his arms. "Why are you desperate to escape the marriage your father arranged? Is your uncle as horrible and disagreeable as your father? "

A soft sigh accompanied the sound of rustling fabric. "No, Uncle is kind and gentle. It's my father. He plans to take baby James away from me, and send..." her voice quavered, "...and send him to Galilee."

Ah. Here was the reason a good Jewish girl was ready to throw in her lot with a godforsaken barbarian. Kadar swallowed his disappointment. "What does your father have against your son?"

Lydia returned to his side. Her dark eyes were sad. "Father doesn't want a bastard to bear the name Onias."

Born a bastard himself, Kadar understood the cruelty of such a fate. He patted the child's swaddling clothes. "Don't you worry, little fellow, I will care for you as if you were my firstborn." Outcasts needed to watch out for one another. The gods knew no one else cared about them. Except James had a mother willing to risk a multitude of dangers to keep him and care for him.

Lydia laid her hand lightly on his arm. "I talked myself out of seeking your help several times before sending the letter. I kept telling myself it was unfair to burden you with my problems. I considered many other possibilities, but my mind always came back to you."

The confession pleased him. "You honor me with your trust."

A burst of noise turned his blood cold. Feet pounded up the hallway, closing in on the bedchamber.

Kadar reached for his sword and almost dropped the baby. "Thundering Thor!"

Lydia grabbed James.

The bedchamber door slammed open.

Kadar drew his sword and stationed himself between Lydia and the child.

Chapter 2

Members of Father's bodyguard stormed into Lydia's bedchamber. Her heart beat double-time, and she couldn't hear anything past the roaring in her ears. "Go," she cried, pushing against Kadar, heartsick over drawing him into trouble.

All muscle and menace, Kadar raised his sword and widened his stance. "I'm not going anywhere."

Vicious oaths peppered the air as grim-faced soldiers fanned out in a wide circle around them, careful to keep their distance from Kadar's long, gleaming blade.

"Stay behind me," he said, his voice deep and heavily accented.

The room brightened. She took a deep breath and peeked around Kadar's broad back. Slaves stood on either side of the door, holding up torches. Father strolled over the threshold, his rich robe swirling about him. Haughty disdain showed on his pinched face. Her insides turned to ice.

She tightened her hold on baby James and tugged on Kadar's tunic. "Go," she begged, desperate to spare him her father's wrath. "There's nothing you can do for me now."

He shook his head. "I'm not leaving. Even if I was coward enough to attempt an escape, I wouldn't get far. I'd bet my last coin your father has men posted at the bottom of the ladder."

"But that would mean—" Father must have seen her letter before it was sent to Kadar or learned of the message saying he had arrived. Nausea threatened to choke her.

Father directed a smug smile at Kadar. "You aren't the halfwit you appear to be, Barbarian." He shook a finger at Kadar. "I gave you fair warning. I promised I'd repay you for your rough treatment of me."

Lydia's mind whirled. *The two men had clashed? But when? And over what?*

Kadar shrugged a shoulder. "I only regret I didn't give you a real beating before I tossed you off Nathan's farm."

Nathan was married to her sister, Alexandra. Lydia knew Nathan and Alexandra had a falling-out with Father some time ago, but hadn't known the details, only that Father was still terribly angry.

Lydia stepped around Kadar and looked up into eyes blue as a summer sky. Her grief redoubled. Asking him to come had been selfish and unfair. "Forgive me for involving you in my troubles."

The fierce lines of his warrior face softened. "It's not your fault. I made the mistake of underestimating your father."

"Cease groveling before that swine," Father commanded her. "Come kneel before me."

All the breathable air deserted the room. She turned to her father.

He pointed at his feet. "If you don't want this barbarian to be flogged, you will beg for my forgiveness."

Baby James fussed and nuzzled against her, his small mouth seeking sustenance. She willed her feet forward, prepared to submit to any punishment necessary to spare Kadar and her baby from harm. Dropping to her knees, she swallowed. "I am sorry I—"

"Speak up," Father demanded.

The guards snickered. She held her head high.

"Laugh again and I'll cut your tongues out," Kadar growled.

The men cursed and shifted in place.

"I apologize, Father." Lydia said hurriedly. "I meant no harm. Please release Kadar. I'm to blame. I was desperate to keep my baby."

Father nudged her with his foot. "You are a disgrace to my name."

Before she could open her mouth, Kadar was at her side.

The point of his sword hovered under Father's nose.

The guards yelled and swarmed around the giant.

Lydia grabbed the hem of Kadar's tunic. "Don't give them an excuse to hurt you."

"Drop your weapon, gentile," her father said. "Unless you want to make this more difficult for her than it's already going to be."

Kadar loosed a string of foreign curses, but sent his enormous sword sliding and clattering across the tile floor. "This is between you and me. Leave your daughter out—"

His words gave way to a sharp hiss, and a red drop plopped onto James's white swaddling clothes. Lydia gasped and jumped to her feet. The head guardsman twisted the tip of his sword into Kadar's muscled arm, and bright red blood streamed from the wound.

Heart pounding like torrential rain, she cradled James against her chest and pulled on the soldier's arm with all her might.

A guardsman shoved her back. She tripped on her hem and fell hard on her bottom, but was able to keep her arms safely wrapped around her tiny son. Frightened wide awake, James gave an ear-splitting wail.

Two soldiers dragged her to her feet. The one on her left snagged James's little foot instead of her elbow, almost tugging him out of her arms. She wanted to continue fighting on Kadar's behalf, but couldn't risk it.

Lungs heaving, she smoothed James's back and cast a sorrowful frown at Kadar. "Did the cut go deep?"

Kadar winked. "It's a small scratch...nothing to worry about."

Tears burned her eyes. Kadar was so brave. So honorable. They were practically strangers, yet he had shed blood in her defense and now attempted to soothe her.

"Bind him," Father said. A thick reed rope was brought forward and coiled tight around Kadar's bare wrists.

Kadar studied his bonds. "I hope you didn't go out of your way on my account."

Father laughed, and the cold sound raised bumps on

Lydia's arms. "I'm glad you appreciate the fetters, Barbarian, because you will go to your grave wearing them."

"Coward," Kadar spat back.

Lydia grabbed her father's sleeve. "You can't kill him. He's done nothing wr—" Father swung his arm wide and backhanded her, snapping her head sideways. She clutched her stinging cheek.

Kadar lunged at Father, but the guards fell on him.

"Touch her again, and I will tear you to pieces!" Kadar bellowed, struggling against his captors.

Father's nose curled as though catching a whiff of foul air. He snapped his fingers, and his faithful eunuch slave Goda stepped out of the shadows. "Kill the barbarian and dump the body in the Nile."

Lydia groaned. The poor, poor man. What had she done?

Kadar heaved and thrashed, trying to reach her father. "Coward!"

The guards hauled Kadar toward the door. He kicked and bucked against them, but to no avail. Goda and the knot of men disappeared with him down the corridor.

Baby James fussed. Stomach roiling over Kadar's fate, she put her knuckle to her son's seeking mouth.

Father stared at her with undisguised contempt. Cold night air poured through the open window. The noise of the struggle slowly faded away, leaving a terrible emptiness in its wake.

Lydia shivered. Baby James settled. She brushed her fingers over his soft, dear face. *I'd risk anything for you, my darling.* She grieved for Kadar, and felt wretched about what she'd done to him. It was unforgivable. But with her precious babe's welfare at stake, how could she have done otherwise?

Two slaves entered the bedchamber carrying reed baskets. Flaxen-haired Brynhild shot a look of concern at Lydia.

"I had to try, Bryn," Lydia said.

The middle-aged slave woman exhaled heavily. "Of course you did, my kitten."

Father swiped his hand at Bryn. "Stop your jabbering,

and pack up everything. I don't want any sign of the bastard child remaining in this house once he's gone."

The other slave, a pockmarked Egyptian, set the basket on the bed and reached for the neat pile of swaddling clothes stored in a small niche above the sleeping platform.

Lydia tucked her infant son against her chest. Legs shaking, she stood. "Don't take my baby. Spit on me, pull my hair out, whip me, I will suffer anything. But don't take him."

"Cease your squawking," Father snarled.

Baby James's small face puckered at Father's harsh comment, and he wailed a complaint. Father's frown soured further.

"Don't cry, my sunshine," she begged, her jaw and neck rigid from the stark fear gripping her. She patted her son's back and made shushing noises.

Uncle Jacob and Aunt Sarah shuffled into the room, wiping the sleep from their eyes. Uncle Jacob wrinkled his nose. "What's all this noise about, Brother?"

Father smoothed his dark blue robe. "I'm sorry to have disturbed you."

"What's upset you, my dear?" Uncle Jacob asked. He had generously taken them in after Father left Jerusalem for Egypt to escape his enemies. Lydia had no idea what long-term plans Father had made for himself, but she was to become Uncle's second wife. Intermarriage between nieces and uncles, though frowned upon by most, was a common practice among the rulers of Israel. Lydia wouldn't dread the prospect nearly so much if she could keep her baby.

She knelt at Uncle and Aunt's feet. They were her last hope. "I beg you to convince Father it is unjust to give James to *that man's* family."

That man being her captor, Judas the Zealot, the criminal who had attacked Lydia's family while they traveled through Galilee, changing her life forever. Kadar and her brother-in-law Nathan had rescued her and killed the crazed bandit, but the nightmare hadn't ended there. Judas's family had gone to court and laid claim to her darling baby. Father refused to contest the matter.

Uncle looked dumbfounded. Aunt Sarah's hostile gaze made Lydia shudder. Little James cried louder.

Lydia grabbed Uncle Jacob's pudgy hand. "I will be a good, dutiful wife and give you many sons. Allow me to keep my baby and I'll never ask for another thing."

"Oh... I don't think...ah...." Uncle stammered, then turned to Aunt. "The child is rightfully the father's. Don't you agree, my dear?" In the normal way of things, children belonged to the father. If the man died, the child then belonged to the father's family.

Lydia shot Aunt a pleading look. "Judas's actions were evil. He and his family have no right to my baby."

The older woman's eyes locked onto Lydia's hand, still grasping her Uncle's. "The court ruled," Aunt said flatly. "Judas's family prevailed."

Lydia pulled her hand back and curled her arms around James. "A baby needs its mother. Please tell them it's wrong to take my baby, Aunt. They'll listen to you." Aunt was the mother of eight. Surely her sympathies would rest with the child and what was best for him.

Aunt frowned. "Your father told us you agreed to marry Judas."

Lydia's heart sickened.

Father looked down his pious nose. "Did I speak the truth, Daughter?"

Lydia squeezed her eyes closed. "Yes, but—" Once again she searched for a way to excuse and explain what had happened during those confusing months of captivity. Lydia's throat constricted. "That crazed bandit would have forced marriage on me whether I agreed to it or not."

Though true, it didn't ease her guilt. At first she had been terribly frightened of the zealots, especially of the man who led them. But Judas had another side. He had a way with words. His fiery preaching and scripture-laced speeches had enthralled her as much as it had his men. Judas's band of followers loved him. After he was finished speaking, they would sit around the fire for hours eating, talking, and laughing. The small caves of Upper Galilee soon became

Lydia's only reality. Though forced to marry Judas, she soon did the unthinkable — she came to think of him as a true husband.

The rustle of her father's robe drew near. "Did you practice your flirtatiousness on Judas the Zealot?"

Lydia gasped.

"You always were too rambunctious," Aunt accused.

"Rambunctious?" Lydia could hear her rising hysteria, but was helpless to stop it. "I love to smile and laugh. How can that be wrong?"

Father's lips pursed. "You draw undue attention to yourself, carrying on so."

"I will be more demure," Lydia promised frantically.

Uncle Jacob patted her shoulder. "Lydia is lively, but she means well. Our girls adore her. They love the new games she's taught them."

Aunt Sarah's face tightened, accentuating the weary lines on her forty-year-old face.

Lydia's compassion for Aunt grew every day. It must be terrible to suddenly find yourself competing against a much younger woman for your husband's affections. The dear woman had nothing to fear. Uncle was quite besotted with his wife. The couple couldn't be more in love, even after so many years. The problem was, fifty-one year old Jacob needed a male heir. After the birth of their eighth daughter, they decided it was time for new measures. And so Lydia was to marry her uncle in two days' time and provide him with a houseful of sons.

She hated the pain and trouble it would cause. Like a cloud of locusts settling over a fruited field, her entrance into the marriage would chew away at her aunt's and uncle's joy, and likely turn their love into a hollowed-out husk of what it had been. The destruction had already begun.

Lydia grasped Aunt's hand. "Allow me to keep my baby and I will stay in my room. You will never have to look upon my face."

"Hand the bastard child over," Father snapped.

Lydia wrapped her body, cocoon-like, around James.

"Please, don't take him," she begged.

The pockmarked Egyptian pinned her elbows. "Give me the urchin."

She hugged James to her chest and pressed her lips to his tiny, soft cheek. "We have no one to protect us. No one to save us." Her thoughts went to Kadar. She ached for him, and hated that a brave, beautiful man would die because of her.

Brynhild spoke in her ear. "You're hurting the baby."

Lydia became aware of James's muffled cries. She gasped and loosened her hold. Her babe was taken from her arms. Her vision blurred. Loud roaring filled her ears. She glimpsed a flash of blue robes and a white bundle disappearing through the door.

She moaned and buried her face against her knees. Anguished sobs shook her. Grief and blackness consumed all.

Chapter 3

The hired guards pushed and dragged Kadar out of the villa. He glanced up at the canopy of stars overhead. *Give me strength, mighty Thor. Allow me to die with honor. Help me take these fiends to the grave with me. And may they suffer in the Underworld.*

They passed the ladder propped against Lydia's window, now guarded by two men. The sound of inconsolable weeping spilled out. Her heartbreak cut him to the quick. He'd failed her. It made his imminent death all the more bitter.

A loud shriek came from close by. The men hoisted their swords. Foul oaths filled the air.

The tiger cat sprang from the shadows, bared small, sharp teeth, and hissed and spit.

Taking advantage of the distraction, Kadar kicked the closest guard. The man's leg broke with a satisfying crack, and he screamed and hit the ground. Amid the surprised shouts, Kadar turned sideways, lifted his leg high, and hammered the sole of his sandal into a face. Blood spurted from a broken nose. He roared triumphant. Regaining his balance, he shoved his shoulder into the next body in his path, then rammed his head into an exposed gut.

A teeth-rattling blow to the skull knocked him to his knees. Staggering like a drunk, he climbed back to his feet. Swords poked into him from all sides. He sucked air into his starved lungs.

The bald eunuch slave named Goda studied Kadar with a dark scowl. "Cease fighting or I will order these men to put you on the ground and cut off your pillar and stones."

Kadar winced. The threat had extra force coming from a eunuch, a man who probably cherished the idea of having others join him in the unhappy ranks of the castrated. Kadar willed his muscles to relax and forced a smile to his face. "You know how to take the fight out of a man. I'll grant you that, eunuch."

The man's hairless forehead wrinkled. "We'll see who will be laughing when this is over."

"I will, eunuch. Because you never smile."

The bald slave ignored the goad and trudged on. Kadar flexed his wrists, measuring the length of the fetters. He'd make his next move at the river's edge.

They reached the end of the lane. The eunuch turned left.

"The Nile is the other way, fool," Kadar said, just to be a jackass.

The eunuch stopped abruptly and turned to him. He narrowed his eyes at Kadar. "I have my own plans for you."

"Plans?" Images of gory tortures and degrading punishments flashed through Kadar's mind.

"It would be a waste to kill you." The eunuch gave Kadar a measuring look. "An oversized barbarian like you will draw a hefty sum on the slave market."

Slave. Kadar's blood ran cold. He'd rather die. "If it's money you want, I can get it to you. But I—"

"Save your breath," the eunuch said. "I have someone who will give me a good price now, and who is leaving Alexandria at first light. Simeon Onias will never know you didn't die. And these guards and I will share a generous reward. It gives me great pleasure to imagine you sweating your last drops in an Egyptian copper mine."

Kadar's temples throbbed like Thor's hammer. A slave. He was going to be a slave. He searched for some argument to save him from the humiliating fate.

"What? No clever insults now?" the eunuch gloated.

Kadar wanted to wring the man's scrawny neck. "Kill me and dump me in the river, as you were ordered, or I swear by the gods, I will come for you and I choke the life out of your miserable body."

The bald man laughed. Kadar roared and lunged for the chortling fool. The eunuch backpedaled, tripped, and fell.

Kadar bent over the cowering man and grabbed a fistful of rumpled tunic.

A solid object struck the back of his head and the world went black.

Western Sinai - *Six Months Later*

Kadar took another step. The fine desert sands shifted underfoot, swallowing his sandal. The yellow glare of the sun burned cruelly on his bare head. He licked his parched lips and peered into the distance. Glaring white sand stretched endlessly. He'd heard tales of snow blindness. Maybe he was suffering from a desert version.

A chill went through him. *A chill?* His brain was cooked, yet his skin felt cold and clammy. You didn't have to be a physician to know it was a bad sign. He lifted the clay water jar over his mouth and shook it. Nothing. Not a single drop.

The donkey caravan he was trying to catch up to had left the copper mine a half day ahead of him. Though the likelihood of him catching up was low, he'd hoped to come across other travelers going either east or west—it didn't matter, so long as he escaped from Sabu Nakht's cruelty.

Kadar reached for the black leather cord hanging around his neck, pulled his silver, hammer-shaped amulet from beneath his tunic, and ran his thumb over the embossed image of Thor. A gift from his father. He longed to experience the cold chill of a crisp autumn morning, to gaze upon vast fields of unbroken snow, and to lift his voice in a battle cry with his fellow Northmen.

He'd know the gods had truly abandoned him if he was forced to breathe his last in this abominable wasteland.

A shimmery outline wavered in the distance, then took form, revealing a line of camels. He tucked away the amulet, crouched down on his haunches, and shaded his head with the empty clay jar. The camels loped closer. Yellow tassels decorated the blue blankets covering the beasts' backs.

Kadar pounded his thigh. "Thundering Thor!" Sabu

Nakht had tracked him down. For the third time. Kadar's knotted calf muscles complained as he pushed to his feet.

The camel drivers dragged their beasts to a halt, boxing Kadar in. Dust swirled up around them. Sour camel's breath spilled over his face, adding to his nausea.

"I told you I'd make you pay if you tried to run away again," Sabu Nakht growled, sliding off his saddle.

Kadar shrugged, pretending indifference. "Do what you have to."

The steward's black, oiled hair clung to his shoulders, leaving mottled stains on his brown, striped tunic. "The champion Persian warrior will be here in three weeks."

Not another fight. Kadar assumed fate had thrown her worst at him when he'd been sold into slavery, but no, the degradation hadn't stopped there. Kadar was Nakht's prize rooster in the overseer's godless cockfights, dueling other slaves in battles to the death, so Sabu Nakht could have the pleasure of betting and boasting against equally bloody-minded men.

Nakht wagged his finger at Kadar. "How am I supposed to punish you and still leave you fit to fight?"

Egyptians were a damnably strange lot. The man's red-painted fingernails made it hard to take him seriously. Kadar rubbed his throbbing head. "I'm sure your fiendish mind will come up with some foul new evil."

Nakht smiled.

Kadar glared back. "Do me a favor and just kill me."

The Egyptian sighed loudly. "Why do you bother to escape? I don't understand you. I give you beautiful women. You turn your nose up at them. I give you a room in my home. You refuse to use it. I offer you a life of leisure. You insist on working in the mines. What more do you want?"

"I want you dead." Kadar would eat dog testicles before he accepted anything from the hand of the man who owned him. *Owned him.* Curse him.

"You've just earned yourself a few more days in the pit. You should have kept your mouth shut."

The pit. Kadar shuddered, and it wasn't because he'd been

out in the sun too long. "The pit makes better company than you."

Nakht clutched the cord attached to Kadar's amulet and yanked it free. "Let's see what you are willing to do to get your prize amulet back."

Hate consumed what remained of Kadar's heart. "I will kill you before I crawl on my knees to you for anything!"

It was good Kadar didn't know then it would take him six long years to make good on his oath.

Chapter 4

Alexandria, Egypt - *Six Years Later*

The end of another *Shabbat* neared. Dread curled through Lydia. She sat on a low couch to the left of her uncle. Aunt Sarah sat to Uncle's right. Brynhild, the pear-shaped slave woman, cleared away the last of the dinner dishes.

Excited chatter from Lydia's five youngest cousins echoed off the brightly painted walls of the dining hall in the heart of the villa. Wearing matching white tunics, and perched atop plump, pomegranate-colored pillows, the girls all had straight black hair and shining black eyes.

"Tell us another story, Lydia," her youngest cousin begged. The others clapped and echoed her demand for a new story.

Desperate to delay what couldn't be escaped, Lydia readily agreed. "I had a strange dream. Would you like to hear it?"

Five glossy heads bobbed.

Lydia pulled her shawl tighter and closed her eyes. "The dream began in Jerusalem. People were rushing through the streets, very afraid. My father, brother, and sister were with me. We were running. But I didn't know who or what we were trying to escape. I kept looking back, straining to see the evil, and I fell. My family disappeared, and I was frightened and alone. Then the dream shifted to a vast wheat field. I saw a man standing amid the waving stalks, his golden hair and white robes swirling about him. He shone so brightly I had to shade my eyes.

"Was he an angel?" one of the girls asked.

"Maybe he was an archangel," the youngest suggested.

"Did he give you his name?" another asked.

The vivid image...vision...dream—Lydia wasn't sure what to call it—replayed through her mind. A golden giant armed with a fiery sword stood guard over her precious baby, who was sleeping peacefully on a bed of blankets amid the vast wheat field.

She didn't mention the part about baby James. The family never spoke of him. She suspected they'd forgotten her sweet boy even existed. No matter. She remembered and prayed for him every morning upon waking and each evening before going to sleep. Her sister Alexandra was neighbors with little James's grandmother. Alexandra sent letters regularly describing Lydia's precious boy in great detail. He'd recently lost his first tooth. But in Lydia's dreams, he was always an infant.

She swallowed back the ache thickening her throat. "The man didn't speak to me." He didn't need to. She recognized him. He wasn't a spirit or an angel. He was the long-dead, blond-haired, blue-eyed barbarian Kadar. She tried not to think about him, since it always made her sad. But the memory of him persisted. Last night he'd come to her in a dream. What could it mean?

She sighed too loudly.

Uncle patted her hand. "You girls have tired our dear Lydia enough for one day." He turned toward Aunt. "You won't mind if we say goodnight now, will you, my dear?"

Aunt's smile was so brittle, Lydia was surprised it didn't shatter. "Of course not."

Uncle Jacob heaved his heavy body off the couch. He held out his hand to Lydia. "Come, my dear wife."

Wife. Her stomach lurched. Though they'd enacted this cruel scene every week for the last six years, she hadn't learned to stop hating it. At the close of every *Shabbat* her uncle called her "wife" and took her to bed. The rest of the time he addressed her as Lydia and slept with Aunt Sarah.

Lydia forced her hand up. Uncle clasped it and, as always, he winked at Aunt Sarah and Lydia. "Perhaps our prayers will be heard tonight. Perhaps the Lord will finally bless us with a son."

Aunt Sarah's eyes caught Lydia's and held. Resentment used to shine in the older woman's face, growing more and more intense as months passed into years and Lydia did not conceive a child. But a new emotion flickered across Aunt's countenance tonight. Pity. Aunt Sarah felt sorry for *her*. Lydia wanted to weep.

Uncle Jacob led her out of the dining alcove and steered her down the long, wide corridor. Doughy fingers stroked over her hand. "You seem out of spirits, my dear."

"I'm not feeling well."

"I'll be quick tonight. I promise."

"Thank you, Uncle."

He chuckled. "You are supposed to call me Jacob or Husband. Remember?"

"Aunt doesn't like me to."

Uncle sighed and slowed. A sheepish look crossed his face. "Promise me you will never tell your aunt how much I enjoy lying with you. It would hurt her."

Sadness scraped at her bones. "You have nothing to fear. I would never purposely hurt you or Aunt." She tried to pull her hand free. "I don't think I am ever going to give you a son. You should divorce me and remarry." She held her breath.

An agonizing moment of silence passed, then Uncle patted her hand. "Your cousins would cry their eyes out if I sent you away. We can't have that, now can we?"

Lydia stared blindly down the long hallway. "Of course not, Uncle."

The next afternoon a loud knock sounded on the bedchamber door and Brynhild rushed in and hurried to Lydia's side. Lydia rubbed her eyes and set down the yellow linen scarf she was trimming with ivory stitches.

"Master Jacob dropped dead at the synagogue," Bryn wheezed. "Come quickly. Your aunt and the girls need your support."

Heart hammering, Lydia jumped to her feet. "Uncle is dead?"

Brynhild led the way out of the room. "Master Jacob's friends carried him home and laid him out in his bedchamber. Your aunt is beside herself. I coaxed her and the girls out of the room so the body could be prepared for burial."

Lydia rubbed her stiff fingers, trying to warm them. Poor Aunt. She and Uncle had been married twenty-five years. *Twenty-five years.* Two years longer than Lydia had been alive. Six years of marriage to Uncle had been too long for her. Thank heaven, thank heaven, thank heaven, the burdensome marriage was over.

She winced. Listen to her. Could she sound more wicked or selfish? Where was her grief? And her compassion for Aunt and the girls? Her cheerful uncle... er... husband had been a gentle soul who would never dream of harming anyone. A respected man among his peers, he would be greatly missed.

Sobs spilled out of the family's combined dining chamber and reception hall.

Lydia hurried forward. Her cousins cried louder when she entered the room. The two youngest ran to her and buried their sweet faces in her skirt. Lydia's heart broke for them. She knelt and put her arms around them. "There, there," she cooed. Then she turned to Aunt. "Please accept my sorrow for your terrible loss."

"I don't want you here." Aunt Sarah snapped back. "Leave us."

Lydia didn't take the sharp words to heart. Aunt was terribly upset. Patting her cousins' small backs, Lydia stood. "What can I do to help?"

Aunt's watery eyes iced over. "I want you out of this house."

Lydia nodded. The request didn't come as a surprise— Aunt Sarah had never wanted her here—but it hurt nonetheless. "Of course. I will write to my father after we sit *Shiva* for Uncle and make arrangements to return to Jerusalem."

She was going back to her childhood home. The idea threatened to set Lydia's head spinning, an indulgence she couldn't afford, since the house would soon be overrun with mourners. A roomful of tasks awaited someone's attention. "Do you want me to speak to the rulers of the synagogue about Uncle's burial?"

"He was *my* husband," Aunt said, her voice rising. "The burial is my duty."

"I'm sorry. I only meant to help. I didn't mean to upset you."

Aunt Sarah pointed at the front door. "Go! I want you out of my house *now!*"

Lydia froze.

The girls began to weep again, clinging to her. Aunt's face crumpled. "Please leave."

Lydia turned and fled. Tears of regret and grief burned in her eyes.

Brynhild caught up to her. "What are you going to do, girl? Where will you go?"

The question stopped Lydia in her tracks. "I will—" Dear heavens above, what would she do after she stepped out the door of this house?

Chapter 5

Idumea - *One Month Later*

Kadar retreated to a corner of the walled courtyard to escape the loud gaiety and press of richly attired guests arriving for the formal banquet hosted by the Governor of Judea, Antipater of Idumea.

Starlight glimmered through the oval leaves of the orange tree overhead. The sweet fragrance of oranges swirled around him. He'd never smelled the like before coming to this part of the world, or tasted anything as delectable and delicious as the tangy, juicy fruit the trees produced. Oranges had once been a favorite of his. But not now. Not since Sabu Nakht.

A middle-aged couple cast nervous glances his way. Kadar plucked a leaf and dug his nail into the waxy surface. Where was Herod?

As if summoned, Antipater's youngest son strolled across the courtyard, his black, curly hair damp from a recent bath. Herod's swagger drew a mix of frowns, smiles, and admiration. The mercurial Governor of Galilee, Herod appeared to be as brash and bold as ever.

Kadar rubbed his weary eyes and stepped out from under the tree's shelter. "Did you speak to your father? He said you'd know the current whereabouts of Simeon Onias."

"What a way to greet an old friend," Herod said, smiling.

Revenge uppermost in his mind, Kadar had little patience for social niceties. "Do you know where Onias is or not?"

Herod slapped Kadar on the shoulder. "I nearly fell off my horse when Father told me you turned up...what was it...three days ago? I had to see your ugly face for myself. We thought you were long dead. My father sent men to Egypt after we didn't hear anything from you for a month, but it was like you had vanished." Herod's eyes swept over him. "You were a slave? Jupiter, you must have hated it. What happened?"

"I was careless."

"You look strong. Not many men walk away from those salt mines alive." Herod's brows rose questioningly.

Kadar didn't bother to correct Herod—salt mine, copper mine—neither was exactly a pleasure cruise on the Nile. And the damnable man would have to remain curious. Kadar would rather be castrated than be forced to confess one word of his shameful behavior after Sabu Nakht finally found a way to break him. Kadar gritted his teeth. "The head overseer set me free."

Herod blinked repeatedly. "He set you free? The fool could have made a small fortune selling you."

"The overseer called it a reward for my faithful service." The truth was Nakht couldn't find anyone to challenge Kadar, after dozens and dozens of contenders had tried and failed. Kadar could still see the overseer's oily grin as he handed over the *manumissio*, the official document given to a freed slave. The stench of Nakht's foul breath lingered from the kisses he planted on Kadar's cheeks before sending him off with a westbound caravan. "I returned in the middle of the night and killed the cretin," Kadar said flatly, his hand going to the silver amulet he had torn from Nakht's broken neck.

Herod laughed and shook his head. "Can I convince you to be my bodyguard? You would scare my enemies witless."

The last time Kadar had seen Herod, the hotheaded man was cooling his heels in Syria after marching an army on Jerusalem. "Your father told me you managed to earn the good opinion of the Jews."

"I can't understand why everyone made such a big fuss over one small army."

"You threatened to annihilate the Sanhedrin."

He shrugged. Although only about thirty years old, Herod had confidence and conceit to spare. "A few months after you disappeared, Hasmond did me the great favor of gathering an army and invading Galilee. He managed to capture three fortresses before I struck back and drove him out of the country. Jerusalem greeted me with a hero's welcome when I returned. The city had a parade in my honor."

"With your luck, you don't need my help anyway."

"My father is disappointed you refused to join his bodyguards. You might reconsider after you hear what I learned today."

Kadar shifted restlessly. "Can you tell me where Simeon Onias is hiding, or not?"

"I figured Onias was involved in your disappearance. The old prude denied it, of course." Herod checked over his shoulders and lowered his voice. "My spies tell me Onias journeyed to Parthia. He is a guest of Hasmond. The two devils probably have their heads together, even as we speak, conspiring against my father and John Hycranus."

The struggle for power between John Hycranus and Hasmond had been going on for twenty-plus years. Kadar didn't think either man was worth the effort. Simeon Onias joining with Hasmond was an inconvenience. It meant a journey far to the east. Then again, Parthia was probably as good a place to go as any.

"I'll set out for Parthia tomorrow. You and your father will have one less thing to worry about once I kill Onias."

Herod's bark of laughter drew curious glances.

Kadar frowned.

Herod's lively black eyes sparkled. "Remind me never to cross you."

Kadar searched for the closest escape route. "I don't have time for your nonsense." The archway leading to the interior of the house was crowded with guests and slaves. It would have to do. A hand circled his arm. He narrowed his eyes at Herod.

No fool, Herod released his hold and stepped back. "There's a thing or two you might want to know before charging off to Parthia."

Kadar blew out sharp breath. "Talk. And make it quick."

"Lydia Onias is a widow."

Kadar clutched his chest, feeling as if a hand had reached in and grabbed his heart. "A widow? What happened?"

"Her husband died," Herod said, flashing boxy white teeth.

"You don't want to see the murderous side of me."

Herod sobered. "I passed through Jerusalem this morning. The city was all abuzz over Lydia Onias's arrival. They say her husband was dead before he—"

"Hold on. Slow down. Lydia Onias is in Jerusalem?" Kadar said.

Herod nodded, then waggled his brows. "She's still in your blood, isn't she?"

Kadar paced in a circle, his body humming with the urge to race to Jerusalem. But then what? Would Lydia want to see him? She'd probably long since forgotten him. He needed to let go of the past. Let her go.

"Will you try to see her?" Herod asked.

Kadar scrubbed a hand over his face. "I don't know. I... ah—" Damnation. Who was he trying to fool? A legion of angels couldn't keep him away from Lydia Onias.

James Onias smoothed the folds of his costly robe and entered the noisy dining chamber. A dozen low, wooden tables ringed by gold-tasseled cushions filled the room. Slaves moved about the room serving food and drink.

He'd visited Antipater's country home a few times. Idumea was an armpit of a place, if you asked him, but he wasn't in a position to say no to this invitation. Estranged from his selfish father at age fourteen, he'd been a member of Antipater's household for over six years now. The Idumean was a man worth pleasing. A wealthy military commander and a friend of Rome and blessed with a surfeit of guile, Antipater had used his influence to gain the office of governor of Judea, making him the second most powerful man in the land.

James took a deep breath, plastered a smile on his face,

and realized he was doing it again—stroking his knuckle over the scar running across his cheek. *Fickle Fortuna!* The jagged purple blemish drew notice enough without him pointing it out.

He pressed his hands to his sides, marched to his seat, and dropped down next to Antipater's oldest son, Phasael.

A slave came right over and poured wine into a silver cup incised with a band of grape leaves. James tapped the rim. "Fill it to the top." He glanced over at the head table. John Hycranus was busy loading his plate with choice cuts from the fatted calf. The High Priest of Israel didn't appear to have noticed James. Thank the seven heavens!

James lifted his cup and sipped. Mmm...the finest wine this side of the Mediterranean. Antipater wasn't sparing any expense to celebrate his son's engagement to John Hycranus's lovely granddaughter. Herod and Mariamne? James shook his head. He wasn't the only one who found the idea incredible. It was all anyone could talk about.

A large hand clapped James on the back. Wine sloshed over his hand and dotted his brown tunic. James gave Phasael a sour frown.

Dark-complexioned like his Nabatean mother, Phasael's white teeth gleamed as he laughed. "What do you think of the place? My father is proud as a peacock about the renovations."

James's practiced eye winced at the garish, faux Doric columns, bulky plaster rosettes, and over bright murals layered over the skeleton of a once-humble farmhouse. He'd spent the last four years in Rome studying construction and design under the tutelage of the world's elite master builders, so he knew good work when he saw it. This wasn't good work, not by any stretch of the imagination.

He picked up his spoon and pointed toward the oasis painted on the wall behind the head table, which featured bloated palm trees swaying like drunkards around a mud puddle. "The artisan responsible for that eyesore ought to be trussed up, coated in honey, and dropped into a camel pen."

Phasael grinned. "My mother adores it."

"Ah...I begin to see its charm."

"You are a clever one."

James shrugged. "I've seen worse." Attempts to emulate the splendors of Rome ran rampant among those granted Roman citizenship, placing the governor of Judea amid good company.

Phasael swiped a chunk of rye bread through an oil and herb concoction. "My father says your tutors couldn't stop boasting about your uncommon talent. He and Herod want to put you to work rebuilding some key outposts."

James still marveled at the drastic turn his life had taken these past six years. Left with a nasty scar on his cheek, thanks to his father's overzealous quest to become High Priest of Israel, James had walked out of his father's house six years earlier, never to return. Jerusalem's gossips had feasted on the scandal for weeks, squawking like elated buzzards when they learned James had gone to live and work in a community of stonecutters.

But for the first time in his life he'd felt whole and alive. He'd relished the burn in his arms when he swung a hammer, took great satisfaction in the sweat pouring off him while he helped slide a block into place, spent hours in fascinating discussions about the art and craft of building. The stone dust had soaked into his pores, mingled with his breath, seeped into his marrow, until he burned with the drive to fashion the finest palace-fortresses the world had ever seen.

James held back the smile he knew might make him appear overeager. "Your father has been most generous with me." Antipater had plucked James out of the community of stonecutters, paid for his education, supported him while he studied in Rome, and was poised to hire James as a master builder.

Phasael stuffed a piece of bread into his mouth. "My mother is clamoring for a big new home in Jerusalem. She wants Father to bring in one of those acclaimed master builders from Alexandria."

James sat up straighter. "Will your mother get her way?"

"What do you think?"

"Wise men keep their wives happy."

"Why, you silver-tongued flatterer. And here I thought you went to Rome to learn how to stack stones."

"I learned many lessons in Rome," James said through gritted teeth. He'd spent time with oxen more clever than this grinning fool.

Phasael lifted a brow. "We heard you grew quite fond of the wine and slave girls."

"Heard?" James's face heated, and rightly so, given the liberties he'd taken while living in Rome. "Heard from who?"

"Our spies."

"Spies?"

Phasael's bark of laughter ricocheted around the room. "You should see your face. We weren't spying on you. Not officially. The information we received was more in the way of gossip. One agent found your misadventures quite entertaining."

"Go hang yourself, you Cretin bast—" The insult stuck in James's throat. High Priest Hycranus and a handful of Temple officers were staring at him.

Hycranus wagged his pudgy finger. "Why haven't I seen you at the Temple?"

James's chin firmed. "I have other matters to attend to."

The answer earned perplexed frowns from Hycranus and the Temple officers. James was a priest by birth, a descendant of Aaron, the first priest of Israel. A priest eschewing the Temple was the equivalent of a farmer refusing to enter his fields.

The mingle of voices and clink and clatter of dishware became quieter and quieter. Heads turned. He saw the pitying looks. Heard the whispers, "The poor boy with the scar."

James's fists balled. It was how he was known from one end of Israel to the other, thanks to his *wonderful, caring* father. Six years ago, Simeon Onias had dragged his children into the wilds of Galilee so he could conspire with a band of deranged bandits. The meeting had gone terribly wrong. One of James's sisters had been abducted and ravaged by the lead madman, and the other sister had been forced to slice James's cheek with a knife. He still had nightmares of the gleaming, sharp blade hovering over his nose. The disfigurement had rendered James unfit to offer sacrifices at the Lord God's altar. The Law stipulated both animal and priest must be without spot or blemish. James had been rendered a damnable freak, listed in Moses' Law beside dwarfs, hunchbacks, and eunuchs.

Though he hated the idea, James would return to the Temple. He owed it to his sisters. Alexandria and Lydia had suffered enough, thanks to his cowardice. He didn't want to tarnish them with his shame.

Hycranus sighed. "You young priests try my patience."

"Leave the boy alone," a firm voice commanded. All eyes went to Herod. The formidable man picked up his goblet and stood. "We are here to celebrate my engagement." He smiled down at Mariamne. "Everyone join me in toasting my lovely espoused wife."

Cups were lifted high, and happy cheers echoed through the rooms. More salutations followed, after which the guests returned to eating and chatting.

James exhaled a relieved breath.

Phasael chuckled. "He's actually lovesick. Can you believe it?"

James uncurled and flexed his fingers. "Who?"

"Herod."

James glanced over at Herod and Mariamne. The newly-engaged pair were whispering into each other's ears and exchanging ardent looks.

Mariamne was a true beauty, with royal blood. No wonder Herod had divorced Doris and banished her and his five-year-old son to a small, bleak outpost overlooking the Dead Sea. A dull-minded girl with a flirtatious smile and large breasts, Doris never had a chance of holding Herod's interest.

Herod and Mariamne's engagement, however, was still a wallop of a surprise. John Hycranus had no business marrying his granddaughter off to a man who was a Jew in name only. Herod's father was Idumean. His mother a Nabatean princess from Petra. All of Jerusalem was outraged over the engagement.

"I see the disgust in your eyes," Phasael said. The burly man's eyes hardened.

James's mouth went dry. He grabbed up his cup, sipped, and chose his words with care. "My disdain is for Hycranus and his cronies. They need your father's army and protection more than ever, now that Hycranus's rat-faced cousin Hasmond has aligned with Parthia. I admire your father and brother for taking advantage of the situation. The alliance can only help your family. I am pleased for you." Running out of platitudes, he drained his cup.

Phasael's smile was twice as frightening as his grimace. "It's good to hear you find the engagement agreeable. My father has a strategic marriage in mind for you."

James choked. "Marriage? For me?" He coughed some more. "Who does he have in mind?"

Phasael pointed to the opposite end of the table. "My mother's cousin, Kitra,"

A petite girl with the same dark, exotic beauty as Antipater's wife batted her eyes at James. *Fickle Fortuna!* Marrying her was out of the question, but he was going to dream of the flirtatious siren for months to come. "She's a pagan," James said.

Phasael grinned. "If you consent to the marriage, Kitra will convert, just like my mother did before marrying my father."

"I'm a priest. I can't marry foreign women. Moses' Law is very clear on the matter."

"Kitra's father has enough riches to build a city full of marble palaces."

The purred words curled around James like the sinful scent of a harlot luring him to delicious, delightful destruction. "I, uh...I need to think about it."

Phasael tore another chunk of bread from the rye loaf. "Of course. Of course. In the meantime, Kitra's father would like to speak to you about the Roman-style amphitheater he hopes construct."

James scrubbed his face. Damnation. Antipater and his sons knew him too well. Were fully aware of his weaknesses.

They'd probably already made his wedding clothes.

"Do you want to hear more?" Phasael asked.

The sinking feeling James had lived with in Rome came back threefold. He nodded and added another bit of self-loathing to the festering pile within him.

Chapter 6

Kadar strode through a smallish atrium of the ancient mansion, past a white marble side table holding a vase bursting with yellow flowers. Lamplight from gilded fixtures reflected off the silver-gray flecks embedded in the black stone floor. The vivid colors almost hurt, due to eyes grown sensitive from too many years in the dim confines of the copper mine. This gem of a mansion was one of Antipater's recent purchases.

Deft at handling people and money, Antipater continued to prosper. Impressive. Very, very impressive, considering the personable statesman needed eight sets of eyes just to keep up with the stream of plots aimed at his demise—the Hasmoneans, the religious zealots, Simeon Onias—they all would love to send Antipater back to Idumea like a whipped dog.

Antipater had earned a life of luxury with his sword. Gaining riches and costly goods was what drove many men to pick up the sword, but not Kadar. He'd always fought for the sheer joy of it. Would he ever experience that roaring joy again in the future? Or would hate be all that drove him?

Kadar stopped before the tall double doors leading outside. His hand curled into a tight fist. He wanted to dig up Sabu Nakht and kill him all over again.

"Where are you off to in such a hurry?" Antipater called out as he came through the archway to the north wing of the house.

Tempted to ignore the inquiry, Kadar cursed under his breath and turned around. "I need to stretch my legs." He'd

41

learned Lydia Onias took the same walk every day. He planned to observe her, assure himself she was whole and well, before approaching her.

Antipater smiled and folded his arms across his wide chest. "You could wring John Hycranus's neck for me if you happen to see him. The High Priest sent a servant by with a message informing me he is hosting a small banquet tonight and he expects me to attend. Tonight! He couldn't have told me this a week ago?" Antipater rolled his eyes. "Now I have to postpone my meeting with my new master builder. Have you seen James Onias? I stopped by his room, but he's not there."

"I haven't, but I'll give him your message if I come across him," Kadar promised, not mentioning he'd already planned to have a word with the Onias boy. Lydia's fate would be in her brother's hands once Simeon Onias was dead. If the spineless boy had become even half as sour and hateful as his father—

"I don't want you to kill him," Antipater said, amused.

Kadar swallowed back the foul taste filling his mouth. "Do you have any idea where James might have gone?"

"We discussed making repairs to the southeast tower of the Baris."

"Good, I had already planned to go by the citadel." Lydia walked that way going to and from her cousin's home. Kadar nodded goodbye and pulled the door open, only to interrupt a lively conversation between the two guardsmen.

"How does it go?" Kadar asked politely as he walked between the soldiers. They looked away and mumbled a greeting.

He exhaled heavily and descended the stone stairs. Heading to the right, he walked by the small barracks housing Antipater's personal guard. Soldiers sat on benches arranged in a circle, shining their swords and swapping stories.

Silence descended. The men eyed him uneasily.

What was their problem? Kadar knew most of the men, and had been on good terms with them years ago. Surely they weren't behaving this way because he'd been a slave. Slavery was rampant in the Roman world. And freedmen were as common as cattle. Rich households might have two or three hundred slaves or more seeing to a family's every need. Fear of a slave uprising made for poor sleep in many wealthy households. Masters dangled the promise of freedom before slaves as one of many methods used to pacify them. Yes, noblemen and the aristocracy frowned on freedmen and women, but on the whole freed slaves vanished comfortably into everyday life.

Kadar stopped beside the captain of the guard. "I hear your boy is the healthy and hearty image of you."

"Thank you for remembering," the captain said, his eyes aimed at Kadar's chest. "Let me know if there's anything I can do. I have connections in Rome and Athens...if you need someone to put in a good word for you...or anything."

Was that pity he heard in the captain's voice?

Old John jumped up from a nearby bench. Armed to the teeth as usual, he held out a knife. "Take it. I have plenty more." The grizzled soldier studied Kadar's sandals instead of looking him in the eye.

Kadar flinched. Was the hate tearing up his insides so obvious? The men were treating him the way soldiers treated the gravely wounded—everyone pretending the man would be going home to his family when they knew his next stop was the grave. "Keep it. I have everything I need," he replied, his voice gruff.

Old John grabbed his arm. "I want you to have the knife. And if you decide to stay, I'll be happy to fight again by your side."

Old John reminded Kadar of his father and the Northman warriors he'd loved like brothers. It had stung soul-deep when he was forced to leave his life and everything beloved and familiar behind.

John's friendly gesture made Kadar painfully aware of the lonely life awaiting him once he departed Jerusalem. But he wouldn't be welcome here after he killed one of the city's elite. The sweet taste of revenge when he watched Simeon Onias die at his hands would go a long way toward soothing that pain.

Kadar took the knife and slid it under his belt. "Thank you, John."

"Be sure to keep the blade oiled and sharpened."

He clapped the career soldier on the back and resumed his walk. Lengthening his stride, he turned down the first alley he came to, then weaved his way through a series of narrow, crowded lanes.

Work-worn tunics hung from the edges of the flat roofs, drying in the sun. Men and women rushed about their daily business. Children's chatter drifted out of the small homes and apartments. The sounds of everyday life pricked at Kadar.

Was there any place in the world for him? The memory of Lydia Onias tucked against his chest came back.

He walked faster, turned corner after corner, and burst out of a narrow alley at the foot of the northwest tower of the citadel Hasmonean Baris. Halting under its long shadow to catch his breath, he squeezed his eyes shut.

Stop. Cease your useless daydreams. Lydia Onias could never be his. Two immovable objects stood in the way. Jewish women didn't marry pagans, and Lydia wouldn't want anything to do with the barbarian responsible for her father's death. He should walk away now. Leave the city immediately.

He ducked down an alley, stopped next to the side entrance to Hasmonean Baris, and slipped a couple of coins to the guards to gain entrance. Once inside, he took the stairs two at a time, exited the tower and hurried to an opening in the crenellated parapet.

The stone citadel served as the second residence of the High Priest of Israel. An underground tunnel connected the Baris to the Temple. The order of men called Levites manned the citadel towers, watching to make sure nothing and no one defiled the sacred ground set aside as holy to the God of Israel.

The north tower overlooked Jerusalem. The city hadn't changed much in the six years he'd been gone. Shabby yellow, white, and light-brown stone buildings in various stages of disrepair leaned on each other for support. A city a thousand years past its glory, Jerusalem had seen better days. No matter what its inhabitants believed. A lowly people with no army or wealth to speak of, the Jews nonetheless believed their God would establish an everlasting kingdom on this very spot, wherein all the nations of the world would bow down before their God.

Kadar shook his head. He admired the Jews' bravado. It was part of what had drawn him to this place.

He sobered the moment he spied James Onias trudging up the wide stone street, followed by two women. The taller, slimmer one's shoulders were squared proudly and her head was held high.

Kadar's gut tightened.

Lydia Onias.

He would recognize her anywhere.

He gripped the waist-high stone wall, and, like a man half dead of thirst, he drank in the sight of Lydia. She appeared healthy and strong. Was she still a beauty? Would looking into her large, sad eyes still slay him? He wanted to strip away the veil covering her face, loosen her hair, and watch it fall about her shoulders. What would become of her? Another marriage, most likely. He growled and ground his teeth, wanting to strangle the fortunate fellow.

James Onias stopped and turned back to Lydia and the other woman. They exchanged words. Then James pointed at the tower. The women looked up. Kadar hesitated. Lydia's eyes swept over the tower and paused on him. His hand rose and he almost waved. Heart pounding and breath short, he ducked out of sight.

What next? He'd seen her. But it wasn't enough. He'd made a promise to her, promised to protect baby James as though the child was his firstborn. He needed to find a way to speak to her. Once he could be sure Lydia and the boy were happy and safe, he'd depart from Jerusalem and never come back.

Chapter 7

James shook Lydia's arm, but his sister continued to stare up at the tower. "What's wrong? You look like you've seen a ghost."

Lydia bit her colorless lips and shivered. "I would like to visit with you at Antipater's today, after you finish inspecting the tower."

People veered around them. Some pointed and gawked.

James glanced over at the other woman with them, Elizabeth Onias. His father and hers were cousins. Lydia was staying with Cousin Nehonya, waiting for word from Father, who reportedly was in Parthia. Parthia? The family had distant relatives in the east, but James doubted his father was there for a friendly visit.

Elizabeth's brow furrowed. "I hope you plan to do your duty by your sister."

James shifted in place. With his father gone, Lydia's care and well-being had become his responsibility. He had failed her when she needed him most—when the bandits attacked them. This time he would do better by his sister.

A desperate look came into Lydia's brown eyes. "Please take me to your home. I want to see where you live."

Antipater's house was no place for her. There was no telling what evils his sister would encounter. Worldly pleasures, drunken revelry and lewd behavior were regular visitors among the Idumean half-breeds. "Take you...to Antipater's home?" James made a face. "Are you mad?"

His sister flinched as though he'd struck her.

Elizabeth wrapped a protective arm around her. Black eyes flashing, she said, "Why do you always have to be so hateful and mean?"

James's instinctive reaction—and more, the way he'd expressed it—had been thoughtless. Lydia had been held captive for months by those same wicked bandits, and the family had feared she might never recover from the strain—but he hadn't meant to insult her. James's shoulders hitched. He opened his mouth, but nothing came out.

The reprimand stung. Once again, Elizabeth Onias was seeing him at his worst. She had already witnessed James's cowardly behavior during a time he tried hard to forget. Plus, she was his father's ex-wife—his pretty, young ex-wife.

Originally, James was supposed to marry Elizabeth. The proposed alliance had been part of an elaborate scheme designed to elevate his ambitious father to the position of High Priest of Israel. Disgusted with his father's incessant, manipulative scheming, James had refused the match, so his father married Elizabeth himself.

James's mouth twisted. The age difference between Elizabeth and his father was obscene. At the time, Elizabeth had been a thirteen-year-old girl, and Simeon Onias had been fifty-three. It was an accepted practice among the Sadducees for old men to marry young girls, but most Israelites frowned on the practice.

Elizabeth crossed her arms. "Well?" she prodded. Spirited and confident, Elizabeth had become a breathtakingly gorgeous woman.

James swallowed. Though modestly dressed, her shapely body would make a fertility goddess appear demure. Large breasts. Small waist. Round hips. And he could be bedding her if he had accepted her as his wife.

"James Onias," she scolded, "don't you shame me with your eyes."

His face burned hotter than Hades. "Why... why aren't you remarried?" he sputtered. "You should have long since married. You've been divorced for six years."

Elizabeth paled.

Lydia revived, and put her arm around their cousin. "It's unkind of you to speak of Elizabeth's sorrow."

James frowned. "Sorrow? What are you..." A faint

memory floated up. Something about Elizabeth being unclean. "You still bleed?"

Both women blushed. Elizabeth clutched her stomach while her eyes filled with loathing.

A woman's monthly flow made her ritually unclean. Eight days after her bleeding stopped she was free to go the Temple and offer sacrifices for atonement. A woman with a continual discharge was always impure. A husband would be defiled every time they had marital relations. She couldn't go to the Temple. Others shunned her.

James could bite his tongue off for throwing Elizabeth's shame in her face. Men didn't discuss such matters with women. Whatever he said now would only add to everyone's mortification. He turned and fled. It was the kindest thing he could do for all of them.

But, *damnation*, he could feel Elizabeth's eyes on his back, watching him play the role of coward. Again. They had both been taken captive by Judas the Zealot. Elizabeth had remained strong and brave, but he had blubbered like a baby and curled up into a frightened ball.

Lungs burning from holding his breath, he stopped at the first available entrance to the Hasmonean Baris. He'd have to cut through the citadel to get where he needed to go, but he didn't care. The sooner he escaped Elizabeth's judgmental glare, the better.

The Levite guarding the thick wooden door inspected him head to toe. "Did you purify yourself at a ritual bath?"

The religious pomposity grated like dirt between James's teeth. He wished he was still in Rome. "I don't plan to go anywhere near the Temple. I'm here to inspect the southeast tower."

The guard made a disgusted noise. "Why do you continue to shame your family by eschewing the Temple?"

Not in the mood for lectures, James slipped past him. Ignoring the loud complaints behind him, he hurried through the entryway. The dark, cold, airless confines of the ancient fortress closed around him.

Elizabeth's stomach churned as she watched James Onias flee down the road. *The spineless snake.*

"I apologize for my brother's callous remarks," Lydia said.

"I've had more bothersome flea bites." But the hurt lingered. Suddenly weary, Elizabeth looped her arm around Lydia's elbow. "You look frighteningly pale. Are you ill?"

Lydia glanced up at the tower. "I'm a bit tired. Would you mind if we turn back?"

Elizabeth patted Lydia's hand. "I hope what your brother said didn't upset you."

Lydia shook her head. "James was a gangly, awkward boy when I left Jerusalem to live in Egypt, and now he is a handsome young man. I'd hoped he would outgrow his prickliness and learn to tame his sharp tongue."

Elizabeth's eyes told her James was fine-looking, and he might be beautiful as a soft summer sky or stunning as a mighty oak tree or striking as an eagle taking flight; it didn't matter. He ruined his attractiveness every time he opened his hateful mouth. Elizabeth wrinkled her nose. "James is like your father. Simeon's sourness has rubbed off on your brother."

Lydia sighed. "I fear you are correct. My father has no inkling of how to be happy. And James seems to be headed down the same path."

A knot of Pharisees came around the corner.

Elizabeth's spine stiffened.

The religious men's lively conversation came to an end. Distaste warped their faces. They crossed the street lest they pass too close to her.

It took every bit of Elizabeth's strength to keep her chin up.

After so many years enduring all the ramifications of her defilement, she should be used to the ignominy, used to the whispers behind her back, used to the pain. She wasn't. The monthly bleeding her mother had warned would come had arrived a month before she married Simeon Onias. Once the cursed blood came, it never stopped. The affliction was a grievous fate for a woman born in a nation dedicated to the worship of God…and worse still for those living in Jerusalem, a city devoted to ritual cleanliness…and particularly onerous for the wife or daughter of a priest, whose life revolved around the Temple.

She carried another equally weighty burden. The continual bleeding was often the sign of a barren womb. The chief purpose of marriage was the begetting of children. It was one of the first commands God gave to Adam and Eve: be fruitful and multiply. Many men divorced their wives for failing to produce children. And it was next to impossible to convince a man to marry a woman with her condition. A burdensome truth Elizabeth lived with every day.

One blessing had come with the bleeding. She'd emerged from her brief marriage still a virgin. Simeon Onias had refused to even touch her because of the issue of blood, much less bed her. *Praise heaven!* She hadn't breathed a word of that particular blessing to anyone, and never would.

James entered a small dining chamber deep within the Baris. Servants moved about slowly, preparing for a banquet. The Baris had been built by High Priest John Hycranus's forefathers. The small fortress sat at the northwest corner of the Temple complex and served as an administrative building and repository for the High Priest's garments, the precious blue ephod, and the jeweled breastplate. Though it was not magnificent or spacious like the royal palace, High Priest Hycranus preferred the fortress and spent a good deal of his time here.

Avoiding the main corridor lest he cross paths with priests and Levites coming and going between the Temple and the Baris, James entered the long, narrow servants' corridor.

The familiar smell of incense mixed with burnt offerings permeated the air. A sour taste tainted his mouth. The odor of the morning sacrifice followed him around Jerusalem, plaguing his every step. Though he hated the idea, he resigned himself to visiting to the Temple soon, for Lydia's sake. She deserved a respectable guardian, someone to present holy sacrifices on her behalf until their father returned to Jerusalem.

If he returned. For all they knew, Father could be dead. And James might never have to look at the horrid man's face again. "Praise Jupiter!" he shouted, grinning like a maddened man.

A cold draft shot up his legs, ballooning his tunic. He clapped his hand over his mouth, and broke out in a clammy sweat. Evoking the name of pagan gods—an evil habit he'd picked up in Rome—was terrible enough, but doing so on ground consecrated to the Lord God of Israel reeked of blasphemy.

He braced his hands on his shaky knees and took some deep breaths. "Forgive me, Lord, for sinning against you." He waited, half expecting the ground to open up and swallow him. Or the heavens to smite him. The ringing in his ears slowly cleared.

Whispered words drifted out of a small storeroom to his left, punctuated by a man's gravelly laugh. "Don't worry. It will be over in a blink of the eye. Next time you do it, you won't be a virgin. You might actually enjoy it."

The salacious comment spurred James to move on.

"Shhh... I hear someone," a high-pitched, skittish voice hissed.

James picked up his pace and nearly collided with young Niv when the red-headed, freckle-faced boy exploded out of the storeroom, his face a picture of guilt.

James frowned. "Slow down. It's only me."

"What did you hear?" barked a tough-looking solder with an eye patch, meaty hands braced on the doorframe to the storeroom.

James couldn't put a name with the face, but was fairly sure the rough-hewn soldier was a high-ranking officer in the Jewish army. One of Malichus's hand-picked men. James mustered a scowl. "What evil are you up to?"

"Did Herod send you here to spy on us?" the patch-eyed man demanded.

"A spy? Are you foolish?" James replied.

"Watch your mouth," the burly man growled.

James turned to Niv. "What are you doing spending time with the likes of this corrupt fellow?" The soldier's name was Laban... or Lazarz... or something close. "Antipater won't be happy to learn you are meeting in secret with his enemies."

The color drained from Niv's freckled face, and he clutched his bulging cloth pouch more tightly. "We—"

"Keep your mouth shut, boy," Lazarz warned.

James reached for the pouch. "What do you have in there?"

Lazarz charged at them.

Blood pounding, James dropped down on all fours and rolled into Lazarz's shins, toppling him. Sprawled out face-first on the stone floor, the brawny man cursed and spit out blood.

James scrambled to his feet. He fled one way and Niv the other. Heavy footfalls thudded close behind James. Fear sizzling through his veins, James raced past wide-eyed servants and zigzagged his way through a maze of corridors. At the end of a long hallway he turned to the right and stumbled into a large reception area. The room was filled with a mix of priests, Levites, and layman, sitting or standing in small groups, all eyeing him with disfavor. He scowled back, smoothed his disheveled tunic, and exited at a more sedate pace.

Satisfied he'd lost the soldier, James worked his way toward the north corner of the Baris. He'd certainly riled up the patch-eyed man. When would he learn to keep his quarrelsome mouth shut? His rude remarks were forever landing him in trouble.

Reaching the southeast tower, he paused at the base of a wide, steep stairway and ran his fingers over the smooth, gray ashlar blocks. The distinctive oblong stones were a hallmark of Seleucid construction. He would have enjoyed working alongside the craftsmen who wrestled these stones into place some hundred and twenty years ago.

He missed having a hammer and chisel in his hands. He should go visit Pinhas and the other stonecutters and work with them for a day or two. Pounding on stone always calmed him.

James heard the rapid slap of sandals on stone coming down the hall. A moment later Lazarz burst around the corner.

Heart slamming, James turned and charged up the stairs. *Coward. Coward. Coward.* His conscience accused while his thighs and lungs burned with exertion.

Why was he running? He wasn't a helpless boy anymore. He was a man.

Hands fisting, he stopped and turned to face his pursuer.

The burly soldier barreled up the stairs.

James braced his feet. "Leave me alone, you big ox," he croaked, his voice breaking like a spotty-faced youth.

Lazarz reached the step below James, grabbed his tunic, and yanked him off his feet.

James slapped and kicked back. "Put me down."

An evil smile spread across the patch-eyed man's face. He swung James in a wide arc and hurled him through the air. A scream stuck in James's throat, and the last thing he saw was the satisfied expression on his murderer's face.

Chapter 8

Less than an hour after catching sight of Lydia Onias, Kadar paced outside the door of the formal chamber Antipater used to conduct business and receive guests. If anyone could arrange a safe, clandestine meeting with Lydia, it was Antipater. Kadar wouldn't rest until he spoke with her. He'd made a promise to Lydia Onias, vowed he wouldn't allow anyone to take her baby. But he had failed her. If she wished, he was prepared to turn the world upside down to make matters right.

Antipater's personal slave, Saad, exited the reception room and limped past Kadar. "The governor will see you now."

Kadar strode into the opulent chamber. Antipater, his secretary, and several prominent members of the religious sect called Sadducees lounged on cushioned couches, surrounding a marble-topped table.

The Sadducees frowned, but Antipater's smile broadened. "Ah...my favorite barbarian." He pointed to an empty couch. "Have a seat and we'll discuss your urgent matter."

The Sadducees' faces puckered with distaste.

The disgust was mutual. Kadar was as unhappy sharing the room with those pompous, bejeweled men as they were to have him there. "I'll stand. This won't take long. I hate to ask for another favor."

"Nonsense," Antipater said. "Tell me what you need. I have a favor to ask in return."

"Anything you want, name it."

Antipater laughed. "You didn't even hear what I want."

Jerusalem's shrewdest merchants would have a hard time competing with Antipater when it came to bartering. Though he drove a hard bargain, Antipater was honest and always delivered what he promised.

Kadar rolled his knotted shoulders. "That's because I'm certain the favor I need is more of a challenge than whatever you might ask." He wanted Antipater to provide safe passage out of Judea for Lydia Onias if the need arose. And safe passage for him as well, if need be.

The religious men were suddenly all ears.

Kadar narrowed his eyes at them. "But I won't discuss details while these obnoxious gossips are listening."

The bejeweled men blinked and sputtered.

Antipater's robust laugh coaxed a smile out Kadar.

The crippled slave, Saad, stumped back into the room and addressed Kadar. "A pair of slaves just arrived asking to speak to you. They say it's of utmost importance."

"Take me to them," Kadar directed, gut instinct telling him the slaves had come on behalf of Lydia.

The crippled man bowed and retreated toward the door with Kadar close on his heels.

"We still have a deal to discuss," Antipater called out.

Kadar smiled over his shoulder at the burly man. "Maybe... maybe not." He might not need the favor, depending on the message the slaves had for him.

"You're a scoundrel, you..." The rest of Antipater's good-natured complaint faded into the distance.

Kadar almost ran Saad over twice before they were halfway down the corridor. The muscle in his jaw ticked at their slow progress, but Kadar kept his impatience to himself. Saad suffered enough unkind remarks because of his lame leg, yet he remained unfailingly cheerful, and he was one of Antipater's most loyal supporters. Both qualities earned him Kadar's respect.

"Do you know the favor Antipater had in mind?" Kadar asked the slave.

"A member of my lord's bodyguard deserted him to go work for the King of Chalcis," the slave tsked. "The fool."

Not sure if the insult was aimed at the bodyguard or the King of Chalcis, Kadar forgot what he was going to say when they reached the small alcove located next to the front door.

Two brown-clad slave women sat huddled together on a stone bench. Kadar dismissed Saad.

They jumped to their feet and the tallest one rushed toward him, dislodging her hood and revealing the mystical, beautiful woman who haunted Kadar's dreams.

Lydia stopped a hair's breadth away from him, so close he could feel the warmth of her breath on his chest. "You're alive," she said, half crying and half laughing. "Brynhild said I was seeing things, but I *knew* I wasn't." Lydia looked at her companion. "I told you, Bryn. I told you I saw Kadar."

Knees weak, Kadar forced his gaze to the slave, a middle aged, pear-shaped woman with long, straw-colored braids.

Brynhild studied him with unconcealed suspicion and disapproval. "We should go back before someone discovers we are missing."

"Who else knows you are here?" Kadar asked, concerned for their safety.

The slave woman's brows furrowed. "What part of Gaul do you come from? I'm familiar with all the dialects, but your accent is new to me."

She spoke with the guttural accent distinct to outer Gaul. Most people assumed he also came from Gaul, and he didn't correct them. But a true native of the region, such as this woman, was unlikely to be fooled by his poor attempts to mimic the language. He touched his hand to the amulet tucked beneath his tunic and saw his father's face and the rugged terrain of his homeland, a country far beyond Gaul, a place so remote the Romans had yet to discover it. He exhaled heavily. "You didn't answer my question."

Brynhild's frown deepened. "My mistress insisted on dressing like a slave to slip out of the house unnoticed."

He scrubbed his face. "What possessed you to do such a thing, woman?"

Lydia's light brown eyes widened. "I had to see you. What happened? I was sure you were dead, but memories of you often passed through my mind, and now I understand why. How did you escape? Or did my father set you free and allow me to believe you were resting on the bottom of the Nile?"

Kadar's mind reeled. Lydia hadn't forgotten him. She actually remembered his name—and thought about him. He swallowed the emotions crowding his throat. "I was enslaved in a copper mine."

Lydia paled. "You suffered terribly, I can see it in your face. I'm so sorry. Can you ever forgive me?"

Forgive *her*? "You weren't to blame."

She reached for his hands. "I shouldn't have asked you to come to me in Egypt. It was selfish."

Her slender fingers grasped his. The sorrow he saw in her eyes wasn't pity. No, she was pained for him, for what he'd suffered. "Don't be sorry. I'm not."

"You are a good man."

Her skin was wonderfully soft and warm. Heart hammering, he forced himself to remain perfectly still. Upright Jewish women such as Lydia kept far away from men who were not a part of their immediate family, but she had never shied from him. She'd never been afraid of him, not even a little. "I'm a rascal, and worse," he said, his voice rough. "Yet from the very first you trusted me. I don't understand."

"Why wouldn't I trust you?"

"I'm a pagan."

Her eyes swept over him, then met his and held. "I feel safe with you."

"But why?"

"I don't know," she whispered.

The air sparked between them.

Brynhild tiptoed toward the door.

"Don't go, woman," he commanded. If he and Lydia were found alone together, Lydia's reputation would suffer irreparable harm. And if anyone saw her touching him—

Damnation! They stoned people to death for less. He untangled their hands. Lydia blushed prettily and, the gods save him, he wanted to kiss her breathless.

Lydia swallowed. The fervor in Kadar's brilliant blue eyes matched the hot heat rushing through her. *Was this how it felt to be truly awakened as a woman?* The two men she'd called husband had unfailingly repulsed her. But Kadar was handsome and well formed and ... and absolutely splendid. If only she was married to him. The glorious, yellow-golden hair brushing his shoulders illuminated an inescapable truth—the daughters of Israel didn't marry pagans. She stepped back and bumped into the marble bench. "We ought to go. I've already caused you too much trouble."

Kadar pressed closer. "Wait. What happened to your child?"

A familiar ache tugged at her heart. "Father sent my baby away. I hope to see him very soon. I have a plan. Not much of a plan, but..."

Like the glory of the sun breaking through black storm clouds, a smile spread across Kadar's rugged face, a visage weathered and lined by years of brutal labor in the confines of a copper mine. "A plan? Let me hear this *plan* of yours."

Loathe to entangle him in more of her troubles, she hesitated.

"I won't stop until I coax the truth from you." His voice was gentle but firm.

His reappearance in her life couldn't be an accident. "My sister and her husband will arrive in Jerusalem soon for the feast days. They will set up their camp next to the family who has my baby. I shouldn't call him a baby. James is six years old now." Tears pricked at her eyes. "My sister has written to me saying James is healthy and well cared for, but I want to hold him and tell him how much I love him." She rubbed her hands over arms that still felt empty. "I want to observe and talk to the woman raising little James to see if she is kind and goodhearted. If she is the mean sort—" She squeezed her eyes closed and trembled at the memory of Judas the Zealot looming over her with a leather strap. "If I find the grandmother unacceptable, I will ask my sister or perhaps my brother James to help me—"

Kadar crossed his arms and widened his stance. "I will help you."

He wasn't asking her permission. The fierce determination stamped on his face told her he was ready to do whatever she asked. He'd been just a young man when he promised to help her last time, probably no more than eighteen or nineteen. Could she justify placing him in danger again? But what if she needed to run away with her baby? She massaged her temple. "I need time to think on the matter."

Bryn slipped a protective arm around Lydia's shoulder. "You will do what you have to. You brave ones always find a way."

Lydia's laugh was brittle. "I appreciate your kind regard, but..." she twisted her hands into the folds of her tunic. "I have no worldly goods; not even the clothes I'm wearing are truly mine."

Bryn wrinkled her nose. "You did just fine when your aunt turned you out into the streets of Egypt, and you'll do fine now."

A chill went through Lydia just thinking about her terrifying flight through the streets of Alexandria.

"Turned you out?" Kadar's face grew stony. "It's what the gossips are saying, but I assumed it was the usual exaggerated horse sh—" He emitted a rumbling growl and raked long fingers through his golden-blond hair. "Forgive my foul mouth. But you were alone? On those streets! Please tell me a neighbor took you in."

Lydia patted Bryn's hand. "I wasn't alone. Bryn begged to go with me, and my aunt consented. I told Bryn she'd be better off with my aunt, but she wouldn't listen."

Bryn narrowed her eyes at Kadar. "Mistress Lydia might look helpless as a wide-eyed kitten, but my dear girl has a quick mind and the heart of a lioness."

Blue eyes swept over Lydia.

Her cheeks heated. "Brynhild is too kind."

"Bah!" Bryn swiped the air with her hand. "I'm spitting angry. I want to clobber your father over the head with a staff.

The wicked man…leaving you without so much as a chamber pot to call your own."

Kadar raised his brows at Lydia. "Your father didn't make any provisions for you, even though he gave you to an old man who would most likely leave you a widow?"

"Simeon Onias is lower than a snake," Bryn answered for her, disgusted. "Mistress Sarah's family made sure she was taken care of, but Simeon didn't set aside a single shekel for his daughter."

Lydia didn't want people to pity her, especially not Bryn and Kadar. She stood taller. "I don't need much." She wanted her baby. Material goods meant nothing.

"Why aren't you under the protection of your father-in-law?" Kadar asked. "Why are back under your father's control?"

Lydia sighed. "My grandfather would have also been my father-in-law, but he died when I was a young girl. My father is the head of the family."

Bryn grunted. "Simeon Onias is the most uncaring man I've ever met."

If Lydia had the strength, she'd smile. Her father would be outraged if he heard people he disdainfully referred to as "uncivilized barbarians" were criticizing *him*.

Bryn's hand rubbed over Lydia's back. "My fierce kitten did just fine on her own."

Lydia did smile then. "The Lord watched over us."

"I prayed to Freyja," Bryn said. "The gods were merciful, and Mistress Lydia guided us to safety, brave as could be."

Kadar's eyes showed approval.

Lydia swallowed. Brave? It was not how she recalled their flight. The smell of her own fear and the garbage-strewn streets and the press of sweat-soaked bodies had lingered in her nostrils for days after. "We walked fast and kept our heads down and reached shelter before night."

"Walked fast?" Kadar shook his head. "Kept your heads down? I want to murder your aunt."

"We were well taken care of," Lydia reassured him.

Matters had moved quickly after she and Bryn found a

safe haven among Aunt Sarah's distant relations. A second cousin booked passage for them on a small trading vessel. Another cousin accompanied her over sea and land to Jerusalem. They had arrived in the city a week earlier and had been taken in by Cousin Nehonya. Suddenly tired, Lydia leaned on Bryn.

Kadar nudged Bryn aside and guided Lydia to the stone bench. He knelt in front of her and said something to her in his native tongue. The rich, deep sound tingled down her spine.

Bryn gasped and chastised Kadar in the same guttural language.

His crystal blue eyes alight with amusement, he winked at Bryn and said something back.

The pear-shaped woman blushed and giggled.

Lydia blinked. *Bryn didn't giggle.*

Kadar grinned. "I think your slave might be sweet on me."

Bryn gave him a slight slap on the arm. "Mind yourself around Mistress Lydia."

Lydia gripped the stone bench lest she give into the urge to throw her arms around Kadar. "I'm so very glad you're alive," she said, her heart bursting with unfamiliar joy.

Desire darkened Kadar's eyes.

Her flesh warmed. "My sister and her husband still pitch their tent in the olive groves east of the city. I hope to spend time with them. If you were to visit when I am there, we could talk…" Was she actually inviting Kadar to meet with her? The thought of never seeing him again made it hard to swallow. "Am I asking too much?"

Loud knocking and shouts came from the front door. Kadar, Lydia and Bryn hurried to the entrance of the small alcove. Hand on the hilt of his sword, Kadar took up a protective stance. Lydia peered past his massive back and watched the doorman pull open the mansion's tall double doors. Four slaves crossed the threshold carrying a flimsy litter bearing an unconscious man covered with blood. A diagonal scar crossed the man's face.

James. Dear angels in heaven, what's happened?

His head almost scraping the low ceiling of the corridor outside James Onias's bedchamber, Kadar leaned against the bare block wall. Rooted in the same spot for the better part of the afternoon already, he refused to leave until he was sure of Lydia's brother's fate.

The bedchamber door opened yet again, and Antipater's personal physician, Avda Hama, stepped out into corridor.

Kadar pushed away from the wall. "Will he live?"

Distracted, Hama barely glanced at Kadar. "Only the Lord can say."

Kadar threw his arm out, blocking the physician's path. "Have you been able rouse him?"

Hama's bearded chin jerked up. An educated man in his early thirties, and surprisingly fit, the physician frowned. "The patient is still unconscious. Now step aside and allow me to go about my business."

Kadar widened his stance and rested his hand next to the hilt of his sword."What other damage did the fall do?"

Hama arched a brow. "What business is it of yours?"

Kadar's concern for James Onias's health was selfish. He needed the young man alive and well for Lydia's sake, so she would have a guardian after Kadar killed her father. He didn't need this arrogant man questioning him. "Just answer me."

"I will...if only to get you out of my way," Hama said in a clipped voice. "Most of the damage was minor. One arm suffered a nasty gash, and he has numerous bumps and bruises. The blow to the head was the worst. It's too soon to tell if the injury will prove fatal."

The bedchamber door opened again, and Brynhild and another slave hurried off on an errand. Lydia stepped into the hall behind them. "Kadar, you're still here?" She sounded pleased. "You didn't have to stay."

Resisting the urge to reach for her, Kadar dug his fingertips into his hips. "I thought you might need help. What can I do?"

"Hmmm...let me think." Her shoulders fell. "Sorry, my mind is a muddled mess. At this point there's not much any of us can do." She gave Avda Hama a weary smile. "I'm glad I caught you before you went too far."

"What else may I do for you?" Hama replied, far too attentive for Kadar's liking. He wanted to punch the damnable man.

Lydia glanced over at the bedchamber door. "I'd like to cleanse the blood from James, if you think it may be safely done."

Hama smiled. "Yes, absolutely. It would, in fact, be a great help. Your brother is blessed to have such a steady and caring sister."

Lydia pushed her hair away from her pretty, flushed face. "I am relieved James is under the care of a skilled physician."

Hama stepped closer to her. "I count it a pleasure to serve you and your brother."

Kadar ground his teeth and thumped Hama on the shoulder. "You are in for a busy afternoon. The household slaves are chattering about Cypros. Reportedly the grand lady has taken to her rooms with one of her crippling headaches."

Hama's smile disappeared. "I haven't heard word of it." Antipater affectionately called his wife a *difficult woman*. Cypros was a hateful shrew, and that was one of the kinder things to be said about her.

Kadar shrugged. "It's what I heard."

Hama combed fingers through his thick black beard. "I should go look in on her. I'll return as soon as possible with a balsam cure for your brother," he promised, then hurried off.

Lydia wrinkled her nose. "I hate to be selfish, but for James's sake, I hope Cypros doesn't take up too much of Physician Hama's time."

"He won't be gone long."

Lydia's soft laugh soothed like a caress. "How can you be so sure?"

"Cypros isn't ill. At least not to my knowledge."

"You lied?"

"It's not the cleverest tale I ever invented. But it served

the purpose."

Lydia's brow furrowed. "What purpose?" The cool breeze wafting through the corridor pushed loose tendrils of hair across her face.

He touched his fingertips to the silky strands. "Never mind." He didn't want to confess his jealousy. "I will stay in Jerusalem until your brother's fate is determined."

Lydia swallowed. "You don't have to."

Yes, he did. "I want to."

"My sister and Nathan should arrive soon."

He brushed her hair back behind her ears. She trembled, and the vibration went straight through him."I'll give you into their care when they come. Until then—"

Brynhild came around the corner carrying a water pitcher and clean rags. He and Lydia stepped apart.

The slave woman nodded. "I'm glad to see a man such as you watching over my kitten."

A rosy blush spread across Lydia's almond-colored cheeks.

Kadar scrubbed his face. Safe as a lamb watched over by a wolf. Except this lamb was strongly attracted to the wolf. Lydia needed a reminder he was a barbarian. He shifted closer to Bryn and patted her pear-shaped buttocks. "Women from Gaul like to take scoundrels to their beds, isn't that so?"

Lydia flinched.

Stomach churning over her hurt look, he rubbed his whiskers over the side of Brynhild's face.

The slave swatted him with the rags clutched in her hand.

Lydia whirled around, opened the bedchamber door, and disappeared.

He stepped away from the slave woman with an apologetic frown.

Brynhild scowled up at him. "You want her. Why are you pushing her away?"

"She deserves a better life than I can give her."

"What makes you think so?"

He exhaled heavily. Lydia deserved a real home and a stable life, not the perpetual nomadic existence stretching out before him.

Brynhild patted his arm, then re-entered James's room.

Kadar stood alone in the empty hallway for a long, long time.

Chapter 9

Later that day, after Physician Hama informed them James Onias might not wake for days or weeks, Kadar went looking for Antipater and caught the governor of Judea coming out of a private reception chamber followed by his loyal slave, Saad.

Kadar nodded in greeting. "Don't laugh in my face when you hear what I have to say."

Antipater flashed a wide smile but kept walking, and signaled Kadar to join him. "You aren't leaving Jerusalem, am I right?"

"There are matters requiring my attention. My business could take weeks or a handful of days. So—"

"You need work," Antipater guessed. "And a place to sleep."

Kadar nodded. "I'll do whatever needs doing for food and a bed."

"I will pay you a wage too. You can start right now."

"Now? Where are we going?"

"To see a man about taxes."

"Do you expect trouble?"

Antipater laughed. "Every hour of every day."

Saad limped past them, grimacing as he opened the front door.

Antipater halted beside the crippled slave. "Your knee is bothering you more than usual, I see."

"It's a bit stiff." Saad's smile was forced. "But the walk will loosen it up."

Antipater stroked his beard and studied his slave for a long moment. "I want you to stay behind. You—"

"I am aware I'm growing old." Saad struggled to stand

erect. "But I'm not feeble."

Antipater patted the slave's arm. "No one said you were. I want you to get regular reports on James Onias's condition. Come find us if the boy takes a turn for the worse."

Mollified, the slave nodded and stepped back.

Kadar followed Antipater out the door and past the curious guards. "Who are we going to meet?"

"Malichus."

"How did that backstabber steal command of your army, anyway?"

"I gave up the post." Antipater smiled again, and a twinkle lit his eyes. "It seems the Governor of Judea can't be spared to fight the occasional war. High Priest Hycranus wanted his good friend Malichus to succeed me. I agreed against my better judgment, and have spent all my time since righting the fool's mistakes."

"Malichus struck me as a man too greedy for his own good."

"Malichus is ambitious to the point of recklessness. Then there's the little problem of him wanting me dead, so he can dispose of Hycranus and make himself king." Antipater led them into the stream of people moving along Jerusalem's main thoroughfare. Broad of chest and robust, he waved or smiled to everyone who acknowledged him.

"I'm surprised you tolerate him," Kadar said.

"I shouldn't." Antipater veered off the road and stopped in front of a jeweler's stall. Sunlight sparkled over polished gold baubles, bracelets, and rings. Antipater draped a diamond-studded headpiece over his bronzed arm. "Cypros is unhappy with me. A shiny new trinket might distract my dear wife, don't you agree?"

The smiling merchant's head bobbed eagerly while he chirped a steady stream of encouragements.

Kadar's eye was drawn to a bright red scarf. The color would look stunning against Lydia's olive skin.

Antipater dangled the jeweled band in front of Kadar. "What do you think?"

Doubting anything would cure Cypros's bad moods for

long, Kadar shrugged.

Antipater sighed, handed the headpiece back to the disappointed merchant, and moved on. The crowds grew thicker as they neared the Temple of the God of Israel. The east wind increased, carrying the scent of roasted meat and rich spices. Antipater's chest expanded. "Ahhh, the aroma of heaven. I never grow tired of the smell of sacrifices. Makes me giddy as when I was a boy, excited at the prospect of our yearly trips to Jerusalem." He slapped Kadar's back companionably. "You ought to convert to Judaism. Marry a good Jewish girl."

Kadar coughed. "Me?"

Antipater laughed again. "Yes, you."

"I say this with all respect. I have lived among your people long enough to have learned you have a worthy God. But your God demands too much." Kadar clutched the amulet hanging from his neck. The Northland's gods were all he had left of his old life. "I would have to give up my gods to worship yours."

Antipater shielded his mouth with his hand. "For the world to see, yes. What you do behind the closed doors of your home is another matter." An Idumean who had married a pagan from Nabatea, Antipater was likely turning a blind eye to members of his household who secretly bowed down to idols.

Kadar made a face. If Lydia Onias was the prize, he might give the ruse serious consideration. But daughters of priests didn't marry ex-slaves with no rank, money or property. "You keep your God and I'll keep mine."

"You don't bend easily to others. A worthy trait."

Kadar raised a brow. "And?"

The Idumean's hearty laugh turned heads. "Aaannnd, Malichus is not aware of it yet, but you two are about to become well acquainted."

"Please tell me I get to punch the fiend if he becomes too obnoxious."

"A tempting offer I wish I could agree to." Antipater's smile fell away. "Malichus has been dragging his feet about collecting the taxes owed Rome. The people love him for it, meanwhile Rome is sending threats." Antipater wrinkled his nose. "The viper did something similar a few years ago, and Rome's reply was to sell four Judean cities into slavery. And, of course, the fractious Romans were occupied with another civil war, so it took me many months to rectify matters. The Roman official sent to investigate the debacle proposed executing Malichus. But I foolishly spared his life, *again*."

They left the road and walked up a stone path to a fairly large home. Antipater lifted his hand to knock at the door. "I plan to send you out with Malichus to collect the taxes. I don't want you to take no for an answer from anyone. What do you say?"

Kadar liked Antipater, and wanted to help him outmaneuver his enemies. "Malichus will learn to hate me."

"I'm counting on it, Barbarian. I'm counting on it."

Come nightfall, after making a point of staying away from James Onias's sickroom and Lydia Onias, Kadar accompanied Antipater to a hastily-arranged banquet hosted by High Priest John Hycranus.

Antipater came to an abrupt halt under the arched entryway to the luxurious hall. "John assured me this was a small, private affair." Heaving a sigh, the governor of Judea followed the slave assigned to escort him to the head table.

Kadar scanned the crowded hall, searching for Malichus. The crafty man had given an obviously-invented excuse when Kadar and Antipater pressed him to make the rounds collecting taxes. Kadar meant to set Malichus straight, make it clear that his time of wiggling out of his responsibilities was at an end.

Huffing and puffing, Saad limped up beside Kadar. "James Onias's condition hasn't changed. His sister has returned to her cousin's home and plans to return to care for him early tomorrow morning. She didn't want to leave, but Physician Hamas promised Onias's sister he would send for her if her brother worsened."

A loud clatter echoed through the chamber. All eyes turned to see shattered plates scattered across the mosaic-tiled floor. The young slave responsible for dropping the reed tray scooped it off the floor, and promptly lost hold of it, again. The boy's freckled face turned red as his hair.

Saab clapped his hands to his head. "Niv! What is the matter with the overgrown clod? He's turning out to be a fumbling ninny."

A one-eyed soldier wearing a patch stopped beside Niv and whispered in the boy's ear. The color drained from Niv's pudgy face. Kadar's muscles tensed when he recognized the soldier. *Lazarz.* The grizzled warrior noticed Kadar's stare and smiled. Lazarz was Malichus's second-in-command, and the cocky, self-satisfied smirk on his face was the very one the arrogant man wore earlier when Antipater introduced Kadar to Malichus.

"I best go help the fool clean up the mess," Saab said stumping away.

Lazarz broke eye contact with Kadar and squeezed Niv's shoulder. The boy winced. The one-eyed man spoke into Niv's ear again. The red-headed boy nodded furiously and patted the bulging cloth pouch tied to his belt. Lazarz moved off and took a seat between Malichus and Avda Hama at the table reserved for household retainers and staff. A slave directed Kadar to the same table.

"Thundering Thor," Kadar grumbled. A pack of wild dogs would make better company than Malichus and Lazarz. Ignoring the pair, Kadar sat beside Hama. "I hear the Lady Cypros is recovered."

Hama's brows rose. "Indeed. I must be a miracle worker, for the Lady Cypros was cured before I entered her presence."

Kadar smiled and nodded his respect, glad to see the man didn't take himself too seriously. "Everyone says James Onias couldn't ask for a better healer. Antipater sang your praises."

The tension went out of Hama's shoulders. "James Onias's head wound is beyond my powers. I have done all I can. He is in the Lord's hands now." The physician turned to Lazarz. "I'm told you are the one who found James. Was he conscious when you came upon him?"

Lazarz lifted his rock-hewn mug, chugged back some wine, wiped his mouth on his sleeve, and loosed a loud burp. "I shook him till his teeth clattered and slapped him hard across the face, but he never roused."

Hama's mouth hardened. "Your brutish actions may have hurt more than helped."

"The boy was half-dead before I laid a finger on him." Lazarz's smug smile made a reappearance. "I'll try to be more careful next time."

Kadar gripped his mug. Wishing it was Lazarz's neck he was wringing, he rescued Hama from the fiend. "How long have you served in Antipater's household?"

Hama blew out a long breath. "Our families go way back. I grew up around his sons. Spent my youth bumped and bruised trying to keep up with Herod, who was five years older."

"Your beard fooled me. You're only thirty?"

"My father was a physician. He started tutoring me when I was ten. Antipater used to haul me in front of his friends, tell them I was a child prodigy and ask me to prove it by reciting the names of rare diseases and exotic cures." Hama smiled fondly. "He wouldn't hear of hiring any other physician after my father's death."

Kadar nodded. "Antipater is loyal."

"I hear you are once again serving as his bodyguard."

"For a short time." Kadar pointed across the table. "Antipater asked me to escort Malichus throughout Jerusalem to help him collect Rome's taxes."

Malichus stared down his pompous nose. "Talk of taxes at the dinner table is crude."

"Crude barbarian," Lazarz mocked, his grating voice loud enough to carry to outer Gaul.

Kadar wanted to beat Lazarz into the ground. Never comfortable at formal banquets, Kadar didn't appreciate having this loud jackass call attention to him.

"I'm the commander of Hycranus's army," Malichus whined. "I should be seated at the head table."

"You deserve a seat of prominence," Lazarz declared. "Where men like these..." the one-eyed man waved his mug, sloshing wine over Hama and Kadar, "...will grovel at your feet."

Kadar reached across the table and grabbed a handful of tunic.

Lazarz pounded on Kadar's arm. "Take your filthy hands off me!"

A guttural groan lanced through general chatter. All eyes went to the head table, to Antipater laying on his side, writhing violently. Screams and panicked shouts followed.

Kadar released Lazarz, jumped to his feet, and sprinted to Antipater.

"Is he sick?" Kadar asked, kneeling down next to Antipater.

"He was fine a moment ago," a shaken John Hycranus said.

Kadar laid his hand on Antipater's rigid shoulder. "Are you in pain?" The ashen-faced man stopped jerking, his eyes rolled up in his head, and he went limp. Kadar had seen death too many times to mistake the signs.

Hama stepped through the circle of onlookers and crouched down next to Kadar.

Sick at heart, Kadar sat back on his heels. "He's beyond help."

Hama nodded. "Poisoned."

"Poison." The word spread like wildfire through the chamber.

"Did you see anyone acting suspiciously?" Hama asked.

Kadar glanced around, searching for the skittish red-haired boy who had dropped the tray. "Antipater had plenty of enemies."

Hama exhaled heavily. "Cypros and his sons will take the news hard. The oldest three are nearby. Do you know where Herod is?"

Kadar wouldn't want to be anywhere nearby when Herod learned his father had been murdered. "Syria, I think."

Hama crouched down beside Kadar, and spoke in his ear.

"With Antipater dead, Jerusalem is quickly going to become a very dangerous place. If you have somewhere else to go, I'd be heading there."

Kadar's thoughts went to Lydia. "Thanks for the warning," he said, but he wasn't about to leave the city.

Saad hobbled up. His face crumpled. "Master Antipater was a good man. He didn't complain when I began to slow down. What will become of me now?"

Everyone associated with the governor of Judea would be asking the same question and scrambling to align with potential successors.

Malichus and Lazarz came and stood beside High Priest Hycranus.

"This is abominable," Malichus cried. "We must mourn him properly. A large funeral, with no expenses spared."

"I'll command the army to go into mourning," Lazarz added, with a barely-concealed smile.

Wary of Malichus already, the tearful performance only increased Kadar's suspicion that Malichus and Lazarz had a hand in murdering Antipater.

"Jerusalem has lost a gem of a man," Hycranus said. "I cannot imagine how I will replace him."

Malichus wiped his tears away. "My assistance is yours to command."

Anger boiled up in Kadar, the same fury he would have felt over the murder of a fellow Northman. He'd do all in his power to punish Antipater's murderers, beginning with beating a confession out of Lazarz.

Kadar climbed to his feet. "Where did Lazarz go?"

The others shrugged. Kadar searched the hall, but the one-eyed man had disappeared.

Chapter 10

Lydia laid a balsam compress across the crown of her brother's head. Though a bit leery over the noisy crowd of protesters outside Antipater's home, she had insisted on being here as usual. James needed family by his side.

Cousin Nehonya wasn't pleased with her. He feared Antipater's death would embolden those who hated the Idumeans. Lydia had listened politely, then informed her cousin she needed to attend to James and would be sure to return to his home before dark.

She tucked a blanket around James. Full of empathy for Antipater's widow and children, and concern for her brother, her mind also continued to go in circles over Kadar's offer to help her steal her son away from Judas's family if need be.

Someone knocked at the door. "I'll wager it's Kadar!" Bryn crowed from her seat by the open window, "I was sure the handsome rascal wouldn't be able to stay away from you."

Lydia's heart skipped a beat. "You are making too much of the matter. When I learned Kadar was alive, I needed to see him. I saw him and I thanked him and apologized for all he suffered on my account. It was nothing more than that."

Bryn hurried to the door. "I hope you're not angry with Kadar for patting my backside. He was just playing."

"Of course not." Lydia readily dismissed the crass way Kadar had behaved, suspecting he'd done it on purpose. She knew he was aware of it, too—the invisible cord pulling them toward each other, present from the first moment they'd breathed the same air. "Kadar must be incredibly busy," Lydia insisted even while she hoped, in her heart of hearts, it was

Kadar standing on the other side of the door.

James moaned.

Lydia forced her eyes back to her brother. Encouraged by this sign of life, she dabbed his hot brow with the wet cloth. "James, wake up," she cooed. "Wake up."

"How is he?" a familiar voice asked.

Lydia gasped and swiveled around. "Alexandra?"

Her sister rushed toward her and Lydia leapt to her feet. They met in the middle of the room, and hugged, holding tight. Lydia didn't want to let go. It had been six long years since she'd laid eyes on her beloved sister.

Alexandra stepped back, her dove gray eyes sweeping over Lydia. "How are you, dear?"

Lydia laughed and hugged Alexandra again. "I'm well. And...I'm so happy you are here." Lydia missed having her sister mother her.

Thick, dark curls held in place by a bright blue scarf, Alexandra glowed with beauty and contentment. "I hope Uncle Jacob and Aunt Sarah were good to you, dear?"

Bryn clucked her disgust. "They could have done better by my kitten."

"It was trying at times," Lydia admitted. Sorrow and loneliness wrapped around her like creeping vines threatening to suck her back into the abyss of despair those years represented. Lydia squeezed her sister's fingers and swung their arms back and forth. "Do you remember the songs we made up when we were girls? I've missed hearing your lovely voice."

The lines of concern etching Alexandra's brow smoothed. "You are the one who made up the fun songs and games and stories."

Lydia hummed a note. Alexandra grinned, and they swayed from side to side while they sang their favorite song. When they came to the chorus, they exchanged wide smiles, and shouted, "Goliath of Gath!" Laughing they collapsed into each other's arms.

Alexandra kissed Lydia's cheek. "I'm so glad to see you haven't lost your gift of joy."

"Your young cousins could sing that silly song for hours," Brynhild tutted.

It was silly, but playfulness suited Lydia better than sullenness. Two years old when her mother died, they had been raised by a father who treated his daughters with either indifference or hostility. Alexandra had been both a mother and sister to Lydia and James, worrying over them like a hen over her chicks. Lydia had done what she could to add a bit of sunshine to the cold, beautifully appointed home they'd been trapped in for countless days and weeks at a time.

Lydia crossed to Bryn, looped her arm around the sturdy woman's elbow, and drew her forward. "Alexandra, this is Brynhild. She fusses over me as much as you ever did."

Bryn made a face.

Lydia squeezed the slave woman's arm. "You will love Alexandra. Everybody does."

Alexandra graced Bryn with a warm smile. "Brynhild, it's a pleasure to finally meet you. Lydia always spoke glowingly of you in her letters."

Bryn snorted. "Sounds like a waste of costly paper, if you ask me."

Lydia and Alexandra laughed.

James stirred. They rushed to his side and knelt beside his raised platform. Lydia removed the compress from her brother's head and set it in a bowl. "This is a good sign. Physician Hama said the sooner James wakes, the more hope there is for a full recovery."

Alexandra patted James's hand. "James, dear, can you hear me?" He moaned.

"Wake up, James," Lydia coaxed.

Nothing.

"He fell down some stairs?" Alexandra asked.

Lydia nodded. "I hardly had any time with him before the accident." She brushed his hair off his brow. "Have you and James resolved your differences with Father?"

Alexandra sighed. "I've tried. But father won't speak to me."

Lydia sat back on her heels and steered the conversation

back to more pleasant subjects. "Tell me about your children."

Alexandra smiled wide. "The boys are five and three. Baby Anna is one. They are wonderful. And excited to meet you."

Lydia grew light-headed. "Is my son here? Did Judith make the trip to Jerusalem?"

Alexandra put her arm around Lydia's shoulders. "Yes, they traveled with us. We arrived late yesterday. Would you like to come visit our camp now?"

Finally, finally, the moment she had dreamed about had arrived—she would soon hold her precious babe in her arms. Lydia clapped. "Oh, that sounds lovely. But..." She bit her lip and looked toward her brother. "I hate to leave James."

Alexandra patted her hand. "He won't be alone. Nathan has gone to ask Elizabeth to come sit with him."

"Elizabeth doesn't like James," Lydia said. So far, Elizabeth had made polite inquiries about James's progress, but she hadn't offered to come sit with Lydia.

Elizabeth arrived a short while later, and Lydia gave the care of her brother over to her cousin and Bryn, then left with Alexandra and Nathan. Anticipating the walk down the winding road to the Mount of Olives, she recalled her and Alexandra's excitement over the annual feasts, when festival pilgrims poured into Jerusalem. Despite the confusion and crowds, Father's mood always improved. Sometimes he went so far as to smile or buy them honeyed nuts.

They hurried out of the house. The mob celebrating news of Antipater's death had doubled in size since morning. Triple the number of guards now stood watch outside of Antipater's palatial home.

Nathan stopped to have a word with the head guardsman.

Lydia surveyed the boisterous throng and spotted a lumbering, bushy-bearded man called Bear. He'd been one of Judas's raiders. A bitter taste filled her mouth at the memory of dank caves and smoldering campfires.

"They continue to hate Antipater," Lydia murmured.

Judas the Zealot's voice still rang inside her head on occasion. *No king but the Lord.* Judas the Zealot had preached impassioned messages calling for the overthrow of Judea's corrupt rulers. Lydia quickly learned it was in her best interest to disavow Antipater and High Priest Hycranus, at least until Nathan and Kadar rescued her from the outlaw band, killed Judas, and put an end to the small rebellion.

Revitalized by Antipater's death, his critics and enemies were crawling out of hiding now.

Lydia welcomed the touch of Alexandra's arm around her waist. "Don't be afraid, dear. Nathan and I are here to watch over you. We won't let anyone harm you."

Lydia forced her shoulders back. "I'm not afraid." But her stomach sickened at the memory of her captivity. She'd started out resisting Judas when he pushed himself on her, but he'd whip her with a strap until she gave in and kissed him and called him husband. Then Judas had abducted Alexandra. And Alexandra had witnessed Lydia go willingly into Judas's arms. Lydia's face heated and she squeezed her eyes shut, imagining her sister's disgust and disappointment.

"Are you sure you want to go to our camp?" Alexandra asked. "You may come across other men you have no wish to behold."

Lydia wanted to believe the past couldn't hurt her anymore, but jolts of panic shot through her. The thought of facing Judas the Zealot's brothers and kin made her want to run in the opposite direction. She shook off her dread and distaste. "I must go. My baby is there." To ease her sister's worries, she smiled and turned the conversation. "How is your new olive grove coming along?"

Alexandra's eyes lit. "The trees are almost mature. If the Lord wills, we should produce double the fruit and oil to sell either this year or the next."

Nathan rejoined them. Alexandra moved closer to him. "Lydia was asking about the orchard."

Nathan ran his hand down Alexandra's arm. "We have a small army of people working for us. But Lex keeps the farm running smoothly, making sure everyone is fed and clothed, and tending the sick and injured. I'm convinced she could command an army." Ruggedly handsome, Nathan was also a man very much in love with his wife.

He gave every evidence of being as good a man, husband, and father as her sister's letters portrayed, but seeing Nathan vividly reminded her of her bleakest hours, and of seeing Nathan run his sword through Judas the Zealot. Her numb desolation afterwards. Her baby being torn from her arms. Lydia fisted her hands in the folds of her tunic.

Nathan turned to her. "I'm sorry for your husband's death."

She ducked her head. Consumed with worries over her brother's welfare and the coming reunion with her son, she'd hardly given Uncle Jacob or Aunt Sarah a thought. She would write to the girls tonight, and make up a lighthearted story about her journey to Jerusalem and describe to them the beauty and wonder of the Temple. "Uncle's death was a difficult time," she told Nathan. "Aunt Sarah and the girls were devastated."

"No king but the Lord!" the protesters chanted louder.

A cold sweat dampened Lydia's palms and forehead.

Alexandra's brow wrinkled with concern. "I promised Rhoda we wouldn't be gone long."

"Don't take Rhoda's grumbling too seriously," Nathan said. "My stepmother has a good heart hiding behind her sharp tongue."

Alexandra clasped her husband's hand. "Did you buy the honeyed nuts?"

Nathan smiled. "I wouldn't dare go back to the camp without them." He led them away from the noisy protestors and down a shaded path. Kadar came barreling around the corner of Antipater's over-sized home, almost colliding with them.

"Job's bones," Nathan exclaimed. "I can't believe my eyes. Kadar?"

"Praise heaven," Alexandra said, then she turned to Lydia. "Do you remember Kadar, dear?"

Two heads taller than Nathan, Kadar's golden-blond hair

shone like an extra sun in the sky. Skin prickling, Lydia nodded.

She half expected him to ignore her, or to turn around and go the other way, but his intense blue eyes locked with hers. "What's troubling you?"

"Nothing's troubling me," Lydia said making her voice cheerful, aware of Alexandra and Nathan's raised brows.

Kadar crossed his arms and waited.

"I'm fine. Truly."

"Don't try to fool me, woman. Now, tell me what's got you worried"

There it was again—a shared, intimate knowledge of each other—one that ought to take years to form. She hugged arms, remembering the comfort she'd experienced when he carried her out of the bandit's camp. "I'm on my way to see my baby."

He moved closer to her and his eyes softened. "Are you? The boy will take to you, straight off."

"I hope you're right." She swayed toward him.

Kadar brushed a stray strand of hair behind her ear. "He will like you just fine, woman."

The tension knotting her stomach eased. "Thank you," she whispered.

Nathan stepped between them and drew Kadar away from her. "Where have you been hiding all these years, my friend?" A tone of rebuke underscored the genial words. "What brings you back to Judea?"

Kadar shot her an apologetic look.

As always, his presence calmed and soothed. She flapped her hand, assuring him there was no reason for concern.

Shoulders relaxing, Kadar nodded a greeting at Nathan and Alexandra. "It's good to see you. How are you?"

Nathan patted the fat coin pouch tied to his belt. "We are healthy and happy. What have you been up to?"

Kadar shrugged. "I was in the desert doing a little of this and that. As to why I'm here..." He exhaled a weary breath and scrubbed his face. "I came to settle some old business, then I plan to leave this region for good."

A lump grew in Lydia's throat at hearing Kadar brush away what he suffered these last six years as easily as sweeping crumbs from a table. Or maybe the discomfort had to do with the idea he would go away and she'd never see him again.

A loud chant erupted from the crowd celebrating Antipater's murder. "Death to foreigners! Death to foreigners!" they yelled at the guardsmen.

A mix of Idumeans and mercenaries, the guardsmen clutched their sword handles and shuffled nervously.

Lydia flinched, seeing the raider named Bear and some others aiming angry looks at Kadar.

Kadar's light blue eyes iced over. "You'll be safer out of my company." He turned to leave.

Nathan put his hand on Kadar's arm. "Would you mind walking back with us to our campsite?"

Kadar frowned. "Are you looking for trouble?"

"No, I'm looking for the use of your sword." Nathan grinned, but it was forced. "Mine's tucked away in my tent." He stared in the direction of the agitated throng. "Antipater used his fierce reputation and a large army to maintain peace in the land for the last fifteen years, but it hasn't been a happy peace. Matters might turn ugly very quickly." Nathan looked back at Kadar. "I'd like an able man at my side if trouble breaks out."

Kadar fixed his eyes on Lydia. "You can count on me. I will stay in Jerusalem for as long as you need me."

Relief coursed through her, even as guilt stabbed at her heart. She gained strength and comfort from Kadar's promise. What did he get? Trouble, nothing but trouble. *Why?* She mouthed.

He winked at her, making her toes curl in her sandals. Then he turned to Nathan. "Herod could give you more protection than a barbarian turned mercenary soldier."

"Herod washed his hands of me," Nathan said, then exhaled heavily. "Herod will be crushed when he hears about his father. My heart died within me when I heard the news. The last time I saw Antipater, he looked hale and hearty. Is it true, was he poisoned?"

Somber, Kadar nodded. "I'm afraid so."

"Herod will burn with murder once he learns the truth," Nathan said glancing around uneasily.

"Herod might not have the luxury of avenging his father." Kadar patted the giant sword hanging at his side. "He may be too busy fighting for his own survival. You should prepare for another war."

Nathan groaned. "More war. The Lord save us."

Alexandra moved closer to Lydia, and they wrapped their arms around each other. Lydia had been seven years old when the Romans invaded Jerusalem. She didn't have many memories of it, other than her terrible fear.

Face ashen, Nathan led them out of the city. Kadar and Nathan talked of war and alliances and best-case, worst-case circumstances during their descent from Jerusalem to the Kidron Valley and then back up to the Mount of Olives.

Alexandra and Lydia trailed behind.

"I'm worried for Nathan," Alexandra confided. "He was a soldier for a short time when he was young. He fought beside Antipater and the Romans and helped make John Hycranus High Priest. He hates what he and others did back then. More war will be hard on him."

Lydia linked arms with her sister. She remembered Judas the Zealot's fiery sermons reviling the Roman intrusion. Judas and his followers had despised Nathan for siding with Rome. Yet Nathan and Alexandra had somehow managed to make peace with Judas's family and the rest of their neighbors. More war would jeopardize everything they'd worked for. "Will Nathan take up his sword again?"

"Only if the war comes to our farm," Alexandra said. "I hope all this worry comes to naught, but if war does break out, our farm should be safe. We live in a very remote spot. Nathan and I were going to ask you to come stay at the farm until your personal matters are settled. Now I'm twice as anxious to have you join us there."

Excitement welled within Lydia. If she went to Galilee, she could be with her darling baby. "What about poor James?

It could be weeks before he recovers from his fall. I don't like the idea of abandoning him."

Alexandra sighed. "I might be able to persuade Nathan to allow me to remain in Jerusalem with you."

Nathan's hearing must be keen, because he jerked around and scowled at Alexandra. "Nobody will be staying behind."

Alexandra smiled sweetly. "We can discuss the matter at more length in private."

Nathan looked like he wanted to argue, but he clamped his mouth shut.

Kadar's laugh was one of sympathy. "I agree with Nathan. It will be some time before Jerusalem is a safe place for women and children, or for men. You should all go to Galilee. I will watch over James."

"But what about you?" Lydia asked. "Who will watch over you?"

Kadar thumped his broad chest. "Do I look like I need protecting?"

Lydia chewed on her lip. She understood loneliness and didn't want that for him. He needed someone to care for him. "You should marry. It would be good for you."

"Marry?" he spluttered. "What has that got to do with anything?"

"You need a wife to worry over you. *If* you won't do it for yourself."

His smile was wicked. "Do you have someone in mind?"

Heat raced up her neck. She almost suggested he return to his homeland to find a wife, but found she hated the idea. "They say Cleopatra is keeping Mark Antony from fighting in Parthia."

Kadar choked. "Cleopatra... I'd rather kiss a crocodile."

Lydia clapped her arms open and closed in imitation of the toothy beast. "I believe Antony's generals would have an easier time prying their amorous commander away from the jaws of a croc than from Cleopatra."

Kadar and Nathan roared with laughter. Alexandra hugged Lydia. "I've missed your company. Come, the children are dancing with impatience to lay eyes on you. And

Judith has promised to come by with little James."

Alexandra led Lydia into an olive orchard alive with activity. A host of men, women, children, animals, and tents flashed by in a blur as her mind whirled with the prospect of beholding her sweet boy. Their journey came to end under an ancient, gnarled olive tree sheltering three black tents. A straight-backed woman and an older youth sat by a tidy campfire, watching a pair of small boys drawing pictures in the dirt with sticks.

"*Shalom*, Rhoda," Nathan called out. "We promised to be back before evening meal, and here we are."

The children dropped their sticks and raced toward them.

Lydia's breath caught. Was one of them her baby?

But the tousled-haired boys ran straight for Nathan. They wrapped their arms and legs around each of Nathan's legs. He patted their small heads. "Have you two monkeys been good for your grandmother?"

"Good, good," they sang together.

Nathan laid his hands on the boys' slim shoulders. "Our sons, Achan and Raziel."

Lydia smiled. "How handsome you are."

Three-year-old Raziel nodded with vigor. Five year old Achan scrunched his nose.

"The babies are napping," Rhoda scolded, rising slowly, eschewing the help of the older youth.

Lydia searched for a name. Timothy, the young man's name was Timothy, and he was Nathan's half-brother.

A young woman emerged from the larger tent, carrying a baby on each hip. "Look who's awake." One of the chubby-cheeked babies smiled and reached out her arms.

Alexandra hurried over and took her. "This is little Anna. How are you, my darling?" she cooed to the child, glancing back at Lydia and Kadar. Baby Anna babbled a merry reply, her little arms and legs waving and kicking.

Alexandra wrapped her arm around the pretty young woman holding the other baby. "Do you remember Mary?"

Lydia frowned. She ought to recognize the girl. The raiders who abducted Lydia had taken Mary captive too. Plus,

Lydia had spent two weeks with Nathan's family after she was rescued. Alexandra's letters were full of stories about, Mary, Timothy, and Rhoda. But none of the faces staring at Lydia looked familiar.

The horrible silence stretched on and on. Lydia hated the sympathy showing in their eyes, and knowing they'd witnessed her plunge into despair during that terribly dark time. Everyone believed she'd come to love Judas the Zealot and had been devastated by his death.

Her desolation had been complete, but it hadn't been because she loved Judas. A delusional man who killed innocent people, Judas had earned his violent death. But he was the father of her child, and by the time of her rescue, Lydia had come to accept him as a husband. And what did it say about her?

Lydia took refuge behind a bright smile. "Mary, blessings to you on the birth of your beautiful babe."

A young, strapping man joined Mary. "This is my husband, Cephas, and our sweet angel, Sameah," Mary said, fairly glowing with happiness. Cephas would be the stonecutter Mary had wed, the one Alexandra heaped praises upon in her letters. Shy as he was handsome, the stonecutter dipped his head in greeting.

"Happy marriage to you both," Lydia said.

Mary and Cephas murmured their thanks. Alexandra beamed with pride and love. Baby Anna reached over and pinched sweet Sameah, who squawked a complaint. Both babies burst into tears.

Everyone's attention turned to quieting the children.

Lydia heaved a sigh of relief, then felt Kadar's warm presence at her back.

"Well done, my *valkyrie*." His guttural voice tingled down her spine. "Brynhild would be proud of her *fierce kitten*."

"*Valkyrie*," she repeated, tangling the foreign word on her tongue. "What does—" Her throat closed. An old, stooped woman and a boy hurried along the path winding through the olive trees.

Lydia stared hard at the boy. Dark-headed and the size of Alexandra's oldest son, the boy was chattering away to the elderly woman. Lydia's heart leaped. It was her dear baby, her own sweet James.

Alexandra's oldest boy, Achan, shouted, "Judas, Judas, she's here! Come meet your mother."

Lydia flinched. *Judas?* A distant memory came back, of a letter from Alexandra saying Judith had given baby James a new name—Judas. Lydia had dismissed the notion and begged Alexandra to call her precious baby "James" in their letters. To Lydia he would always be *little James.*

"I meant to warn you," Alexandra apologized.

The boy turned toward them. He was all large brown eyes. He gave her a lopsided grin, reminding Lydia of her own brother's rare but beautiful smiles.

"Achan," little James said. "I have a new sling." He held up the prized possession. His grandmother took his other hand and directed him to a long, oblong-shaped tent sitting opposite Nathan and Alexandra's campsite. The tent walls were drawn up. Twenty or so individuals milled about under the shade of the canopy.

"Judith," Nathan called, but old woman continued her retreat.

"Wait," Lydia cried out, rushing after Judith.

Bearded, sober-faced men stepped out from the shade of the tent. Judas the Zealot's brothers. They stared at her with fiery, fearsome eyes.

Lydia froze.

Kadar and Nathan, radiating danger and a readiness to commit violence, positioned themselves on either side of Lydia. Though tempted to fight her way to her child, Lydia didn't want little James or Alexandra's children to witness such ugliness. Believing the brothers were cut from the same cloth as Judas, and would turn surly with a woman who wasn't properly humble, she lowered her eyes. "May I visit with my son?"

"My mother has changed her mind," a hard voice replied. "She doesn't want you to meet her grandson. She fears your presence will upset Judas."

Judas? They'd had the gall to name her dear boy after a maddened outlaw? Lydia fisted her hands in her tunic, and barely held back a screech of frustration.

Alexandra stepped forward. "May I speak to Judith?"

"Not today," a gruff voice said. The men turned and departed.

Lydia watched Judas's brothers file back into the oblong tent. She searched for little James, eager for another glimpse of her heart, her sunshine. He was surrounded by a group of boys inspecting his sling. Oblivious to her, he laughed and smiled with the others.

The side walls of the tent thumped to the ground with a finality that echoed through her bones, filling her with a heaviness as grim and black as the curtains cutting her off from her son.

Chapter 11

The first hour of Elizabeth's vigil over James Onias's sick bed passed quietly, so she sent Brynhild off to find a bit of food and wine.

At the sound of the door snapping closed, James's eyelids fluttered open and his black eyes met hers.

Elizabeth knelt beside the bed and held her breath, waiting for the inevitable complaint, insult, or rude remark.

The corner of his mouth quirked up. "I've been dreaming of angels, but you aren't an angel, are you?"

She shook her head.

James's eyes drifted closed. "You are the lovely Elizabeth. I must have been close to death's door, or you wouldn't be here, would you?" He lifted his hand to his head. "Keep the fragile state of my health in mind before you reply."

Her lips twitched. "Your sisters asked me to come, and I was happy to help."

"You're not a very good liar." He grimaced and rubbed his head. "Ouch. My thick skull hurts like sin."

She took his hand to keep him from reopening the nasty gash. "Physician Hama left an herbal remedy for the pain. Would you like a sip?"

His fingers wrapped around hers. "You are a strong woman."

She blinked. A compliment? Could the bump to his head have done him some good? She bit back her wry smile. "Physician Hama says you will be back to your old self in no time."

"Good gods, I hope not. I'm an unpleasant jackass most of the time."

She laughed. "I would disagree, except you told me I was a terrible liar."

He smiled wide, then screwed up his face in pain. "Right. Did I mention my head feels like it's about to explode?"

"Let me get the wine and herb drink." She tried to pull her hand free, but he tightened his grip.

"Don't go." Desperation edged his voice.

She patted his hand. "Don't fret. I'll stay as long as you need me."

James opened one eye. "Men don't fret. We exhibit wise concern."

"Sensible men follow their physician's advice."

"Normally, I refuse to cede an argument, but..." he released her hand "...something tells me I won't get any peace until I allow you to pour whatever vile concoction Hama has cooked up down my throat."

She picked up the stone cup and swirled the dark liquid. "It smells horrible."

"I'd be disappointed if it didn't."

She grinned. "Can you sit up?"

He struggled briefly, then collapsed. "No, not even if my life depended on it." He touched his brow. "My head is heavy as an ashlar block."

"Let me help." She tucked her hand under James's head, lifted it a bit, and brought the cup to his mouth. He sipped slowly. She massaged the nape of his neck.

When he had finished drinking, he sighed. "Your touch feels wonderful."

"Rest now," she said.

The tense lines crossing his face smoothed. Soon his breathing turned even and deep. Satisfied he was asleep rather than unconscious, she relaxed and shook her head.

James Onias wasn't always gruff. Who would have guessed? Better yet, he had a humorous side. She continued to massage his neck. Minus his scowl, he was quite handsome. His smooth brown beard distracted from the scar marring his cheek.

What would it have been like to be married to him?

Probably horrible. But maybe not. He had been quite young then. Perhaps she could have influenced him, taught him to laugh and smile.

Listen to her! Who was she trying to fool?

Normally sulky and unhappy, James would have insulted her. Irreverent and over-spirited, she would have laughed at him. Perfect ingredients for a truly miserable marriage.

His lips parted and closed again. He had a nice mouth. Gorgeous, actually. What would his kisses be like? Would they be soft and caressing, then turn hard and demanding? Warmth speared through her.

"What in the name of Beelzebub are you doing, Sister?"

She hadn't heard the door open, but she didn't miss it slamming closed. "Gabriel? You shouldn't be here." Her brother was a Temple Officer, which required him to remain ritually clean. Her bleeding made her, and anything she touched, unclean. As a result, she almost never saw Gabriel since he'd been appointed to a minor post requiring his daily presence at the Temple.

"Is everything well at home?" She couldn't imagine what else would bring him into a sick room, especially one in Antipater's home. The defilement she caused would end at sunset, but by coming into a dead man's home Gabriel had condemned himself to an unclean state lasting a full week.

Her brother's frown didn't diminish his regal air. "Why do you have your hand tangled in James Onias's hair?"

She turned and stared at James's black hair, which lay feathered over her ivory-white wrist. How odd, she hadn't given a thought to her uncleanness when James held her hand or when she helped hold his head up. When was the last time that had happened?

"Elizabeth," Gabriel said louder, sounding more frustrated than angry.

She pulled her hand free and cradled her fist, cherishing the warmth. "James needed to drink a healing potion. I was helping him."

Gabriel strode across the room. "It looked more incriminating from my perspective." He brushed his fingers through his leonine mane of hair. "Mother of misery! Do you want to be further condemned?"

"Condemned?"

"For one, you are in a room alone with a man. And it looked like you were about to kiss James Onias, who happens to be your former stepson. One of those reasons alone would be enough to stir up the gossips."

Her face heated. "I'm sorry. I don't mean to cause you trouble."

Gabriel knelt beside her. "I'm worried for you. You suffer enough as it is."

She glanced at James, then back at Gabriel. "You never cared for James." Maybe it was the age difference. Her brother was five years older.

Gabriel made a face. "James is a coward."

She winced at the uncomfortable truth. "He seemed a bit more likable today."

Her brother gave her a doubtful look. "As fond as I am of Lydia and Alexandra, I'm annoyed with them for asking you to venture out." Gabriel pointed at the open window. "The mob surrounding Antipater's home is growing larger and louder. The streets aren't safe. I plan to escort you home when you're done here."

She patted his hand. "You are a good brother."

Gabriel usually smiled or made a humorous remark when she flattered him, but he grew grimmer. "I also have news to pass onto our cousin. A letter just arrived at the house from Simeon Onias. He has found a husband for Lydia...a man from Parthia. The poor woman will be going to live in yet another distant land."

Kadar gritted his teeth as he watched Judas the Zealot's family lower the tent curtains, cutting Lydia off from her son. He couldn't imagine how she remained on her feet. "May Thor smite them," he growled, pressing closer to Lydia, ready to catch her if necessary. He touched her elbow. "Once you're steadier, I'll invite myself into Judith's tent and *convince* the wretched woman to hand over your son."

Lydia shuddered. "Your offer is tempting, but I don't want to do anything to frighten little James." Her large, sad eyes met his. "His name *is* James. I can't call him the other."

He clasped her arm. "Let's find you a place to sit." He wanted to thrash someone, break some necks, shatter some teeth.

Nathan's stepmother and Mary beckoned for them to sit by the fire.

Kadar put his mouth to her ear. "Rhoda has a reed mat set out for you."

"Let me help you, dear," Alexandra said. She passed baby Anna to Nathan, took Lydia's hand. "I'll take care of my sister."

Alexandra was a good woman with a keen mind, someone Kadar knew had Lydia's best interests at heart, and yet he remained rooted in place.

Alexandra glanced around, then her solemn eyes returned to him. "It's best if you allow me to support Lydia."

Kadar surveyed the nearby campsites. Greeted by a multitude of frowns, his muscles tightened.

Lydia pressed her arm against his hand, trapping his fingers against her warm body. "They fear you more than they hate you," she murmured.

Relieved to see a bit of color return to her face, he squeezed her elbow. "I'm sorely tempted to give them good reason to fear me."

Lydia shook her head. "It would only make matters worse. Promise me you will stay far away from them."

He flexed his sword hand. "They are safe from me, unless I see them mistreat you."

Alexandra cleared her throat loudly. "Come and eat. Nathan will go smooth matters over."

Lydia straightened. "Rhoda and Mary and Cephas are waiting for our company." Head high, she pulled free, made her way to the small fire, and knelt down on a mat.

Kadar rolled his shoulders and turned to Alexandra and Nathan. "I should go."

Nathan patted baby Anna's back. "Don't be running off just yet."

"You will always be a welcome guest around our fire," Alexandra assured him.

Kadar gave the couple a pointed look. "You are good people, and have always treated me well. But..." he jabbed his thumb in the direction of the closed tent, "...you know Judas's grandmother won't allow Lydia to meet with the boy if Lydia is seen keeping company with a pagan."

Baby Anna's small hands grabbed at Nathan's nose. He smiled at his daughter. "My neighbors are aware that I have gentile friends. But leave Lydia's welfare to me." Nathan's voice grew gruff. "Keep your distance from Lydia and all will be well."

Kadar had no quarrel with the reprimand. The problem was his good sense vanished when he came anywhere near Lydia.

"I will be more careful," Kadar promised.

Nathan passed the baby to Alexandra and clapped Kadar on the back. "You are a good man. It's too bad you weren't been born a Hebrew."

Kadar let the insult pass, knowing Nathan meant it as a compliment.

Alexandra gave Kadar a kind smile. "Have you ever considered putting away your gods and turning to the Lord God of Israel?"

Kadar touched the amulet hidden beneath his tunic and laughed. "Why would I? You declare your God is the God of gods, yet your nation is weak and poor. If I ever gave up my gods, it would be to turn to the gods of mighty empires such as Rome or Parthia."

Looking distinctly uncomfortable, Nathan and Alexandra fussed over the baby.

Taking pity on them, Kadar turned the conversation back to Lydia. "I'll stay if you are sure it won't cause problems."

"I'm glad to hear it," Nathan said. "I'd like your company when I return Lydia to Nehonya Onias's home. We will leave well before dark."

Kadar remembered why he liked Nathan. He had a warrior's mind and instincts, and handled a sword like a champion. "You'd have made a good barbarian, olive farmer. Too bad you were born a Jew."

Nathan's jaw dropped. Kadar laughed and clapped him on the back.

Alexandra and Nathan's sons raced past them, and skidded to a halt beside Lydia.

"Mind your manners," Alexandra called out.

The boys' small heads bobbed in unison.

"Will you tell us a story, Aunt Lydia?" the oldest begged breathlessly. "Mother said you'd tell us stories. How about the talking donkey? Mother said you make funny animal noises."

The younger boy clapped and hopped in place. "Talking donkey, talking donkey."

Lydia's smile was fragile. "The talking donkey? Why, that's my favorite, too."

The youngest climbed into her lap and tipped up his dirt-smudged, angelic face. "Talking donkey."

Lydia hugged the boy. "Your mother wants you to say please."

He stuck out his lower lip.

Lydia tickled him.

The boy squirmed and giggled. "Please, please, please."

Rhoda, Mary, and Cephas joined the laughter while Nathan and Alexandra made their way to the fire. Lydia plunged into the story, braying like a donkey, and buzzing like a honeybee, and barking like a dog as needed, delighting her adoring audience.

Kadar marveled at Lydia. She must be dying inside, but you couldn't tell.

Her eyes met his. She beckoned, inviting him to join the others around. He made his way toward them. The aroma of roasting meat and the joyous laughter swirling up reminded him of his youth and time spent next to a roaring fire in the company of his father with his half-brother and sisters. He missed it. Coarse jesting and sour wine shared with fellow soldiers couldn't compare.

He sat opposite Lydia. She spun more tales, taught the children games and songs, and generally kept up a brave front. Kadar participated in all the fun, which, for some reason, the others found amazing. The children begged to sing Goliath of Gath, again.

Familiar with the lyrics, Kadar sang with relish. Everyone quickly covered their ears. When the song ended, accusations rained down. "You can't sing." "You call that singing?" "Who brought out the broken horn?"

Lydia said nothing, but her hand covered her mouth to hide her smile.

Kadar shrugged. "I can't hum, either. Whistling," he rocked the flat of his hand "I'm so-so at whistling. Do you want to hear me try?"

"No!" the others chorused, shaking their heads and covering their ears again.

Too soon it was time to go. Everyone stood. Achan and Raziel clung to Lydia's skirt. "Don't go, Aunt Lydia," the oldest begged.

Raziel waved his chubby finger. "One more game."

Lydia tousled his hair. "You said that three games ago."

Alexandra interceded. "Aunt Lydia will return in two days to share the *Paschal* meal with us."

The boys jumped up and down. "Will you sit with me?" Achan pleaded. "Sit with me," Raziel echoed.

Lydia tucked a boy under each arm. "I will sit between you. How's that?" She received wide grins in reply.

Chapter 12

A short time later Kadar, Nathan, and Lydia climbed the road back to the city and passed through the ancient arched gates. People scurried about, intent on finishing their business and returning home. Many shops had closed early. Doors and gates were barred. Danger and uncertainty hung heavy on the air. Kadar's muscles tightened like they did before a battle.

He heard the protesters before he saw them. The next turn of the narrow, crowded street revealed men shouting and raising fists at Antipater's massive home.

Nathan stopped. "I think we should take the long way around." Boxed in on all sides by stone buildings here, escape would be difficult if trouble arose.

Hand at the ready on his sword handle, Nathan scouted for danger as he led them down a series of narrow, deserted alleys. Kadar followed close on Lydia's heels.

She looked back at him. "Is my brother in danger? Maybe we should move him to my cousin's house."

"I plan to scout out the situation after seeing you home. Tell me you won't step outside until I report back."

Lydia nodded, then frowned. "I hate this unrest. I sometimes wonder if Jerusalem will ever find peace."

He touched the back of her arm. "Peace has the substance of a cloud. It provides a bit of shade and rain until a good wind blows it away."

"This is going to sound selfish, but I'm afraid this trouble will prevent me from seeing my son."

A penniless widow, with an injured brother to care for, a son she couldn't visit, and now worry the city would erupt into violence around her, she deserved a ray of light.

Kadar moved closer to Lydia and put his mouth to her

ear. "Don't go to the Temple for *Pesach*. Make an excuse to stay home, and I will come for you and take you to see your boy."

Lydia slowed. "Little James? Truly?"

"Bring Byrnhild with you. You don't want to be caught sneaking off alone with a pagan."

"I'll risk any danger."

He wanted to pull her to his chest and wrap his arms around her. "Not much frightens me, but your courage puts the fear of the gods into me. Promise me you will act with your wits and not your heart."

"Me?" Her elbow jabbed into his gut. "You are always putting yourself in danger."

He laughed. Good gods, how was he supposed to walk away from this woman?

The rhythmic pounding of sandals slapping against stone spurred them forward, with Lydia close on their heels. Kadar took point. A few moments later the lane emptied out onto the main thoroughfare, throwing them directly into the path of an approaching army. Kadar's hand went to his sword. He signaled for Lydia to stay back. Tension bristled off Nathan.

Kadar relaxed when he spotted Herod at the head of the armed contingent, with his brother Phasael at his side. The brothers were on a collision course with the protestors.

"Barbarian!" Herod called out, raising his hand to bring the soldiers to a halt. "I could use another sword."

Kadar relished the idea of battle. It had been too long since he'd lifted his sword. "Why are you leading Hycranus's army? Where's Malichus?"

Herod scowled. "The worthless dog refused to send troops to disperse the hatemongers, declaring the people should be allowed to express their grief in any manner they see fit. Which is a stinking pile of bull dung."

"When did you arrive in Jerusalem?" Kadar asked.

Herod exhaled heavily. "A few hours ago."

"My mother begged Herod to ignore the troublemakers until after we buried my father," Phasael said, his words choked and his eyes red-rimmed and puffy. "But Herod insisted on dispersing them immediately."

Kadar pointed at the protesters. "At the rate the throng is growing, you're just asking for more trouble by waiting." Herod's brothers had arrived in Jerusalem yesterday and gone into mourning, even as the family's enemies grew bolder. But Herod had recognized the danger and now moved to overturn the threat. Antipater would approve.

Nathan coughed and cleared his throat. "Please, except my deepest condolences for your father's death."

Phasael bowed his head in thanks. Herod didn't acknowledge Nathan. No dirty look. No sharp reply. Nothing.

The color drained from Nathan's face.

An uncomfortable silence ensued, finally broken by Herod. "Are you coming with me, Barbarian?"

"Give me a moment," Kadar said, pulling Nathan aside. He glanced around quickly. Nehonya Onias's home was close by. "My first loyalties lie with..." he caught himself before saying Lydia "...your family. But I owe it to Antipater to aid his sons."

Nathan nodded. "I'll take Lydia home and wait with her until you send word the city is safe."

Kadar's eyes went to Lydia. "Don't change your *Pesach* plans. I'm confident Herod will put a quick end to the unrest."

Her lovely eyes widened. "Don't worry about me. Watch out for your own safety."

It had been a long time since anyone cared about his sorry hide. He swallowed. "I'll do my best, woman."

Nathan and Lydia departed, and Kadar fell in beside Phasael.

Herod gave the signal for the soldiers to move ahead.

Kadar cinched his sword belt tighter and glanced over at Phasael. "What did Herod say to Malichus to get him to hand over the control of the army?"

Phasael grimaced. "Herod didn't ask. He just commandeered them. Took the best soldiers, too."

Kadar laughed. "Did the men balk?"

"No. They couldn't pour enough insults on Malichus and Lazarz." Phasael sobered. "Herod will want to talk to you after this is over. He wants a full account of events from everyone present at my father's death."

Kadar ground his teeth. "Lazarz disappeared right after your father's death. I haven't been able to track the one-eyed fiend down."

They turned a corner and the small plaza teeming with angry men came into view.

Swords hissed from sheaths. Kadar drew his weapon. They closed on their prey.

Herod wouldn't need skilled soldiers to turn this small arena into a death trap. The unarmed protestors would clog the few lanes of escape if they tried to flee, leaving the majority ripe for slaughter.

One by one the protestors turned away from Antipater's home to face Herod's army. Shouting mellowed to grumbling, then to murmurs, then to silence. But face after face remained full of hate.

Kadar's blood hummed. He longed to swing his sword until he was too exhausted to lift his arm. He wanted to be enveloped in air saturated with the smells of sweat and blood. He yearned to feel his throat burn from yelling. "What are you waiting for?" he asked.

"I'm waiting for an apology from these scummy turds for slandering my father's name." Herod's white-toothed snarl radiated pure loathing "I don't hear any apologies. What about you?"

Kadar grinned and shrugged. "I don't hear a thing."

Phasael griped Herod's arm. "You can't cut men down in cold blood without giving them the opportunity to leave peacefully."

Herod pulled free. "They need a hard lesson. Father and Hycranus coddled them, and look where it's led."

Phasael sheathed his sword. "I want no part of this."

"Phasael, trust me," Herod pleaded.

"Do you want Father's death associated with a massacre?" Phasael countered. "Think of Mother."

The spark went out of Herod's black eyes. "Go. Give them a warning. Tell them to leave the plaza immediately."

Phasael exhaled a relieved breath and hurried forward.

"Don't go anywhere, fools," Kadar muttered, watching Phasael plead with the leaders of the protest.

Herod pulled Kadar aside. Resting his sword on his shoulder, he said, "I want to hire your services."

"I don't want to be your bodyguard. I plan to take up soldiering in some other part of the world."

"It involves avenging my father's death," Herod purred.

Kadar straightened. "Everyone in your father's inner circle believes Malichus had a hand in the poisoning."

"And what do you think?"

"I was at the same table with that one-eyed jackass Lazarz and Malichus when your father was killed." Kadar saw the mob begin to disperse. Disappointed, he rolled his shoulders and sheathed his sword. "I'd bet my life they had a hand in the poisoning."

Herod's face hardened. "I plan to pursue my father's murderers to Hades if I have to. I want your help. What do you say?"

Kadar flexed his sword hand. "I've been meaning to pay a visit to Hades."

Herod clapped him on the back. "Good. We will start by having a talk with Malichus."

Chapter 13

The next morning, after tossing and turning almost the whole night, and hardly sleeping a wink, Lydia rose early, woke Brynhild, and set out to check on her brother. They stepped outside. The air hung cold and wet over Jerusalem, trapping the smoke from the daily sacrifice over the Temple compound.

They walked quickly through the quiet streets. Kadar had sent word saying it was safe to go out. Still, she breathed a sigh of relief when they reached Antipater's grandiose home and there was no sign of the protestors—or bloodshed. It was foolish to have worried for Kadar's safety. He was an experienced warrior, able to hold his own in a fight against farmers, laborers, and merchants, but she'd been frightened nonetheless as she watched him march off with Herod.

She arrived at her brother's bedside and was informed he had woken several times during the night and become agitated when trying to recall his accident. Physician Hama had given James a sleep potion a few hours earlier. She sat vigil beside James all morning, unable to stop thinking about her little boy. Her heart ached that he was so close but still out of her reach. Except Kadar had promised to take her to see her precious child. An incredibly kind offer, which she hated to accept, since she'd already robbed him of six years of his life. She prayed Judith would change her mind, and Alexandra and Nathan would arrive with little James in tow, or with an invitation to Judith's tent.

By midafternoon, after a small break to stretch her legs, Lydia excused Brynhild. "Go take a stroll. The fresh air will do you good, and the garden is full of spring blossoms."

The door clicked closed, then reopened. "I smell baking bread," Bryn crowed. "I mean to find the baker, convince him to give up a few loaves, and stuff myself full while I can."

Bryn detested unleavened bread, and complained about the lack of raised bread every time *Pesach* rolled around. "The week will be over before you know it," Lydia consoled her.

Bryn made a face and banged the door shut.

James stirred.

Lydia fussed with the bedcovers.

Her brother opened one eye and managed a weak scowl. "Physician Hama mixes a foul-tasting drink with more kick than a mule." He touched his brow.

Relief washed through her. "You look better. You have more color."

James held his hand out and inspected it. "Hmm, yes, I'm simply pale instead of my usual pasty whiteness. Fabulous news indeed."

She smiled. "You became upset. Physician Hama wanted you to rest."

"The concoction was more pleasant than a hit to the head with a hammer, but not by much."

Lydia gave her brother a quick kiss and a hug.

"Lydia," James spluttered. "Was that necessary?"

"Absolutely. I love you and I'm happy you are alive."

He wiped his cheek. "Our family isn't the kissing and hugging kind."

"We could be. Perhaps you could learn to enjoy it."

He pulled his blanket up to his chin. "I highly doubt it."

Oddly enough, James's grumpiness was a comfort, making her feel at home for the first time since she'd arrived in Jerusalem. She poured a cup of wine and mixed in some honey. "Drink this. It will help strengthen you."

James grimaced and massaged his forehead. "I remember falling, but everything else is fuzzy."

"Accidents happen to all of us," she said, then changed subjects before he worked himself up again trying to recall the particulars. "Physician Hama predicts you will be on your feet soon."

"I think I might have been pushed."

Lydia gasped. "Pushed? Are you sure?"

"No, I'm not. But, I'm fairly sure someone replaced my perfectly-functioning mind with mashed grapes."

"Don't make light of it, please. You could have died."

"I think that was the point."

"Who pushed you?"

"I can't quite hold onto the culprit's image. A picture starts to form, but dissolves before I can make it out."

"Why would someone want to kill you?"

James gingerly fingered the gash atop his head. "A good question, and one I will puzzle over when my head doesn't feel like it's about to explode."

She swirled the wine and honey around in the cup. "Physician Hama says this will help dull the pain."

Eyeing the cup with suspicion, James propped himself up on his elbows. "I want to apologize for the thoughtless remarks I made to you and Elizabeth when we were out walking. I don't understand what drives me to be so thoughtless and unkind."

Lydia brushed back his bangs. "Some matters are hard to explain to ourselves, much less to others."

"You are thinking about your time in Judas the Zealot's camp."

She nodded. "Down deep, you have a good heart. I wish you would let go of your anger and allow your goodness to shine through."

James exhaled heavily and looked away. "I should have done more to protect you and Alexandra from Judas."

Their guilt over the nightmare they'd survived was a shared bond. "Shhh," Lydia soothed, her eyes going to his mottled scar. "The past is best left in the past." She held up the cup clutched in her hand. "Drink this and rest."

James downed the wine, lay back, and soon fell into a deep sleep. A short time later the door opened, and Alexandra slipped into the room accompanied by Brynhild.

Lydia stood. "I'm happy to report James is much better."

Alexandra crossed the room. They hugged, and Lydia

blurted out the questions clamoring through her mind, "Did you speak to Judith? Did she change her mind? Will she allow me to see my son?"

Her sister sighed and shook her head. "We talked to her all last night and today, and didn't get anywhere."

Lydia could only manage single-word replies to Alexandra's concern and gentle queries, until Nathan arrived to walk them home. Her mind whirled, inventing and discarding dozens of fruitless plans to run away with little James, even while she assured Alexandra and Nathan she would share the *Paschal* meal with them the next day and waved goodbye to them outside Cousin Nehonya's home.

"I know what you're thinking," Brynhild said as soon as the couple was out of hearing.

Lydia studied her feet. "What choice do I have?"

"The festival lasts one week. Your sister and brother-in-law promised to do everything in their power to make Judith see reason. Promise me you won't rush off and do something rash."

"You won't change my mind about going with Kadar to visit little James."

"Go, if you feel you must."

Lydia hugged Bryn. "I knew you'd understand."

"Just don't do anything foolish," Bryn repeated, then frowned. "There's your pretty cousin."

Gabriel was Cousin Nehonya's oldest son, and a bit of a fancy dresser. He lived close by with his beautiful wife and baby daughter. The yellow hues of the setting sun haloed his regal mane of brown hair. Bejeweled and clothed in rich robes, he could be easily be mistaken for a prince. But never a princess, not with the hint of granite will showing through his elegant surface.

Gabriel paused at the foot of the porch. "Greetings, Cousin. You are taking the news well. I feared the marriage your father arranged would make you unhappy."

"News?" Lydia asked.

Gabriel sobered. "You haven't read Cousin Simeon's letter? I'm sorry, I assumed—"

A wave of nausea rolled through Lydia. "Your father and mother were visiting with your mother's family when I returned last evening. Excuse me. I'm—" She raced up the stairs, grabbed the door latch, wrenched the door open, and tumbled into the small atrium, where she was greeted with astonished looks from Cousin Nehonya, his wife, Chloe, Elizabeth, and other cousins gathered just inside the doorway.

"Take a deep breath," Bryn whispered, her sturdy hand cupping Lydia's elbow.

Cousin Nehonya stared at her and smoothed his robes in much the same way her father did. "You are just in time to join the search."

Lydia blinked. "Search?" She cleared her throat and tried again. "Gabriel told me you have a letter for me."

Cousin Nehonya frowned. "Actually, you have two posts. I planned to give you your father's note this morning, but you'd already left the house by the time I arose. The one from your Aunt Sarah arrived a short time ago."

Lydia clasped her shaking hands. "I'd like to take the letters to my room."

Cousin Nehonya shook his head. "The bad ne—"

"The news will have to wait," Cousin Chloe said, shaking her head at her husband.

Cousin Nehonya cleared his throat. "It is time to begin the search for leaven."

Lydia finally noticed the oil lamps and feathers the others held. Today was the day all leaven must be removed from one's home in preparation for *Pesach*. Drat! How had she forgotten?

"If you will just tell me where the letters are, I will—"

Cousin Nehonya stopped her with a firm look. "I may not be as fastidious about religious matters as your father, but I take care to keep the commands in the manner of the Sadducees. We don't search the house for leaven for days on end like the Pharisees, but we do make a proper inspection."

Lydia's shoulders hitched up. "I did not mean to disparage anyone. However, I am anxious to learn what my father and Aunt Sarah have to say."

"I promise you will have your letters the moment we finish." Cousin Nehonya produced a piece of raised bread and set it on the bench next to the front door. "Now, do you want to search or sweep?"

Chloe held out a small clay lamp and three slender gray feathers.

Lydia chose a feather. By far the safer option—tense as she was, she might well set something ablaze.

Lamps were held up to every nook and cranny of the atrium. Those brandishing the feathers swept up any crumbs revealed by the search.

"Looks like plain old dust to me," Bryn muttered in Lydia's ear more than once.

Lydia shrugged. "We wouldn't even find dust if my cousin was a Pharisee. I remember Goda and the other slaves spent two or three weeks cleaning our house in preparation for *Pesach*. When I was young, the search for leaven seemed a delightful game. It wasn't until I lived in Egypt that I understood the significance of *Pesach*. I never felt at home there, and I never stopped asking the Lord to deliver me from Egypt. And he did."

Bryn snickered. "It does my heart good thinking of you Jews as slaves who bested Pharaoh and escaped from Egypt."

"I dreamed of celebrating *Pesach* in Jerusalem once more, but not under such strained circumstances."

The hunt moved to the main house. Lydia noticed Elizabeth hung back behind everyone else, a habit of hers, most likely stemming from the stigma of her constant bleeding. Lydia wanted to hug Elizabeth or give her a word of encouragement, but feared it would only call more attention to her plight.

But then Cousin Nehonya waved Elizabeth forward. "Libi, come. I need your help." Affection filled his voice. Libi, meaning *my heart* in the Hebrew, was the family's pet name for Elizabeth. The only daughter among five sons, she was the apple of her parents' eyes and much beloved by her brothers.

The tight lines crossing Elizabeth's face smoothed. She

moved to her father's side. Talking and laughing, they worked together, with Nehonya holding the lamp up to dark corners and Elizabeth inspecting for crumbs.

The noisy procession moved to the bedchambers and Lydia found herself paired with Elizabeth.

"You have a wonderful family," Lydia said.

Elizabeth held the oil lamp next to a niche. "They are very good to me."

Lydia swept her feather over a collection of small vials and jars. "Your father is nothing like mine. Cousin Nehonya is so warm and generous. My father would have sent me and Alexandra away if—" Lydia cringed over her thoughtlessness. The last thing her cousin needed was someone reminding her of her affliction. "I'm sorry. I didn't mean to—" Drat. She almost did it again. "Please forgive my clumsy mouth."

The glow from the lamp lit Elizabeth's face. "My curse is not something you forget, so there is nothing to forgive. And some good came from the affliction. Your father wouldn't come near me because of it. He shut me up in your bedchamber, where I spent long, dreary days thinking about you and your sister, and the dismal life you must have had, and how blessed I'd been to have a loving, happy family."

They moved to a tall niche. A striking painting of a blue vase filled with bright yellow flowers adorned the alcove. Lydia's eyes met Elizabeth's. "I forget about the marriage. Everything from that time is still a confused jumble." She swallowed back the foul taste in her mouth and summoned up a smile. "You slept in my room? Did you sleep in the soft bed or the hard one? Alexandra always complained mine was too hard."

Elizabeth laughed and shook her head. "I alternated between the two, but soon decided it was hopeless. The beds could have been fit for a queen, but I was never going to be comfortable in Simeon Onias's home."

"I'm so sorry for what you suffered."

Elizabeth wrinkled her nose. "My father must have apologized a thousand times for agreeing to the marriage, even though I reassured him there was no long-term damage done."

Lydia stroked the feather across her palm and glanced over at Nehonya Onias. Her father and Nehonya shared the same profile, height, build, and age, but their dispositions couldn't be more opposite. "Why did your father agree to the marriage if he already suspected it would prove dreadful?"

Elizabeth sighed. "I wondered the same thing, and asked a few times, but it made my father very upset. He wept the last time I brought it up. I decided I can live without the answer."

A few moments later the family returned to the spot where they'd begun and assembled in front of the bench holding the chunk of raised bread. Sweeping up the crumbs and placing the bread on a spoon for burning, Cousin Nehonya prayed the prayer coming from every home in Jerusalem. "Blessed be Thou who has commanded us to remove the leaven."

The spoon and feathers were tied together and suspended over a lamp, and Lydia shuddered, as though flames were licking at her own feet, when Cousin Nehonya turned to her. "Do you want me to read the letters to you, or would you prefer to read them by yourself?"

Lydia closed her eyes briefly. *Give me courage, Lord.* "I will take them to my room."

Chapter 14

The crippled slave Saad hobbled into James's drab bedchamber. "The household is leaving for the Temple to observe the *Paschal* sacrifice. Is there anything you need before I go?"

James flapped his hand at the offer. "Go. There's no need to fuss over me." Rubbing his aching head, James reexamined his father's high-handed letter informing him he had arranged a most favorable marriage for Lydia to a man from Parthia.

"The old goat," James muttered. "Advantageous. For Father."

"The guards Herod posted outside your door will change shifts soon," Saad added.

James reread his *favorite* line, "Be prepared to take up your rightful duties as my son, or suffer harsh consequences."

The slave sighed and the door clicked shut.

James tossed the parchment aside. "Threaten all you want. It won't do you any good." He had more immediate worries, such as remembering who had tried to kill him.

The wooden door creaked open again.

Tired of the constant stream of people tramping in and out of his room, James pinched the bridge of his nose. "Leave me to my peace."

"Would you like a back rub?" a tinkling voice said.

James bolted upright, then clutched his spinning head.

Kitra crossed to his bed. An overpoweringly sweet smell filled the room. "You look lonely," she said with a girlish giggle.

He pulled the bed cover up over his chest, baring his cold feet.

Almond-eyed Kitra wet her red lips. "Would you like a

foot rub instead?"

The sheer ivory gown Cypros's niece wore hugged every last one of her mouthwatering curves. "What are you doing here?" James croaked, hiking his knees to his chin.

Kitra fluttered her long lashes. "I thought we should get to know each other better."

He should send her from the room, tell her he had no interest. Except her lush body practically had a sign on it, saying *enter here*. He swallowed hard. "I suppose it wouldn't hurt for you to sit beside me."

"I had a feeling we would get along just fine," Kitra purred, climbing onto the bed. She nudged her rounded bottom against his rigid thigh. "I told my father he shouldn't give up hope of having a master builder for a son-in-law."

James sucked in a strained breath. "Kiss me, and we'll find out if we suit."

"I'll need you to teach me. I've never kissed a man."

James didn't believe it for a moment. Kitra was no innocent. She was the embodiment of the foreign temptress the scriptures warned against. And wouldn't his father have a royal fit when he learned James was bedding a heathen seductress and planned to marry her? He crooked his finger. "Come closer."

Kitra smiled, straddled his lap, and lowered her red lips to his.

He groaned and tasted her pouty, succulent mouth.

She pushed him back on the pillow. Eyes flashing naughtily, she reached for the hem of her gown.

Loud snickers interrupted. Two leering guards stared unabashedly at James and Kitra. A third man joined them. But the patch-eyed soldier wasn't smiling.

James's guts turned to ice. In a flash he remembered the incriminating conversation between patch-eyed Lazarz and red-headed Niv. Saw Lazarz chasing him through hallways. Recalled his abject fear when the beefy soldier tossed him head-first down the stairs. And finally the world going dark.

James struggled to sit up. "Get off me."

Lazarz shot James a nasty smile, then strode out of sight.

"I don't care if they watch," Kitra cooed, running her hand up his bare leg.

He pushed the shameless girl off his lap. "Tell your father to find another master builder."

Kitra slapped him across the face, slid off the bed, and raced weeping past the amused guards.

Ears and head ringing, James stood. "Call for a litter," he ordered the guardsmen.

"Where are you going?" one of them asked.

"Out." James wasn't going to wait for Lazarz to bribe his way past his *guardians*.

"Did you hear that?" Lydia asked Bryn, jumping off the plush reclining couch she was sharing with the slave. Lydia raced to the door, and placed her ear to the polished wood.

Brynhild's fat, flaxen braids scarcely budged as she shook her head. "For my sake, I hope it's Kadar. I'm worn out from watching you flitter about every time you hear the slightest noise."

Lydia began pacing, clenching and unclenching her hands. "I haven't even gotten a glimpse of him for the last two days. Maybe he changed his mind." Unable to eat or sleep, the wait to see her son seemed like an eternity.

"Kadar has been busy with Antipater's funeral. If he said he would take you to see your boy, he'll keep his promise."

Lydia rolled shoulders against the knot of tension lodged between them. "I don't know how you convinced Cousin Nehonya to leave me behind. One moment he was insisting the whole household must go observe the sacrifice of the *Paschal* lamb, and the next he was happily waving goodbye to me."

Bryn flapped her hand. "Nehonya Onias is much cleverer than your uncle Jacob, but neither of them is Plato or Aristotle."

Lydia laughed. "Plato? Aristotle? You probably even know interesting facts about the Greek philosophers, don't you?"

"I like hearing about places and people and stories from the past." Bryn's eyes twinkled with mischief. "Conveniently for me, others like sharing what they know. The trick is to ask the right questions, otherwise you'll hear more than you want to about sore knees and lame backs or cheating husbands and unruly children. Slaves excel at gossip and complaints, mostly because we're bored. I believe in making the best of a situation."

Lydia returned to the couch, sat down next to Bryn, and clasped the old slave's chapped hands. Aunt Sarah's letter had delivered a blow almost as devastating as Father's announcement of her impending marriage. Regretting the loss of a skilled, useful slave, Aunt demanded that Lydia send Brynhild back to Egypt. "I hate knowing you are a slave. I promise to do everything in my power to make you a free woman before I go to my new husband."

Lydia swallowed. No, she wouldn't think about the marriage her father had arranged. Not now. Not today. She squeezed Bryn's fingers. "I'm sure my sister or brother will lend me the money to buy your freedom."

Bryn patted her hand. "I doubt your sister and brother-in-law have spare coins clinking around in their home."

Nathan and Alexandra had tripled the size of their olive orchard, but the trees were still maturing. Prosperity might come to them, but it would be too late to do Bryn any good. Lydia sighed. "I suppose I'll have to ask James."

"Your brother can hardly keep his eyes open. It will be some time before he'll be allowed to agree to anything."

"You heard Physician Hama. He is pleased with James's progress."

Bryn wrinkled her nose. "Hama is pleased with something, but it isn't your brother."

Lydia rolled her eyes. "Bryn, you think every man who lays eyes on me falls in love."

"They don't need to see you to fall in love. The blind man we pass coming and going from Antipater's house asked you to marry him, didn't he? You have a special way about you. A room brightens when you walk into it."

Lydia made a face. "Blind Saul is older than Methuselah."

"I will soon be as old as blind Saul." The light went out of Bryn's eyes. "You mean well, making plans to free me, but I'd prefer to remain a slave."

"You can't mean it."

Bryn held her hands out and flexed her crooked fingers. "My bones are growing frail. Where would I go? What would I do to earn money? If I was younger I could turn to harlotry, or—"

Lydia gasped. "What about your family? You could go back to Gaul."

Bryn let out a bleak cackle. "Family? Go Home? I come from a harsh land. Everybody I knew is either dead or old like me. If the long journey to Gaul didn't kill me, my people probably would. They'd see me as a burden. I have no place there." Bryn bent her head. "I'd rather stay with you, if it's not too much of a bother."

"Bother?" Lydia was aghast. She wrapped her arms around the slave and took note of the plentiful white hairs woven through Bryn's thick braids. "You are my dear Bryn. I will find a way for us to be together again."

Bryn returned Lydia's hug, then set her at arm's length. "I don't like the look I've been seeing in your eyes. I know you're hurting because of little James and fearful of the marriage your father has planned for you. I'm worried about what you'll do."

Lydia gulped back her tears. "Parthia, Bryn. I don't want marry a man from Parthia. I want to live in Jerusalem or in Galilee. I might have been able to resign myself to going back to Egypt, but not this. I won't go. I can't."

"What difference does it make?" Bryn asked. "Parthia and Egypt both have large communities of Jews. You'd be among your own kind."

Lydia's stomach hadn't stopped churning since she read her father's letter, which informed her she was to marry a man of great importance from Parthia. "Father didn't name the man I am to marry or give me one jot of information about him. It isn't a good sign. I can't endure another dismal marriage, Bryn. I can't."

Brynhild patted her back. "You have no choice but to endure it."

Lydia straightened. "I won't."

Bryn exhaled heavily. "You look like a cornered kitten, all big eyes and claws. And make no mistake, you are in a corner. Think girl. What would you do? Where would you go? No one in Judea will go against your father to help you."

"Alexandra and Nathan would take me in." Lydia winced. "But father would simply take me back, wouldn't he? And he'd probably find a way to make them suffer for taking me in."

Bryn nodded. "The law is on his side. Your father owns you, as surely as your Aunt Sarah owns me. Neither of us is free to follow our hearts."

"I will leave Jerusalem and go to another country."

"And do what? Women with no means end up as whores."

Lydia's head began to throb. "Someone would marry me. You said yourself men would line up to marry me."

"What if you choose wrong, and you marry a man who beats or abuses you? With no family nearby, who is to stop him?"

"I'll be careful."

Bryn grabbed Lydia's arm. "Tell me why an uncertain path out in the world sounds better to you than marrying the man from Parthia?"

"I'm afraid I'll never see little James again."

"If you steal your baby and run, you will have your father and all of Judas the Zealot's family chasing you down." Bryn shook her. "Are you paying attention to me?"

A knock announced a visitor. Lydia broke away and hurried toward the door.

"Fool-headedness doesn't suit you," Bryn called after her.

Lydia had accepted her fate in the past, and what good had it done her? She grabbed the door handle and yanked.

Kadar filled the doorway. Hair freshly washed and tied

back with a leather thong, he smelled of sandalwood oil. His intent blue eyes swept over her. "Are you ready?"

Lydia barely resisted throwing herself at him.

Chapter 15

Kadar led Lydia and her slave woman, Bryn, through Jerusalem's near-empty streets. Lydia was unusually quiet. He might be able to ease some of her worries. "I made a quick trip to the Mount of Olives. Your boy is there with Judith, but almost everyone else has come up to the city. I don't anticipate running into any difficulties on that end. And you should have plenty of time to visit. The first group of worshippers is only now entering the Temple grounds to sacrifice their lambs. Alexandra and Nathan and their neighbors from Rumah are waiting their turn with the second group. It would be better for us if they were more slothful and had showed up last, so they had to enter with the group of the lazy."

"The group of the lazy? I like the name," Brynhild said in her native tongue, chuckling. The heavy rasp of her voice and her thick braids conjured up images of the elderly women from Kadar's home village, who would sit around blazing fires spinning tales of wildly successful hunting expeditions, or of bloody raids on neighboring lands yielding mountains of silver and gold.

Brynhild's loyalty to Lydia earned her more favor in his eyes. Knowing it would please, he replied to Brynhild in her language. "Almost all Jews cringe at the thought of being counted among the group of the lazy, nonetheless the assembly grows larger and larger. Some say the nation is growing indifferent, but Herod says it's because more and more pilgrims are coming from afar and the Temple compound isn't large enough to house the expanding crowds."

"What does the group of the lazy have to do with

Mistress Lydia?" Brynhild asked.

Lydia poked him with her elbow. "If you are going to talk about me I would like to understand what you're saying."

Kadar purposely kept to the Gaul. "Is she always this feisty?"

Bryn puffed up like a peacock strutting its colors. "Oh yes, lively and spirited, and then some."

Lydia growled, but they both knew there wasn't a menacing bone in her willowy body.

He stifled a laugh, lest he embarrass her, even if only in front of Brynhild. "It will be some time before the second group leaves the Temple, so you should have a good hour or more to visit with your son."

Lydia sobered. "You've had a busy afternoon, what with checking on both Judith and Nathan. Thank you for everything you've done."

He didn't want her to read too much into his actions. "I was just being careful."

They entered a narrow lane, forcing them to walk single file. Brynhild tapped him on the back. "Before you go feeling all proud of yourself, I think you should be aware that my feisty mistress plans to steal little James and run away."

Kadar halted, did an about-face, and glared at Lydia.

"Brynhild," Lydia complained, sounding more aggravated than angry. "Don't burden Kadar with any more of my concerns. He's suffered enough because of me."

Kadar gritted his teeth. "Brynhild, go wait for us at the end of the alley while I have a word with your mistress."

The pear-shaped slave squeezed by them wearing a satisfied smile.

Kadar backed Lydia against a whitewashed plaster wall. "What's this nonsense about running away?"

She swallowed. "Don't be angry."

"I'm not, but the thought of you out in the world on your own frightens me half to death." He touched the back of his hand to her long, slender neck. She trembled, and not because she was afraid of him. His gut tightened.

"I overreacted to some bad news." Her voice was

breathy.

He skimmed his fingers over her smooth, olive skin. "What frightened you?"

"My father sent word I am to marry a man from Parthia."

His hand curled into a fist. "Marry. How soon?" He loathed the idea down to his last fiber.

"Too soon, I fear." Sorrow brimmed in her brown eyes.

He stroked her dusky cheek, desiring her with a soul-deep craving. She was beautiful and refined and utterly tantalizing. And another man was going to take her away.

A feral growl swelled his chest. He took her mouth.

Lydia whimpered, but it was a sound of desire, not fear. His blood heated. Cupping her head, he pressed his lips more firmly to hers. She kissed him back, her mouth hot and desperate. Nectar from the gods couldn't taste sweeter. Her kisses should be for him alone, but another would have her. He nipped at her mouth, her lips parted, and he thrust his tongue deep. Her arms circled his waist and she pressed against him. He lifted the hem of her tunic and ran his hand up her slim, bare leg.

Gasping for breath, Lydia spoke against his mouth. "Kadar, someone might come upon us."

He broke off the kiss. *What was he doing?* He was close to fornicating with an upright Jewess in broad daylight, in the middle of Jerusalem, during one of their holy days, for anyone to witness, crawling all over her like an animal. He set her at arm's length. "I shouldn't have kissed you. I swear it won't happen again."

Lydia collapsed against the clay brick wall. "I don't want to go to Parthia. You said you are going away. I want to go with you."

The gods knew he wanted to say yes. "I won't do that to you. I know the cost of leaving everything familiar behind. I don't want you to suffer the same fate."

Lydia frowned. "I was sent to Egypt."

He exhaled heavily. "Did you go among people who worshipped other gods, spoke a different language? A place with no family, friends, or acquaintances. Egypt and Parthia have large Jewish communities. Living among pagans would be very different."

"We would have each other."

"I shouldn't have kissed you. I was—" Admitting he was insanely jealous wouldn't help his argument. "I was curious."

Her chin lifted. "We both know the truth. You desire me." A red flush crept up her neck. "And I desire you."

Jupiter, she was beautiful and desirable and quick-minded and refined, and had absolutely nothing in common with the ill-favored, desperate women who threw in their lot with soldiers. Six years ago he'd been more than ready to help her escape. But he'd been a young stud, ruled by lust. He hadn't given thought to how a highborn Jewess would fare in his rough-and-tumble world. He tried imagining Lydia as a camp follower. "I won't take you to live in an army camp."

She watched him out of wide, innocent eyes. "Why not?"

"Army camps are filthy, lewd, dangerous places, and that's when troops aren't at war."

"I promise I won't complain."

"You have no idea what you're asking. Military life is uncertain, involving marches to far-off lands, sieges lasting for months or years amid pestilence and disease. Women end up following their men from one dusty end of the world to the other. Soldiers die by the hundreds and their women are passed from man, to man, to man." He reached out and traced his finger over her soft, delicate cheek. "I would rather kill you than turn you into a camp follower."

"Are you trying to frighten me?"

He wanted to shake her, then kiss her breathless. "Everything about me should frighten you."

"Take me with you."

He blew out a frustrated breath. "Woman. I'm a warrior. There's no place in my life for you."

"We could go to Gaul, to your family."

His gut contracted. He clutched his tunic and the amulet beneath. "It's impossible."

"Why?"

"It just is." *Home.* He'd give anything to go back and

bring her with him. And then what? Get them both killed. He stepped back. "Do you want to spend your time arguing with me when you could be with your son?" He was being unfair, but he was desperate.

Lydia flinched, pushed away from the wall, and hurried down the lane, a graceful, bounding gazelle narrowly escaping the jaws of a ravenous lion.

He swiped is hand over his face. The sooner Lydia married the better. Their mutual attraction was stronger than the pull of twenty oxen.

And curse Simeon Onias for arranging another distasteful marriage for his daughter. If anyone deserved a bit of happiness, it was Lydia. Kadar clasped his sword. When the time came, he was going to doubly enjoy killing the detestable man.

He shook his head and laughed mirthlessly. He'd allowed jealousy to render him deaf and blind to a pertinent detail—Lydia wouldn't be marrying the man from Parthia, because Simeon Onias would die before the wedding could take place, even if Kadar had to sacrifice his life, safety, and freedom to make it happen.

Lydia marched up to Judith's tent. Her agitation over the kiss—an unsatisfying description for what had passed between them—and the subsequent conversation, left her frustrated and exhausted. She took a deep breath and lifted her fist to knock but encountered a hide flap instead of a door. Kadar and Brynhild stood close behind her. Lydia cleared her throat. "Come forth, Judith of Rumah. You have visitors."

"Grandma, someone's here," a boy's bright voice said. Lydia's heart beat faster.

A moment later Judith's wrinkled face peeked around the tent flap. "I wasn't expecting you until later. But it's probably best for you to meet Judas while it's quiet."

Lydia blinked repeatedly. "You were expecting me?"

"Alexandra and Nathan visited me this morning. They said you are to marry a man from Parthia and your visits to

Judea would be infrequent at best." The stooped woman frowned. "They also said my grandson would be unhappy with me if he never got to meet you."

Lydia clamped her mouth shut. Who cared what motivated Judith? Nothing mattered except seeing her son.

Judith waved them away. "Go sit by Nathan's tent and I will bring the boy to you."

Bryn put her fists on her pear-shaped hips. "Don't make my mistress wait too long, or—"

"Bryn," Lydia warned, pulling the slave woman away from the tent.

When they reached the woven mats, she met Kadar's eye for the first time since the alley. "You don't have to stay. Nathan will escort me home."

He regarded her from inscrutable blue eyes. "Do you want me to go?"

"No."

"Good. Because I wasn't going anywhere."

She exhaled a relieved breath. "I was afraid you were angry with me."

"I'm angry with myself."

"Did I miss something?" Brynhild asked.

"No," Lydia and Kadar both said emphatically.

Young Mary came out of her tent and joined them, cradling her daughter in one arm and a swaddling blanket in the other. "Blessed *Pesach* to you."

Lydia kneaded her tunic. "Blessings to you. I came early. I'm so eager to see my son, I couldn't wait any longer."

Mary invited them sit on the mats circling the cold coals from yesterday's fire. "We are all so happy Judith had a change of heart. You might have a hard time believing it, but Judith is usually very kind-hearted."

Lydia recognized the yellow stitches edging the swaddling blanket as her own handiwork. "Is she good to...to my son?"

"If anything, she is overprotective. Judith says she prevented you from visiting with Judas because she was afraid it would upset or confuse him."

"I don't want him frightened, either."

"Of course you don't." Mary kissed her baby. "You are wonderful with children. Alexandra's boys have talked nonstop about *Aunt Lydia* and your fun games and stories. We believe Judith is afraid or worried Judas will love you more."

Lydia ran her hands over her empty lap. "I will never forgive her for taking my son away from me."

A pained expression crossed Mary's face. "No, I don't see how you could."

Kadar snatched up a blackened stick resting against the rock-rimmed fire pit. "Little James will learn the truth someday, and woe to Judith of Rumah then."

"Grandma," A boy's voice rang through the campsite. "How come Achan got to go up to the city and I didn't?" Achan was Alexandra's oldest son and little James's best friend. Of course he'd be unhappy about being left behind.

Judith approached them, leading little James by the hand. "Because you have a visitor."

Lydia held her breath.

Little James's brows shot up. "Me? Wow, I must be important. Important men have visitors."

Judith chuckled. "Says who?"

James tipped his head back and smiled. "Grandma, you know. You keep telling me I'm growing up too fast."

Judith embraced him. "Yes you are." She sobered and pointed a finger. "Your mother has come to visit. Go and greet Lydia."

Lydia smiled and waved, and tried not to look overeager.

Suddenly shy, little James clung to Judith's skirt.

Judith and Mary took turns trying to coax him out of hiding. His lower lip began to quiver.

Lydia's stomach sickened. She'd imagined this moment thousands of times, convinced it would be wonderful. Instead, disaster loomed.

Kadar pulled a small knife from his belt and buffed it on his sleeve.

Little James sniffed, wiped his hand across his watery eyes, and inspected the knife with interest. "I can throw a knife real far."

"Is that so?" Kadar said. "Achan told me he could throw a knife twice as far as you, but I don't believe it."

"Achan is bigger than me."

Kadar held the knife out. "Do you want to show me how far you can throw?"

James raced to Kadar's knee. "I'm way stronger than Achan. See—" He made a fist and held his arm up.

Kadar squeezed his arm. "Weeping crocodiles, you must be strong as Hercules. Go show your mother."

Little James scooted around the fire, hopped onto Lydia's lap, and made a fist again. She circled her hand around her son's small, solid arm, and pressed. Tears stung at her eyes. "My, you are strong."

His angelic smile revealed a lower tooth hanging by a thread. "Do you want to watch me throw Kadar's knife?"

She resisted the temptation to hug him tight to her chest. "I promise to pay close attention."

Kadar stood. "Watch? I think we should teach your mother to throw a knife."

Little James leaned back into her and giggled. "Girls don't throw knives."

Kadar grinned. "They do where I come from."

Lydia tousled her son's baby-fine hair. "What do you say?"

Little James hopped off her lap, took her hand, and pulled. "Come on. It's easy. I'll go first to show you how to snap your wrist at just the right time."

Heart bursting with love, Lydia jumped to her feet.

"I wish the others were here to watch," Mary said.

Bryn hooted her support.

Lydia paused. Taking knife-throwing lessons on a feast day from a barbarian was not the way to win Judith's approval. The old woman was probably searching for reasons to limit the time Lydia spent with little James.

Her son tugged on her hand. "Are you coming, Lydia? Do you want to me to call you Lydia or Mother? Achan says you are the best storyteller. Do you know any stories about sea serpents?" He blessed her with a hopeful smile.

Happiness flooded in. "Mother sounds lovely. Do you want to hear about scary sea serpents or friendly ones?"

Little James scurried over to Judith, wrapped his arms around the hunchbacked woman, and scrunched his face in mock fright. "Scary! I like scary stories best. Grandma knows, don't you?"

Judith patted his back. "You and your scary tales."

He gave Judith's wrinkled cheek an affectionate peck. "Do you want Kadar to teach you to throw a knife, too?"

Judith chuckled. "No child. You go, and I'll watch."

He raced to Kadar. "Do you want me to go first?"

The giant man turned his piercing blue eyes on Lydia. "Who should go first, you or your son?"

They both knew the question went beyond knife-throwing lessons. Little James cast her a hopeful look. There was no denying he was happy and well-loved. Though relieved and glad for his sake, there was a small, dark corner of her heart that wished it weren't so, because then she wouldn't have to make a decision. She would have no choice but to take her son and run. Could she justify taking him from a safe home for a future filled with uncertainty and dangers too numerous to count?

She forced a false smile to her lips, one years in the perfecting. "My son must go first. I wouldn't have it any other way."

Kadar raised a brow.

She smoothed her tunic. "Have we chosen a target? Or may I throw the knife wherever I like?"

He threw his head back and laughed.

Her face heated.

Little James clasped her hand. She squeezed his small fingers. She couldn't remember the last time she was this happy.

Kadar led them away from the others and propped a sack of barley against a large stone. Little James took aim and hit the target on his first try. She clapped the loudest while he ran to retrieve the knife. "Thank you for everything," she murmured to Kadar.

"You didn't need me. Judith had already decided to allow you to see your son." Kadar tugged on the neckline of his tunic. "Ah. About what happened earlier."

Little James returned and pressed the bone-handled weapon into her hand. Kadar and little James peppered her with a slew of advice, but the only suggestion she remembered as she prepared to hurl the surprisingly heavy dagger was to keep her eye on the target.

She threw the knife, it sailed true, but dropped just short of the barley sack. Little James whooped and clapped and went to pick up the knife.

Kadar's chest puffed. He crossed his arms. "Well done, my *valkyrie*, for a first attempt."

She frowned. "*Valkyrie?* You called me that before. What does it mean?"

A faint flush showed beneath his fair skin. "Brynhild's people believe *Valkyries* are birds of prey hovering over the battlefield deciding who will live or die. But among my people they are seen as virgin warriors who arm themselves with helmets and swords and ride horses into battle beside Northmen." He shrugged. "Watching you brings those beautiful, unattainable creatures to mind."

"I'm not a virgin." She gulped. Why had she felt it necessary to point out the obvious?

Little James came skipping back, handed the knife to Kadar, then pointed. "Here comes Nathan with the *Paschal* lamb." He raced off, and the campsite came alive with joyous exclamations and hectic activity.

Lydia hugged her arms and watched little James talk excitedly to young Achan. "He's absolutely wonderful."

Kadar's warm breath filled her ear. "Woman, you're still a virgin."

Her face heated. "You are aware I'm a twice married—" She stumbled over her words. No one, except her, viewed her forced marriage to Judas the Zealot as a legal union. "I was married—"

"Marriage be damned," Kadar hissed. "Have you ever

taken a man between your legs willingly?"

Vivid recollections of Judas the Zealot and Uncle Jacob's suffocating weight pinning her in place made the air back up in her lungs. "No, never willingly."

"Then you remain a virgin in spirit. You'll know it to be true when you finally marry a man of worth."

The conversation should mortify her, but as always, Kadar's rough voice and calm presence soothed instead. "My father's idea of a man of worth and mine are not the same."

Kadar drummed his fingers against his sword belt. "Don't worry about the man from Parthia. My gut tells me the scheme will fall through. Promise me you won't do anything drastic in the meantime."

She stared at his sword hand. "I want to believe you, but—"

"If you run, I will track you down and haul you back here, so don't even try."

"Me?" Her eyes went back to his sword, and her stomach pitched. "Are you going to kill my father?"

"Go to your family and your son, and don't worry over what I might or might not do."

Torn between wanting to run to little James and never stop hugging him and wanting to spend as much time as it took to convince Kadar not to seek revenge, she gripped her shaking hands together. "Don't kill him. Not for me. I—"

"It has nothing to do with you." Kadar's eyes remained cool. "Your father did me a great wrong."

"Kadar, please—"

"There's nothing to discuss." He stepped back. "Go celebrate *Paschal* with your family."

"Wait. Don't go. Just because you can't eat the *Paschal* lamb with us doesn't mean you need to leave."

Kadar pointed toward the others. "Your sister is coming this way, and she's not pleased with us."

"Look at me," Lydia demanded.

Beautiful, ferocious blue eyes locked with hers.

She swallowed. "This talk is far from finished. Come for me tonight, after everyone has gone to bed."

"Do you recall what happened last time I tried sneaking into your room in the middle of the night?"

"Tell me you will come."

Kadar expelled an exasperated breath. "Bring Brynhild with you, and wait for me by outside the back door."

She nodded. "Where will you go till then? I hate the idea of you walking around Jerusalem alone while everyone is feasting." Idol worshippers could not share in the sacred rituals commemorating the day God freed his people from Egyptian bondage.

He broke eye contact. "I'll make out fine. I've been alone for almost all of my life. I'm used to it." Then he turned and walked away.

Alexandra came alongside Lydia. "What's wrong? I thought you'd be overjoyed at seeing little James."

Lydia searched for her son among the throng of people amassing in the campsite. "Where is he?" What a horrible mother she was, already losing track of her dear boy.

Alexandra kissed her cheek. "Boys don't stop running. They could be anywhere, but I think I saw Nathan, Achan, and James walking Judith back to her tent."

Lydia rubbed her arms and watched Kadar until he disappeared behind a screen of olive trees. He never looked back, not even once. "Do you need help with the *Paschal* lamb?"

Alexandra frowned. "Did you and Kadar argue?"

Lydia shook her head. Why did her heart keep telling her Kadar was the man for her when reason and experience screamed otherwise? She'd been wrong before. "We've never spoken about..." a chill went through Lydia "... about what happened with Judas the Zealot."

"I didn't want to upset you."

"I wanted to explain. Why I went willingly to Judas."

"He beat you." Alexandra clasped Lydia's hand. "You had no choice."

"He hit me with a strap. That was not so terrible, but when he drank too much..." Lydia shuddered. "After months went by...and I was with child, I started to believe those hills and caves were my destiny, and I accepted my fate. *He* was the father of my baby. So I went to him and tried to be a good wife." The confession opened up wounds that refused to heal. "Were you..." Lydia's voice broke "...are you disgusted with me?"

Alexandra hugged her. "No. Never. You did nothing wrong. Your strength amazes me. Father abandoned you to the rebels, and you did what you had to do to survive. Don't waste a moment feeling shame."

"What I did makes me doubt myself."

Alexandra set her at arm's length. "About Kadar. You are in danger of losing your heart to him?"

Lydia nodded. Truth was, he already owned part of her heart.

"I admire Kadar, and am very fond of him, but he is an idol-worshipper." Kindness and sympathy gentled Alexandra's voice. "It can never be."

Lydia's throat closed. "It can never be," she repeated. But her heart beat for him, repeating the same melody—*she and Kadar were meant for each other, she and Kadar were meant for each other*.

But how could she love the man who planned to kill her father? Had the time she spent in captivity warped her thinking? Was her heart leading her astray again? How could she be sure of anything ever again?

Her eyes strayed to the path Kadar had taken. He'd promised to come to her. A spine-tingling mix of anticipation and apprehension pulsed through her. If she was already condemned because of her past, did it really matter what she chose to do now?

She hugged her arms. She would meet him alone, without Bryn. For one night of her life, she was going to enjoy the kisses of the man of her choosing.

Chapter 16

The inner gates of the Temple opened and the second wave of worshippers spilled into the outer courts, bringing the pungent smell of blood with them. Men brushed by James's sedan chair, hauling skinned, gutted carcasses strapped to wooden poles. The baaing of the lambs and kid goats next in line to be killed took on a frightened keening, as they sensed they would join the thousands of animals put to death today in accordance with the Law directing every family to offer a sacrifice to the Lord.

After spilling the animals' blood, the priests removed the choice meats for burning on the Altar of the Lord, and the worshippers were then required to take the remains home, roast the meat, and consume a feast to the Lord in remembrance of the day the Lord delivered His people from bondage.

Another round of nausea hit. James managed not to gag. Roasted lamb. He hated the very smell. Through force of will he choked down his allotted portion, but the block of meat always sat like a rock in his stomach. Today, the way he felt, eating the *Paschal* meal might be the death of him. He leaned back in the sedan chair, rested against the cushioned chair back, and massaged his pounding head.

Physician Hama crouched down next to his chair. "I told you it was too soon to leave your bed."

"Stop worrying. You are worse than an old woman."

"I liked you better when you were unconscious."

"Which means you won't take offense when I say the foul concoctions you keep pouring down my throat are better company than you are."

Hama exhaled a heavy breath. "I don't understand why

you insisted on leaving your bed."

James recalled Lazarz's smug smile. "I want the culprit who pushed me down the stairs to see I am very much alive, and mostly alert, just in case he's thinking of paying me a visit with the intention of finishing the job."

"Guards are posted outside your door."

James sat forward and waited for the dizziness to pass. "A few coins slipped into the guards' hands, and there goes my protection."

The inner court emptied and the third group of Jews, the group of the lazy, shuffled ahead. James took an instant liking to the odd collection of people—Jews like him, who didn't quite fit in or conform. In Moses' day, these people would have been the last stragglers to sprinkle blood on their doorpost to ward off death, the last to leave Goshen when Moses led his people out of captivity, and the last to cross the Red Sea after Moses parted the waters.

James's amused pondering came to an end when he spied Saad limping toward them. Wonderful. Just wonderful. Talkative company was the last thing he needed.

Saad stumped to a halt. His eyes were red and swollen from the plentiful tears he'd shed over Antipater's death. "How are you? Can I serve you in any way?"

"The last thing I need is anyone else fussing over me." James put his hands to his head, sure it was about to split open.

Saad's shoulders sagged. "Forgive my meddling. I don't know what to with myself since—"

"Don't apologize," James said sharply, then exhaled. How did his sisters manage to always be so pleasant and kind? It was exhausting. Simply exhausting. He started over. "Come by my room later today. It could use a good tidying."

Saad brightened. "As you wish."

"As I wish," James muttered, then signaled the litter-bearers to move on. The two over-sized servants lifted his chair and, performing their duty too enthusiastically, they pushed through the crowd and deposited James in front of the line of priests holding blood-slicked bowls of gold.

James struggled to stand. Hama and Saad helped him to his feet. In no shape to reject assistance, James leaned heavily on Physician Hama and surveyed the priests.

The fire from the altar blazed in the background. The bawl of lambs and kid goats competed with the chanted prayer from the Levites lining the Temple stairs. James gritted his teeth against his own bitterness. Born into a priestly family, he ought to be standing with them.

He spotted his old friend Pinhas. James nodded a greeting. Pinhas smiled warmly. A country priest and experienced stonecutter, Pinhas had tutored James during the short time James had lived and worked with the stonecutters and developed his passion for the art and craft of building.

Those designated to offer up the animals approached the priests. The hiss of blood splashing into bowls soon replaced the baaing.

James touched the ugly scar that marred his face. Like the lambs sacrificed to the Lord, priests must be without blemish. He would never serve as a priest, thanks to his father's corrupt dealings with Judas the Zealot.

His chest tightened as he watched Pinhas catch blood in a rounded bowl and hand the steaming vessel to a waiting priest. The bowl was passed from priest to priest until it reached the last man, who sprinkled the blood over the roaring fire burning on the altar. The fire spit and crackled, and smoke billowed heavenward.

Then the dead carcasses were hoisted onto hooks, and gutted and skinned. Just the way James had been hollowed out and stripped of purpose the day the outlaws attacked his family, sliced his cheek open, and wreaked havoc on his sisters' lives. James's fist balled. Curse his father and his blind ambition.

Pinhas separated out the fatty portions of meat from the entrails and placed the choice morsels in a bowl. Another priest salted the meat, and another carried the bowl to the altar for burning. The aroma of roasting meat soon overlaid the coppery smell of blood.

Pinhas's eyes met James's. The stonecutter had spent

hours encouraging James to forgive. Forgive? Hah. Pinhas and others could lecture until they were blue in the face. James's father could say, promise, or threaten all he liked, but James was never going back home, and he was certainly never going to forgive the man.

The ceremony came to end. James continued to stare at the flaming altar. A hand squeezed his shoulder, and Herod's gruff voice filled his ear. "I heard you were half dead."

James swung his head around. Stabbing pain lanced through his skull. He clutched his forehead. "You heard right. However, my love of proving others wrong pulled me through, and here I am."

"I'm glad you survived." Lines of grief showed on Herod's face, making him appear older and somewhat vulnerable.

James flopped down onto the sedan chair. "I am sorry for your loss."

Herod paled.

"We need to speak," James said hurriedly, to cover the awkward moment.

"I can't spare the time." Herod turned to go.

James slid forward on his seat and spoke urgently, just softly enough that only Herod would hear. "I know who provided the poison."

Herod swung around. His eyes were two narrow slits. "What did you say?"

James swallowed, and his vision blurred at the edges. "I'd rather discuss this in private."

Herod jerked his thumb over his shoulder. "Follow me. I want my brothers to hear what you have to say."

James gave the gesture to move out and the litter bearers obeyed.

Saad fell in beside him, but Physician Hama blocked the way. "James should retire to his room."

Herod's chest puffed. "Why?"

Hama wasn't intimidated. "It will be more convenient for me if my patient is in bed when his body gives out."

James sat up straighter. "For heaven's sake, I'm not made

out of eggshell."

Herod frowned. "I won't keep him long."

Hama shrugged and moved aside. "You know where to find me when he collapses."

"Very well. Go with Hama, then. I will meet you—" Herod's voice receded into the distance.

James's vision blurred sickeningly, he swayed, and then tumbled off the chair.

A terrible smell startled James awake. Hama loomed over him. Herod and his three brothers stood behind the physician, staring down at him. James clutched the blanket laid over his chest. He was in his room. In his own bed. He squeezed his eyes closed. No, he hadn't. He couldn't possibly have fainted in the middle of the Temple grounds. "I must have made quite the spectacle sprawled on the stone floor."

"Saad said you looked like a dead bug," a guttural voice said from across the room. "I'm sorry I missed it."

"I'm sorry to disappoint." James said peevishly. "You exhibit an inordinate amount of interest in our family, Barbarian."

Kadar's rumble of laughter didn't improve James's mood. "Someone has to watch over you."

"Why is the barbarian here?" James asked.

"Forget Kadar." Herod's implacable tone made it clear Kadar would be staying. "Tell us what you know."

"James should rest," Hama said.

Herod widened his stance. "He talks, then he rests."

Hama headed for the door. "I need to check on your mother."

"What did you see?" Herod demanded.

James's eyelids felt heavier than Corinthian columns, but he managed to pry them open. "I stumbled upon Lazarz while he was handing Antipater's cupbearer a vial." James had his reasons for protecting red-headed Niv. The lie couldn't hurt the cupbearer, as that dolt had already been put to death. As for Lazarz, the murderous fiend could rot in Hades. "Lazarz spotted me and chased me through the Baris. I thought I lost him, but—" James shrugged. "When I woke I heard about your father and I put the pieces together. Lazarz didn't throw me down those stairs because he was in a bad mood." James smoothed the bedcovering. "I saw him snooping around outside my room this morning. I imagine he came back to finish what he started."

Herod's black eyes burned with hate. "Kadar suspected Lazarz."

"Half of Jerusalem is searching for the murdering fiend," Kadar added.

Herod exhaled heavily. "My brothers and I promised our mother we wouldn't be gone long."

James thanked Herod and watched him and his brothers file out of the room with satisfaction. Turnabout was fair play—Herod employed spies to watch James, and now he would have a spy in Herod's camp. Freckle-faced Niv didn't realize he had a new master, but he soon would.

Saad hobbled in with a plate of food. "Physician Hama wants you to eat."

James frowned. "Let me see, do I want to eat roast lamb and unleavened bread...or unleavened bread and roast lamb?" Unmoved by knowing every family in Jerusalem was serving and eating the same meal, he stuck his tongue out at the unappetizing gray lumps on the plate.

Kadar continued to lean against the far wall. James scowled at the enormous man. "I overheard my sister and her slave talking about you. My father will burst a blood vessel when he learns Lydia is in love with a barbarian."

The giant's blue eyes iced over. "Your father has arranged a marriage for Lydia to a man from Parthia."

James made a face. "I hope for Lydia's sake this husband isn't older than Adam or bow-legged and toothless."

Kadar pushed away from the wall, raised his tree-trunk sized arm, and pointed. "I want a serious answer from you, Onias. If something happens to your father, and you become Lydia's guardian, will you choose a husband she finds acceptable?"

James gripped his blanket. His father, dead or out of the way. Wouldn't that change everything? Could he stand back and allow his father's murder? He chewed on his lip. His father had a penchant for making enemies. Was James supposed to spend his life thwarting murderous plots? Kadar's blue eyes burned a hole through him. Did the giant ox actually think he'd be allowed to marry Lydia? Insulting a man four times one's size was a good way to end up dead, so James selected his words carefully. "Lydia must marry a devout man."

Kadar smirked, but not in a good way. "Say it. I know you're thinking it."

"Hell and damnation," James muttered. Taking a deep breath, he hurried his words. "Lydia can't marry a pagan barbarian. But if she could marry a gentile, you would be at the top of the list." He waited for the eruption.

The Goliath-sized man didn't flinch. "Do you have a devout Jew in mind?"

James shook his head, relieved to still have his thick skull on his shoulders.

"I'll marry Lydia," a calm voice said.

James and Kadar turned. Physician Hama stood in the open door exuding confidence and boldness in enviable abundance.

Chapter 17

Nehonya Onias's darkened home might well have been death's door. Kadar had suffered his fair share of difficulties, but none as burdensome as resigning himself to the proposed marriage between Lydia and Avda Hama. Knowing it was for the best didn't lessen the hurt. Kadar dreaded delivering the news, a duty rightfully belonging to James, who had the tact of a charging boar. Kadar could at least spare her that.

Lydia stepped out of the shadows and rushed to him. His arms opened for her of their own accord. She buried her face in his chest and wrapped her arms around his waist. The scent of white jasmine filled his nose. Her voice was breathy. "Kiss me."

His blood heated, and he crushed his mouth to hers. Cupping her round bottom, he tasted of her moist, supple lips. Mouths and tongues slipping and sliding together in mutual plunder threatened to send them places they couldn't go. He broke away. "Where's Brynhild?"

Lydia tipped her head back. Yearning glistened in her hauntingly beautiful eyes. "I wanted to be alone with you."

His loins tightened and his heart beat faster. "Holy gods, woman, do you have any idea what you do to me?"

"Don't talk. Kiss me, again...please."

Sweet stars in heaven and moon above, he *knew* she wouldn't be a passive lover. With very little encouragement, she would be stunning and glorious. He wanted to be the one to unleash the banked passion vibrating through her more than he craved life itself. "I'm tempted, woman. I truly am. But, you know as well as I do it wouldn't stop with kisses."

"I ache for you. I want the pain to go away."

"It wouldn't be fair to you."

"For this one night, make me forget everything but you," she begged. "You want me. I know—"

"Jupiter and Mars, woman. Of course I want you. If I thought only of myself I would take you now, right up against the wall of the house, and the world could go to Hades."

She blushed bright red. "Why are you being so noble?"

Images flashed through his mind, of his fellow Northmen armed for a hunt, of snowcapped huts wreathed in smoke, of the night sky alive with waves of shimmering light. He exhaled heavily. "Because I don't want you to have to live with regret and guilt."

"I'm afraid I will be sorry if I turn my back on this."

"I understand. I'm drawn to your body, to your presence, to your heart. But I care too much for you to allow you to throw away who you are."

"What do you mean?"

He took her hand, pulled her to the end of the lane, and pointed toward the moonlit Temple. "Are you a daughter of Abraham, Isaac, and Jacob?"

Lydia sighed. "I am."

"Are you a daughter of the Lord God of Israel?"

"I am."

"Are you a righteous woman?"

She dipped her head.

A surge of red-hot anger arose. "You are a righteous woman, but you doubt it because of that ungodly business with Judas the Zealot. Am I right?"

Her silence proved he had guessed correctly.

The door to a nearby house creaked open.

He drew her into the shadows, and directed her southward. "I have a safe shelter where we can talk about this and other matters."

Keeping their heads down, they moved quickly and quietly through dark alley after dark alley, and emerged near the city's outermost wall. They passed through the arched Dung Gate and trod the road leading to the Hinnom Valley. The rot of dead animals filled the air. Morta's small hovel sat a stone's throw from the smoking hell-fires of Gehenna, the burning pit used to dispose of Jerusalem's filth. This dark underside of Jerusalem was a place Kadar was very familiar with, but one he doubted those of Lydia's class ever visited.

Kadar knocked on a rickety door. He didn't like the idea of bringing Lydia to Morta's, but Jerusalem didn't have many safe places for a barbarian to meet, even innocently, with an upright Jewish woman. He'd given Morta extra coins to ensure he was the only visitor she had that night.

The door creaked open, and the middle-aged widow waved him in. A worn bedroll topped with a frayed cover dominated the one-room hole. Morta's coy smile vanished when she spotted Lydia. "I'm not that low a sinner."

Kadar made a face. "I'm not looking for that. I told you I need a safe place to talk."

"Kadar," Lydia stammered. "What... where... who is this woman?

Kadar hated himself, truly, truly hated himself for hurting Lydia this way, even though he knew it was for the best. "Lydia, this is Morta. Morta is a harlot."

The widow straightened and pointed at the ramshackle door. "Go, Kadar. Leave now."

Kadar liked Morta, and was glad to see the whore had some pride left. He wagged his brows. "Return my coins and I'll go." The widow gripped the pouch at her waist and exhaled an exasperated breath.

He shifted his attention.

Lydia's complexion had turned sallow. "Why did you bring me here?"

The misery in her eyes cut to the quick. He longed to hold her, comfort her, but he was doing what had to be done. "Do you know about harlots and what they do?"

A single tear rolled down Lydia's pale cheek. "I know."

He swallowed. "I brought you here because I want you to see what kind of man I am. If you gave yourself to me, you would change in here." He put his hand over his heart. "You are a righteous daughter of Israel. And I am a man who enjoys the comfort of harlots. We come from different worlds."

Lydia hugged herself. "I don't care."

"You should. Morta, how many times have I lain with you?"

The harlot sighed. "Kadar was one of my best visitors."

Lydia's chin came up. "She said *was*. How long has it been since Kadar *visited* you, Morta?"

Morta chuckled. "Many, many years."

Kadar strode to the door and yanked it open. "Go, woman." Morta walked outside wearing a smile wide enough to trip an elephant.

He slammed the door shut.

"I don't care about Morta," Lydia repeated.

He rolled his eyes. "You are the most stubborn, frustrating, drive-me-straight-out-of-my-mind woman I've ever met. Nothing is going to happen between us, because I won't let it, and because Hama would kill me."

"Physician Hama? What does he have to do with us?"

Kadar paced one way, and then the other. This wasn't the gentle approach he'd hoped to take. "I spoke to your brother about you. I wanted to make sure he would do right by you after I kill—"

"I know he doesn't deserve mercy," Lydia said hurriedly. "But I beg you to reconsider."

"Your father holds his life in his own hands."

"You changed your mind? You don't plan to kill him?"

"I will allow him to live if he calls off your marriage to the man from Parthia and gives you to Hama instead."

"What about your revenge?"

"Your father's bald eunuch slave will die, that's non-negotiable."

"Negotiating? Has James heard from Father?"

"James and Hama worked out the terms of a marriage contract, which becomes void if I harm a hair on Simeon Onias's head. So, if your father knows what's good for him, he'll agree to a marriage between you and the physician."

"I have no idea what to say." Lydia buried her face in her hands. "I never hoped for so much."

He pulled her to his chest and rubbed her back. "I made a few stipulations of my own. Money will be settled on you if

Hama dies. The physician has agreed to move to Sepphoris in Galilee so you can be close to little James." Lydia's shoulders shook as she wept silent tears.

"Hama is a good man. He will treat you with respect and kindness." Kadar squeezed his eyes closed. It would have hurt less to rip his heart out and hand it to her.

Lydia wrapped her arms around him. "Where will you go? What will you do?"

He patted her back. "I'll land on my feet somewhere." Knowing Lydia was with her son and her sister in the quiet wilds of Galilee would sustain him in the long years ahead. Would it be enough? No, never. He buried his nose in her silky brown hair and inhaled deeply of white jasmine. "Don't trouble yourself about me."

She pulled away. Tears glistened in her eyes. "Promise me you will marry. I don't want you to be alone."

He brushed his knuckle over her warm cheek. "I am fated to be alone."

"No, you are stubborn."

"I'm used to making my own way. I don't mind it."

Lydia swatted his chest. "Don't! Don't say that."

She was gorgeous when she was angry. He laughed, and she raised her fists.

He grabbed her wrists. "I say it because it's true."

She tried to pull out of his grip. "I don't believe you."

"I'll explain, if you promise to settle down."

She wrinkled her nose. "You are alone because you want to be."

"Look who's calling who stubborn," he said, but released her hands.

The corners of her mouth rose. "I was promised an explanation."

Tempted to kiss her, he moved as far away from her as the cramped room allowed, and leaned heavily against a cracked clay wall.

Lydia eyed the whore's bed with distaste, then perched on the very end.

He scrubbed his face and exhaled heavily. "I wasn't

always at peace with my fate. When I was young, I believed the problem rested in the fact I was born a bastard."

"You're a bastard? That's why you've been so good to me and little James?"

"It's part of the reason."

She touched her fingers to her lips and blushed.

His male pride gloried, knowing she was recalling the kisses they shared. He pushed the thought away. "Little James shows great promise."

"Thank you for taking me to see him. He is amazing and clever, and his smile is so precious."

"I thought little James ought to know his mother."

"Because you never knew yours?"

Kadar rarely ever thought about the woman who had given birth to him. "My mother was a slave girl in my father's household. My father's wife sold my mother when my father was away raiding. I was two years old at the time. Seeing your pain made me wonder about my own mother. Did she grieve for me the way you do for James? I never tried to find her, so I'll never know." Watching Lydia and little James together made him regret not trying.

"Who took care of you after you lost your mother?"

He scuffed his sandal over the hard-packed dirt floor. "The villagers treated me like a stray dog, some were kind, others chased me off or scolded me. My stepmother Gerta and my half brothers and sisters went out of their way to make my life miserable."

Lydia hugged her arms. "I used to dream about little James being alone and frightened."

"From what I could see, your boy is well cared for and has plenty of aunts and uncles and cousins watching over him." Kadar was happy for the child. The contempt heaped on bastards was burdensome enough without the added strain of begging for your every need or fending off constant threats.

"You said you couldn't go home. Was it because you were wronged, or because you wouldn't be welcomed back?"

He scrubbed his face. "Both. I should have seen it coming. I finally found a place where I belonged. My father was a fierce warlord, and I grew to be every bit the warrior he was. I bested everyone, at whatever I put my hand to. And my father came to favor me over his other bastards and his true sons. The happiest days of my life were spent fighting and raiding by my father's side. But the good days ended when he died."

He touched his hand to the amulet hidden beneath his tunic, the one his father had carved for him. "Afterwards, I pledged my allegiance to my half brother, Jokul, but he and Gerta feared me." Kadar laughed grimly. "I was eighteen years old and believed my ability with a sword made me invincible, but Gerta disposed of me without lifting a finger. The sickness that killed my father continued to ravage our village. Whole households died. Our priests sacrificed a handful of slaves in hopes of warding off the curse, but more people became ill. A greater gift was called for. Gerta whispered in the priests' ears and I and a priest's daughter were chosen."

Lydia looked horrified on his behalf. "I don't blame you for fleeing and leaving your land behind."

His flesh crawled, remembering his terrible anger and the sinking dread of that dark day. "I have my doubts now that it was the right thing to do. Under other circumstances, I would have submitted to the priests and counted it an honor to lay down my life to Thor and Odin. Your people count human sacrifice as an abomination, but it's not what troubled me. Gerta's trickery irked me. I wasn't about to allow Gerta and Jokul to get the best of me."

"How did you escape?"

Vivid memories returned. "I fought my way out of the village, then I ran and ran and ran. I slept by day and moved by night, until I reached an unfamiliar land. The whole time I wracked my mind for a way to escape the trap Greta had set, and I kept coming back to the same inescapable truth. I was doomed. No warlord would risk the displeasure of the gods or his people by taking me in. So I did the only thing I could."

He dug in his pouch and pulled out a coin stamped with the image of Julius Caesar. Lamplight danced over the silver disk. "My father gave me a Roman coin when I was a boy and told me it came from a faraway land. The markings fascinated me. I'd never seen letters or writing of any kind. Alone with no other place to go, and cloaked in youthful confidence, I decided to find the people who had made the coin and make my home among them."

"You were so young." Lydia's voice was a soft whisper. "How did you survive?"

He thumbed the silver *denarius*. "Desperation pushes a man beyond what he thinks he can endure. I ate berries and small animals and I just kept walking. The loneliness was the hardest part, worse than the bitter cold, blinding rain, and wild beasts. Months and months later I came upon a pack of *Cimbri* hunters, who treated me a bit roughly, but I eventually escaped, still driven forward by a vague notion of a great city called Rome."

Lydia's huge eyes couldn't get any wider. "Did you make it to Rome?"

"I did. And I wasn't there two days before I hated it."

"Why?"

He tucked the coin away. "I came from the remote wilds. Rome was too crowded and noisy and busy for me. Imagine one hundred Jerusalems crowded within the walls of Rome, with ten times the animals, markets, and rubbish."

"You could be describing Alexandria. I never learned to like Egypt." Lydia sighed. "How did you end up in Jerusalem of all places?"

"I was thinking of returning to Gaul when I heard about a soldier from the east hiring mercenary soldiers. Antipater's man, Obodas, took a liking to me, and by the time our boat crossed the Great Sea I had a working knowledge of Aramaic. I admired the harsh beauty of your land, but the heat from your sun was too strong for my blood." He withheld the prime problem—he'd felt utterly friendless and adrift as a pagan among Jews. He also didn't share how the brief hours he'd spent caring for her after the rescue had soothed like a cool breeze on a hot day. He cleared his throat. "I was on the point of returning to Gaul when your letter came."

Lydia drew her knees up to her chest and hugged them. "I'm so sorry. It wasn't fair to ask so much of you."

Her forlorn frown killed him. He pushed away from the wall. "Thundering Thor, I can't stay away from you now, any more than I could then."

He scooped her up, sunk down onto the bed, and sheltered her in his arms. "Don't torture yourself," he said into her ear. "What happened, happened."

She pressed her head into his chest. "You are a good man."

"I'm not good. I killed Sabu Nakht."

"Who?"

"Nakht owned the copper mine, and was my master, and an evil snake of a man."

"You suffered terribly there, didn't you?"

The hole of loneliness at his center expanded to become a crater. "The backbreaking labor, meager food, and filthy conditions were as bad as you might imagine. It would have worn me into the ground eventually, as it did everyone else. But I was singled out by Nakht for special treatment." Kadar's muscles bunched. "Nakht didn't buy me to work me to death, he bought me to be his champion in the fight-to-the-death matches he arranged. I slept in Nakht's home, shared his food, wine, and women…and I hated every moment."

Lydia hugged him. "Don't blame yourself. You did what you had to survive."

"Death would have been less painful. At first I refused to play Nakht's foul game. I refused the food, wine, and the women. So Nakht killed or tortured those I was friendly with. I stopped talking to others, and Nakht threatened to skin alive a young slave girl to gain my cooperation. I gave in and killed and drank and whored until I stank with it. But Nakht was worse than a jealous woman. He maimed a slave woman I made the mistake of staring at too long, and cut the throat of a servant pouring my wine after I nodded my thanks, and—"

Lydia's soft whimper stopped him. He kissed the top of her head. "Forgive me. I didn't mean to go on like that." It was the first time he'd uttered a word of this to anyone. "I don't

144

know how else to make you understand. Those years taught me what it meant to be alone until it ran through my veins like blood and became the marrow filling my bones. I don't just think I'm meant to be alone. I know it."

Any lingering doubts he'd had vanished with Lydia. He loved her. No, he didn't just love her, his heart ached with longing for her. Yet he must give her to another man. Hama would hold Lydia in the night, not Kadar. Hama would plant his seed and his children in Lydia's womb, not Kadar. Hama would hear Lydia's beautiful laugh and look into her lovely brown eyes, not Kadar. Thoughts destined to haunt him for the rest of his life. What more proof did he need? The gods couldn't have made the message more plain if they'd risen from their thrones and spoken directly into his ear.

Lydia pulled away from him. "I'm glad you killed Nakht."

"I thought avenging the evil done in my name and spilling Nakht's blood would give me peace." He touched his finger to Lydia's face and traced her delicate jaw. "Knowing you will be happy and well cared for means even more to me. Nothing is more important."

Lydia's lower lip quivered. "I don't want you to go away."

"I'll stay until you are married to Hama."

"Physician Hama seems very kind, but...I wish I was marrying—"

Kadar surged to his feet, making Lydia yelp. Some confessions were better left unspoken. He set her down and pointed a warning finger. "You need to be more guarded. You need to stay far, far away from me. No more sneaking out of the house in the middle of the night. I brought you to a whore's den to open your eyes and to scare some sense into you. Morta didn't start out to be a harlot. One or two false steps, and you could fall as far as Morta. Please don't let it happen. Promise me you will be more careful."

Lydia swatted his hand aside, surprising a laugh out of him. She held up her finger. "One kiss. I want to share one more kiss with you."

His gut tightened. "One kiss, and then we can never meet alone again. Do you agree?"

She bit the corner of her rosy lip and stared at him for a long moment. "I agree."

His blood flowed hot as melted gold. No good could come of this. But he couldn't resist. He held out his arms. "Come here."

She shook her head. "Come to me, warrior."

Instantly aroused, he caught her hands and shackled them behind her back. When their lips were almost touching, her warm breath sent a tremor down his spine. "You slay me, woman. You truly do."

Her mouth curved up. "Stop talking and kiss me."

The torturous weight of his bleak past and stark future fell away. *Thundering Thor, she was perfect, absolutely perfect!*

Hands trapped behind her back, Lydia slid her mouth over Kadar's lips and nibbled on the soft, bare skin behind his ear.

He sucked in his breath. "You said one kiss."

"Release my hands first."

His husky laughed vibrated through her. "Not on your life."

She flicked her tongue in his ear, and nipped his earlobe. "Mmm...I could do this all night."

He laughed.

Lydia pulled back and concentrated on Kadar's grin. She wanted to cry her heart out for all he'd suffered, but it was a selfish indulgence she refused to give in to. Instead, she batted her lashes. "I will feast on your neck next," she purred.

His smile widened, and he freed her wrists and cupped her bottom. "I'll make you pay, woman." His fingers dug and kneaded. She ran her hands over thick, powerful shoulders, pulsing with restrained strength. He could easily hurt her, but there was nothing brutish about him.

Her heart sang with joy for this man, and ached. She

hated the thought of him spending the rest of his life alone, but feared he would. He believed loneliness was his lot in life. She'd seen it in his eyes. A few moments of argument wouldn't put a hole in his conviction. And their time together was quickly running out.

Her false smile fell away. "I don't want you to leave."

He sobered. "And I don't want to go, my *valkyrie*. But we both know I must. Now kiss me," he demanded.

She stared in to his light blue eyes and laced her fingers through his golden-blond hair. Their hot breaths mingled and she moved her mouth over his. Tongues and lips slipped and slid together. His shoulder-length hair brushed over her collarbone, sending waves of pleasure to her core. Unused to the touch of a generous lover, she kept waiting for him to turn greedy, but he gave and gave. His sandalwood scent saturated her pores and Kadar's physicality filled all her senses.

He broke away first, and their panting breaths echoed off the crumbling plaster walls. They clung to each other for a long, long time, neither willing to let go of the moment. Tonight was the end for them. This would be the last time she could touch him and he could touch her.

Tempted to beg him to stay, or beg him to take her with him, or beg him to hold her forever, she already grieved the loss him.

He thumbed away the tears rolling down her cheeks. "You will be in my heart wherever I go."

"I will never forget you," she promised, and squeezed her eyes shut. Now all she had to do was teach her heart to accept what couldn't be changed.

Chapter 18

The next morning Lydia took away the bowl of broth her brother had barely touched and set it on a tray next to James's bed. "May I get anything else for you?"

James's lips pursed. "I'll take more wine. Then I can pretend my head aches because I drank too much, a malady I'd have hope of recovering from in mere hours."

Lydia reached for the wine pitcher. "The fall from the sedan chair couldn't have helped." The dark red splotch on James's cheekbone was new, thanks to an ill-advised outing to the Temple.

"I'm told the sound of my face smacking against the paving stones could be heard all the way to the Mount of Olives."

"I'm glad you weren't hurt more seriously." She poured a generous portion of wine into James's cup, and reached for the water pitcher.

"I'll take the wine straight," James said.

She frowned. "I wish you'd treat your body more kindly."

"You sound like Alexandra. One sister fussing over me is enough. You are supposed to make me laugh or tell me a story to help me forget my troubles."

Stifling a sigh, she handed over the silver goblet. "I'm sorry. I didn't sleep well." Kadar had delivered her back to cousin Nehonya's a few hours before dawn. She had lain in bed and cried until she couldn't cry anymore, then slept fitfully for a bit before making her way blindly to James's bedside. "I received a letter from Father," she choked out. "He is on his way here. Cousin Nehonya expects him to arrive within the week. You know about Father's plan to marry me to a man from Parthia?"

James's nose curled. "I received a letter as well, and I'm happy to help thwart whatever nefarious plot he has dreamed up now."

It saddened her to know her brother always referred to Father as *he* or *him*. "Do you have any idea what Father is up to or what he hopes to gain?"

"I'd bet my inheritance he is still scheming to be named High Priest." James tapped the raised, red scar on his face. "And we both know he doesn't care how many lives he destroys to get what he wants." James's solemn eyes met hers. "You have suffered far too much as a tool of his ambition. My hope is you will be as happy in your next marriage as Alexandra is with hers. Does the thought of marrying Physician Hama please you?"

Grateful and touched by her brother's concern and thoughtfulness, yet still heavy of heart over parting with Kadar, Lydia managed a small nod. "Your support and help mean the world to me."

James wagged his brows. "Your barbarian wanted to kill...*him*, but Hama wouldn't hear of it."

She winced. "He's not *my barbarian*."

"I hope you don't plan to sneak out of Cousin Nehonya's house again to meet him in secret."

Her face heated. "What...I don't...that is—"

James rolled his eyes. "Don't fret. I won't tell anyone."

Unnerved, she glanced repeatedly over her shoulder. "How did you know? Who told you?"

"You knew about the talk I had with Hama and Kadar, and only your future husband or the barbarian could have told you. I hope nothing untoward happened. Hama wouldn't be pleased."

"What wouldn't please me?" Physician Hama asked entering the bedchamber.

Lydia's heart skipped a beat. Aware she still smelled of sandalwood, with her lips still burning from Kadar's kisses, she'd have preferred to put off this awkward meeting until she was steadier.

"Ah, my favorite physician," James lifted his cup in

greeting. "Lydia insists on remaining by my side all day. I was telling her you wouldn't be pleased." Her brother didn't bat an eyelash at the lie. "You ordered me to rest. Isn't that so? I have a perfect solution. In light of your happy prospects, you two should stop pestering me and take a long walk so you may become better acquainted."

Lydia wanted to swipe the smirk off her brother's face and see him dropped in donkey dung.

Physician Hama came closer. "You can start by resting your over-busy mouth," he said mildly.

James pretended to be indignant. "I was just trying to be helpful."

Physician Hama grunted. "Helpful? Maybe I should mix you up one of my special remedies."

"No, not that," James howled.

Lydia covered her smile.

"Did you have a happier *Pesach* celebration than your brother?" Physician Hama asked.

Lydia forced her chin up and met Physician Hama's calm brown eyes. He was a man in the prime of life, with a fine face and figure; she knew she should be rejoicing over her prospects. "The day brought many joys."

Physician Hama smiled.

Embarrassed because her thoughts were not of the proposed marriage but of little James and Kadar wrapping their warm arms about her, she looked down and dug at her tunic with her fingernail. "Did you spend the day with family?"

Physician Hama exhaled heavily. "No, Cypros was in a terrible state. I attended her and administered medicine, but nothing helped. Her grief has turned into anger. She is pressuring her sons to find and punish her husband's murderer."

Lydia had heard little about Antipater's widow, except for her reputation as a difficult woman. "Thank you for taking time to check on James."

James sat forward. "Have Malichus and Lazarz been apprehended yet?"

The physician shook his head. "Malichus denies the charges and continues to shed copious tears over Antipater's demise. And Lazarz has disappeared without a trace."

James lay back against his pillow. "So I still have to worry Lazarz might show up at my bedside in the middle of the night and slit my throat."

"I imagine Lazarz has fled and won't be heard from again," Physician Hama said.

Lydia rose to her knees and fussed with James's blanket. She'd heard Cousin Nehonya and Gabriel discussing the poisoning and palace intrigue. It made her frightened for her brother. "It's too dangerous here. I'm sure Cousin Nehonya will take you in."

"I'm not a stray puppy in need of rescuing," James replied sourly. "You are the one putting yourself in danger. You should go back to our cousin's home and stay there until the dust settles. Tell her, Hama."

Physician Hama looked down his nose at James. "You look more like a wet cat than a stray puppy to me. Now, if your sister would be so good as to move aside, I will take a closer look at your injuries."

Lydia scooted to the foot of the bed.

Physician Hama placed his reed basket of ointments, herbs, and small jars of liquid cures onto the marble-topped bedside table, then leaned over the bed and inspected her brother's head. "Antipater's death has placed this entire household at risk. It's best if everyone behaves with extra caution." He glanced over at her.

She squirmed. Physician Hama's word would soon be law for her. He already saw himself as her protector. Though he meant well, she prayed he wouldn't tell her to go back to Cousin Nehonya's, because she'd have to obey or risk appearing headstrong and unruly.

Physician Hama turned his attention back to her brother. "Herod has doubled the guard, and he has eyes and ears everywhere, ready to report any trouble."

James pulled his blankets higher. "Herod has many talents. He appreciates well-built buildings and women."

Physician Hama dabbed clear cream onto James's newest wound. "Watch your mouth in your sister's presence."

"Go poke someone else," James said, swatting the physician's hand away.

Physician Hama sat back on his heels. "With your permission, I'll take your sister for a walk about the gardens and allow you to sleep. I doubt it will improve your disposition, but it can't make it worse."

Misery shone in James's eyes. "Thank heaven. Some peace and quiet at last."

Lydia ached for her brother. She realized his prickliness came from years of fending off barbed criticism from a father who never found anything good to say about his children. "Don't get used to it," she said sternly. "I plan to take my dinner with you and make you listen to one of the stories I learned during my stay in Egypt."

James smoothed the bedcovers. "Come back if you like. And bring along someone who will make better company than me. Perhaps Cousin Elizabeth. I imagine she would be glad for an excuse to get out of the house."

Lydia blinked repeatedly. "Cousin Elizabeth?" The faint blush spreading across her brother's face told her he hadn't picked the name out of the air at random. "I'll ask but—" She searched for a nice way to say Elizabeth detested him.

"Forget I said anything." James sank down lower. "Go have your walk with Hama."

Physician Hama gathered up his basket. The collection of jars and vials clinked and rattled as he retreated to the door.

Lydia's limbs felt rooted in place. She squeezed her brother's hand, slowly climbed to her feet, and made her way to the man who would soon be her husband.

Physician Hama led her through a series of shiny-floored corridors, and showed himself to be incredibly kind by carrying on a one-sided conversation about the obsession the previous owners of the house had with menorahs. The seven-branched candelabrums were everywhere, in images painted on the walls, and inlaid on tile mosaic floors, and cast in gold or silver in custom-made niches.

The thought of a future without Kadar opened a dark pit in Lydia, one a thousand burning lamps couldn't dispel.

They exited a side door, emerging into a flower-filled courtyard. The sky overhead was blue as Kadar's eyes, but the bright rays of the sun spilling into the walled garden failed to warm her. She came to a halt beside a clutch of purple and white blooms. She forced her eyes to Hama's. "Forgive my directness, but why...why do you want to marry me?"

"Don't apologize. I admire your forthrightness, and I will be equally open. I have two boys." The life went out of his eyes. "I lost my wife. My sons need a mother."

"I didn't know. I'm honored by your offer, Physician Hama."

"Call me Avda."

"Avda," she said softly, the first step toward greater intimacies waiting over the horizon. A chill went through her. "But why me? Jerusalem abounds with young, fruitful women. I may not be able to give you more children."

Avda stared into the distance. "I hope it is so, and I will pray fervently you never conceive. My youngest is four, and his mother died giving birth to him." His voice turned forlorn. "I loved Mary. She was my whole life. The truth is, I'm a coward. I don't want to go through such pain again."

Lydia's heart opened a bit. They shared a common bond. They both were familiar with loss. Perhaps, over time, the comfort they gave one another would grow into something deeper and richer. "Tell me about your sons."

His smile reached his eyes. "They are boisterous and noisy and busy and perfect."

"I predict we will get along wonderfully."

"Did your brother tell you I plan to take you to Galilee?"

"I hardly dared to believe it." She twisted her hands together. "Your kindness is overwhelming."

"I'm not a saint. I have my own selfish reasons for wanting to leave Jerusalem."

"You sound worried."

"Antipater's death means years of woe for Judea. I want better for my family. Plus, I'd like to use my skills to benefit the poor. I've had my fill of pampered fools complaining of sore stomachs and headaches brought on by an excess of self-pity or self-indulgence."

She smiled. "You've done nothing to convince me you aren't a good, good man."

He ducked his head. "All I ask for is a joyful, peaceful household to come home to." He turned hopeful eyes to her. "Do you believe you could be happy living with me and my sons? Do you want to marry me?"

"I...I..." She should accept the proposal and count herself abundantly blessed. She cleared her throat. "Of course. What objections could I have?"

"Marriage contracts are drawn up between men, but a man and a woman must live with the marriage. I don't want to force you into something you don't want."

She swayed, suddenly a bit dizzy. What was the matter with her? She should be leaping for joy over this man. "Forgive my hesitation. Everything has happened so quickly. My mind hasn't had time to get used to the idea." Memory of the passionate kisses she'd shared with Kadar intruded. Her throat closed.

"You don't have to commit to anything today," Avda said gently. "If you like, I can come by your brother's room at the same time over the next few days, and take you to walk about the gardens so we can become better acquainted."

She nodded. "Thank you."

Chapter 19

One week after Lydia had hugged little James and watched him begin the trek back to Galilee with Alexandra and Nathan, her heart was still heavy. She paced around James's bedchamber to the beat of his soft snores. She hated waiting. Waiting for her father to arrive in Jerusalem so she could confront him over the proposed marriage to the man from Parthia. Wondering how long she would have to wait to see little James again. Anxious over what her life would be like as Avda Hama's wife.

As promised, Avda arrived and escorted Lydia out of James's room for their daily walk. The time they spent together helped make her more comfortable in her proposed husband's company, but if she was being honest, she had to admit part of her jitters came from yearning, hoping, and obsessing about catching a glimpse of Kadar. True to his word, he had stayed away. The heaviness in her heart over the loss of Kadar, and now little James, cast a dark shadow over the rest of her life.

Avda went straight to her favorite spot in the garden, a curved niche molded into the outer wall, which sheltered a small marble bench and was shaded by a citron tree heavy with waxy white buds.

She plucked a flower and inhaled its lemony fragrance. "Do Ori and Benjamin like their new tutor?" Well-mannered, quiet boys, ages six and four, Avda's sons had taken to her almost immediately the one time they'd met.

Avda rolled his eyes. "My sons tell me their young rabbi tutor is quite unreasonable, expecting them to read from the Torah for two hours each day. I told them I planned to pay Rabbi Saul double what I'd promised."

The tender care Avda showered on his sons deepened her respect and admiration. She trusted he'd treat little James equally well. "I would like to visit them again."

Avda sobered. "I want to settle matters between us before allowing Ori and Benjamin to become attached to you." A hint of vulnerability entered his eyes. "Do you want to marry me? Is the marriage acceptable to you?"

She swallowed. "I...I—"

"This is difficult for me too." He held out his hand.

Trembling, she forced her hand toward his. His palm met hers. She made herself look at him. "I'm not sure what it is you want me to say."

He reached for her other hand and linked their fingers. "The wedding contract will be a mere formality. What's said between us now will be the true promise, binding us together. I want a promise as simple as the one I'm ready to give you." He squeezed her hands. "Lydia Onias, in the sight of the Lord, I, Avda Hama, pledge myself to you."

Two broken souls in need of a simple, peaceful life, bound by an honest vow. How could she say no? What was there to dislike? She took a deep breath. "Avda Hama, in the sight of the Lord, I pledge—" Her heart slammed, telling her she couldn't commit herself to Avda. It wouldn't be fair. His wife was dead, but the man she loved still lived and breathed. She loved Kadar. Loved him with everything within her. She couldn't pledge an oath to another. The words would be a lie. A huge, tragic lie.

"Lydia?" she heard Avda say.

She blinked and the garden came back into focus.

Avda's brow creased with concern. "You've lost all your color. Come and sit on the bench until the spell passes."

She nodded, and backed up a step.

A group of soldiers spilled out of a side door, putting an end to the quiet. A golden-blond head stood out from the others. Kadar. His penetrating blue eyes clouded and locked onto her and Avda's joined hands.

She tried to yank her hands back, but Avda's firm grip held her in place.

"All will be well," he assured her.

His calm steadied her. "I'm sorry. They surprised me."

He released her hands and moved to her side.

She stared at the ground, listening for the quiet that would signal the men, *and Kadar*, had moved on.

A shadow fell over the yellow clutch of flowers surrounding her sandals.

"Hama," Kadar said in greeting.

Kadar's deep voice reverberated through her. She continued to study her feet.

"You and your men are armed to the teeth," Avda observed. "Where are you going?"

Kadar grunted. "Syria."

Lydia's head snapped up. "Syria? But you'll be gone for weeks." He'd promised to stay in Jerusalem until her father arrived, whereupon Kadar would *persuade* Father to sign a marriage contract binding her to Avda.

Kadar's square jaw tightened. "They arrested Malichus. Herod asked me to accompany him."

"I hear the Parthian army is wreaking havoc in Syria," Avda said.

Kadar nodded over his shoulder at the soldiers. "Herod is willing to risk the danger. He is determined to see Malichus put on trial for murdering Antipater. Herod won't rest until he lays out his charges to the governor and Malichus is condemned."

Lydia twisted her hands together to keep from reaching for Kadar. "But you said—"

Kadar's blue eyes flashed ferociously. "Antipater was murdered while under my protection. Herod asked me to go with him. I cannot refuse." He pointed a large finger at Avda. "Hama, can you handle Onias?"

Avda straightened. "I am well able to protect my own."

"That's what I wanted to hear." Without a word of farewell, Kadar turned and walked away.

Lydia chased after him and grabbed his sleeve. "Wait!"

He whirled around. "What do you want, woman?"

His ice-cold voice stung sharp as a slap to the face. "Will

I see you again?"

"Go back to Hama. He's your protector now."

"But I lo—"

"Go!" Kadar barked, yanking his arm free. His strides long and steady, he caught up to his fellow soldiers and disappeared through a gated archway.

Lydia's knees gave out. Avda Hama scooped her up before she hit the ground. Sitting on the bench, he cradled and rocked her. She squeezed her eyes closed. Her chest ached as she struggled to hold in her tears. Avda's mouth brushed her ear. "The heart needs to mourn. So mourn him. You won't be able to move on until you do."

Tears welling, she wrapped her arms around his solid chest. "Thank you, Avda. Thank you for understanding."

Kadar made it as far as the stables, then turned back. He was ashamed of how he'd just treated Lydia. He had been undecided about accompanying Herod to Antioch, until he saw her try to pull away from Hama when she saw him. He had warned her to be careful lest she fall into disgrace. Hama couldn't have liked her practically throwing herself at a barbarian. Sick at the thought she was endangering her future, Kadar had overreacted and been unnecessarily cruel.

Herod blocked his path. "Are you coming with us or not?"

"I am, but I have to see to something. I'll be right behind you."

Herod grinned. "Let me guess, this urgent errand concerns Lydia Onias?" Herod shook his head. "Simeon Onias will have your pillar and stones, Barbarian, if he catches you within sniffing distance of his daughter."

"Shut your mouth," Kadar said without heat. Herod's ribald laughter followed Kadar as he made his way back to the walled garden.

Kadar paused beside the arched entryway. His heart died in his chest at the sight of Lydia clinging to Hama, crying her heart out. Hama and Lydia, body to body. Kadar wanted to beat Hama to a bloody pulp. But this was the direction Kadar had pushed her. He should be happy she was turning to Hama for comfort.

Except the sight crushed him. *Merciful gods*, why did he have to actually witness them together? It had already been torture just thinking about it, and now the image would be burned into his mind.

Lydia's crying slowed and Hama stroked her back, comforting her. Kadar's hands itched with the need to hold and soothe her. She said something, and Hama laughed. Kadar's gut twisted, but he wouldn't expect less. She was his *valkyrie*. Then she stared off in the distance and her large brown eyes looked so damnably sad.

Chest tight and vision blurred, Kadar felt his way along the rough-hewn wall and slid to the ground. He buried his face in his knees and, for the first time since he was a child, he wept.

Tyre - *Four Days Later*

The forlorn travel party came to a halt yet again, because Malichus's troublesome donkey decided it was a good time to lie down and roll in the sand.

Kadar ground his teeth and climbed off his horse. The gray sky stretched into the distance over the choppy waters of the Great Sea. Two-thirds of the journey still lay ahead of them. At this rate they'd be old men by the time they reached Antioch.

"Obodas," Herod called to the commander of his guard. "Ride ahead and tell the head tribune to expect us. I believe his name is Aemilius." He tossed a bag of coins to Obodas. "Tell him to prepare a banquet."

Obodas wheeled his horse and galloped off. Malichus clambered to his feet cursing.

"A jackass riding a jackass!" Herod accused.

"It's not my fault," Malichus whined, beating the dirt from his white linen robe.

Kadar shook his head. *White?* The man was a fool from the top of his oiled head to the soles of his impractical sandals. Mealy-mouthed besides, Malichus wouldn't stop yapping, proclaiming his innocence in the matter of Antipater's poisoning to everyone and anyone.

Herod's face reddened. "Nothing's your fault, is it?"

Malichus shifted in place. "If you would just listen, I could clear up this misunderstanding, and we could return to the comfort and safety of Jerusalem."

"Get back on your donkey," Herod growled.

"John Hycranus believes I'm innocent. I don't—"

Herod urged his horse forward. "I will tie you on to your donkey myself if I have to."

Malichus's face puckered. "You can't treat me like this. I have friends." But the sniveling coward coaxed and prodded his donkey.

Braying a complaint, the sturdy beast rose.

Not wanting to watch the lifelong city dweller's clumsy climb onto the donkey, Kadar walked to the water's edge, wet a rag, and washed the cloying smell of harlots from his body. If his stomach wasn't already empty from voiding it repeatedly when he woke outside the whore's den this morning, he'd be vomiting again. He massaged his aching head. Drinking himself into a stupor every night since leaving Jerusalem hadn't helped him forget Lydia. Last evening had been particularly bad. Mind full of her, he'd gone searching for a harlot wearing nothing but white jasmine, only to find all the usual smells associated with whores, and after kissing a few limp-lipped mouths tasting of sour wine he'd given up. *Thank the gods!*

Lydia and Hama. It was for the best. So he kept telling himself, except no amount of rubbing up against whores, or throwing back strong spirits, or heaving his guts up in dark alleys, had dulled the pain or taught him to stop wanting Lydia Onias.

He slapped the water with the rag, and returned to his horse. The trek resumed at the same snail's pace. Herod's horse fell in beside Kadar's brown steed. "You look like you want to kill someone," Herod observed.

"I'd like to start with Malichus."

"I couldn't agree more."

"What's the latest word from your spies? Will we be able to get through to Antioch without running into the main body of the Parthian army?"

"Did you hear about Julius Caesar's assassination while you were in the salt mine?"

"Yes. We had word of the outside world." The caravans delivered a steady supply of news and gossip. "I heard Sextus Caesar was killed as well." Herod winced. Herod and Sextus had been great friends. Kadar cleared his throat. "Sextus was a good man."

Herod's mouth was a grim slash. "Caesar's death was a blow to my father, and to Jerusalem's pro-Roman faction. And it sparked another round of civil wars in Rome. Mark Antony and Octavian are still at odds. In the meantime, Parthia is breathing down our necks."

The two empires were mortal enemies. Rome dominated the west and Parthia the east.

Herod made an obscene gesture. "Curse Mark Antony. If he was beating back Parthia's invasion of Syria instead of chasing Cleopatra from one end of the Nile to the other, we wouldn't have to worry."

"Does Antony love the fratricidal nymph, or does he just want access to Cleopatra's armies and wealth?"

"The gods know he'll need every soldier and coin he can lay his hands on when he and Octavian finally go for each other's throats. That aside, I think the damnable fool actually loves her." Herod shook, dog-like. "I don't know how he stands her. The woman makes my skin crawl."

An hour later they came to halt again so Malichus could empty his bladder.

Kadar tightened his grip on the reins to keep from wringing the fool's neck. "I'm surprised you didn't just hand Malichus an empty bottle."

"I won't begrudge the man a last—"

A dozen Roman soldiers burst out of a scrubby stand of

pines. They fell on Malichus before the murdering fool saw them coming. Swords slashed. Malichus flopped to the ground, a bloom of red spreading over his white robe.

Herod's men stared in shock.

Unfazed, Herod slid of his horse and headed toward the Romans.

Dismounting, Kadar followed Herod across the uneven ground to the soldiers circling Malichus's still body.

The men parted. Herod put his hands on his hips and surveyed the damage. "Wrap the body in a blanket and tie him to his donkey."

"You knew the legionaries were coming, didn't you?" Kadar asked.

Herod chuckled. "Knew? I sent Obodas to fetch them."

Kadar remembered the bag of coins. "Did you bribe the Romans to kill him?"

Herod toed Malichus's sandal. "My father was a friend of Rome. They don't forget their friends. And I don't forget those who wrong me and mine. Malichus's death will send an appropriate message to my enemies. Hurt or injure my family, and I will make you pay with your life."

Kadar grunted. "That's some message."

Herod clapped him on the shoulder. "A banquet awaits us in Tyre. I'm hungry enough to eat a bull."

Kadar winced. "Don't mention food."

Herod led him back down the beach. "I hear you've been drinking and whoring with the vehemence of a Roman army celebrating a victory."

Kadar shrugged. "Too much time in Jerusalem. The uptight piety would make the Vestal Virgins weep."

"Their sanctimonious zealousness drives me foolish, too. A problem I intend to remedy in the deliciously sinful city of Tyre. You pagans know how to have a good time, but I'm going to show you how to do it right. And I've got something in store far better than whores. Slave women." Herod poked Kadar's ribs. "The head tribune promised me a whole boatload of slave women fresh from outer Gaul. A buxom, blonde barbarian girl will help you forget your woes."

"Stop smiling," he warned Herod. "Or I'll knock those large white teeth of yours down your throat."

Herod sobered, and climbed back his horse. "Take a slave girl to your bed. It will help you move on."

Kadar exhaled heavily. A thousand slave girls wouldn't erase Lydia from his memory. He had no choice but to move on. "Fine. You choose one for me, because I plan to be too drunk to see."

Chapter 20

Jerusalem - *Three Weeks Later*

Kadar stared up at the ceiling of Morta's small hovel. The middle-aged harlot's soft snore blended with the low clucks coming from a henhouse butted up against the far wall. The income from eggs was ostensibly Morta's means of living, providing her protection from those who would stone her to death if they knew the truth about how she actually earned money for food, clothes, and shelter.

Kadar was paying Morta so he could hide in her home until Simeon Onias arrived in Jerusalem, but it was all his money was buying. *Move on,* Herod had advised. But Kadar couldn't force himself to touch another woman. He had tried in Tyre with the slave girl from Gaul and failed. Desperate to forget Lydia, Kadar had ordered the slave to touch him, thinking lust would take over, but his stomach had curdled with the first stroke, and he had stumbled and crashed his way out of the barracks given over to the drunken orgy.

His celibacy would come to an end. Eventually, his needs would drive him to another woman's bed. But not here. Not in Jerusalem. Not while he was within a thousand miles of Lydia Onias.

He saw the future, knew what it held—he'd make his way to an army camp, find someone like Morta, and make her his woman. Then he'd move on to another camp and the pattern would repeat itself. Then he'd move on again.

Kadar had decided to leave Judea after coming across Lydia and Hama in the garden, but when it came right down to it, he couldn't. Not until he was sure of Lydia's fate. He wasn't going anywhere until Simeon Onias showed his insufferable face. It wasn't that he doubted Hama's abilities, but when it came to *her*—

Kadar ran his hand over his stubbled chin. He had turned down a position among Herod's elite guards, and said no to briefly remaining a guest in Antipater's home. Lydia believed he had left Jerusalem, and it was best for everyone for her to remain ignorant of his whereabouts. But the waiting was wearing him down. The temptation to sneak out and catch a glimpse of her grew and grew, until he was ready to climb the walls.

When he wasn't obsessing about Lydia, he was pacing the room over her father, certain Simeon Onias's delay meant the devil was up to no good, and not being able to do a single thing about it was beyond maddening.

Someone pounded on the door.

Kadar rolled out of bed, ready to tear the butcher's head off. Morta kept sending the lusty man away, but the fool showed up regularly, begging for a quick *favor*. He yanked the door open, and found Herod's guardsman, Old John, staring up at him, armed to the teeth.

"What's the trouble?" Kadar asked pulling on a tunic, sure something of significance must have happened to cause Herod to seek him out.

The grizzled soldier hitched his thumb over his shoulder. "The Parthian army marched down the Phoenician coast. Ptolemais and Sidon welcomed them. Tyre resisted, but the Parthians made quick work of them and have invaded Galilee."

Morta pressed up against Kadar's back. "The country is at war?"

Kadar squeezed her arm. "Get dressed, woman." He planned to find a safe spot for Morta. Images of how a war would impact or endanger Lydia raced through his mind. Kadar strapped on his sword. "What's being done to stop the Parthians?"

Old John fidgeted. "Hycranus's army is racing to meet them on the plain below Mt. Carmel. We are waiting for word of how they fared. Herod is preparing to ride to Galilee with a small company of men, but the bulk of the guard has been charged with defending Jerusalem. He ordered his household to move to the palace. Commander Obodas sent me to ask you to join us in defending the royal palace."

Kadar peered out the door at the smoldering fires of Gehenna. Jerusalem might soon be reduced to a pile of ashes. The Hasmonean palace would be the last to fall. He reached for his sword belt. "Take Morta to the palace and I'll be there shortly." He planned to rouse Lydia and take her to Hama and James. He assumed the two men were making the move to the palace, or soon would, if he had anything to say about it.

"I want to stay in my own place," Morta said.

Kadar could tell from her cross-armed, stubborn stance she wouldn't be budged. He couldn't say he blamed her. He remembered her mentioning the name of a Temple official who paid her an occasional visit. The palace of the High Priest was the last place a harlot would feel safe.

Kadar sent Old John on ahead, finished dressing, and pressed the last of his coins into Morta's steady hand. "Come find me if you change your mind."

"Save your worry for yourself." Morta said placing the coins in her prized alabaster box, given to her by an elderly whore she had once cared for. "Anna lived through the last three wars. She assured me harlots survive war better than most. Anna said soldiers bent on rape become thoroughly flummoxed when they break down a door and find a naked, willing woman waiting for them."

"I hope you don't plan to demand a fee," he quipped, not the least fooled by the brave front.

Morta shrugged. "The coins will come. Once the dust settles, soldiers will line up at my door. War makes men very lusty." She stretched up on her toes and pecked his cheek. "You love her. I see it in your eyes."

He blinked repeatedly. "I...who—"

Morta laughed. "The coming fight isn't yours, Barbarian. You should spirit your Lydia away."

"And what? Subject her to years of lonely wandering?"

"Where is it written that you have to be alone?" The

whore's solemn eyes held a life's worth of disappointment and solitude.

He hugged her. "You never used to be this sharp-tongued, woman."

Morta opened the door and pushed him outside. "You, however, remain as pig-headed as ever."

The acrid stink from the nearby burning trash heap stung his nose. Dawn's early light outlined the dark edges of the low clouds hovering overhead. *Thundering Thor,* he was going to miss Morta. He turned back to ask her to reconsider coming with him. The door snapped shut with finality.

Head down, he trudged up the rutted road, entered the city, and made his way to the red-tile-roofed homes of the wealthy district. He was debating whether or not to wake Nehonya Onias's entire household with the news of war when the wavering lamplight shining through the home's latticed windows saved him the trouble of deciding.

He knocked on a thick, carved-wood door. A heavily armed guard, backed by a dozen more sword-wielding men, greeted him.

Kadar cursed, and clasped the hilt of his sword. *What in the name of Odin had he walked into?*

"Find out who's there," an impatient voice directed from an interior room.

Kadar recognized the surly voice. *Simeon Onias.* The selfish, grasping man had finally turned up.

Nehonya Onias poked his head out the door and grimaced. "The visitor is a very large gentile, carrying a tremendous sword," he reported.

"Does he have name?" Simeon Onias demanded. Kadar didn't have to see the detestable man's face to know it was puckered.

The lead guard hefted his sword and pointed it menacingly at Kadar.

Kadar grinned, earning some nervous twitches from the guards.

"The name's Kadar," he said, wishing he could see Simeon's face. "But you probably remember me as the barbarian you wanted drowned in the Nile."

Nehonya Onias, looking like a lamb amid snarling wolves, retreated inside.

"Rubbish," Simeon Onias countered, but a hint of caution edged his doubt.

"Kadar, go! Run," Lydia shouted, sounding very distressed.

Kadar sobered.

"What's this?" Simeon squawked.

"It's not safe," Lydia warned. "Leave before my father—"

The crack of a loud slap echoed through the house. A muffled cry and frightened shrieks followed. His Northman's blood icing, Kadar batted aside the blade blocking his path, barged past the stunned guards, and stormed into the home's inner sanctum.

Lydia stood in the middle of the richly appointed reception chamber clutching her face. Simeon Onias's arm was poised to strike his daughter a second time. Kadar hurdled one of the cushioned reclining chairs crowding the room and knocked the wicked man's hand aside.

"Leave her alone!" he roared.

Simeon Onias yelped and raised his arms to shield his head.

The guards fell on Kadar, depriving him of the pleasure of giving the Onias a well-deserved beating. Terrified screams and jumbled shouts burst out around him. He threw off two attackers, and pulled at the arm locked around his neck in a choke hold. A hard blow to the gut bent him in half, and a sword hilt smashed against his head. While he was still reeling from the blow, his hands were pulled behind his back. A different hand fisted in his hair and yanked his head up.

Coughing and wheezing, he sought out Lydia.

Tears streamed over the red welt on her cheek. Flanked by Nehonya's daughter, Elizabeth, and the slave Brynhild, Lydia strained against the protective pair's firm hold, trying to get to him. Off in a corner, Nehonya Onias watched over his wife and a handful of household slaves, trembling and clinging together.

"Why didn't you escape while you could?" Lydia sobbed.

"I would never leave you unprotected."

"Daughter, do not speak another word to the godforsaken pagan."

Though in no position to threaten anyone, Kadar was too angry to care. "Hear me, Onias, if you hit your daughter again I *will* kill you."

The point of a sword dug into his back. "Watch your mouth, heathen," a guard growled.

"You?" Simeon Onias sputtered, eyes jumping between Kadar and the bald eunuch at his side, Goda, the man who had sold Kadar into slavery. The cretin who was owed a painful death at Kadar's hands.

The eunuch's eyes bulged. "Nobody gets out of those mines alive."

"Why isn't this man dead?" Simeon Onias demanded.

The eunuch's jaw tightened. "Death was too good for the damnable pagan. I sold him into slavery."

Kadar smiled. "I thought you were going to use the coins to buy your freedom."

"Goda," Simeon Onias scolded. "You told me your family raised the money."

Sweat pearled on the eunuch's shiny head. "My brothers sent what they could, which amounted to next to nothing. I'd have died a slave waiting for them to collect enough coins. I did what any man would do."

Simeon Onias didn't look convinced.

The eunuch wrung his hands. "I could have found work anywhere after I became a freedman, but I agreed to be your secretary. And I agreed to convert and be circumcised. If those sacrifices don't prove my loyalty, what will?"

Circumcision was required of male converts to the Hebrew religion, a stipulation separating the truly dedicated from the merely respectful. Those unwilling to part with their foreskin called themselves God-fearers, worshipping the God of Israel from afar, but with all their manly parts intact.

Kadar usually had nothing but respect for converts, but he'd bet his last *denarius* the bald eunuch's motives arose from pure greed. "I hope the clipped cretin is stealing you blind," Kadar said. The corrupt pair deserved each other.

"Shut up!" Goda hollered. The irate man grabbed up a pitcher from a nearby bench, swung with all his force, and cracked Kadar across the head.

Pain exploded behind Kadar's eyes. Frightened and shocked shouts ricocheted around the room. He staggered. The guards cursed and grunted in their struggle to keep him on his feet.

Hate burning bright as a consuming fire in his eyes, the bald man drew the pitcher back again.

"Goda, stop," Simeon Onias commanded.

The eunuch ignored Onias.

Kadar braced for another blow.

Lydia broke free and her willowy body pressed against him. "Don't hurt him," she cried, and raised her arm to block the hit.

"I'll break every bone in your body if you strike her," Kadar hissed.

Squawking like a flock of demented seagulls, Brynhild, Elizabeth, and Nehonya Onias swooped down on Goda and tackled him to the floor. The eunuch cursed and kicked. Nehonya's wife and slaves shrieked and wailed. Derisive remarks spewed from the guards' mouths. The eunuch stopped to draw breath, and Bryn stuffed a waded rag into his open mouth.

Though it felt like Thor's hammer was pounding inside his head, Kadar grinned. "I'm glad someone finally shut that jackass mouth of yours."

The soldiers hooted even more raucously.

The red-faced eunuch glared back.

"Cease this nonsense," Simeon said pucker-faced, then snapped his fingers at the guards. "Help the fools up."

Suffering another round of insults, the eunuch was hauled to his feet and the rag was ripped from his mouth. The bald man shook his finger in Kadar's face. "You will regret humiliating me."

Lydia hugged Kadar.

He pressed his mouth to her ear. "You are supposed to watch out for your own safety. Remember?" Northmen prized fearlessness in their women, and would boast about having a warrior-like wife, but the opposite was true here. Any defiance from Lydia toward these men would be viewed, at best, as meddling. "I can fend for myself, my *valkyrie*."

"Daughter!" Simeon Onias said sharply. "You are as bad as your harlot sister, shaming me by throwing yourself at this dog."

Tempted to fight off the guards and strangle the detestable man, Kadar resisted for fear Lydia would get hurt in the scuffle. He straightened and puffed out his chest. "Leave her alone."

Onias's pinched red face held all the attraction of congealed blood. "You're acting very possessive. Have you dallied with my daughter?"

"Kadar is an honorable man," Lydia shot back.

Her father's eyes narrowed. "Step away from the overgrown barbarian this instant or you'll suffer double punishment."

Kadar felt a tremble pass through Lydia. "Do as he says," he whispered.

Lydia lifted her chin and held fast to him.

He forced his eyes away from Lydia to her mean-spirited father. "Don't harm her, or..."

Simeon Onias paled. "Goda, take *my* prisoner to the storage room. And don't misplace him this time."

Lydia gasped and turned to Nehonya. "Tell Father to release Kadar."

Clothes and hair righted following his tussle with Goda, Nehonya Onias stepped forward. "The gentile has done nothing wrong. Let him go."

Simeon Onias smoothed his robes. "I will release him, but after I teach him to stop sniffing around my daughter."

Lydia blanched.

"Watch your mouth," Kadar growled.

"Step away from the heathen scum," Simeon said.

Lydia pressed closer to Kadar. "Kadar is ten times a

better man than you."

Her father's face turned purple. "You whore."

"Go to Brynhild," Kadar begged.

Lydia kissed his cheek, and then flew into Brynhild's arms.

"See? She is a whore," Simeon said.

Nehonya winced. "And I'd ask you to be more careful with what you say around my wife and daughter."

Simeon cocked a brow. "I'm the soul of discretion. *You* know it better than anyone, *Cousin*."

Kadar recognized a threat when he heard one.

So did Nehonya, who paled and turned his attention to Kadar. "What brings you to my house, gentile? Especially at such an early hour."

Nehonya and Simeon could pass for one another from a distance, but Nehonya was a thousand times more likable—a contest he won easily by not making Kadar want to vomit every time he opened his mouth.

Kadar regretted having to lie to Nehonya, but knew he'd do far worse to protect Lydia. "James sent me. He wanted Lydia to join him at the royal palace. A Parthian army has invaded Galilee."

Nehonya staggered back as though he'd been pushed. "An invasion? How much of a threat do they pose?"

The members of Nehonya's household clucked over the news like a clutch of panicked hens.

Fear flicked through Lydia's large brown eyes. "Galilee? Will the fighting reach as far north as Rumah? Is little James in danger?"

"Little James and Alexandra and Nathan are far safer in upper Galilee than they would be in Jerusalem," Kadar assured her.

Simeon Onias made a sound of disgust. "The boy's name is Judas. Don't refer to the bastard using your brother's name."

Lydia flinched.

Like a spider thoughtlessly devouring its young, Onias continued remorselessly, "It will serve your sister and her miserable husband right if the Parthians rob and kill them."

Kadar's fists balled. "Shut your mouth, old man. We both know the Parthian army will push south to Jerusalem." Hearing himself, a suspicion formed. Simeon Onias and his guardsmen hadn't so much as flinched when they heard the news about the Parthians. Inspecting the guards more closely, he saw they were heavily armed. Guards? No, they were probably mercenary soldiers.

"But you know all about the damnable invasion, don't you?" Kadar said. "Did you return to Jerusalem to be on hand to welcome your Parthian friends into the city?"

The obnoxious man shrugged. "There was nothing I or anyone could do to stop Parthia. I have merely taken steps to ensure the Onias family fares well. I have made an alliance with King Orodes."

Lydia groaned. "You mean the marriage contract? Who am I to marry?"

Her father bristled. "Silence! I won't stand for any more of your impertinence."

Kadar intervened. "Answer her."

Nehonya Onias stepped forward. "Lydia has had to wait long enough. Your dealings affect me as well. Tell us what you've done."

"What I've done?" Simeon mocked. "Riches and honor will flow to us, and to our children, and to their children, thanks to my...*dealings*."

Nehonya sighed. "What alliances have you made? Give us a name. Is it Hasmond Mattathias?"

Kadar gritted his teeth. Hasmond—he should have realized the whiny, rat-faced nephew of High Priest John Hycranus was behind the invasion. With Antipater dead and Rome on the brink of more internal warfare, Hasmond had seen an opportunity and rushed to side with Parthia.

Simeon Onias shook his head and smiled smugly. "Guess again, Cousin."

Kadar 's skin crawled with the sick certainty the husband Onias had chosen for Lydia would prove a great deal more detestable than Hasmond. "Spit it out, old man," Kadar said.

A hideous smile blossomed on Simeon Onias's face.

"Lydia will wed King Orodes's son, Crown Prince Pacorus."

"But Orodes and Pacorus are gentiles," Nehonya objected, as though stating the obvious.

"A gentile?" Kadar said, the word hitting with the force of a battering ram, forcing the air from his lungs. Impossible. Jewish fathers didn't give their daughters to heathens.

"You can't do this, Father," Lydia exclaimed.

"I won't let *him* send you to Parthia," Kadar promised.

Lydia nodded and exhaled a relieved breath.

"Barbarian," Simeon Onias called out sharply.

Kadar forced his eyes back to the insufferable man. "What now?"

"You have to be alive to stop me." Simeon said, pleased with himself.

"You plan to murder me?"

"Father, you can't," Lydia cried.

Nehonya moved to Kadar's side. "You will have to kill me first."

Simeon stared at his cousin for a long moment, then made a face. "The Parthians will cut him down soon enough." He turned his nose up at Kadar. "You will deliver a message to my son. Tell him if he reconciles with me, I will make him the master builder of a great kingdom."

Kadar stood taller. "If I learn you have harmed Lydia, I will find you, and tear you from limb to limb, and feed you to a pack of crocodiles."

Simeon swiped his hand at the threat. "Goda! Escort the barbarian outside and release him."

Nehonya joined Goda. The soldiers hustled Kadar toward the exit. He looked over his shoulder and caught a last glimpse of Lydia. Their eyes met in a silent farewell.

Goda threw open the front door. The guards released their hold and the chilled morning air hit Kadar's face. Gray clouds hung over Jerusalem. A horn trumpeted in the distance, a low, insistent sound, warning of danger.

Kadar rolled his stiff shoulders and descended the stairs.

Nehonya followed.

Impressed by the brave stand the man had made on his

behalf, Kadar nodded his thanks.

"What do you plan to do?" Nehonya asked.

Doors up and down the street were opening. Men and women stepped outside, faces full of fear and concern. Kadar wanted to take Lydia and go far, far from here. "I'll stay and fight."

Nehonya frowned. "Can you win?"

Kadar gripped the handle of his sword. "If you need me, find Herod. I'll be fighting beside Herod and Phasael." Would Antipater's sons prevail? Unlikely. But Kadar would stand by them.

Chapter 21

Elizabeth pushed her breakfast plate away. The finest dishes adorned the table. Fragrant flowers filled the vases. A dozen golden lamps flickered, sending light dancing over the multicolored mosaic tiles decorating the floor and walls. But the food tasted like ashes in her mouth, and Simeon Onias's revolting presence robbed the dining chamber of its luster.

Married to the malicious man for the three most miserable months of her life, Elizabeth had been tempted to hide under her bedcovers when he barged into her home a mere two hours earlier, but she wasn't going to allow him to intimidate her the way he had during their brief, hideous marriage.

The slaves tiptoed about as though navigating a snake pit. Her brother Gabriel and sister-in-law Talitha were doing their best to be polite, but Simeon's sharp tongue didn't make it easy. Elizabeth and her mother had placed Lydia between them to watch over her. Elizabeth gritted her teeth again over the miserable fate awaiting Lydia. A marriage to a foreigner, serving a foreign god, in a foreign land. What had tempted Simeon to sink so low?

More frightening noises intruded. Sounds of men battling for control of Jerusalem. A chill of dread went down her spine.

Her father frowned. "How much longer will the fighting last?"

Simeon broke off a piece of bread from a rye loaf. "Stop fretting, Cousin. We are perfectly safe. Hasmond's soldiers won't come anywhere near us."

"I would like to hear the details of this deal you've made with the devil," Gabriel said, making his disgust plain.

Simeon dipped the chunk of rye bread into a small bowl of olive oil. "Once the Temple grounds are secure, Hasmond has promised to make me the Captain of the Temple." He pointed at her father. "You will be named the Temple Overseer. And Gabriel will become a Temple Treasurer."

Her brother's brows rose. "Overseer? Treasurer? How many bags of coin did you give Hasmond?"

Simeon pursed his mouth. "Don't be crass."

"Crass?" Gabriel repeated incredulously. "You sold your daughter to a heathen king, and you have the gall to call me crass?"

Elizabeth wanted to hug her brother.

Simeon smoothed his resplendent robe. "King Solomon the Wise married foreign wives to secure his kingdom."

Elizabeth rolled her eyes. Always as arrogant as he was obnoxious, Simeon's regard for himself had reached new heights.

Gabriel choked on his wine. "King Solomon? Are you going to compare yourself to Abraham and Moses next?"

"I won't join a harem," Lydia said softly but firmly.

Simeon exhaled exaggeratedly. "Why did the good Lord give me fools for daughters?"

Elizabeth wanted to stomp her ex-husband's spotless robe into the mud.

The self-satisfied man merely returned to nibbling his bread, then waved the remains at them. "The prince has hundreds of wives. Most he never looks at again after the wedding night. And he will soon have five hundred more wives, chosen from among Jerusalem's finest families."

Elizabeth blinked. He couldn't be serious.

Gabriel made a face. "Pacorus won't find five families willing to give their daughters over to a heathen, even if he is a prince."

"They won't have a choice." Simeon dabbed a linen square to his oily lips. "Hasmond promised the Parthians the women, plus one thousand talents. A small price to pay to rid the country of the Idumean interlopers riding roughshod over John Hycranus."

Her father looked skeptical. "Antipater is dead and his sons have very few supporters."

Simeon put on his superior face, the one Elizabeth had learned to hate. "The only way Phasael and the ambitious Roman-lover Herod will go quietly back to Idumea is if they are carried home on their shields. Parthia was eager to overthrow the devils. Hasmond made his deal with King Orodes, and I have made mine. Lydia will marry the prince, and my new, young wife will teach her to pleasure her husband." Simeon narrowed his eyes at Lydia, who had turned deathly pale. "And you will make every effort to please Pacorus."

Elizabeth's pity for the unhappy woman forced to call Simeon Onias "husband" warred with her anger and disgust. "Leave Lydia alone." All the fear, frustration, and helplessness from when she was under this dreadful man's power came back in a sickening, roaring wave. "You are a wicked, unprincipled man. I pray the Lord will strike you dead!"

Simeon's brow knotted. "Hold your tongue, woman."

Elizabeth's hands balled. "I won't hold my tongue. You have no say over me anymore!"

Her family stared wide-eyed. Simeon's dark look warned her she'd earned an enemy. Good! Let him hate her.

"Cousin," her father interjected in his best placating voice. "You married again?"

Simeon looked away first, and she gloried in the small triumph.

"I have married one of King Orodes's nieces," Simeon said, then pointed a finger at her brother. "When the battle is over I will send for my wife. And I expect you and James to marry Parthian princesses for the good of the family."

Talitha gasped and a shadow crossed her beautiful face. "Gabriel promised he would never take more wives." Marrying multiple wives was a fairly common practice among Sadducees, but the ancient custom was slowly falling out of favor.

Gabriel patted his wife's hand and glared at Simeon. "I

don't want anything to do with your grasping schemes."

Simeon smiled.

All too familiar with that knowing grin, Elizabeth shuddered.

"Your father might say differently, won't you, Nehonya?" Simeon purred.

Looking miserable, her father shifted in his seat. "Gabriel, we will talk about this later."

"Father, send Simeon away," Elizabeth begged, at a loss to understand why her father hadn't put a stop to Simeon's bullying. "He's nothing but an evil, poisonous man."

Simeon reached across the table and slapped her hard across the face. "Silence, woman."

She cried out, flinched back, and rubbed at her stinging cheek.

Gabriel leaped off his couch. "You damnable man!" He rounded the table, and stood over Simeon. "Leave before I throw you out!"

Unperturbed, Simeon folded his hands. "Control your children, Cousin."

Her father looked ill. "Gabriel sit down. Libi, please be silent."

Elizabeth's heart broke. *Why? Why was her father permitting this travesty?*

Gabriel pointed a warning finger at Simeon. "If you ever strike my sister or Lydia or another woman of my acquaintance again, I will break every bone in your body." She'd never seen her brother so angry. He usually treated Father and his elders with the utmost respect.

Simeon exhaled heavily. "You disappointment me, Gabriel."

Gabriel touched his hand to Elizabeth's shoulder. "Good. I plan to make a habit of it."

Simeon rose and tugged his robe into place. "I will give you one week to get your house in order, Cousin. I plan to bring my son back under my control, and you would be advised do the same with yours."

Elizabeth smiled wide, sure James's mule-headed

stubbornness would stymie Simeon's best-laid plans.

Simeon narrowed his eyes at her. "You always were a proud, disrespectful shrew. Your defilement brings shame to your father's house and to our family. I refuse to suffer your presence any longer." He turned to her father. "Cousin, you will send your daughter away. I don't care where she goes, so long as I never have to look at her face again."

Trembling from head to toe, Elizabeth waited for her father to rebuke his cousin.

Her father's shoulders slumped and his face caved in on itself, aging him before her eyes.

Her breath burned in her lungs with the dawning truth. Simeon would prevail. Whatever secret he held over her kind, gentle father was awful enough to give her father no choice but to turn her out.

"Father," Gabriel pleaded. "Why aren't you telling Cousin Simeon to go to Hades?"

Ashen-faced, her father appeared on the verge of collapse.

"I want to go away," Elizabeth said hurriedly, anxious to ease her father's suffering. "I'm ready for a change." It was half true. Part of her hated the idea of leaving her home and family, but the other part wanted to run far, far away from her father's terrible secret.

"I can't do it any longer," her father choked out. "I can't keep lying."

Simeon heaved a large sigh and dropped back down onto his couch. "Confess already, if you must."

Father ordered the slaves out of the room. Elizabeth gripped her seat, dread eating a hole in her stomach.

Father's face was laced with the taut pain of a man stretched upon on a cross. "When I take my regular trips to our farm in Galilee, I also stop in Samaria. I visit a woman. Her name is Anina. We have two children."

A roaring sound filled Elizabeth's ears. Another woman? Her father wouldn't do this to them, to her mother.

"Two daughters," Simeon crowed.

Elizabeth flinched. *Girls. But she was supposed to be her*

father's beloved, lone daughter.

Gabriel curled in on himself and covered his head with his arms. Talitha patted his back, comforting him. Tears streamed down her beautiful face.

Unmindful of the cup dangling from her hands, her mother looked as fragile as a flower gone to seed, ready to shred into a thousand pieces. "Was I a bad wife?"

"No, my dear," her father said with the same warm affection he always used. "This is all my fault."

"Who is she?" Mother whispered.

Father swallowed. "Anina is a widow. She runs an inn, and I came to love her. I love you both."

"Tell them the girls are the same ages as your two youngest boys," Simeon added with glee.

Elizabeth's stomach rolled. Her father had been carrying on with another woman for over fourteen years? But that would mean— *No, no, no! Father wouldn't have, couldn't have.* But she saw the truth in Simeon's gloating smile. To protect his dark secret, her father had abandoned her to a painful marriage to the most wretched man to walk the streets of Jerusalem.

The room whirled. Her mother's soft weeping mixed with her father's desperate pleas for forgiveness. Elizabeth dropped her face into her hands and rocked in place.

James slipped past the tense guards in defiance of Phasael's order that the entire household go to the royal palace and remain there. The battle for Jerusalem had been going on for hours. The reports were grim. He couldn't stand waiting any longer. Wanting to see how matters stood, he climbed the stairs leading to the fortress-like wall surrounding the palace, went straight to the chest-high stone parapet with spectacular views of the Temple compound, and surveyed the battlefield.

Soldier fought soldier outside the citadel situated at the far end of the Temple complex. Smoke from the daily sacrifice hovered over dead bodies strewn across the sacred ground. White-robed priests scurried about.

James had been five years old the last time war came to Jerusalem, but had no real memory of it. The old priest who lived next door shared grim stories with James and the other boys about the bloody battles. Terrible sadness would overcome the frail man while he recited the names of fellow priests who'd been slaughtered as they were going about their sacred duties.

James would have said the Temple, the priesthood, and Jerusalem meant nothing to him. But the sight of the hallowed ground under siege flayed open his heart, exposing the truth. He cared about his people, his home, and his God. He cared very deeply.

A piercing scream close at hand made him jump. Recognizing the sound of a man dying, James swallowed back the bitter acid taste filling his mouth. A fierce battle raged in the market down below. A soldier put his foot on a blood-soaked body and yanked his sword out of the dead man's chest.

Herod entered the fray at the head of a large band of men. A golden-haired soldier stood out from his dark-headed companions. Kadar. Wearing battle armor and carrying heavy shield and sword, the giant looked as though he'd crashed his way out of a fable. Fighting side by side, Herod and Kadar cut down enemy soldier after enemy soldier.

More of Herod's men arrived and joined the fight. They slowly pushed the Parthians back to the oldest of the city's walls, the First Wall. The Hasmonean palace and a third of the city were enclosed behind the First Wall. If Herod couldn't retake and hold that line, all would be lost.

James agonized over whether to join the fight. Swords and shields lay beside dead men, there for the taking. He licked his lips. Kadar, a barbarian heathen, was risking his life for the city, yet here he stood, hiding behind a wall, praying others would save his sorry neck.

A flash of movement caught his eye. A half dozen enemy soldiers crept along the base of the wall, making their way to an ancient, narrow gate leading to the bowels of the palace. The men assigned to guard the little-used entrance had either deserted their post or been killed.

James searched about, ready to shout out a warning, but no one was close enough to hear. A stack of building stones for a construction project sat nearby. He ran, fetched two stones, and took up a spot above the grated metal gate. The soldiers closed in cautiously. A patch-eyed man led them. James's heart jumped. Lazarz. Antipater's murderer was back, and trying to sneak into the palace.

Hands shaking, James set one stone atop the wall. He raised the other stone high above his head and held his breath. A loud roaring filled his head. Lazarz stepped into his line of fire. James flung the stone down. "Die, you brute!" The block whizzed by Lazarz's head, grazed his leather cuirass, and crashed uselessly to the ground.

Lazarz spun around, peered upward and bared his teeth. James ducked out of sight, then thumped his palm against his forehead. *What a quivering, gutless, coward.* Was he afraid Lazarz would *stare* him to death? James hopped to his feet, plucked up the second stone, and hurled it. The heavy block clipped a helmeted head. The soldier cursed and shook his fist at James.

Feet pounded up the stairs at James's back. He swung around. Red-headed Niv and a handful of stable boys surged onto the landing. "What's happening?" Niv asked more excited than afraid.

James exhaled a relieved breath. "Hurry. Come help." He picked up two more stones. "Lazarz is trying to break through a gate into the palace." He peered back over the wall.

The soldiers kicked and heaved against the locked metal gate. James pitched another block, and struck Lazarz's forearm.

The patch-eyed man yelped and grabbed his arm. "I'm going to kill you," he yelled, black anger blazing in his eyes.

Niv and the stable boys started hurling stones. The soldiers covered their heads and cursed. The boys laughed and heaved block after block. Disgusted and defeated, the soldiers moved out of range, only to run into two palace guardsmen. Swords clashed. James held his breath, praying Lazarz would be cut down. But he and a companion retreated to safety.

James leaned heavily against the wall. Niv joined him. They watched the battle unwind. Herod, Kadar, and the palace guard pushed the last of the enemy soldiers back behind the First Wall.

Niv rested his plump, freckled cheeks in his hands. "Herod is the best soldier who ever lived. I wish I was a soldier."

James tried to imagine wielding a sword in battle. "Soldiers die by the dozens."

"I'd rather die fighting than die of boredom serving wine and food at banquets. If Lazarz doesn't kill me first."

James gave the boy a nudge. "I almost soiled my clothes when I spotted him. How about you?"

"I kill rats all the time. I hardly ever miss, but I didn't come close to hitting One-Eye."

The stable boys gathered around. "We won," one of them announced in awe. The feat was impressive. Herod's few hundred men had held off a much larger foe.

"We won this battle," James said.

Niv's eyes widened.

James pointed toward the Temple, then north and south. "Herod holds the First Wall, but the Parthians have overrun the rest of the city. They'll be returning in force." And James would be at the mercy of his father and Lazarz.

The boys buzzed with speculation and swapped stories about the blood they'd seen spilled.

Half listening, James watched Herod organize and encourage his men. Though outwardly calm and collected, Herod kept glancing at the antiquated walls. Walls that wouldn't keep the enemy out for long. He could guess Herod's thoughts, because they were his own. *Trapped. Trapped like a cornered rat.*

Simeon Onias swept down the stairs outside Cousin Nehonya's house in a swirl of blue robes, leaving behind a wake of destruction as deadly as a flood, fire, or earthquake.

Lydia was torn between wanting to stay to give her cousins what comfort she could and wanting to distance herself from the pain filling every crevice of the lovely old home.

Brynhild scanned the area. "You'd never know the city was overrun by an army."

The morning-long battle had ended, the street was quiet and deserted. Lydia looped her arm through Bryn's and prayed for the hundredth time that James and Kadar were safe and well.

Escorted by two dozen soldiers, her father's triumphal march home drew cautious stares from those courageous enough to peek out their doors.

Bryn's hand pressed against Lydia's elbow. "Someone needs to wipe that pleased look off your father's smug face."

"Shhh. He'll hear. "

"I don't care if he hears."

"You don't know what he's capable of."

Bryn tossed her thick, flaxen braids off her shoulders. "The man has no idea what he's up against. I can't be pushed around as easily as that soft-bellied eunuch."

"Bryn, promise me you won't talk back."

"Your foul father will have to step over my dead body to take you to Parthia."

Lydia's steps slowed outside her father's palatial house. The gray, weathered stones waiting to entomb her looked the same as the day her father fled to Egypt. "The thought of disappearing into a harem makes me remember...you know."

Raiders swarming. Blood and terror. Damp caves. Dark degradations. Deep, deep despair. A chill went through her. "Last time I was weak. I gave in, resigned myself to my fate." Afterward she'd escaped into herself. Covered herself in blessed numbness. "I have to stay strong, for little James, or I might never see my baby again."

Gripping Bryn's arm tightly, Lydia followed her father inside. The cold and damp of the house wrapped around her.

Father halted in the middle of the large, barren atrium. "Goda, go gather your belongings and leave my house."

Goda's shoulders hitched. "You're letting me go because of the barbarian?"

"I won't do business with a man I can't trust."

"How can you do this, after all I've done in your service?" Goda begged.

"Service?" Father frowned. "I should have you flayed."

Taking Bryn's hand, Lydia headed for the stairs, relieved her father was raging at the deceitful eunuch instead of her. She led Bryn to her bedchamber, crossed the room, threw open the shutters, and rested her face against the cool latticework. Priests and soldiers scurried about the outer courts of the Temple. The smell of the incense and burnt sacrifices was surprising, and gave her a new appreciation for the faithfulness of the Lord's priests.

"The room needs a good cleaning," Bryn announced, running her hand over a tabletop, sending a cloud of dust drifting through the sunlight.

Lydia stared down the street at the Hasmonean Palace, situated atop a small rise behind the First Wall. Men attended to the dead and fallen on both sides of the ancient barrier. "Don't bother with the dust. We won't be here long." Kadar would come for them, unless—she searched for a blond head. *Let him be alive. Please let him be alive.*

"Daughter."

Lydia spun around. Bryn yelped in surprise.

Father stood in the open doorway, smoothing his robe. "I'm not through with you, Daughter."

Lydia's breath stilled. "I was tired."

Brynhild moved to her side and glared at father. "Haven't you done enough damage for one day?"

Lydia clasped Bryn's broad, weathered hand and squeezed hard. "What else did you want with me, Father?"

"Stop treating your slave like a friend."

Bryn screwed up her face. "You are the nastiest man I've ever come across."

"Hush, Bryn," Lydia said under her breath.

Father smiled, sending a wave of dread through Lydia. "My ex-steward is waiting in the atrium for your irksome slave. I've paid Goda a generous sum to escort her back to Egypt."

Brynhild paled.

Lydia slipped her arm around Bryn. "Father, don't take Brynhild from me."

"Go, woman," Father said. "Get out of my sight."

Bryn charged forward. "You miserable man."

Lydia chased after Bryn, wrapped her arms around the pear-shaped woman and dragged her to a stop.

Father stood his ground. "Go, before I have you beaten."

"Leave, Bryn, please," Lydia begged. "He means what he says."

Bryn's face crumpled. "Who will watch over my kitten?"

"I'll be fine," Lydia said with far more confidence than she felt.

Bryn hugged her and pressed her lips to Lydia's ear. "Don't do anything rash," she whispered. "Wait for Kadar. He will keep his promise." Bryn gave Lydia a parting peck on the cheek, and fled down the stairs.

Father shook his head. "Impertinent slaves are the bane of my existence."

Tears blurred Lydia's vision. She had suffered many losses, and ought to be used to them, but she wasn't. *God go with you, my dear Bryn.*

Father strolled to the window, looked through the lattice screen, and nodded his approval. "Come, Daughter. Come witness the truth."

Lydia swallowed, straightened her shoulders, and went to the window.

His blue robe draping like a curtain from his arm, Father pointed to the enemy soldiers pouring into the city. "Nobody is coming to rescue you. Herod and your pet barbarian are the ones in need of rescuing."

She gripped the cold stone of the windowsill. Father hadn't uttered one word of sympathy over Uncle Jacob's death, hadn't asked after her welfare, and hadn't even greeted her. She meant nothing to him. Whatever love or care she still had for him died in that moment.

Father retreated to the door. "Prepare to leave for Parthia."

She threaded her fingers through the diamond-shaped openings in the lattice and stared at the Hasmonean Palace. The door clicked closed. The lonely existence looming ahead of her in Parthia frightened her more than ten armies.

The wind shifted and carried the heady fragrance of orange blossoms to her window. Determination took hold. She wasn't going to sit around waiting for Kadar to be killed, waiting for her father to send her to Parthia, waiting for help to come. That's what she'd done when the rebels abducted her. She was no longer a helpless, quivering sixteen-year-old. No, she was a grown woman able to fight back. One way or another, she'd find a way to escape her present troubles.

Chapter 22

The stale smell of boiled leeks and lentils lingered in the palace reception chamber. Kadar leaned against the gold-painted wall and blew out a frustrated breath. John Hycranus sat slumped in a chair, his chubby arms clinging to his wide belly. Herod paced the room.

Four days into the war, the palace guards had beaten back two assaults on the First Wall. Matters were currently at a stalemate, but it wouldn't take much to tip the scale in Hasmond's favor.

"Sit down before you wear a hole in the floor," Phasael said, drawing circles on the polished wood table with his finger.

"Are we going to surrender?" Pheroras asked again before going back to tapping his foot and chewing his nails to nubs.

"No!" Herod and Phasael answered together.

The door banged open, and Obodas barged in looking grim as the grave. Not a surprise, since the thick-necked career soldier was the man charged with defending the thin ribbon of stone and mortar separating them from Hasmond's swarming horde.

"Our army was slaughtered on the plains below Mount Carmel," Obodas announced bluntly.

Kadar banged the wall with his fist.

The color drained from John Hycranus's face.

Herod punched the air. "Damnation! There goes our last hope."

Phasael shoved back his chair and stood. "Have our spies reported back about Hasmond's reinforcements?" Hasmond's army was made up of Jewish rebels and foreign mercenaries.

If the Parthian army descended on Jerusalem, there would be no stopping them.

Obodas nodded. "That's the one bright spot. Hasmond has sent message after message to General Barzaphranes, begging him to march on Jerusalem, but Barzaphranes has set up camp in Galilee."

Herod went back to pacing. "Barzaphranes is no fool. He is waiting for me and Hasmond to tear each other to pieces."

Pheroras's foot tapped faster. "It's hopeless."

Herod came to a stop behind Pheroras and massaged his timid brother's shoulders. "Don't give up. I need you to stay strong."

Obodas held out a scroll bearing an impressive seal. "Barzaphranes sent a message for High Priest Hycranus."

John Hycranus held out his hand.

Herod reached over Pheroras's head, grabbed the document, tore it open, and scanned the contents. "The Parthians want John, and us, to go to Galilee to negotiate a peace. What a bunch of horse —"

"I think we should accept," Phasael said taking the message from Herod.

Herod grimaced. "It's a trap."

Hycranus fished a stuffed olive out of a bowl. "I'm going to accept."

"Didn't you hear me?" Herod growled. "Barzaphranes wants to flush us out of hiding."

Hycranus blinked a few times, then popped the olive into his mouth. "I don't see any other option."

Phasael exhaled heavily. "I agree with John."

Herod turned on Phasael. "You can't be serious?"

Phasael scraped his hand through his curly black hair. "Hasmond has the upper hand."

"How will turning yourself over to the enemy help?" Herod asked frustration souring his voice.

"I want to make a deal now," Phasael said, "while we still have something to bargain with."

Herod clapped his hands to his head and looked as though he was going to be sick. "Phasael, don't go. Please, I'm begging you."

Pheroras cast a pleading look at Kadar.

Kadar frowned. Nothing he could say would help. There was no right answer. Both paths held danger. Every man would have to decide for himself. If it came to it, Kadar would choose to go down fighting.

Phasael squeezed Herod's shoulder. "I'm going to Galilee. I'd like you to come."

Herod's arms fell to his sides. "Someone has to stay with the family."

Phasael glanced quickly at Pheroras, but the timid man tended to be more of a burden than a help. Phasael sighed. "I need to say farewell to my wife and to Mother."

John Hycranus rose with effort, and he, Phasael, and Obodas took their leave.

Herod turned his black eyes on Kadar. "You were no help."

"I'm still here," Kadar said. Every instinct he had told him he should get out of this country. Slipping away on his own wouldn't be overly difficult. But he couldn't leave Lydia behind. Would he stay if she wasn't a consideration? He wanted to say *No. Not a chance.* Except he missed the company of other warriors. Missed having a people to live and die for.

The faces of those he had loved and lost flashed though his mind. A pang of guilt hit, and he realized his hand had gone to the amulet his father had given him. "What's next?" he asked. "What are you planning?"

Herod always had a plan.

Kadar smiled. They made quite a rescue party—a Northman, the would-be master builder James Onias, and a handful of Idumean soldiers, sneaking through Jerusalem's dark alleys to spirit highborn Jewish girls to safety. The unlikely alliance had been brought about by the news Hasmond Mattathias planned to choose five hundred women from good families to join the Parthian prince's harem. Herod was welcoming the girls into the shelter of the palace. Most of the wealthy families residing inside the confines of First Wall had accepted. Families living outside the safe haven needed assistance moving their daughters to safety. Kadar had spent the last three nights smuggling the young women past Hasmond's undisciplined troops.

More reinforcements had arrived in the late afternoon, a development which made tonight's outings a bit more interesting. This was their third trip of the night. Hugging the shadows, Kadar checked around a corner. Finding the way clear, he waved on James Onias and the Idumeans.

Old John slid in line behind Kadar. "The place we want is near the end of the lane. Supposed to be six girls waiting. Six. That's a lot of frightened, fidgety women to deal with." As usual, the grizzled man bristled with weapons.

"One look at you, and half of them will run off screaming," Kadar said.

Old John chuckled and jerked his thumb over his shoulder. "That's why we have this respectable rascal along."

James Onias frowned. "Respectable is probably too strong a word."

Old John tugged on the scabbard strapped to his side. "Me and Kadar, here, would rather face down an army of giants than cajole and console teary-eyed mothers. Isn't that right?"

Kadar grinned. "Absolutely." He hadn't been happy when Herod had given James the task of quieting the fears any concerned parents might have about handing their daughters over to a barbarian and a crew of Idumean soldiers. But James had handled himself well so far.

Men's voices carried to them. Kadar lifted his hand, and the Idumean soldiers halted. Swords hissed from sheaths. Kadar's blood rushed through his veins and his nerves hummed. Thundering Thor, he missed this. Missed the heady rush of taking up arms with battle-hardened men.

A moment later a large band of enemy soldiers moved by the entrance to the alley. Everyone held their breath, waiting...waiting. The low murmur of voices slowly faded away. Swallowing his disappointment, Kadar glanced back.

Stark fear showed on James Onias's face, but still his weapon was drawn and held at the ready. James swallowed and lowered his dagger. "Fickle Fortuna! I nearly wet myself."

A rumble of laughter rippled through the group, dissolving the last of the tension. Kadar gave the signal to move out. The men crept ahead. Each of them clapped James on the back in passing and gave him a word of encouragement or praise.

Earning respect from men who made their living with sword was not an easy feat. "You did well," Kadar said when it was his turn. "Next time, remind yourself to breathe." It was the advice Kadar's father had given him when he'd gone out on his first raid.

James pushed aside the black bangs hanging in his eyes, his lopsided grin faded. "Alexandra and Lydia would be amazed I didn't curl up in a ball and cry my eyes out, which is what I did when the zealots attacked."

"You were a boy then. Young men don't always act as they should." A truth Kadar knew from experience. Try as he might, he had trouble justifying his decision to run away from his homeland. There were many who would call him a coward for refusing to sacrifice his life for the good of his people. A charge he'd be hard-pressed to refute if he came face to face with the men from his village.

Kadar clapped James on the shoulder. "Obodas is ready to knock at the Levite's door. The man is a singer at the Temple?"

"The Head Singer. A highly coveted post."

They reached the door as it opened. A bug-eyed man wearing a tunic two sizes too small for his round body waved them into the multi-storied home. Obodas, James, and Kadar followed the Levite into a lavish reception room. The costly furnishings gave Kadar a new appreciation for the importance the Jews placed on the office of Head Singer. A notion the Northman in him found laughable.

The young women awaiting rescue stood bunched

together next to a table heaped with untouched food. The girls' parents gathered around James and the Levite singer.

The bug-eyed Levite pounced on James. "I can't believe your father would turn on us like this. He's visited all the members of the Sanhedrin, asking the members of the court to support Hasmond."

James stood taller. "Don't trust my father. He is a liar."

The statement earned nods of agreement.

"So far the Sanhedrin is divided," the Head Singer continued. "Some are for John Hycranus. Some are for Hasmond." The bug-eyed man patted James's arm. "I passed judgment when you left home, but your father's present actions cast the matter in a new light."

A red flush crept up James's neck and face. "Herod needs your support. He promises to be very generous to those who act as his friend."

The Levite Head Singer blinked repeatedly. "Um...ah...tell Herod I will do what I can."

The vague offer of help sounded familiar. Fear of backing the wrong side in this little war was making almost everyone cautious.

"Don't work against Herod," James warned. "Don't forget, Herod marched an army on Jerusalem after he was put on trial for murder. Just think what he'll do to those dealing treacherously with him now."

The Head Singer paled. "Assure Herod I won't lift a finger to aid Hasmond."

Kadar smiled to himself. He thought Herod had gone a bit soft in the head when he picked Lydia's prickly brother for this mission. But James was the absolutely perfect choice. He came from a priestly line, and he was the son of Simeon Onias, giving him clout and credibility among the people who mattered. What's more, James's hatred for his father made him an extra-zealous messenger.

A short time later, the young women, after shedding many, many tears, and exchanging second and third hugs, were finally coaxed out the door. Old John and the Idumeans walked ahead of the skittish girls and Kadar and James guarded the rear.

"I noticed some of the girls we've rescued making eyes at you." Kadar was careful to keep his voice low. "And not just the ugly ones. Have you seen any who interest you?"

James made a face and shook his head. "Per my usual habit of doing the exact opposite of what's good for me, I find myself attracted to the last woman in the world I should set eyes on."

"It better not be Mariamne. Herod will kill you if he catches you lusting after his intended bride."

"Wouldn't my father love to see me married to the High Priest's granddaughter?" James crowed, then exhaled heavily. "My damnable father can propose all the marriages he wants for me, and I will go on rejecting them. My poor sister doesn't have the same luxury. I expected him to choose an old, toothless groom, but he has sunk to a new low."

James wasn't the only one to think so. Simeon Onias was the only man eager to give his daughter to a foreigner. The other four hundred and ninety-nine fathers were doing all they could to avoid the sin.

Old John held up his hand a short way from a main thoroughfare. The groups halted, and a soldier crept to the end of the alley to make sure the way was clear. The young women formed a tight knot and held hands.

Kadar rubbed his tired eyes. "I've spied on your father's house every night, searching for a way to get by the guards, but the place is sealed up tighter than a drum. It's maddening. Here I am smuggling dozens of women by Hasmond's army, but I'm powerless to help your sister."

"I've given the problem some thought. I could tell my father I want to meet at my cousin's house and insist he bring Lydia along."

"Your father would be accompanied by guards. And what makes you think he'd take Lydia with him?"

"Because he's bent on talking to me. He sends messages every day demanding my presence. I'll tell him if he wants to meet with me he has to leave the guards behind and come with Lydia, or I won't go. Then I'll make sure Lydia is in my cousin's garden, and I'll distract my father long enough for you to spirit her away."

Kadar came wide awake. "It's a good plan. I'm impressed. But it's likely to cause you a pile of trouble."

James shrugged. "A man is born unto trouble, the scriptures say. What's a little more suffering, if it enables Lydia to find a bit of happiness and peace?"

"How soon can you arrange the meeting?"

Kadar heard a whisper soft noise behind him. The hair on the back of his neck rose. He spun around and hefted his sword. A dark shadow moved toward him.

"Stop right there," Kadar ordered.

Old John and James took up a position beside him. The pre-dawn light danced over the blades of their dark daggers.

The tall form stilled. "I spy for Herod. I have vital information to pass on."

Kadar's shoulders relaxed. "Come with us. We'll take you to him."

They moved on. A few alleys away they came upon the home of a Herod supporter. Old John knocked. The door opened and the ladder they needed came sliding out. Two of the Idumeans grabbed the ladder. The rescue party continued on.

Kadar kept a close eye on the messenger. The tall man looked very grim. The news he brought couldn't be good. A moment later they reached the tricky point—a lightly defended section of the First Wall guarded by a roving patrol.

After making sure all was quiet, the Idumeans propped the ladder against the wall, then took up defensive positions. Kadar climbed up the ladder first. Reaching the top, he whistled, gaining the attention of palace guards awaiting their return.

Herod, who always seemed to be everywhere at once, showed up to help guide the women over the wall.

After the last of the rescue party reached safety, Kadar escorted the messenger to Herod.

"I have news about your brother and High Priest Hycranus," the tall man said.

Herod straightened. "Tell me."

The messenger frowned. "They've been arrested and put in chains."

Herod's calm dissolved. "Damnation, I knew it! I told them not to go."

Pheroras came from the direction of the palace. "What's wrong?"

"We need to go to Mother," Herod said his voice pained. "Phasael has been arrested."

The timid man shook his head. "It will have to wait. The Parthian commander is at the front gate. He's calling for a truce."

"Truce. Ha!" Herod smacked his fist into his palm. "They want me to surrender, and then they'll arrest me, too."

Feeling the walls of their small refuge closing in around him, Kadar flexed his shoulder. They were running out of time and options.

The light of the rising sun spilled into the enclosure. Herod dismissed the messenger and gave Kadar, James, and Pheroras a grave look. "I've made a decision. I plan to fight my way out of Jerusalem tonight."

Kadar's heart beat harder.

"You're going to leave Mother behind?" Pheroras asked, his eyes wide.

Herod squared his shoulders. "I'm taking the entire household."

James pointed toward the palace. "What about the young women we've been taking in?"

Herod nodded. "We will take them too."

"You're taking a big risk," Pheroras said.

"I'd make the same decision if I was in charge," James said, drawing a surprised look from the others.

James jerked up his chin. "Well, I would."

Herod's sharp eyes focused on Kadar. "You're being awfully quiet. What are your thoughts?"

Kadar liked Herod's boldness. "It's a risk, but doing nothing is just as risky. I say we go."

Herod's brows rose. "This isn't your fight."

A calm came over Kadar, similar to the peace that usually settled over him before a big battle. "James and I will be going for his sister." He turned to James. "Arrange the meeting with your father."

"I'll go write the note now," James said and hurried away.

Herod squeezed Kadar's shoulder. "Lydia Onias will be accorded all the protection and honor due a member of my family."

Invigorated, Kadar asked, "What do you need me to do in the meantime?"

Herod grinned. "Wagons. Bring me every wagon and beast you can lay your hands on."

Chapter 23

The cool of the evening gathering around them, Lydia and Elizabeth and Chloe sat in a close circle in the open-air atrium, each lost in her own thoughts.

Lydia poked her needle through the soft cloth of the pillow cover she'd begun to decorate upon her return to Jerusalem. The needle jabbed her finger, drawing blood. "Ow...I used to be good at stitch work, but lately my fingers go to war with each other every time I pick up a needle."

Elizabeth and Chloe didn't acknowledge her. Devastated to learn her husband had been unfaithful, Chloe had kept to the confines of this small walled garden from sunup to sundown for the past week, rarely eating or speaking.

Lydia sucked on her finger, annoyed with herself for trying to mend her cousins' aching hearts with trifling wit.

She blamed her jitters on her father. He had charged into her bedchamber an hour earlier and dragged her with him to Cousin Nehonya's house. Father had then directed Gabriel and Cousin Nehonya to the reception chamber and told Lydia and Elizabeth to go find something useful to do. *What are you up to, Father?*

Lydia tossed aside the cloth cover, walked to a small marble table, and poured wine into a carved stone goblet. She glanced about the garden, searching for a means of escape. A prisoner in her room since the day her father sent Brynhild away, this might be her only opportunity to escape before Father locked her away again. *Bryn. My dear Bryn, I miss you.*

The tang of the new wine slid down her throat and into her belly, but it did nothing to warm her. *Where was Kadar? Was he whole and well? What danger was he risking for her sake?* Questions, and more questions. She couldn't keep them from racing around her mind.

The doves roosting in the fruit tree shading the arched entryway took flight in a swirl of beating wings and high-pitched cooing.

Her heart swelled upon spotting the reason for the commotion. "James." She rushed to meet him. "James. How are you? You look stronger." The red scar wasn't as noticeable now he had more color.

"Listen closely, there's not much time." The cold determination in his voice belonged to a man.

Lydia tensed. "Time for what?"

"Herod plans to fight his way out of the city tonight. I am here to distract Father so you can escape with Kadar."

Her heart sped up. "Tonight? Now? With Kadar and Herod?"

James gently pressed his finger to her lips. "Shhh." She sensed a confidence in her brother that gladdened her heart. He took his finger away. "What Herod proposes to do is very dangerous. Kadar is coming for you, but you don't have to go."

"Tell me what to do." She trusted Kadar, and felt safer with him than she would with ten thousand angels by her side.

"Wait here. I'll keep Father busy until you are out of the city."

"How will you escape?"

His perpetually sad eyes clouded. "I'm staying."

"No! Please come."

"I failed you once, and you suffered terribly. I want to do this for you."

"You didn't fail me."

James's sad smile held a lifetime's worth of hurt and grief. "The old goat is waiting."

Her throat thickened. "Thank you for sacrificing yourself."

"I can't keep running from him."

She hugged him. "Will you reconcile with Father?"

James laughed. "Jupiter, no! Not even if he turns out to

be the next Moses. I can't believe you have to ask."

"You called him Father."

"I did it out of deference to your delicate ears, Sister."

Just beginning to appreciate how clever and witty her brother was, she prayed these weren't the last words they ever shared. "Father cares only about himself."

James nodded, but she no longer had his full attention. He was watching Elizabeth walk to a table supplied with the bread and wine. Pretty cousin Elizabeth lifted the pitcher to her cup, then looked up. Her cheeks pinked, and she stared at James. And he stared back.

Leave it to James to take an interest in the last woman in the world he should be looking at. Heaven help them! Elizabeth had been their stepmother. Lydia poked her brother in the ribs. "Libi has enough problems without you adding to them."

"What problems?"

She poked him again. "Stay away from Libi."

Her brother kissed her cheek.

Surprised and pleased, she reached for him.

James backed away. "Take care, Sister," he said, and he turned and hurried inside.

She smiled and shook her head.

Elizabeth joined her. "What does your brother want? Why is he here?"

"He came for me, to help me."

"I always wished you had a brother as kind and good as Gabriel."

"James has a good heart. He just needs to learn to listen to it more often."

Elizabeth's brow furrowed. "James would never be warm and caring the way Gabriel is."

"There's still hope for him. If he can distance himself from my father's poisonous grasp, he might learn to be happy."

A clatter sounded overhead. Lydia looked up to see Kadar come sliding down the porch roof, and land next to them with a small thud. His eyes were bluer and his hair more golden than she remembered.

Lydia threw her arms around his neck and took comfort in his solid, wide chest.

His warm breath curled around her ear. "Are you sure you want to do this? We could be on the run for a long time."

She pushed closer to him. "As long as I'm with you, I won't mind."

His mouth moved over hers as soft as a whisper. "Brave *valkyrie* that you are, I should have known you would agree without hesitation."

"I missed you," she said against his lips.

He cupped her head and kissed her long and deep. A tingling warmth spread through her.

Elizabeth made a loud, throat-clearing noise.

Lydia and Kadar broke apart.

Lydia gasped for breath. "I'm leaving with Kadar. Please don't tell father. I'm sure he will scream and stomp about, but—"

"Let him yell," Elizabeth said, and stood taller. "I will be deaf to it."

Chloe joined them. Frail and drawn, she appeared to have aged ten years. "The Lord go with you, dear Lydia." Chloe took hold of Lydia's hand and placed it in Kadar's. "I've followed a righteous path all my life. I thought I married an upright man. But this gentile is ten times more honorable than my husband. The Lord go with you both."

Lydia's eyes widened. Was Chloe encouraging her to listen to her heart instead of following the path expected of her?

Kadar shifted restlessly. "I promise to do all in my power to protect Lydia."

Unnerved, Lydia hugged Chloe and Elizabeth. "Thank you for taking me in. I'm sorry for the trouble I brought you."

Elizabeth sighed. "My father and your father are to blame, not you."

Kadar touched his hand to the small of Lydia's back. "We should go." She nodded and he directed her to the porch, and made a step with his hands.

She lifted her foot. Kadar boosted her onto the sun-warmed tiles, hauled himself up beside her, then guided her to a waiting ladder. Stars twinkled overhead. Lamplight winked behind lattice-shaded windows below. The campfires of the invading army sparked at the edges of Jerusalem.

Her breath caught. "Herod is deserting Jerusalem?"

Kadar helped her onto the ladder. "He has no choice. Even so, I'm not sure we'll be able to escape. I could be leading you into disaster."

She climbed down. "Don't try to talk me out of going with you."

"Are you sure you're not a Northwoman?"

She smiled. Safely back on the ground, Kadar led her down a narrow alley. The thick walls of the Temple Treasurer's lumbering home rose overhead. The jovial man wouldn't be laughing when he learned his prestigious post was being taken from him and given to Gabriel. They skirted a wagon full of clay tiles for the new roof John the Younger's fretful wife insisted they needed. Passing a moss-covered well dating back to the days of Solomon, she couldn't help but wonder if she was seeing this and other familiar sites for the last time.

Defying her father would have grave consequences. If Parthia and Father prevailed, she could never return to Jerusalem. She wouldn't be able to worship the Lord at his Temple. She might never see James, or Elizabeth, or Chloe, or Cousin Nehonya again. She wouldn't have to go to Parthia, but the results might be the same.

She pressed closer to Kadar. "Can he do it? Can Herod raise an army and defeat Hasmond and Parthia?"

The comforting weight of Kadar's arm slid around her and settled on her hips. "Herod believes it, and he's is the grittiest, most tenacious fighter I've ever encountered."

She slipped her hand into his. Their fingers intertwined. "But what if he fails? What will happen? Where will I go?"

He squeezed her hand. "Herod will win. And you will come back to Jerusalem."

"But—" Her voice cracked and hot tears stung her eyes.

"But what if he doesn't?"

Kadar pulled her to a stop. His callused fingers stroked over her jaw. "It's not too late. You can go back."

She shook her head. James was subjecting himself to Father's vicious harangues so she could escape. "I won't allow myself to be used again by Father for his ugly purposes."

Kadar's lips brushed over her forehead. "Ah, my *valkyrie*, you have the heart of a warrior."

"I'm not brave. I'm terribly, terribly afraid."

"Of course you're afraid." His soft, guttural voice skidded down her spine. "I'm always afraid at the start of a battle."

"You?" All hard-bodied muscle, he dominated any room he entered. "I can't imagine you being afraid of anyone or anything."

His mouth trailed over her ear and down her neck. "I'm more afraid now than I've ever been in my life."

She dragged his face up to hers and kissed him with a fierceness she hadn't known she possessed. Stepping back, she struggled to slow her breathing enough to speak, then said, "James warned me we would face grave danger."

Kadar's blue eyes glittered. "Helping Herod fight his way out of Jerusalem doesn't make me half as scared as the thought of walking out the end of this lane, where Avda Hama is waiting to take you into his care."

She squeezed her eyes shut. *Avda.* She hadn't given the physician a second thought during the last week. "You're afraid Avda won't be able to protect me?"

"No. I fear I won't have the courage to leave you with him."

"If only there was a way for us —"

Kadar's mouth covered hers, pressing and pressing, until she gave in. They tasted and touched one another till they were wild with it. Kadar broke off the kiss. She buried her face in his chest.

Breathing hard, he said. "You will marry among your people. You will marry Hama." He set her gently away from him, and strode ahead.

Her blood pounded through her veins and hammered loud in her ear. Avda was her destiny, not Kadar. So why couldn't she make her heart believe it?

Chapter 24

Kadar waited with a small cadre of soldiers in the shadows of the First Wall. A diversionary force, they planned to attack the main body of Hasmond's army, hoping to draw men away from the south end of Jerusalem. When the way was clear, Herod would escape out the Dung Gate, leading an eight-hundred-person-strong caravan to Idumea.

Still stinging from leaving Lydia with Hama, Kadar had the comfort of knowing a good man would watch over her. He had left her behind, ready to sacrifice his life to secure her future.

Obodas and Old John flanked Kadar. His body hummed with the familiar tension and anticipation he'd experienced before battles large and small. The Idumean soldiers backing him were every bit as able and hardened as his father's Northmen. He relished the solid weight of the sword gripped in one hand and the shield in the other.

Obodas slowly rose to his feet. A hundred men stood as one. Silent as death, dreadful as the dark, lethal as a speeding dart, they moved forward.

Hands cooperated to lift away the beam locking the gate. More hands eased the gate open. Obodas raised his sword above his head, slashed the blade down, and charged. A trilling ululation, the war cry of the Idumeans, rang in Kadar's ears, firing his warrior's blood. He threw back his head, loosed a mighty bellow, and raced forward.

The small patrol guarding the gate fell back, but the Idumeans chased the Parthians down. Kadar caught up with a meaty soldier. The man turned and raised his sword, Kadar swung with all his strength, cut the man down, and roared his satisfaction.

Enemy reinforcements arrived to join the battle, and Obodas called for his men to fall back. The Idumeans and Kadar retreated behind the First Wall to a waiting redoubt. Horses stood ready to help them make their escape as soon as the odds turned in favor of the enemy.

Kadar and Old John worked in tandem to hold the right flank. The grizzled man battled with a vengeance, his face full of fierce determination born of knowing failure meant the loss of his family, his tribe, and his land. Kadar had fought by his father's side to thwart the enemies of his people, and his blood sang today the way it had then. This fight was his fight. These men were his men. Come life or death, victory or defeat, they would meet their fate together.

———→·—→‡←·——·—

The half moon dipped in and out of dark clouds hovering over the Hasmonean palace. Lydia sat in the back of Avda Hama's donkey cart, atop sacks of grain covered with blankets. A teeming mass of people, animals, and wagons surrounded them. A baby cried in the distance, a counterpoint to the soft lowing of oxen and urgent whispers filling the night. Avda's sons, four-year-old Benjamin and six-year-old Ori, huddled against her, though they hardly knew her. The threat of imminent danger had formed an instant bond between them.

The crowd parted. Well-worn leather armor strapped to his muscled body, Herod strode forward leading his betrothed wife, Mariamne, and some of her close family members to a covered carriage ornamented with gold-painted carvings. A famed beauty, Mariamne's bright red lips and ivory-white skin accentuated her perfect cheekbones…and her utter terror.

Wearing bold confidence like a second skin, Herod whispered comforting words to his betrothed while he helped her settle onto a cushioned seat.

Avda appeared next, escorting Herod's mother, Cypros, and an entourage of young, frightened nieces.

Cypros halted beside the workmanlike wagon awaiting her. Her exotic eyes narrowed with disdain. "Where's my travel carriage?"

Avda glanced away and back. "Herod set aside the nicest wagon for you."

Cypros's chin firmed. "Mariamne is traveling like a queen, while I am stuck with a donkey cart?"

"This is a fine, sturdy wagon," Avda persisted.

Impressed with Avda's patience, Lydia wanted to shake some sense into Cypros. Their lives were in danger. What business did Antipater's widow have worrying about her status, about something as silly being shown up by her future daughter-in-law?

Herod shut the door to Mariamne's carriage and crossed to his mother. "Ima, what is wrong?" he asked, glancing over his shoulder repeatedly

"Do you expect us to sit on top each other? This wagon isn't half the size of my carriage."

"I have room in my cart, if one of your nieces would like to ride with me," Avda said.

Herod took his mother's hand. "Kadar was ready to retrieve your carriage, but we decided against it, lest it raise suspicions. I gave you the best wagon of the dozens Kadar managed to collect."

Lydia gazed about at the multitude of carts. Kadar was responsible for all this? And yet he'd made time to come after her. He believed he was just a simple soldier, but his capabilities went beyond swordsmanship and warfare.

Cypros's petulant frown deepened. "I don't like this business. Maybe we should try to make peace with Hasmond."

Herod glanced over his shoulder again. For an instant he looked every bit the man whose enemies were breathing down his neck. He blinked, and the veil of bold confidence slid back in place. He petted his mother's hand. "Have faith, Ima. I'm doing what's best for the family. Father would have done the same." He helped his mother into the sturdy wagon. "That's not so bad, is it?" He draped a finely woven blanket over his mother's lap.

"I will need a warmer blanket," Cypros said.

Herod snapped his fingers and a household slave jumped to do his mother's bidding. "I promise you, Ima, no harm will come to you."

Lydia took comfort in Herod's quiet determination.

Avda escorted a pretty, almond-eyed young woman to his wagon. "This is Kitra."

Lydia gave the terrified girl an encouraging smile and patted a cloth-covered grain bag. "I'm glad for your company."

Ori murmured a shy greeting. Benjamin pulled his thumb out of his mouth. "We're going to Idumea. Do you want to come?"

"I hate Idumea," Kitra grumbled, climbing into the cart.

Avda rested his arms on the sideboard. "Is everybody comfortable?"

Lydia and the boys nodded.

Kitra pouted her red lips. "The remedy you made for my upset stomach has worn off already."

"Give it more time to work," Avda advised patiently.

Kitra wrinkled her nose and plunked down next to Benjamin.

Avda's calm brown eyes settled on Lydia. "I may not be able to stay by your side if duty calls. Do you want a weapon to defend yourself?"

Kitra gasped. "A weapon?"

"Um... I have had a knife-throwing lesson," Lydia said. The brief, wonderful time she'd spent with little James seemed as though it had happened ages ago instead of mere weeks. Avda's sons looked up at her with the same awe as little James. She pushed away her grief and hugged Ori and Benjamin until they squirmed, then tickled them. Raising her voice above their squeals of laughter, she said, "A small dagger or a large knife will do."

Avda managed a weary grin. "I knew you would be good with them."

"I'm honored to have earned your trust."

"And I promise to do all in my power to help you reunite with your son."

Lydia pictured little James's happy face. "For the first time, I'm glad he is in Galilee."

Kitra leaned between them. "Herod has called for his horse."

A low buzz filled the air. Herod stood apart, tall and broad-shouldered. A white stallion was brought forward. He mounted the tall warhorse with ease, and rode to the soldiers assigned to clear a path through the Dung Gate.

"Can he do it?" Lydia asked. "Can Herod get us away safely?" The plan called for them to dash south to Idumea, to join forces with Herod's brother Joseph.

Avda nodded, dug through a small clothes basket, and drew out an old, old dagger. "It belonged to my grandfather, who was a friend to Antipater and a supporter of John Hycranus long before Herod was born. Our families have been aligned for many, many years."

"Then you have no choice. You must go with Herod. You must leave Jerusalem."

"Yes. Our fortunes rise and fall together." His eyes searched hers. She was aware of what he wanted. He wanted her to say the words back to him—*our fortunes rise and fall together*—but she couldn't. Her heart whispered one name over and over again—*Kadar, Kadar, Kadar*. She looked away.

Avda exhaled heavily, laid the dagger beside her, climbed up onto the cart's small bench, and readied the reins.

Silence descended over the caravan in anticipation of the signal to move out. Ori and Benjamin pressed up against her. Stark fear froze Kitra's face. Tension built like a billowing storm cloud over the palace courtyard. Herod rode up and down the line, throwing out words of encouragement and assurance to his nervous followers—close to eight hundred souls counting the women promised to Pacorus's harem.

The wait seemed interminable. The tension intolerable. Then a terrible noise filled the night. The high-pitched trilling of the men assigned to distract the enemy and allow Herod to escape. Lydia's breath backed up in her lungs. *Kadar.* He was risking his life for them, for her. *Keep him safe, Lord. Please keep him safe.*

"To Idumea," a soldier roared, and Herod and his men dashed toward the gate.

Clanging noises and gruesome cries arose, then the donkey cart lurched forward. Lydia tightened her arms around Ori and Benjamin as they rolled through the Dung Gate. Dead bodies littered the ground. The wagon in front of them slowed. Herod's white horse appeared out of nowhere and whirled in a circle. Sword dark with blood, Herod waved them on. "Go! Don't stop. Go. Go."

They bumped and rumbled onward. The night closed around them. Lydia and Avda and Kitra kept looking back, expecting to find their enemies bearing down on them. How soon before Hasmond's soldiers gave chase? Could they outrun Hasmond? When would they reach safety?

Herod galloped by on his horse, sitting tall in his saddle. "Be of good cheer, Hama. All will be well."

"Keep leading and we will follow," Avda called back.

The sound of weeping came from a nearby wagon. Kitra burst into tears.

Lydia felt Benjamin's little shoulder begin to shake.

"I want to go home," Ori confided, his voice small and frightened.

Lydia patted their slim backs.

"I want my mother," Kitra wailed, burying her head in

her lap.

Lydia bit back a rebuke. Kitra was still a girl. Lydia hadn't been brave at that age, either.

Realization struck.

Lydia had been the same age as Kitra when Judas the Zealot had taken her captive. Tremendous guilt smothered Lydia every time she recalled how she had cowered before Judas, and later had given in and behaved toward him as one would a true husband. Now she could see she'd merely behaved like the young, frightened, sixteen-year-old girl she was at the time. Her burden crumbled and scattered like dust on the wind.

The wagons slowed. Herod swept by again. "Press on. Press on!" A moment later the pace quickened.

Lydia pulled Benjamin onto her lap. "Kitra, come sit with me."

The distraught girl scooted under her arm. "I hate this."

"I do too," Lydia assured her.

"Try to sleep," Avda said over his shoulder.

Lydia leaned back against a sack, settled the boys and Kitra, and closed her eyes. Where was Kadar? Why hadn't he and the diversionary force caught up to them yet? Captured. Injured. Dead. Countless scenarios darted through her mind. *Spare him, Lord. Please spare him.*

The rattling of the cart slowly lulled her, and she fell into an exhausted sleep. The next thing she knew, she was startled awake by the sound of a loud crack.

The caravan ground to a halt.

Heart racing, she sat up. "What's wrong? Where are we?"

"A wagon tipped over," Avda said, sounding bone-tired.

A sliver of yellow flickered across the dark edge of the horizon. They had made it to morning without being caught. "Do you think Hasmond decided not to give chase?" she asked.

Avda rolled his shoulders. "The coming day will tell the full story."

Kitra and the boys woke.

Word of the trouble ahead rippled back to them. A wheel had come off Cypros's carriage. Herod's mother was dead. Kitra gave a strangled cry. Lydia hugged her.

Avda jumped to the ground and raced forward.

An old woman in a cart ahead of them swayed back and forth in time to her mournful keening. Lydia cringed and foreboding filled her. Was the terrible accident the start of the evil that would befall them?

Herod's white horse clopped up beside them. "What's wrong?"

"Your mother is dead," someone announced tactlessly.

Herod howled like he'd been stabbed. Sliding off his horse, he fell to his knees, and beat the ground with his fist. "No! No! No!"

Avda's sons pressed up against Lydia. She comforted them, wishing she could do the same for Herod.

Avda came running back and knelt beside Herod. "Do not despair. Your mother is alive."

"Praise heaven," Lydia said, echoing the relief of those around her.

Wild-eyed, Herod clasped Avda's arms. "You spoke to Ima?"

"I did," Avda said with an exhausted smile. "She reprimanded me for not having my basket of ointments for her scraped hands."

Herod scrubbed his face. "Scrapes?"

"All minor," Avda assured him. "No one was seriously hurt. But I think we should abandon the carriage."

Looking like he had an ox strapped to his back, Herod heaved to his feet. "Get what you need while I move my mother and sister to a new wagon."

Avda shot a relieved look at Lydia. "Eat," he instructed before leaving to attend to Cypros.

Lydia fed the boys and prepared a small meal for Avda. She glanced behind the caravan. Why hadn't Kadar and the other men caught up with them yet? What had happened to them?

Avda and Herod returned. A loud murmur swept through the caravan at the same time. People were pointing and staring. Lydia stood. The glow of the rising sun cast an orange glow over riders and horses racing across a barren wilderness, a vast wasteland stretching for miles in all direction.

"Our men or theirs?" Herod asked.

Lydia held her breath and stretched up onto her tiptoes, straining her eyes, hunting for *him*. For Kadar. *Lord, let him be alive.*

A rear guardsmen raced toward them on a gray horse. Throwing up a cloud of dust, the man brought his horse to a halt next to Herod. "Obodas and his men made it out."

A rousing cheer went up.

The riders came closer and closer. She still didn't see him. He wasn't with them. Her stomach knotted.

Avda hopped onto the wagon and stood next to her, then lifted his arm. "See, at the very back? He made it."

A short distance behind the main body of soldiers came a few stragglers. Two men shared one horse, accounting for their slower pace. Beside them a soldier rode slumped over his saddle, and another man was leading his horse, the sun glancing off his yellow-golden hair.

She hugged her arms and smiled until it hurt.

Horses and men pushed upstream through the jubilant throng. Dirty-faced and bleary-eyed, the soldiers managed tired smiles and nods of acknowledgement.

The brawny, thick-necked commander of the bloodied band left his horse with another soldier and hustled over to Herod. "Hasmond is hard on our heels. He will be upon us within the hour."

Lydia's smile crumpled.

Fear and doubt flashed across the faces of those around her.

Herod squeezed the commander's shoulder. "You and your men get some food and rest." Herod leaped atop one of the large boulders scattered across the low knoll. His supporters gathered around. "We can't outrun those who want us dead." Herod was a commanding and reassuring leader. A thirty-five year old man in the prime of his life, Herod's voice was firm and assured, his gestures and attitude strong and masculine. "We will make our stand here. Together we will fight for our lives, fight for our families, fight for our destiny."

A roar of approval went up. Avda remained silent.

Lydia rubbed her arms. "Is Herod as good a soldier as people say?"

Avda exhaled heavily. "I'd be more confident about the coming battle if we had more men. Herod and his soldiers are experienced and battle-tested, but he's asking a lot from his three hundred and fifty men, a hundred of whom haven't have had time to recover from last night's contest."

Herod raised his battered sword. "Men, take up your weapons if you have them. Arm your wives, arm your aged men and women, arm your children. Prepare to battle to your last breath." High-pitched trilling filled the air. Grinning fiercely with affection for his followers, Herod sheathed his sword, jumped to the ground, and strode off, issuing orders to his aides.

In his wake, still mounted, came Kadar, leading two horses.

The sight of his pained face and blood-soaked tunic sent another wave of fear through Lydia. "Are you hurt?" she called out, jumping to the ground.

Kadar climbed off his horse. "No, but Old John nearly had his arm cut off."

Men swarmed around the injured man and carried him off. Stable boys took charge of the horses.

Kadar walked toward her.

"I couldn't stop worrying about you," she confessed.

Kadar stopped close to her, so near his long golden hair brushed over her shoulder and his warm breath spilled down her neck. "Didn't anyone tell you, my *valkyrie*? Barbarians are hard to kill."

He was trying to tease a smile out her, but she wasn't fooled. The exhaustion and anguish in his bright blue eyes told the true story. She reached her hand to his face and stroked his stubbled chin. "I'm just glad you're safe. That's what I know."

"Lydia?" a child's querulous voice called out.

Ori's summons brought Lydia to her senses. She bumped up against Avda's wide chest and spun around. "Old John is hurt."

"I heard," Avda said avoiding her eyes. His many friends and admirers, however, glared at her with open disapproval.

Her face heated. "I wasn't thinking. I didn't mean—"

"We will speak of it later," Avda said, his voice clipped.

Kadar interceded. "Don't hold this against her, Hama."

Hands fisted, Ori stood beside his father, glaring up at her. The boy might not understand she'd just shamed his father in spectacular fashion, but he was clearly aware she'd hurt Avda. And in turn, she'd failed at the sole task Avda had asked of her—to make a happy home for his sons.

"Forgive me," she whispered.

Avda's broad shoulders sagged. "Go join Cypros and watch over her while I tend to Old John."

She turned and fled. Father and Aunt Sarah had called her boisterous, said she was overly flirtatious and forward. They were half right. She was too lively and open for her own good. And a kind, decent man had been hurt and his reputation besmirched because of it.

Winded and wretched, she paused outside Cypros's

wagon. She knew what she had to do. She would release Avda from his promise, and encourage him to find a woman who could control her impulses.

Chapter 25

Kadar helped Herod push the last wagons into place. "Did you have to bring along all five hundred of Pacorus's proposed harem?" He could hardly hear himself over the babble of questions and suppositions batted around by the worried women circling them. Kadar shook his head again, amazed a man running for his life would burden himself with a pack of frightened women.

Herod laughed. "At the moment it doesn't seem like the best tactical move I ever made, but if I manage to deliver these girls to safety, their fathers will remember and will be indebted to me."

Kadar stared over the women's veiled heads toward the cloud of dust boiling closer and closer to the ring of wagons standing alone in the middle of a vast desert wasteland. "You have to be alive to collect the debt."

Herod cinched his sword belt. "Walk the perimeter with me. I want to see for myself it's secure."

They moved off a short distance to observe the camp from the enemies' vantage point. Herod held the high ground—if the miserable mound of land could be called that. And shelter? The small boulders and bushes scattered about couldn't provide cover for a good-sized deer. Water and feed for the animals were both in short supply. Of course, Hasmond wasn't any better supplied than they were, and his army was three times the size of theirs. There would be no long, drawn-out standoff.

"What do you think?" Herod asked.

"The battle could go either way."

"I keep asking myself what my father would do." Herod turned grim. "But it's no help. I'm going with what my gut tells me. Today is either the end or the beginning for me. If I fail, at least I will go down with a sword in my hand." He narrowed his eyes at Kadar. "What I can't figure out is what you are doing out here."

Kadar opened his mouth, then clamped it shut.

Herod laughed and thumped him on the shoulder. "It's too late to run now. I'm going to go check on Old John and my mother and Mariamne. You should go speak to the Onias girl. And don't tell me you don't want to, because I know you do." Still smiling, Herod dashed off toward the makeshift enclosure.

Kadar massaged his clammy forehead and studied the sturdy wagon where Lydia was sheltered.

He wanted to go to her, but he wouldn't. *Thundering Thor!* What had she been thinking, stroking his cheek for everyone to see? Her obvious feelings for him were damaging her reputation and her future prospects. He needed to keep his distance for her sake.

A swirl of wind kicked up the dust, spraying fine grit into his face. He turned his back on the makeshift camp and frowned at the small army closing in on them. How was Lydia holding up? The desolate surroundings had to be stirring up memories of when she'd been held captive by Judas the Zealot.

Then there was Old John. The grizzled soldier, who stroked and touched his weapons with a lover's caress, had lost his arm. His soldering days were over, *the poor devil.* Kadar scrubbed his eyes with his palms. He couldn't imagine what he'd do if such a thing happened to him.

When he went into battle today, he'd be fighting to avenge Old John and Antipater, and to destroy those determined to destroy Antipater's sons. Kadar's loyalty to Herod, Phasael, Joseph, and Pheroras flowed as strong as it once had for his fellow Northmen.

He pulled the hammer-shaped amulet free and clutched it. "Thor, Odin, and Freyja...hear me now! Give me the strength of ten warriors."

His gods seemed far, far away. He tucked the amulet

back under his tunic.

He wanted to pray to Lydia's God, to Old John and Herod's God.

Kadar stared at his wilderness surroundings. Would the God of Israel even hear him?

An all-encompassing calm settled over him. And he knew beyond all doubt he was meant to be here, meant to answer this call, meant to fight this battle.

⟶ ➤❖◀ ⟵

Another death scream pierced the clang and clash of swords. Lydia covered her ears and pushed back against the unyielding wagon wheel. The battle had been raging for what seemed like hours with no sign of slackening. Cold and frightened, she couldn't stop shaking and worrying.

The enclosure formed by the wagons was surprisingly large. Avda, Ori, and Benjamin were at the opposite end, and her view of them was blocked by the draft animals milling about the center ground.

She pushed herself to a crouching position, and waited for her dizziness to pass. First, she'd check to make sure the boys were well, and offer her help to Avda again. If he refused, she'd return her attention to helping and comforting others.

The noises from the battle came closer. She rose to her feet, and saw a ball of men and swords and shield clashing. A blond head appeared and disappeared in the middle of melee. Her heart pounded harder. Praise heaven. He was alive. *He was still alive.*

A great thundering sound came from behind. She whirled around. Soldiers charged at a wall of men and shields. Herod and his broad-shouldered warriors didn't buckle. Their swords plunged, then re-emerged dripping blood.

Revolted and horrified, Lydia looked down at her feet and willed them forward, and stopped alongside the women from Herod's household. Kitra had said Herod's mother and sister didn't get along with Herod's espoused wife and future mother-in-law. But they were sitting close together now, comforting one another, providing a good example to the young, highborn girls huddled together around the borders of the enclosure.

Horses and mules shifted from foot to foot and flicked their tails. Lydia dodged the hind legs of one jittery donkey, then another. The foul smell of manure made her eyes water. Grateful the warhorses were penned separately, she quickened her pace and collided with someone. She swallowed a cry.

Avda caught her by the arms. "Where are you going?"

"I was worried about you and the boys."

"I was on my way to you, to ask a favor. Would you take Ori and Benjamin with you? They have witnessed too much already."

She peered past his shoulder at the line of bodies stretched out on the bloodstained ground. A stable boy was busy tending to a soldier with a wide gash across his upper thigh. Sickened, she squeezed her eyes closed. "Do you need help?"

"I'll manage here. Just, please, take the boys elsewhere."

Avda went to a blanketed corner and ushered the boys to her. Four-year-old Benjamin was sucking his thumb. Ori's chin wobbled as he worked to hold back his tears.

Avda squeezed their slim shoulders. "Take good care of Lydia," he said with a wink for her.

Lydia wanted to wrap the boys in her arms and never let go, but feared it would only make them more upset. She held her hands out. "Have I told you the story about a brave young shepherd who brought home a wolf pup?"

Benjamin's thumb popped free. "Where'd he find the wolf?"

Lydia smiled and blinked back tears. "In a bear den, of all places, under the shadow of a tall mountain."

Benjamin put his small hand in hers, but Ori pressed up against his father.

She'd lost his trust and would have to work hard to gain it back. Her arm fell. "I could use your help finding a stash of honeyed nuts. I want to have some ready for Herod's soldiers."

Ori continued to hang back. Avda whispered something in boy's ear. Squaring his little shoulders, Ori crossed to them and took hold of Benjamin's hand.

Avda's eyes met hers. "You are a good woman."

"I will keep them safe." Honored to be trusted with his precious children's lives, she shuddered at the thought of failing him, or them.

Two soldiers appeared off to the right, dragging a bleeding man. Avda hurried to assist them.

Lydia led the boys away, peppering them with questions to distract them from the terrible cries coming from all directions. She reclaimed her spot next to the wagon wheel and put the boys to work searching for the honeyed nuts. They were successful too quickly, so she directed them to a blanket. The boys sat at her knees, waiting for the promised story.

A soldier's loud death scream came from close at hand, and several bodies crashed against the wagon that sheltered Mariamne, Cypros, and Kitra. The women screamed and scrambled away while the five hundred girls of the proposed harem shrieked and clutched each other. Ori and Benjamin scooted under Lydia's arms and huddled against her.

Nausea nearly overwhelmed her. The shouting and confusion plunged her into vivid memories of the day her family was attacked, the sheer terror of that day and this, clashing within her, froze her, mind and body. If Kadar and Herod couldn't hold off Hasmond's men, she'd be taken captive again, would be at the mercy of armed men who could do whatever they wanted to her. She slipped her hand under the blanket and pulled out the dagger.

A jubilant, victorious cry reverberated throughout the enclosure—a sign the battle had shifted in favor of one side or the other. The cacophony of swords clashing faded. Joyous hoots and hollers filled the air. Who had won? What if she was taken captive again, and found herself at the mercy of drunken soldiers delirious with victory? Men's hands pushing and pulling at her. Taking deep breaths, she gripped and re-gripped the dagger.

The wagons opposite her were pushed apart. Her heart

pounded harder. Ori and Benjamin pressed closer to her, sobbing and trembling. Men poured through the opening. She wanted to cover her eyes and scream until it was over. She stood and shielded the boys.

Herod and Kadar's broad chests and muscled arms filled her vision. Relief nearly brought her to her knees. They'd won. Kadar was whole. Ori and Benjamin were safe.

Herod swept Mariamne up in his arms and kissed her soundly to rousing applause.

Kadar came to Lydia and tapped the point of the dagger clutched in her hands. "You don't need it now, my *valkyrie*."

Hands numb, she lowered the dagger. "What of Hasmond's army?"

"It was a total rout. They won't be back."

She longed for his embrace, to be held secure in his strong arms. "You should get some food and rest."

"Not yet. Our dead need must be buried and the injured tended to. Then we'll move on."

"Move on?" The monumental task of readying the caravan for travel seemed too exhausting to contemplate, never mind the actual doing of it.

"We need water. The next oasis is two hours away. Even if we didn't need water, the sun will soon fill this place with the stink of rot."

"But you said the dead would be buried."

"Our dead."

Another wave of nausea hit. She dropped the knife and covered her face with her hands, rocking slightly.

Kadar's warm breath pooled at the nape of her neck. "I hoped you'd never have to witness this kind of ugliness again."

The sound of his low, guttural voice soothed, just as it had when he rescued her six years ago and carried her away from the decimated rebel camp. Determined to resist the pull of the dark oblivion she'd escaped into last time, she lifted her chin and squared her shoulders. "What can I do to help?"

"Lydia," Ori said. He and young Benjamin took hold of her hands.

Kadar's eyes clouded, and he backed away. "You have these two boys and your little James to care for. That is enough."

Was it? A sadness filled her, grief for what might never be between them.

A deafening, exuberant cheer went up. The boys pulled her around so she faced the cause of excitement. Herod stood atop a boulder as he had earlier in the day. His white teeth gleamed under the bright sun. "I promised we would defeat our enemies and we did."

His followers trilled and yipped joyously. He sobered, and the people quieted. "Before you, and before the Lord, I make a vow." Hands held palms up and his eyes pointed heavenward, Herod's voice rang out. "I vow to rid Jerusalem of the Parthian invaders. And after I do, I will return to this place and build a grand monument to commemorate this great victory." Another roar of approval accompanied Herod as he stepped down from his stone throne to graciously accept and share the outpouring of praise and adulation.

Lydia realized she was smiling. A monument out here? They were in the middle of a vast wilderness. The promise was as brash as it was bold. A foreign army occupied Jerusalem. Herod was without home, position, or wealth. Yet he envisioned a time in the future where he would have the means and leisure to construct a shrine to memorialize this desert stand. The strange part was, she believed him, believed he could deliver on his outsized promises.

Avda appeared at her elbow. She stiffened.

Kadar and Avda stared at each other over her head. Ori and Benjamin jumped with joy their words tumbling, one on top of the other's, describing the night's dangers to their father.

Avda patted the boys' heads, quieting them, and met Lydia's eye. "How did you and my sons fare?"

She clasped her hands tightly. "You should be proud. They were very brave." Watching over Ori and Benjamin had been easy compared with what lay ahead. She needed to release Avda from his promise to marry her, but couldn't imagine finding a good time and place to proceed. He looked spent, yet he must have hours of work remaining ahead of him.

"We were good," Ori assured his father.

Benjamin stuck his thumb in his mouth and bobbed his head in agreement.

Kadar pointed his finger at Avda. "I was the one who sought Lydia out. I needed to see for myself she is well. Don't blame or punish her."

Avda straightened. "I don't need to be lectured on about how to treat Lydia."

"I'll be watching," Kadar warned.

Aware of the curious stares from nearby, Lydia's face heated. "Please don't argue."

Sparing her a final, sidelong glance, Kadar strode away.

Realizing she was staring after Kadar, Lydia forced herself to look into Avda's eyes. "Do you want me to watch the boys until you finish with your work?"

Avda exhaled heavily. "I will ask Rabbi Gabini's daughters to look after them." He took hold of his sons' hands. "Say good bye to Lydia and thank her for taking good care of you."

Ori turned his large brown eyes up to her. "Lydia, come with us."

She shook her head. "I can't."

Benjamin pulled his thumb out of his mouth. "I want to stay with Lydia."

Tears pricked at her eyes. She patted his small head. "I promised your father I would take care of the lady Cypros."

"I want Lydia," Benjamin sobbed.

Ori scrubbed his sleeve across his teary eyes. "Please, Father. We want to stay with Lydia."

Avda gave her a sad smile. "I knew they would love you."

"I'm sorry," she whispered. Hurting Avda and his boys was the last thing in the world she wanted.

Avda sighed. "The last day has been very trying. It wouldn't be wise to rush important decisions. For now... if it pleases you, I will leave Ori and Benjamin in your care. And when the caravan gets underway again, I hope you will continue the journey in my wagon."

She knelt and wrapped her arms around the boys' small bodies. "When you are through with your work and have had time to eat and rest, we should talk."

Avda gave her a long look, then retreated.

Lydia kissed Ori and Benjamin on the head. Releasing Avda from his promise was for the best. But it would be far harder to do now.

Chapter 26

By noontime the next day the caravan had crossed into Idumea. Lydia was amazed at how quickly the mood had gone from desperate to festive. The news of Herod's unlikely victory spread like wildfire, drawing hundreds of supporters along the way, swelling their ranks threefold as entire families and small villages chose to throw in their lot with Antipater's sons.

Lydia half-listened to Kitra, who had asked to ride in Avda's cart. Giddy and lively, the almond-eyed beauty could talk of nothing but the young soldier she'd taken a fancy to. The boys were seated with Avda, going over their daily lessons.

Lydia wished she'd resisted when Avda had summoned her and the boys to the wagon. But with no time to talk matters over, they were carrying on as if nothing was amiss. Her only recourse now was to wait for a better time and place to press the matter.

She tensed at the sound of clopping hooves and creaking leather approaching. Herod rode by in the company of his inner circle of confidantes. Kadar's golden-yellow head towered over the darker, smaller men. His blue eyes were trained on her.

Kitra leaned closer, and her voice dropped to a conspiratorial whisper. "If I were you, I'd ask the barbarian to convert. He would do it for you."

"To what purpose?" Lydia snapped, her face heating. She glanced up. Avda and his sons were busy chatting.

Kitra smiled slyly. "So you could marry."

Lydia winced. "Marry? My family would never consent."

"You have left your family behind. Who or what is to

keep you from taking what you want? And don't tell me you don't want Kadar."

"But the marriage wouldn't be legal."

"Says who? If Herod can raise an army, and oust Hasmond and the Parthians, he will reign supreme in Jerusalem. Herod will decide what is legal."

Lydia's heart beat faster. Kitra's suggestion wasn't nonsense. Herod's escape from Jerusalem, the flight across the wilderness, and their successful stand against Hasmond's army changed everything.

But what if Herod couldn't raise an army? What then? He would be an exile. If he wasn't caught or killed. What about her? If her father's side prevailed, she would most likely end up back in her father's power. The thought of facing her father after defying him in such a glorious fashion chilled her. The other alternative would be to go into hiding. Kadar would help her escape if she asked.

Kitra looped her arm around Lydia's elbow. "My aunt and cousins like the idea of a marriage between you and Physician Hama, but not me. Tell me you will choose Kadar."

"You make it sound like a contest."

Kitra made a purring noise. "A battle I would thoroughly exploit if I were in your place."

"Physician Hama is a devout Jew and a good, good man," Lydia said.

"But you don't love Hama."

"Shhh," Lydia said putting her finger to her lips and checking over her shoulder. But Avda was busy schooling the boys in the Law of Moses.

"You love Kadar," Kitra whispered.

"It's hopeless. Kadar would have to give up his gods for the one true God."

Kitra pouted her red lips. "He would do it for you."

"But belief should come from the heart. I don't want Kadar to convert to please me."

"My mother says a clever woman uses her charms to influence a man's heart. Aunt Cypros put away her idols to marry Antipater. And I will do the same when I am betrothed." Kitra sighed. "Herod had high hopes your brother and I would marry."

Lydia groaned. This explained Kitra's friendliness. "Is James aware of that?"

Kitra nodded and smiled her beguiling best.

Heaven help James. He'd be doomed if this sneaky temptress ever sank her claws into him. Lydia brushed at the dirt staining her tunic and worked to regain her composure. "I would never ask Kadar to forsake his gods for me. I'd want him to convert for the sake of his beliefs, and not as a mere convenience."

"If you won't have him, I know someone who will."

Lydia's stomach soured. "Who?"

"My cousin. She talks nonstop about the blue-eyed barbarian."

Lydia remembered the girl. Beautiful and exotic like Kitra, she was also twice as flirtatious. Lydia wanted to protest, but she had no right. Kadar wasn't hers.

Kitra crawled to the end of the cart, hopped off, and raced back to her own carriage.

Avda turned and smiled back at Lydia. "There's a girl on a mission. What did you say to her?"

Lydia swallowed her misery. "If Kitra asks to ride with us again, please say no."

"What's the matter, Lydia?" Benjamin asked. "Are you hurt?"

She shook her head, even as she ached with longing for Kadar. "I'm tired."

Concern clouded Avda's face. "We will reach En Gedi within the hour. Try to rest."

Desperate to escape scrutiny, she lay down on the bed of blankets the boys had abandoned and pulled a cover over her head. Sorrow engulfed her. A tight ball of pain twisted in her belly from trying to hide her grief at thought of another woman with Kadar. She bunched her hands in the blankets and stuffed a bit of the rough wool into her mouth to stifle her sobs.

Kitra's words played and replayed through her mind. *If I*

were you, I'd ask the barbarian to convert. He would do it for you. Who or what is to keep you from taking what you want? Herod will decide what is legal.

The idea was tempting. Very, very tempting. But it would make Lydia no better than Kitra.

Except Kitra had been correct about one thing—the flight from Jerusalem changed everything. Marrying Kadar wasn't totally out of the question, if he was willing to put away his gods.

Listen to her! Would she put aside the Lord God of Israel if Kadar asked?

No. No she wouldn't. She couldn't.

She believed the words of the Law and the prophets. The Lord of Abraham, Isaac, and Jacob was the one true God. And no one and nothing would dissuade her from her belief.

It was hopeless.

Unless.

Dare she?

She spit the blanket out of her mouth and took a deep breath. She would go to Kadar and tell him she loved him and wanted be his woman. He loved her. She was sure he did. Together they would find a way to make it work.

But first she must speak to Avda.

Near sunset the bloated caravan ground to halt outside the dusty village of En Gedi, sheltered by the foothill of the stark mountain plateau of Masada. Herod's brother Joseph, accompanied by his family and two hundred soldiers, received them with much relief and affection.

Herod, Joseph, and Pheroras retreated into a swayback-roofed inn, inviting their closest aides to join them. Kadar and Obodas took a seat on the end of a rickety bench. Antipater's three sons sat on the other side of the scarred plank table. Their father would be proud of the hard fight they were waging to save the family's fortunes. But the task was scarcely begun. Kadar was eager to hear what they planned to do next.

His smile fading, Herod put his arms around Joseph and

Pheroras's shoulders. "Phasael should be here."

A wilder, untamed version of Herod, Joseph scratched his scruffy beard. "Hasmond's men had better not touch one hair on Phasael's head, or I swear I will cut the mealy-mouthed man up and feed his worthless remains to my dogs.

Pheroras winced. "Herod warned Phasael it was a trap, but he insisted on joining High Priest Hycranus in negotiating with the Parthians."

"Talk never did any good," Joseph growled. "I say we regroup and strike back at Hasmond immediately, and we hit him hard."

Herod picked up a clay pitcher and poured wine into the chipped mugs scattered across the table. "We'll need an army to take back Jerusalem."

Joseph chugged back his wine, and dragged the back of his hand across his mouth. "An army?"

Kadar, who always believed Joseph was too rash for his own good, watched Herod mull over the problem. Everyone thought Phasael was the level-headed one of the brood, but Herod had a keener mind.

Herod tapped his fingers against his mug. "Nabatea owes us favor and money. I'll have to go to Petra and pay King Malichus a visit, and *convince* him to help us."

"I dare Malichus to say no to me," Joseph said lifting his mug to his mouth.

Herod stayed Joseph's hand. "I want you to escort Mother and our supporters to Masada and guard them until I return."

"Maybe we should go live in Petra," Pheroras suggested. "We would be safe there."

Herod and Joseph ignored their next-to-youngest brother.

"The first thing you need to do is send the bulk of your followers home," Joseph said.

Herod nodded. "I'll give the needy ones what money I can." He pointed at Kadar and Obodas. "You two will go to Petra with me."

Kadar wasn't going anywhere, but he let the point slide, preferring to argue the matter in private.

The meeting ended a short time later. Kadar went straight

to his horse, and relieved the stable boy of the feedbag. The enormous brown steed, named Valiant, bobbed his head and whinnied. Kadar stroked the horse's smooth, sleek neck, and held the bag under the animal's flaring nostrils. The bold name suited his spirited steed. Kadar regretted having to give him up, but Masada's steep, narrow ascent must be made on foot.

Avda Hama's wagon was parked a short distance away. Lydia sat with Hama's boys, gesturing spiritedly, telling them a story by the look of it. Festive music filled the air thanks to a band of Levite musicians. Wine, food, and good cheer flowed freely through the temporary camp.

Spotting Herod striding toward him, Kadar put the feedbag down and prepared to set the mule-headed man straight.

Herod smiled wide. "What are doing over here by yourself?"

"Obodas stopped at the latrine. Once he returns, we'll set the night watch."

"Make sure to get some sleep. We will leave for Petra at first light."

Kadar widened his stance. "I'm not going."

"Damnation!" Herod blew out an exasperated breath. "I was sure you'd kick up."

"I'll go to Masada and help Joseph guard your family."

Herod swiped a dismissive hand. "Two hundred men are more than enough to guard Masada. There's a single, narrow path to the top. Those trying to assault the summit have to approach single file. Joseph and his archers will cut them down like a scythe felling rye...if Hasmond is foolish enough to attempt it."

Kadar scratched Valiant behind the ears and feigned boredom. "I won't be any help to you in Petra, either."

Herod's black eyes flashed. "When I return to Masada, I will do so at the head of an army. I want you there leading one of the flanks. Obodas will lead the other.

Not too long ago Kadar would have jumped at Herod's offer, but his loyalties lay elsewhere now. "I promised Lydia Onias I'd guard and protect her."

"I swear you're blind as a lovesick pup."

"Stop the foolish talk."

A malicious grin spread across Herod's face. "You know what I think? I think you need Lydia Onias more than she needs you."

"Leave it alone," Kadar warned.

"Lydia will be perfectly safe with Avda Hama at Masada. It is the prospect of Simeon Onias ruling alongside Hasmond which poses the true danger to her. Tell me I'm wrong."

Kadar wanted to drive Herod's smirk down his throat. "Damnation. I need a good night's sleep."

"Bed the Onias girl. It should take care of what ails you."

Annoyed by the truth, Kadar replied through gritted teeth. "That mouth of yours is going to get you killed."

Herod smiled. "We leave at sunup. Don't be late."

Kadar wanted to protest, but Herod was already halfway to Mariamne's wagon. Kadar draped his arms around Valiant's neck. "I don't need Lydia Onias." The accusation was pure dung. Everything Kadar had done was for Lydia. Going to Egypt when she wrote to ask for his help. Sneaking her out of her cousin's house so she could visit little James. Arranging for her to marry Hama. Helping her to escape from Jerusalem. All for her.

Valiant sniffed at Kadar's tunic. Kadar exhaled heavily. "Do I look like a lovesick fool?"

The warhorse shook his withers and swished his long tail.

"Traitor," he said without heat. He dug a chunk of honeycomb out of the leather pouch tied to his belt and held the treat out on the flat of his hand. Valiant's soft muzzle brushed over his palm.

A reexamination of the recent past proved uncomfortable. When the diversionary force had caught up with the caravan after escaping from Jerusalem, Kadar could have gone around Lydia when he'd seen her smiling and watching him. Instead he headed straight to her, and by doing so created trouble between her and Hama. Afterward he'd vowed to stay away, but following the bloody battle with Hasmond, he'd immediately sought Lydia out, then made matters worse by threatening Hama.

"Kadar?" a soft, urgent voice queried.

He twisted around.

Lydia moved toward him, her long, willowy body outlined in the orange of the setting sun, her large brown eyes gazing at him intently. His heart sped up.

Lydia stopped beside him, too close for comfort. She patted Valiant. The steed nickered and flicked his ears. "We must talk." she said.

Kadar spotted Obodas marching toward him. The brawny man halted a short distance away.

"Can you give me a few moments?" Kadar asked him.

The career soldier scanned the darkening sky and gave a curt nod.

Not sure what to make of Lydia's visit, Kadar took a small step back. "Did you come to say goodbye?"

"No, I want to talk about us."

"Us?"

Obodas grinned knowingly, probably thinking along the same lines as Herod. How many others were calling Kadar a lovesick pup? His lack of restraint was jeopardizing Lydia's future. This had to end.

Kadar crossed his arms. "Go back to Hama, woman."

Valiant bumped Lydia with his head. Unfazed by the size and strength of the warhorse, she patted the steed's long nose. "I can't."

Kadar tensed. He glanced about the makeshift camp, searching for Hama, and saw the physician tending to a sick child. "What happened? Did Hama send you away?"

"No, not yet."

"But you're afraid he will?"

She moved closer to him. "I can't marry Avda. I love you, and I want to be your woman, and I won't take no for an answer."

Stunned and exhilarated, he blinked. "You're talking foolish."

"Foolish? Charging into the wilderness with Herod was foolish, but here we are, alive and well and free to do what we will."

"What exactly are you saying?"

"You and I can have a life together."

"We've already been over this. I won't take you to live in an army camp. What about little James?"

Her rose-tinged cheeks paled. "If Herod can't take back Jerusalem, I'll never see my precious boy again. You know it's true. But if he succeeds, he will reward those loyal to him. If you asked, Herod might give you command of a fortress in Galilee."

Certain he'd soon move on to another country, to another army after ensuring Lydia was safe from her father's selfish schemes, he hadn't given any thought to the full implications of a victory by Herod. His chest tightened. "You're assuming too much. It could take months or years to drive out the Parthians. What will you do in the meantime? If Herod loses, or if I am killed, what then?"

"Avda could be killed," she shot back. "What then?"

Obodas was tapping his thigh impatiently, restless to be off. Hours of talking wouldn't be enough to discuss matters, much less resolve them. Kadar scrubbed his face. "Have you brought the matter up to Hama?"

"No."

"Why not?"

Her chin rose. "You are avoiding my question."

He smiled, loving the spit and fire in her eyes. "What did Hama say?"

"You are plain mulish," she complained crossly, then her shoulders sagged. "I planned to tell him I don't want to marry him before I came to you, but he has been busy with his work."

"Tell him?" Kadar laughed. "I don't think Hama would have any idea what to do with the likes of you." Kadar knew exactly what he'd do. Loins heating, he swallowed. "Stay with Hama until we see which way the war goes."

"I don't love Avda. I love you."

The end of his lonely, bleak existence stood before him. Joy and beauty and a future with meaning were his for the taking. Mightily tempted, he grabbed at the one sure weapon he had. "You can't marry a pagan."

She grasped his hand. "My heart tells me otherwise."

Aware of a multitude of watching eyes, Kadar pulled Lydia to the opposite side of Valiant. He backed her against the horse. "It can never be."

"You love me. I know you do."

"Love doesn't change the truth."

"We are meant to be together."

He wanted to kiss her breathless. "If I said I was going away and I was never coming back, you still wouldn't marry Hama, would you?"

Solemn and serene and absolutely beautiful, she shook her head.

"Obodas," Kadar called stepping around Valiant. "Tell Physician Hama I need a word with him."

Obodas rolled his eyes, but obeyed.

Kadar gave Lydia a stern look. "Herod and I could be gone for weeks or months. Promise me you will take time to ponder matters carefully. If your desires change, we—"

Lydia beamed. "They won't." Her smile fell away. "Why did you send for Avda?"

He ground his teeth at her use of Hama's given name. "I won't leave you the ugly task of breaking off with Hama. If he wants to be angry he can unleash his fury on me."

Obodas and Hama made a wide circle around the steed's hind legs.

Kadar turned and squared his shoulders.

Hama trained his fierce gaze on Lydia. "You couldn't stay away from him, could you?"

Lydia clasped her hands. "I couldn't. I'm sorry, I—"

"Save your apologies for my sons," Hama snapped.

Lydia fell back, and bumped up against Valiant. The steed snorted and pawed the ground. Kadar took Lydia's arm and led her over to Obodas. "Take her to Cypros." Kadar gave Lydia's hand a slight squeeze. "You'll be part of Herod's household now."

Large brown eyes swimming with misery and guilt,

Lydia glanced between him and Hama.

"Leave us," Hama told her.

"Let me deal with Physician Hama," Kadar urged.

She ducked her head. "Don't be hard on Avda. He has every right to be angry."

Obodas ushered Lydia away.

Kadar turned and narrowed his eyes at Hama. "Treat her well while I'm away or..." *Or what?* He couldn't kill or maim the man. He was a father of two boys and the physician caring for Old John. And he liked Hama.

"I'll continue to treat Lydia with the utmost respect." Hama snarled. "Worry about yourself. If you want to spare her hurt, you will marry her properly, but before you marry you ought to put away idol worship and turn to the Lord God of Israel."

Kadar clamped his hand over the amulet beneath his tunic—the last connection to his father and his Northland home. "I wouldn't make a good Jew."

"Why not?"

"Look at me. People will laugh when a blue-eyed, blond-haired giant tells them he is a Jew."

"You don't seem like a man who cares what others think. What really bothers you is the thought of circumcision."

Kadar's buttocks and thighs clenched tight. "Thundering Thor, is there any way around getting clipped?"

Hama's grin was malicious. "No."

"You might get more converts to your faith, if you set that little gem aside."

"You have to say one thing for our Law, it weeds out the committed from halfhearted."

Kadar shifted in place. "Would calling myself a God-fearer be good enough?"

Hama shook his head. "We welcome the company of strangers and foreigners who abstain from idol worship and revere the Lord God of Israel. But we don't allow our sons and daughters to marry so-called God-fearers. You either are a Jew or you're not. There's no halfway. To do right by Lydia, you must sacrifice your foreskin."

The hidden amulet lay heavy on Kadar's chest. "I promise to give the matter serious thought."

Lydia lay awake staring at the starry sky. Cypros had invited her to sleep in one of the rooms Herod rented from the villagers, but Lydia hated the idea of being cooped up with near strangers. She would have enough of that starting tomorrow, when she and the friends and followers of Herod imprisoned themselves atop the towering heights of Masada.

She and a few girls from the harem had made their beds in a large wagon. Surrounded by soft snores, Lydia thought of Brynhild. She missed the sturdy woman's company, and her mothering. She hoped and prayed Bryn was healthy and content. Aunt Sarah wasn't cruel to her slaves, so Lydia had no fears in that respect. The problem was, Bryn was loyal to a fault, making it likely she would risk running away to return to Lydia. The thought of Bryn falling into trouble or coming into harm's way made Lydia sick.

Her worry didn't stop there. She wondered over and over what Kadar and Avda had said to each other after sending her away. Neither of them had come to her afterward. She feared Avda would never speak to her again, and who could blame him? The worst was not knowing when she would see Kadar again. She longed to have his strong arms about her. She didn't regret confessing her love, but wished they'd had more time to discuss their future, especially concerning little James.

A shadow blocked the starlight. Her breath stilled.

"Lydia," Kadar whispered.

"I'm awake."

"Come with me, my *valkyrie*."

His guttural voice wound through her. She swallowed and sat up. "Where are we going?"

He reached over the side of the wagon and skimmed his knuckles along her jaw. "We didn't share a proper farewell."

Skin tingling, she rose to her knees. Gentle, strong hands circled her waist, lifted her out of the wagon, and set her on her feet. Kadar took her hand and led her into the shadows of the tumbledown wall enclosing the village. Two large warhorses stood a short way off, overseen by a soldier who turned his back to them.

Her heart ached with worry for Kadar. "Promise me you won't rush into danger."

He pressed her body back against the warm stones. His husky laugh tickled her ear. "I'm not reckless, except when it comes to you."

"I will hate myself if you are injured or—"

He crushed his mouth to hers and pressed until she surrendered. She tasted of his lips and salty skin.

He kissed his way down her neck and bared her shoulder. His hair cascaded over the sensitive slope of her collarbone, eliciting a loud moan from her. He captured her mouth and his tongue swept over hers.

Need burned through her. She ran her hands down his wide back and over his firm buttocks, and pulled him closer. His fingers tangled in her hair, and they devoured each other's mouths.

Kadar groaned, stepped back, and pinned her shoulders to the wall to keep her from following. His breaths were labored. "We better stop while we can."

"It might be months or years before we can marry."

He gave her a roguish smile. "Even though it's likely to kill me, I refuse to dishonor you. I want to do what's proper."

She bit her bruised lip. "You're ruining my image of barbarians. I thought your people excelled at rape, robbery, and pillage." Teasing was the only way to avoid weeping.

"We reserve that for our enemies. As for our friends..." he wagged his brows "...we kill them before they know we are there." His smile faded, and he released her shoulders and traced his finger along her jaw. "You must have a touch of the barbarian in you, my *valkyrie*, for you pierce me to the heart every time I lay eyes on you."

A raw ache filled her throat. "What will happen if Herod isn't able to raise an army?"

"No matter what, I will come for you, and take you where your father can do you no further harm."

She would always be safe and well cared with Kadar. "We can go to the ends of the worlds, and it won't matter, as long as we are together. But, I couldn't—"

"You couldn't leave little James behind," he finished for her. "We can snatch him away from the Zealot's family and take him with us, if you decide it's best."

"For little James? Why wouldn't it be?"

Kadar exhaled heavily. "Being separated from everything familiar is difficult."

She flinched. "Difficult?"

The clopping of dozens of hooves put an end to the interlude.

They embraced. "Forget I said anything," Kadar said in her ear.

"But—"

He kissed her, then led her from the shadows.

The warm amber of dawn haloed the wives, children, loyal followers, and servants gathered in the middle of the village to heap blessings and farewells on Herod and his handpicked delegation. The hopes and welfare of the eight hundred exiles rested on the shoulders of fewer than fifty men.

Herod mounted his white stallion. Lydia hugged her arms and watched Kadar ride off, his last words tumbling through her mind. She'd assumed, whatever the outcome of the present trouble, she'd enjoy a life that included both Kadar and James. What if Herod failed? What if she and Kadar were forced to flee abroad? What if the only way to be reunited with her son was to steal little James away from Judith? Could she do it? A shiver went through her. She prayed she never had to make such a gut-wrenching decision.

Chapter 27

Jerusalem - *Later That Day*

At the knock, James lifted his stylus from his drawing of a resplendent palace.

The crippled slave Saab poked his head into James's bedchamber. "You have a visitor."

"Whoever it is, tell him I can't buy them favor with my father. Tell them to seek help elsewhere."

One of the few people from Antipater's household to remain in Jerusalem, James had been given a room in the Hasmonean palace, affording him the dubious pleasure of watching Hasmond strut around like a rooster, crowing over his victory, while the populace waited for the main body of the Parthian army to arrive and occupy the city. If that wasn't bad enough, James had been besieged by a continuous flow of men begging for assistance or favors, assuming he had influence with his father, even though he kept rejecting his father's demands for reconciliation. Reunite? The heavens would roll up like a scroll first.

"Your visitor is a woman," Saad said.

"A woman? Don't tell me they're sending their wives to beg." James rubbed his weary eyes. "I'll be down shortly."

Face reddening, Saad hitched his chin over his shoulder. "She insisted on coming to your bedchamber."

Bribes of gold and beautiful daughters to wed hadn't won his goodwill, so now they were sending him slaves to bed? James's fists balled. "I don't want another man's slave whore."

A cloaked figure pushed by Saad. "I hear you've enjoyed the comfort of many slave girls," a familiar voice taunted.

James shot to his feet "Elizabeth? What in the name of

Beelzebub are you doing breaking into a man's bedchamber?" Memories of his base behavior when he studied in Rome arose and heated his face. A reminder of his own sins was the last thing he needed to recall in the middle of a rant against the corrupt company his father was keeping. What stung more, though, was learning Elizabeth had heard about his unsavory past.

Saad smiled and pulled the door closed.

James marched around to the front of the desk. "You shouldn't be here."

Elizabeth pushed back her hood. Ivory skin framed by jet black hair emphasized her stricken demeanor.

James moved to her side. "What's happened?"

Tears welled in her lovely black eyes. "Your father wants to send me away. He said I'm a disgrace to the family. I wouldn't mind so much for myself, but my mother isn't well. She needs me."

James's jaw tightened. "I hope your father told him to go to Hades."

Elizabeth's face crumpled before she could hide her expression with her hands.

His anger over his father's hatefulness gave way to pity and concern. He wrapped his arms around Elizabeth.

She pulled away. "Don't. I'm unclean."

A soft breeze blew through the open window, carrying the smell of myrrh and cinnamon from the Temple's altar. He tightened his hold. "Damnation! Don't push me away. I don't care one iota about clean and unclean."

She lifted her chin. Tears ran down both cheeks. "You don't?"

Filled with unfamiliar tenderness and love, he kissed her forehead. "Tell me what's troubling you."

Elizabeth wiped her tears and inhaled a shuddering breath. "My father has been keeping a terrible secret." She laid out the whole sordid story.

The sight of her long black eyelashes sweeping over pink cheeks did more to undo him than the particulars of her father's sins. James had witnessed hypocrisy aplenty among men he'd admired. He was finding it harder and harder to be shocked.

"I didn't know who else to go to for help," she confessed.

He smoothed his hand over her shapely back. Proficient at pushing others away, he was surprised at how much pleasure and comfort he gained from the close intimacy with Elizabeth. "I won't allow my father to send you away."

"Truly?"

"Truly," he assured her without the faintest idea how he'd keep the promise.

She smiled up at him, filling him with unfamiliar warmth.

The door crashed open.

James and Elizabeth broke apart.

Saad limped in. "They're coming! The whole Parthian army is swarming through the city gates."

Elizabeth ran to the window, leaned out, and gasped.

Nauseous, James glanced at the shiny sword wedged between his bed and the wall. Hasmond had assured everyone from wealthy merchants, to skittish Pharisees, to skeptical Sadducees, that all would be well if they cooperated with their new overlords. Carrying a weapon might get him killed. James left the sword where it stood and joined Elizabeth.

Soldiers armored in black leather poured like ants through the streets and alleys, overrunning homes and shops, hauling off armloads of loot.

Elizabeth clutched his sleeve. "Soldiers are breaking into my brother's house. Your father said our family would be safe from marauders."

Her agony and fear stabbed at him. "There's been a mistake, or a miscommunication." He grabbed her hand. "Gabriel will need our help."

They raced out of the room, ran down a series of hallways, and bolted out a side door. Screams and shouts came from all sides. The tall double doors at the main entryway stood wide open. Soldiers flooded into the palace.

James pulled Elizabeth across the paved courtyard. A bloodied, beaten body lay in a heap at the bottom of the first stairway. Elizabeth froze.

James slid her hood over her head and wrapped his arm around her back. "Keep your eyes down. Don't look. I'll guide you the rest of the way."

He led her to the roadway and they picked up their pace.

Outside the Temple Treasurer's grand home, a soldier slashed at the elderly priest with a thick bullwhip, demanding gold and jewels. James slowed. Elizabeth pushed back her hood. Two warhorses charged around the corner, forcing him and Elizabeth to leap out of the way. The cavalry men raced on without a backward glance.

The goldsmith's three lovely daughters tumbled out of a nearby house. They wept and clung to each other, unable to escape the trio of drunken soldiers who pawed at them and shoved them toward the road. Both arms hanging broken, the goldsmith stood in his doorway sobbing. His quiet, dignified wife begged for help.

James didn't know who to assist first. Hatred for his father welled up. His father's selfish ambition was to blame for this. All of it. How could James possibly atone for the evil wrought today?

A bloodcurdling scream came from Gabriel's house, and Gabriel's wife Talitha burst out of the two-story home and fled in the opposite direction.

James and Elizabeth hurried forward. Gabriel's desperate shouts came from within the elegant house, underscored by baby Helen's loud wails. James and Elizabeth hurried up the stairs, rushed through the door, and came to a halt.

Four muscled soldiers grappled with Gabriel, holding him in place. A fifth blunt-nosed man held two-year-old Helen by the heel. Purple-faced, curly-headed Helen screeched and howled.

"Put the child down!" James yelled.

The blunt-nosed man shook baby Helen. "I'll crack the brat's head against the wall if you don't tell me where you're hiding your gold and jewels."

Baby Helen began to choke on her tears.

Gabriel bucked and kicked. "I will kill you if you hurt

her!"

The blunt-nosed man hammered his heel into Gabriel's belly.

Gabriel struggled for air, the baby bawled louder, and Elizabeth cried out and leaped forward.

James caught her, hauled her back, and narrowed his eyes at the soldiers. "Get out. Leave."

The blunt-nosed man grinned, revealing a row of black, rotted teeth. "Or what?"

Elizabeth squeezed his hand. "Please don't rile them up."

James had to try. If he didn't, who would? Legs shaking like dried reeds, he lifted his chin. "My father is Simeon Onias. And this man is his nephew."

The black-toothed smile faded. "We didn't see a red strip of cloth tied to the door."

"Liar!" Gabriel choked out. "I tied the red flag there myself."

Swearing viciously, the blunt-nosed man swung the baby in an arc and released her. Sweet Helen sailed toward James. He dragged his hand free from Elizabeth and managed to catch the flailing child. Heart lodged in his throat, he hugged curly-headed Helen.

The soldiers released Gabriel and fled.

Eyes red and puffy, nose running with goo, baby Helen held her arms out toward her father. Gabriel took the child and cradled her against his chest. Grim-faced, he headed to the door. "I need to find Talitha."

James and Elizabeth followed.

"We saw her run down the road toward Father's house," Elizabeth said. Her calm amidst the chaos reminded James of the valor she'd displayed when they'd both been held captive by rebel outlaws. She was a remarkable woman. He would be proud if he were only half as brave and noble as she.

Gabriel trotted down the porch stairs. "She must have gone to Father for help. Or maybe to her parents' home."

"There she is," Elizabeth pointed across the road.

Talitha spotted them at the same time. A relieved smile crossed her beautiful, tear-streaked face. Nehonya Onias walked a few paces behind his daughter-in-law.

A band of cavalry men rode hard up the wide thoroughfare. Talitha left Nehonya behind and sprinted across the road.

James cringed. "Stop! Wait."

Talitha's brilliant eyes remained fixed on Gabriel and little Helen. A rider carrying a blue and yellow pennant ran Talitha down. Her crumpled body tumbled and rolled beneath the heavy hoofs of a second horse, then a third.

James clapped his hands to his head.

Gabriel's anguished cry shattered the air.

Elizabeth hiked her tunic up and raced forward.

The Parthian soldiers galloped on.

Elizabeth, Gabriel, and Cousin Nehonya converged on Talitha's bloody, twisted form. Baby Helen's breathless wails and Gabriel's harsh weeping twisted in James's soul like a knife. Sounds of terror and grief sprang from all quarters of the city, and rang in his ears as if heaven itself was weeping.

A tidal wave of resentment crashed over him. His hatred for his father redoubled. He peered toward the Temple. Where was the Lord in all of this? Why did He look the other way as Jerusalem suffered more strife, more death, more war?

Chapter 28

Petra in Nabatea - *One Day Later*

The Arabian city of Petra was impressive, its temples, treasury, and palace carved into the faces of towering, pink-hued cliffs. Markets overflowed with goods supplied by the camel caravans plying the ancient trade route. Exotic, almond-eyed women smiled alluringly from behind silk veils. The heavy scent of rich spices saturated the air.

Kadar stood in a throne room beside Obodas and the small retinue of soldiers hand-chosen for this mission. Herod, accompanied by his brother, Pheroras, and Pheroras's seven-year-old son, had finished presenting their impassioned plea for aid to the king of Nabatea.

The king was a relative of some sort to Herod, whose mother, Cypros, had been born and raised in Nabatea. A nervous, simpering man, King Malichus presided over a throne room dripping with gold and pretension.

Surrounded by numerous white-clad slaves waving large fans of palm fronds, and a cadre of pompous advisors who eagerly agreed with every word he uttered, the king frowned at Herod's request for money and an army. "If I give you half my army, I'll be vulnerable to attack from Cleopatra."

Herod laughed without humor. "Are you two still sniping at one another?"

The king shifted uncomfortably on his filigreed throne. "She is a greedy harpy, eager for more lands, more gold, more power. She'll pounce on me and my kingdom if she senses the least weakness."

"You owe my father money and favors."

"It will take some time to gather the coins."

Herod tapped his thigh with his sword hand. "How long?"

The king conferred with his advisors, then straightened. "Six months, at the least."

Herod's eyes flashed. "Have the Parthians warned you not to cooperate with me?"

King Malichus's face reddened. "I would help you if I could. Your father was a good man. If he was the one asking..."

Kadar winced. Insulting Herod was pure foolishness.

Herod speared the king with a withering look. "If I didn't need your help securing Phasael's release from the Parthians, I'd wash my hands of you right now."

Malichus spluttered and blinked. "Help? What kind of help?"

Herod patted his nephew's shoulder. "Lend me coins for a ransom. And I will leave my nephew behind as a hostage until the funds are repaid."

A stricken frown crossed Pheroras's face. But the sturdy seven-year-old puffed out his chest, proof he was cut from the same audacious cloth as his uncle.

The king nodded and jumped up. "Agreed. Now, come and share a feast with me in honor of Antipater."

The king's cronies followed him out of the throne room.

Herod pulled Kadar aside. "We will leave for Egypt at first light tomorrow."

A foul taste tainted Kadar's mouth. *Egypt.* Vivid memories of the six years he'd slaved away in Sabu Nakht's copper mine roared to life. He'd sworn he'd never step foot in the damnable country again. He swiped a hand over his face. "Will Cleopatra give you an army?"

Herod made a noise of disgust. "I've stopped trying to figure out what goes on in her fiendish mind. But I don't have any other good options. Hers is the only kingdom east of Rome with armies and wealth enough to take on Parthia. So, even though the thought makes my skin crawl, I'm prepared to kiss her pretty backside, if that's what it takes."

Unease and foreboding about the journey oozed through

248

Kadar. *Stop thinking like a worried old woman.* He didn't have anything to fear in Egypt. "I'd like to see to a personal matter while I'm in Egypt."

Herod's brows rose. "Are you hoping to repay an enemy?"

Kadar shook his head. Simeon Onias was the only foe Kadar wanted to get his hands on. "Lydia was very fond of a slave woman who was recently sent back to Egypt. I want to check on her. Make sure she is being treated well." Kadar planned to pay to free Brynhild and give her enough money to live out the rest of her days doing whatever she pleased.

Chapter 29

Masada - *One Day Later*

A small Parthian army had arrived at the base of the sheer-walled plateau the day before. Surrounded by her fellow refugees, Lydia peered over the crumbling wall edging a cliff and held her breath. The steep drop to the rocky plain below, though dizzying, didn't scare her half as much as the sight of the Parthian soldiers trooping up the narrow, winding trail.

As the soldiers drew closer, she saw they were a mixed force of both Parthians and Jews. A tightness filled her chest. She didn't understand her countrymen's eagerness to kill one another over the matter of who would sit as High Priest of Israel. How long would the warring and hatred go on? How many people would have to die before peace was reestablished? How would the nation heal from the gaping wounds of yet another war?

A cheer went up, and Herod's brother Joseph marched into the midst of the men, women, and children who depended on him to safeguard them until Herod returned. Cypros and Mariamne and the rest of Herod's household followed Joseph.

Kitra broke away from her cousins and rushed toward Lydia. Her diaphanous Roman-style stola drew the eye of every man she passed. Arriving breathless at Lydia's side, Kitra leaned out over the fortress wall for a closer look at the advancing soldiers. "This is all so thrilling, don't you think?"

Engulfed by Kitra's cloying cloud of perfume, Lydia wrinkled her nose. "Aren't you even a little frightened?"

Kitra's tinkling laugh earned her more stares. "Joseph took the time to hold my hand and assure me we are perfectly safe."

Certain the flirtatious girl's sheer dress was responsible for Joseph's attentiveness, Lydia merely nodded.

Rough of dress and demeanor, Joseph jumped up onto a large, flat boulder. "Don't let the size of the Parthian army worry you. They don't stand a chance against my archers."

Kitra looped her arm around Lydia's and spoke into her ear. "Joseph terrified me half to death when I first came to Idumea to live with Aunt Cypros. But I think he would make an interesting bed partner, don't you?"

Inclined to believe the rumors circulating about the debauched behavior of Herod and his brothers was the work of exaggerated gossip, Kitra's behavior was causing Lydia to have second thoughts. Lydia pulled her arm free. "I *think*...we should listen to Joseph."

"The enemy is coming to test us." Joseph's voice was confident and bold. "But those Parthian devils and their pet dogs are about to learn what bloody work it will be to take Masada."

Earsplitting trills and yips filled the air. Cypros and Mariamne smiled and applauded. Lydia followed suit, but she found it hard to believe Joseph and his paltry two hundred soldiers could hold back an army of thousands.

Joseph smiled wide, revealing yellowed, overlapping teeth. "Don't lose faith. I will keep the enemy at bay. And Herod will come back for us."

A roar of approval went up.

Joseph jumped to the ground and strode off.

Lydia turned and leaned out over the wall to check the progress of the men sent to capture Masada. They were coming fast and strong. Her muscles still ached from the one-hour trek up the steep Snake Path. Once the Parthian soldiers and Jewish fighters reached the summit, they would have to dig deep into their reserves to find the extra strength to enter into battle.

Joseph positioned his men at a choke point. A brown-clad Jewish fighter rounded a blind corner. An arrow whizzed through the air, and struck home. The man keeled over, crashed against a sloping boulder, and slid off into the wide-open blue.

A collective gasp went up. Lydia winced.

Whoosh after *whoosh* sounded below. Death cries rang out. Men fell. Herod's followers cheered each time the archers' arrows found a target.

Both horrified and mesmerized, Lydia swallowed back the sour remains of the rye bread from her breakfast and prayed the battle would come to a quick end.

Close to fifty men on the Parthian side went down without striking a single blow against Joseph's fighters.

The flow of enemy soldiers slowed to a trickle, then stopped. Joseph's men watched and waited. Soldiers up and down the Snake Path hunkered in place. Herod's followers held their breaths. Lydia twisted her hands in her tunic.

A forlorn note from a horn drifted up the Path. The Parthian soldiers turned and fled back down the winding trail.

Joseph's men cheered. Herod's followers embraced and cried out their joy. Cypros was heaped with praise for bearing such courageous sons. Kitra hugged Lydia. Relieved, Lydia set aside her dislike and hugged the girl back.

Cypros approached them, looking more cross than usual. "Lydia Onias, you will mend your relationship with Physician Hama. I won't tolerate having him distracted from his work."

"I promise to stay far away from Avda," Lydia said employing the respectful tone she used with her father.

Cypros's lips pursed. "You mistake my meaning. You were promised to Physician Hama. I expect you to do your duty and marry him."

A warm flush raced up Lydia's neck. "I appreciate your concern, but the matter is a private one."

Kitra fidgeted next to her.

"You are a member of my household," Cypros said snappishly. "Which means you answer to me." The imperious woman strode off, confident her command had settled the matter.

Lydia blew out a frustrated breath. "Your aunt doesn't care for me. I'm surprised she is pushing for me to marry Avda."

Kitra pointed to the main cistern. "Physician Hama is staring at you with large, sad eyes."

Water jar in hand, Avda frowned.

Lydia tensed. "Physician Hama is not happy with me."

Kitra waved at him. Her translucent stola shimmied over soft curves. "Maybe I should go try to cheer Avda up."

Lydia's shoulders hitched upward. What made the irritating girl think she had a right to call him Avda?

Avda's face reddened and he turned his back to them.

Kitra's tinkling laugh stopped a pair of soldiers in their tracks. She crooked her finger at them and sauntered off. Entranced, the slack-jawed men trotted after her. Lydia half expected to see their tongues hang out.

Lydia massaged her forehead and surveyed the narrow strip of dirt which comprised the tiny fort. Today's lopsided victory proved Masada was safe as a cloud floating high over danger. Regrettably, it was a very small, cramped, crowded cloud. Parthia posed no immediate threat. No, the real trouble awaited her within the hemmed-in confines of the plateau. Unpleasant run-ins with Avda and Kitra and Cypros would be a daily affair.

Avda lowered his pitcher into the round stone cistern, the frayed rope sliding through deft hands capable of tending wounds and mending broken bones.

She hated the uneasiness between them. She wasn't sure the hurt could be mended, but she had to try. Stomach churning, she crossed to the cistern.

Avda's frown smoothed. "How are you? I'm sorry you've had to suffer the lady Cypros's displeasure. I've asked her to leave you in peace, but she's not the peaceful type."

Avda was apologizing to her? She hugged her arms. "You're not angry with me..." her voice broke, "...I was afraid—"

"Oh, I'm angry." His eyes darkened.

His words stung like pin-pricks. "Forgive—"

"Don't apologize. I'm aggravated with myself, not you."

"But, why? You are the one who was wronged."

He pulled the water jar from the cistern, set the pitcher on the ground, and gave her a sad smile. "You and Kadar love each other. You can't unlearn what your heart knows. And you shouldn't have to apologize for the truth."

Her face heated. "I tried. For a long time I tried to deny my love for Kadar, but it continued to grow deeper and more consuming."

"My real problem is I'm eaten up with regret and longing, watching you with him, remembering the love and closeness I shared with my wife." He stared skyward, put his hands on his hips, and she could tell he had to work at gathering his composure.

His pain became her pain. "Everyone says your wife adored you."

He exhaled heavily. "I want to love again. I thought I didn't. I was afraid to suffer more grief and heartache. I thought an arranged marriage of duty and respect would be enough. But I want to marry someone I love and who will love me back." He shook his head and chuckled. "If my father was alive, he would pull his beard out if he heard me talk such foolishness."

She thought of her father, who regarded marriage contracts as stepping stones to influence and power. "Foolishness takes much worse forms than what you're proposing. And let me give your wise advice back to you. You don't have to apologize for the truth."

He smoothed his neat beard. "My boys miss you. Would you mind...?"

"I miss them too. Bring them along when you come to wait on Cypros, and the boys can keep me company while you listen to poor woman's latest complaints. "

His brown eyes sparkled. "Ha! Poor woman, indeed." He sobered. "How are you getting on? Herod's household isn't for the faint of heart."

Healing the rift with Avda made everything else immaterial. "I have a gift for tolerance and for finding joy where I can. Kitra's tinkling laugh aside." Lydia wrinkled her nose. "Promise me you won't fall for Kitra's rather blatant charms."

He made a face. "I plan to marry a good Jewish girl."

"Thank you for not judging me for pledging myself to a pagan."

Avda frowned. "I told Kadar he needs to convert and be circumcised and marry you properly."

Lydia winced. "What did he say? Never mind. It doesn't matter."

"It does matter. That is, if you hope to live in Judea or Galilee."

She picked up the water jug. "May I help you draw more water?"

"Have you asked Kadar to convert?"

A cool draft swirled up from the well. "The water level is quite low. Are the other reserves this low?"

"Changing the subject won't save you. I'm going to keep at you until you vow you won't marry a pagan. As for the water," the bluster went out of Avda's voice, "the unusually dry rainy season couldn't have come at a worse time. Joseph is concerned. Actually, he is more worried about the water supply than the Parthian army nipping at our heels."

Lydia looked between the cistern and the clear blue sky. "Kadar and Herod hoped to be back within weeks."

Avda returned to looking grim. "In the meantime we will pray for rain."

Chapter 30

Pelusium, Egypt - *Later the Same Day*

The unforgiving sun beat down on Kadar's head. Sweat trickled over his scalp and down his back. Valiant twitched his mane and swished his long tail in an unsuccessful attempt to chase away the relentless cloud of gnats hovering around them. The brown sand walls of Pelusium blended into the drab, flat horizon.

Herod's white stallion stopped alongside Valiant. "Pheroras keeps asking me how long we'll have to wait for Hasmond and the Parthians to release Phasael." Haggard-faced, Herod shifted in his saddle. "I told him these things take time. But Pheroras is understandably anxious to get his son back."

Unsettled and edgy ever since they'd crossed into Egypt, Kadar welcomed the conversation, despite having discussed the matter to death since their pre-dawn departure from Petra. "I think Hasmond will trip over himself trying to appease you if you win Cleopatra's support."

"I hope you're right. But just to be safe, I'm going to ask Her Royal Highness for extra coin for the ransom. Parthia will have emptied Jerusalem's coffers. Hasmond will be desperate for money. Though I relish the idea of the viper crawling on his belly to Parthia, begging for crumbs and dregs, I'd gladly give the snake all my wealth to free Phasael."

Kadar touched his hand to his amulet. He envied the love and loyalty between Herod and his brothers. Kadar had enjoyed the same strong bond with his father. Kadar wanted sons who would stand by each other, no matter the cost.

Obodas rode up on his speckled white horse. He gestured

back over his brawny shoulder. "A lone horseman is closing in on us. I think it's that new Samaritan messenger. The unsavory, gapped-toothed fellow."

A shadow crossed Herod's face. He held up his hand, bringing the fifty-man contingent to a halt. An eerie quiet replaced the usual banter. The Samaritan messenger was actually a spy.

Impatient with delays, Kadar rubbed the back of his neck.

The spy's stiff, ungainly posture marked him as a man with little experience riding a horse, but discomfort alone didn't account for the rigid slope of his shoulders and his jerky movements. His tight-lipped expression said he brought bad news.

The color drained from Herod's ruddy cheeks. Reins clasped tight in his hand, he brought his white stallion alongside his brother's slender gelding. Herod and Pheroras dismounted and waited.

Obodas leaned forward. His saddle creaked and groaned under his great weight. "What deviltry has Hasmond been up to now?"

Kadar felt like he had a pair of oxen sitting on his chest. "If some evil has touched Phasael..." He and Obodas exchanged grim looks.

The spy halted and swung down off his haggard mount.

Obodas spat and straightened. "That poor old girl has been ridden hard. Too hard."

Kadar's fists tightened. "If I had a whip in hand I'd teach the careless fiend a painful lesson."

The spy beat the dust from his tunic. Studying the results, he said, "You directed me to come if I had any news about Phasael."

"I'll rip your wretched limbs from your body if you don't get on with it," Herod ground out.

The spy stood to attention. "The Parthian army handed your brother and High Priest Hycranus over to Hasmond."

Herod cursed. Pheroras bent at the waist like he was about to heave up his guts.

The spy stared straight ahead. "Phasael threw himself off

a rooftop while he was being moved and suffered a severe gash to the head."

Herod clasped his wooly head. "Please, God, no!"

Kadar exhaled a heavy breath.

"Noble fool," Obodas said, his voice rough with emotion. "He'd rather kill himself than allow Hasmond to use him to get to Herod."

Herod's arms dropped to his sides. "Is Phasael dead? Did he—"

"He survived the plunge, but died a few days later," the spy answered. "Rumor has it the physician sent to treat Phasael poured poison into the wound. The slave attending your brother said it was a slow, painful death."

Pheroras collapsed to his knees, buried his face in his hands, and wept bitterly.

Vicious intent hardened Herod's eyes. "First my father. Now Phasael." He thrust his chin out. "I'm going to kill Hasmond with my bare hands. He will look upon my pleasure while I choke the life from his scrawny body."

The spy flashed a gap-toothed smile. "Now there's a spectacle I'd pay to see."

Caught up in his own pain, Herod paid no attention to the spy's thoughtless remark. "Do you have any more information about Phasael's..." Herod 's voice thickened. He coughed. "Phasael...did he wake after the fall?"

"I spoke to the slave woman who was with your brother when he died. She told Phasael how you'd escaped from Jerusalem and about your wilderness victory. Joyful at the news, he said to her, *I can now die in comfort, since I leave behind one who will avenge me of my enemies.*" The spy shrugged. "That's all I know."

Eyes wet, Herod helped Pheroras to his feet and led him a short distance away. Surrounded by tall, yellowed tufts of desert grass, Herod and Pheroras put their heads together and consoled one another.

"Stop your gawking," Obodas ordered the other guardsmen. The tough-as-leather man rubbed the back of his hand over his eyes, dismounted, and took an inordinate amount of interest in the items stored in the sacks hanging from his saddle.

Kadar wanted to hurt someone. Phasael was too good a man and soldier to die at the hands of cowards. He plucked off a black bug climbing through Valiant's mane. "Damnable pests," he muttered, crushing the bug with his thumbnail. Tossing the loathsome creature aside, he noticed the spy staring at him. The look of interest on the man's face raised Kadar's hackles. "What's your problem?"

The spy's lips twitched with amusement.

Kadar reached the spy in two strides. "You have something to say, so say it."

The spy's lecherous smile framed the wide gap between his front teeth. "You must be the barbarian. Simeon Onias has offered a large reward for your head." He winked. "A reward large enough to make men drool."

Kadar stuck his finger into the obnoxious man's face. "Collect your fee for the information you delivered, then go. You have a long walk ahead of you."

"Walk?"

"Be grateful I'm not taking a whip to you. You abused your horse...the poor beast might be permanently lamed. I won't let you finish the job."

The spy's eyes turned dangerous. "It's a horse, you dim-witted barbarian. You talk like the bag of bones is the Lord Almighty come down from heaven."

Kadar slugged the spy, and took satisfaction at the sound of bone crunching.

Blood spurted from the man's nose. "You're a dead man. Do you hear me?"

Guardsmen swarmed around, sending Kadar's mind back to the copper mine and the battles to the death. He beckoned the spy forward. "Let's finish it. You and me, barehanded."

Panic flashed through widened eyes. The spy backpedaled. "Stay away from me."

Rollicking laughter filled the air.

"You will pay for this," the spy threatened.

Kadar reached for his sword.

A thick hand clasped his wrist. "Let the coward go," Obodas said.

The commander's reasonable tone doused the white heat licking Kadar's blood. Uncurling his fingers from his sword, he exhaled heavily. Self-conscious, he resorted to banter. "Spies are lower than maggots."

Obodas slapped him on the back. "Maggots have their uses."

The spy stalked off toward Pelusium. The guardsmen dispersed.

The grit-laced wind scoured Kadar's skin. A sulfurous smell filled his nostrils. The desert sun sucked at his bones. Though they'd barely set foot in Egypt, they couldn't leave soon enough to please him.

Chapter 31

Alexandria Egypt - *Two Days Later*

The queen's royal confines glittered and gleamed with gold. The dimly-lit room looked more like a bedchamber than a banquet hall. Herod sat tight-lipped next to Kadar. Obodas couldn't stop ogling the Queen Cleopatra, whose sheer gown left nothing to the imagination. Herod's guardsmen indulged in the plentiful food, wine, and slave girls for the taking.

A small delegation of merchants from Athens, hoping to seal a trade agreement with the Queen, were fawning over her like dogs licking their master's feet. The regal woman appeared wholly unimpressed.

Kadar drummed his fingers against the yellow-striped reclining couch. Her Royal Highness could be naked or gold-plated for all he cared. A harem's worth of women wouldn't sway or distract him. An army and weapons, those were his priorities.

A tall slave with the blackest skin Kadar had ever seen approached their low marble table. "The Queen will hear your petition next."

Herod sat up, swallowed down the remains of his wine, and pointed at Kadar and Obodas. "You two better come too, you can stop me from tearing my hair out if her Royal Highness tries any of her tricks."

Obodas tossed aside a half-eaten roasted pigeon. "She is a wily one, but you are as skilled a manipulator as they come."

Herod shot him a dirty look. "You meant it as a compliment, I suppose?"

The thick-necked man laughed. "Or you could blind her

with your dazzling smile. One white-toothed grin and you will have her eating out of your hand."

Herod rose to his feet and tightened his belt. "I'd rather kiss a crocodile."

Kadar glanced at the slight woman reputed to be able to make grown men quake. "Is she that much the man-eater?"

"She beguiled Julius Caesar and Mark Antony," Herod said with a note of grudging admiration. "And all the while she's managed to keep Rome from plundering her riches and commandeering her armies."

Kadar stood and stretched his cramped limbs. "Her hawk-like nose is too big for her face. I was expecting a real beauty."

Obodas jabbed Kadar in the ribs. "Queen Cleopatra appears to like what she sees of you."

Kadar whipped his head around, and found eyes full of worldly knowledge and seductive secrets roaming over him, eyes that ought to belong to a much older woman. His mouth went dry. Cleopatra's amused gaze slid back to the Athenians.

Obodas slapped Kadar's back. "I say we give our oversized barbarian friend to Her Royal Highness as her next plaything."

Lydia was the only woman Kadar wanted. But saying no to a queen, especially this Queen, would prove awkward, and maybe dangerous. Resisting the urge to flee, Kadar scrubbed his hand over his face. "I'll kill you both if you throw me to the slaughter."

Herod sobered. "I wouldn't force you, but you and I both know I'll do what I must to secure an army."

Kadar ground his teeth and followed the tall, black-skinned slave to Cleopatra's luxurious, bed-sized couch. Surrounded by amethyst pillows atop a violet-blue cover, the Queen's slinky diamond gown shimmered mesmerizingly. Reclining on her back, with her head pillowed on a drawn-up arm, and one knee bent, she smiled up at them with lips painted siren red.

"Herod of Idumea..." her hushed voice was as sultry as her black eyes "...Parthia has treated you infamously."

Herod bowed his wooly head. "It gladdens me to have your sympathies."

Cleopatra ran her tongue over the edge of her teeth. "What would you have me do for you, Herod of Idumea?"

Obodas crossed his arms and shifted in place. Kadar's gut tightened. Cleopatra exuded a white-hot sexuality a blind man would find impossible to ignore.

Herod cleared his throat. "Seven years ago my father and I came to your aid. We helped you overthrow your brother and take the throne you now sit upon. I have come to ask you to return the favor."

"I would dearly love to assist you, my old friend," Cleopatra purred. "However..."

Cleopatra sat up and slid her legs over the side of the couch, sending her shimmery diamond gown gliding over her lithe body.

Kadar, Herod and Obodas backed up.

The Queen's black eyes sparkled knowingly, pleased by evidence of her power over them. "...I fear if I send my armies to Jerusalem, King Malichus will take advantage of the situation and invade Egypt."

"Malichus wouldn't dare invade Egypt," Herod said. "He well knows Rome would crush Nabatea like a bug if he tried."

"True..." The Queen held out her dainty hand. "I am able to lend you funds to raise an army. Would that do?"

Herod took her hand and helped her to her feet. "That will do nicely."

Red lips curved in a silky smile. "Wonderful! But, I do have one small stipulation."

Herod remained patient and attentive. "Of course. Name your price."

Kadar wanted to wring the Queen's pretty neck.

Cleopatra ran her gold-flecked nail over her full red lips. "We should discuss the terms in private."

Herod didn't flinch. "This is private enough."

The Queen's throaty laugh rippled upward. "You will need to take your army to Nabatea and dispose of Malichus before you see to your own business."

Kadar gnashed his teeth. "War with Malichus could take months or years—"

"I'm sure we can reach a compromise," Herod said calmly.

Cleopatra's shoulder brushed Herod's. "Be prepared to use your famed persuasive powers on me, Herod of Idumea. And remember, I won't concede anything without gaining favors in return." The Queen strolled off, her translucent gown rippling over smooth curves.

Obodas rocked back on his heels. "Holy heavens, how is a man supposed to resist her?"

Kadar raised a brow at Herod.

"By not forgetting Mark Antony," Herod said. "Antony would have my head if I lay one finger on his mistress."

"What about the war she wants you to wage against Malichus?" Kadar asked, afraid he would hate the answer.

Herod crossed his arms over his broad chest. "Though I'd love to repay Malichus for turning his back on me, I won't be talked into fighting the Nabateans."

Kadar massaged his knotted neck muscles. Their plan called for them to go to Rome if Cleopatra proved unhelpful, a few months' journey they'd hoped wouldn't be necessary. "So, it's on to Rome now?"

"I want to work a little longer on persuading *Her Royal Highness* to see things my way."

"You're a braver man than I am," Obodas said.

The gilded chamber closed in around Kadar. Egypt didn't suit him. Not one bit. "Can you do without me tomorrow? I want to check on Lydia's slave woman."

Herod frowned. "Take Obodas along with you. We wouldn't want you to fall into trouble the way you did last time you visited Alexandria."

An image of Sabu Nakht's oily face and lank hair loomed. Kadar swallowed. "Nothing will go wrong. It's just a simple errand."

Chapter 32

Kadar and Obodas walked under the spindly palms guarding the two-story villa he'd sneaked into six years earlier when he came to rescue Lydia. Had he really been so young and reckless?

He didn't regret coming to Alexandria, despite the loathsomeness of the copper mine and slavery. Yes, he'd suffered, but he'd gained Lydia. A more than ample reward for his troubles.

Kadar knocked on the villa's wooden door. The bread and cheese he'd eaten for breakfast curdled as he imagined Lydia married to her old, fat uncle.

"I entered through a window the last time I was here," Kadar said.

Obodas rumbled with laughter. "Sneaking back out the window didn't work so well?"

"Simeon Onias knew I was coming. I never stood a chance."

The door creaked open. A freckle-faced slave maiden stared up in awe. "You must be Brynhild's blue-eyed giant. Bryn said you were brawny enough to lift an ox." The slave's wide eyes moved on to Obodas. "Are you his brother?"

Obodas winked. "Do I look sufficiently ugly to be his brother?"

The girl giggled and a hint of pink showed through her freckles.

Kadar held onto his patience for the young maiden's sake. "I would like to speak to Brynhild."

"Bryn isn't here. Our mistress sold her."

Kadar winced. "Is Brynhild still in Alexandria?"

Turning skittish, the slave maiden glanced back over her

shoulder. "Her master is staying in rented rooms at the Sandbank Inn."

Kadar dug a coin out of his pouch. "I hope we don't cause you any trouble."

The freckle-faced girl grabbed the coin and snapped the door closed.

Kadar and Obodas retreated to the street, stopped a passerby, and asked for directions. A half hour later they were two blocks from the reeking Nile, standing in front of a dilapidated three-story building. Kadar knocked on its faded red door. The door creaked open on its own.

A woman's panicked voice came from an inner room, screaming something unintelligible.

Kadar barged in and ran down a long, narrow hall. Obodas followed on his heels. A crash and a jumble of yells and curses came from the left. Kadar and Obodas veered down another hall, charged into a dimly lit bedchamber, and skidded to a halt. Eight armed men surrounded them. Kadar and Obodas drew their swords and assumed a defensive stance.

"What the devil?" Obodas said, breathing heavily.

Heart slamming in his chest and blood pounding through his head, Kadar tried to make sense of what he saw.

At back the room, a man had a choke hold on Brynhild. The pear-shaped woman's arm was pinned behind her back at an unnatural angle. Hair stood out in all directions from her disheveled blond braids. Tears streaked her ruddy cheeks.

Had they interrupted a robbery? The swordsmen surrounding them were dressed in a mix of armor, making them look more like a collection of mercenary soldiers than a band of thieves.

Then a bald-headed man wearing rich robes stepped out from behind a decorative reed screen.

Goda.

Simeon Onias's bald eunuch strolled forward wearing a broad and pleased smile. "Barbarian, you leaped into my trap just as I knew you would. You oversized giants are so predictable."

Kadar frowned. "How did you learn I was in Egypt? How did you know I would come here?"

Goda laughed. "Word of Herod's arrival, accompanied by a blond giant, spread like wildfire through Alexandria. And a freckle-faced angel flew here as quickly as she could to collect her generous reward."

Hate rekindling for the man who had sold him into slavery, Kadar pointed the tip of his sword at the eunuch. "Release Brynhild."

"Goda blames you for his troubles," Brynhild warned. Arm yanked higher, she screamed pitifully.

Kadar charged. A wall of swords blocked his path. He glared at the gloating eunuch. "I'll kill you if your man hurts her again."

Goda paled.

Obodas put a hand on Kadar's shoulder. "Everybody remain calm."

"Drop your weapons," Goda demanded, hate gleaming in his eyes. "Or I'll order my man to break the loud-mouthed woman's other arm."

Brynhild's whimpers rang in Kadar's ears. "Thundering Thor," he growled as he threw down his sword.

A moment later, Obodas's heavy blade clattered against the stone floor. "What did you do to offend this toad?"

Kadar shook his head. "I made the mistake of not dying in the copper mine. Simeon Onias wasn't pleased when he found out the eunuch hadn't killed me as he'd been ordered to do. Onias dismissed him."

Goda waved his hand at the lead soldier. "Get on with it."

"Down on your bellies, scum," the man barked.

Obodas frowned, but dropped to his knees and stretched out on his stomach.

Kadar's muscles tightened. Memories of his helplessness and vulnerability as a slave flooded back. Resisting the urge to fight his way free, he laid down beside Obodas on the spongy wood floor stinking of urine.

The soldiers bound Kadar's hands and feet with horsehair rope.

Goda came and stood over them. "I'm going to enjoy humiliating you, Barbarian."

Grains of sand rasped along Kadar's skin. "Release Brynhild and do what you will to me."

"Are you sure you want to hurt one of Herod of Idumeas's commanders?" Obodas asked in a reasonable tone.

"You heard him," Goda replied. "The barbarian promised to hunt me down and kill me."

Kadar detested the bald eunuch, but seeking revenge ranked low on his list of priorities. "Do you ever laugh or share drinks with friends? Oh, that's right, you don't have any friends."

A smattering of laughter came from the mercenaries.

The eunuch's lips pursed. "Oh, I have something *special* in mind for you."

A sinking feeling rolled through Kadar.

Goda snapped his fingers and a morose, sallow-faced man stepped out from behind the reed screen, clutching a bulky bundle in his gnarled hands.

"The fiend has hired an unscrupulous Egyptian priest to carve you up," Brynhild choked out, then yelped in pain.

Kadar strained against his bonds. "Just what do you have in mind?"

Goda's smile was wicked. "Flip him on his back and bare his private parts."

Kadar kicked and bucked, but was easily outmatched by four rugged soldiers. Rough hands clamped onto his arms and legs, hauled him over onto his back, and pulled at his tunic and loin cloth. Cool air struck naked skin.

"Leave him alone!" Obodas yelled, struggling to get on his feet. Two men fell on the burly commander, knocking him back to his belly.

Brynhild alternated between screaming curses and cries of pain.

A leather band dug into Kadar's forehead, forcing his head back. A hammer and nails secured the strap to the floor. Arms already pinned behind his back, Kadar's bound legs were fastened to the floorboards next.

Once they'd finished trussing Kadar like an animal pelt to a drying rack, the men stepped back, remarking enviously over his great size.

A white silk slipper kicked Kadar's side. The eunuch smiled down at him. "Who's laughing now, Barbarian?"

Kadar's blood boiled with hate. "I won't grovel for mercy or beg your forgiveness, if that's what you're hoping." A quick death was starting to look good. Very good.

"What I want?" Goda scoffed. "I want the princely reward Simeon Onias will give me for your head after my mercenaries lop it off your shoulders. But first I want to watch as your foreskin is peeled away."

Kadar's stomach roiled. "My foreskin? You don't mean to...you can't truly mean to—"

"Circumcise you?" Goda gloated. "I can't wait to hear you scream louder than old Brynhild."

Kadar broke out in a cold sweat and his loins curled up tight. "As long as you don't kiss me, I don't care what you do."

The soldiers chuckled.

"When will you learn to shut that big mouth of yours?" Obodas hissed, breathing heavily.

Goda's face turned bright red, looking like his head was going to explode. He waved the priest forward. "Cut him. Feel free to make it slow, painful and messy."

The sallow-faced man knelt down, unrolled his bundle of tools, pulled out a silvery, hooked instrument, and inspected the working end.

Kadar's head spun sickeningly and his breath backed up into his lungs.

The priest's hot, sweaty hand seized Kadar's leg.

Kadar twisted and thrashed. The leather straps cut into his forehead and ankles. "Get away from me, you filthy dog!"

Strong fingers squeezed Kadar's stones, ripping a guttural cry from his gut. Unable to curl up, his muscles strained against the blinding pain shooting through him.

The priest's hot breath raked Kadar's face. "Stay still!"

Kadar struggled to draw a breath. Then searing pain knifed through him. Warm blood pooled on his belly and oozed down his thighs. Through a thin blanket of black dancing before his eyes, Kadar watched the priest wave a red-smeared strip of flesh in the air. Watched Goda grab the bloodied foreskin away. Watched the damnable eunuch smile triumphantly.

Kadar groaned. His manhood burning hot as fire, and his insides good as dead, he tipped his chin up, baring his neck for the mercenary's deadly sword.

Shouts and confused scrambling rang through the room. Kadar saw Brynhild knock the eunuch to the floor. Taking advantage of the hired soldiers' inattention, Obodas jumped to his feet, scooped up his discarded sword, and struck down one man, then another.

Kadar strained against the leather bands, found a small amount of give in the tie holding his head in place. He yanked his head up repeatedly, felt the band loosen. His eyes watered at the searing pain stinging his flesh. He took a deep breath, and straining, he pulled and pulled. A nail gave way with a *pop*.

Obodas's sword sliced through a wide-eyed soldier. Goda had gotten a stranglehold on Brynhild. Kadar's legs remained pinned to the ground. He sat up. A sharp stab of pain shot through him. He gritted his teeth and twisted toward Goda, slipped the horsehair rope binding his hands around the eunuch's neck, and yanked and pulled.

Goda kicked and tugged on Kadar's hands, but the spiteful man received no mercy. The eunuch's life ebbed away, then jerked to a stop.

Heart beating double time, Kadar shoved Goda aside, then searched for a sword to defend himself. A sandaled foot kicked a sword his way. He grabbed up the weapon, held it at the ready, only to see Obodas standing alone in the middle of the room. Four bodies lay sprawled on the floor. "What happened to the rest of the men?"

Obodas made a face. "Hired soldiers always run away after the man paying them dies."

A cool draft blew over Kadar's bare skin, raising his flesh. He stared down at his bloody, maimed manhood. Anger surged, then gave way to despair. He tugged his tunic down over his hips.

Brynhild grasped her broken arm and crawled over to Kadar. "It's just a bit of tissue," she reassured him. "You're alive, and you can return to my Lydia. That's what's important."

Obodas knelt beside Kadar, and worked on freeing him from the leather bands. "Leave him in peace, woman. Give him time to recover."

All the time in the world wouldn't give Kadar a new foreskin. He touched his hand to the heavy amulet lying against his chest. And he felt as lonely and lost as the day he left his village behind and set out into the unknown.

Chapter 33

Two weeks after his forced circumcision, Kadar no longer experienced burning pain with every move he made. Now all he had to contend with was the blatant stares whenever he left his bedchamber. Herod and Obodas kept assuring him Cleopatra's household would soon find something new to gossip about, but the whispers and giggles continued to plague him.

Kadar slowed when he reached the arched entryway to the private Roman bath Herod was using. The very bath Mark Antony used when visiting Alexandria. The sound of water lapping against stone mixed with the drone of male voices. A wreath of fragrant almond oil wrapped itself around him. He tugged on the neckline of his tunic. Leave it to Herod to hold a vital staff meeting in a Roman bath.

Kadar entered the vaulted chamber and walked softly across a sea of blue and green mosaic tiles.

"Don't tell me you think you can actually sneak in unnoticed," Herod called out, his booming voice echoing off murals depicting the green banks of the Nile, flourishing with exotic water birds and blue lilies.

Herod, Pheroras, and Obodas reclined on the benches lining the perimeter of the pool. Kadar exhaled heavily and lowered himself onto a marble stool sitting next to a table holding a pitcher of wine, silver cups, and bowls of bread, cheese, and grapes. He plucked up a red-veined grape and stared at it sightlessly. "Have you made any progress with Cleopatra?"

"Take off your tunic and join us in the pool," Herod ordered in a tone that said he wouldn't take no for an answer.

Never bothered by nudity, be it his own or others, Kadar

couldn't look at his own nakedness now without his face heating. He was far from ready to expose his altered state to the world. "I suppose you're trying to help. Don't!"

"Get in the pool," Herod growled.

Kadar flung the grape at the image of a black-beaked Ibis staring from a spindly stand of bulrushes. He yanked his brown linen tunic over his head. Resisting the urge to turn his back, he glared at the other three men, unwound his loincloth, and tossed it aside. Dank air rushed over exposed skin.

"Glad to see the physician didn't cut off any of your important parts," Herod observed dryly.

Obodas wagged his brows. "The women will still like you just fine."

Pheroras glanced down at his nether region, then back at Kadar's face. "I can't imagine why you're hiding. You have no reason to complain, if you ask me."

The ribbing from his fellow soldiers didn't sting as much as Kadar had feared. He walked to the edge of the pool. "Shut your mouths before I shut them for you."

His friends grinned like fools.

Kadar allowed himself a small smile before diving into the cool pool. He swam underwater to the opposite wall, reemerged, and wiped the water from his face. "Will Cleopatra help you raise an army or is she still toying with you?"

Herod's black eyes lost their glitter. "Her Royal Highness is still insisting I fight Nabatea and King Malichus before she will help me retake Jerusalem. My spies tell me Mark Antony won't return to Egypt until next spring at the earliest." Herod pushed a wall of water away from his body with his arms. "I don't think I have any choice but to go to Rome."

The trip meant their loved ones would be stranded atop Masada for months longer. Time Hasmond and Parthia would use to strengthen their defenses. Time enough for people to forget about Herod.

"I think you should continue to work on changing Cleopatra's mind," Pheroras said.

Obodas scratched his trim beard. "Going to Rome is a big

risk."

Kadar hated the idea of going even farther away from Lydia. "Will Antony help us?"

Herod looked like he had bitten into a sour grape. "Antony should be here himself, ridding his provinces of the Parthian menace, instead of traipsing about Rome whoring and drinking and scheming against Octavian. With civil war looming between Antony and Octavian, we might not merit an audience with either of them, much less squeeze support out of them."

Kadar rolled his shoulders. "We don't have any other options, do we?"

"No," Herod said and blew out a frustrated breath. "I agree with Pheroras. Cleopatra is our best hope for now."

Obodas climbed to his feet. Water sheeted off his massive body. "I'll shrivel up like rotted fruit if I stay in this pool any longer."

"I need to write a letter to my son," Pheroras said, following Obodas out of the pool. The two men strolled off toward the dressing chamber.

Herod swam to Kadar's side of the bath.

Kadar lowered himself further into the refreshing water. "I'm going to stay a bit longer."

Herod reached out and tapped the hammer-shaped amulet hanging on a black leather cord around Kadar's neck. "Still holding onto your pagan ways, I see."

"I am a pagan."

"Are you?" Herod gaze slid down, then back up. "You can find a physician who can restore your foreskin."

Kadar winced and covered himself. "Don't jest, you big ox."

A white-toothed smile lit Herod's face. "I'm not. Some Hellenistic Jews resort to epispasm."

"I don't care what you call it, I won't allow a physician to come anywhere near me with needle and thread in hand."

"You giants are all big babies."

Kadar batted the water. "Go bother someone else."

Herod laughed. "The difficult part is behind you."

"What do you mean?"

Herod made a clipping motion with his fingers.

Kadar winced again. "Circumcision?"

Herod sobered. "I thought getting cut might have been holding you back from converting. You are with us in heart and spirit. I can see it in your eyes, hear it in your voice. Your problem is, you haven't admitted it to yourself yet."

Kadar frowned. "I'm a pagan."

Herod shook his head. "Tell yourself that all you want...if it makes you feel better."

"What do you know—"

Herod lunged for the edge of the pool, dragged himself out, and strode off.

"I'm a pagan!" The words echoed uselessly around the empty chamber. Kadar surged through the water and thrashed his way to the opposite wall. His breath heavy in his ears, he plucked the amulet up and ran his thumb over the embossed medallion.

Traitor. A traitor to his gods, to his father, to his people for even thinking about converting.

He studied the amulet.

Water lapped against tile, mocking him. His gods were silent, his father was dead, his people would kill him if he tried to return.

He'd been telling himself, all this time, that everything he was doing was for Lydia's sake. Lydia needed his help. He was fighting beside Herod and Obodas for her benefit. He wanted to restore peace in Jerusalem so she would have a safe homeland.

The truth was, if he dropped dead, Lydia, Herod and Obodas would still have their families, their people, their God. He, on the other hand, would be alone and friendless without them, with no people or God to call his own.

He wrapped his fingers around the hammer-shaped amulet, but the object that had previously been a source of comfort now felt foreign to his hand.

But could he do it? Could he stop calling himself a Northman and start calling himself a Jew?

Chapter 34

Jerusalem - *One Day Later*

James pulled red-headed Niv aside before entering the airy judgment hall. "Are you sure it was Lazarz?"

The multitude arriving to witness Hasmond Mattathias strip John Hycranus of power filed past.

The boy rolled his eyes. "I saw Lazarz when High Priest Hasmond paraded High Priest Hycranus in chains up the street. Who is the true high priest, anyway?"

The spectacle was all everyone in Jerusalem wanted to talk about. "Who cares?" James snapped. "Worry about your neck, if you want to worry about something."

"At least, we spotted One-Eye before he found us," Niv said.

"Lazarz must have joined Hasmond shortly after he poisoned Antipater and vanished from the city."

"You mean after I poisoned Antipater."

"Shhh," James glanced about. "Do you want to lose your head?"

"What does it matter? It's just a matter of time before Lazarz kills me...and you."

"Remind me again why I bothered saving your sorry neck."

"You wanted me to spy for you." Niv's freckle-faced smile faded. "Here comes your father."

James's stomach pitched. "Keep your mouth shut and follow my lead." He stepped into his father's path. "I need to have a word with you."

Simeon Onias blinked his surprise "Here?"

"The matter is urgent. It involves Talitha's death."

"Why are you coming to me instead of Gabriel and Cousin Nehonya?"

"You have influence and connections."

His father smiled with satisfaction. "Ahhh, you *have* been paying attention to my messages and letters."

James bit back an insult and placed his hand on Niv's shoulder. "This boy saw a man wearing a patch over his eye, and who is named Lazarz, remove the red warning flag from Gabriel's front door. The men who attacked Gabriel said they didn't see a flag."

A strange look entered his father's eyes, then vanished. "Did he?"

Red-haired Niv nodded vigorously. "I will swear an oath if—"

"Save your confession for a trial," James said, jabbing Niv. "I'm concerned for Niv's safety. Lazarz already tried to kill him once." The lie was a small one. Lazarz had actually tried to kill James. But Lazarz probably also planned to send Niv to an early grave.

His father folded his manicured hands. "I'm familiar with this Lazarz fellow. He is Hasmond's new commander."

"He was Malichus's man," James said. "I would watch your back around him."

"Why the sudden interest in my welfare, Son?"

James's hands balled. "It became my business when your so-called allies caused Talitha's death."

"You can stop worrying. I'll deal with Lazarz."

"You'll have him arrested?"

"There's a war going on. People die."

Stunned at the lengths his father was willing to go to reach the heights of power, James covered his ears. "I don't want any part of this."

"James and I threw stones down on Lazarz's head when Hasmond's army invaded," Niv announced proudly.

James winced. "That was different."

His father examined Niv with interest. "As I said, people die all the time in wars."

The appearance of the royal procession put an end to the

uncomfortable conversation.

His father tilted his chin toward the high-ceilinged chamber. "Cousin Nehonya and Gabriel saved a seat for you."

James dismissed Niv and hurried to a stone bench at the front of the room, a place of honor reserved for their family thanks to his father's mischief-making. James sat beside Gabriel. The strain of Talitha's death showed in the heavy lines etched on Gabriel's handsome face. Feeling guilty and stained by his father's sins, James's mood became thoroughly morose when his father sat down next him.

King Hasmond wore a triumphant smile as he rode by on his plush sedan chair. Lazarz and other close aides followed on Hasmond's heels.

Lazarz aimed a nasty smile at James.

James slouched in his seat, disgusted with himself and his father.

A rattling sound came from the back of the chamber. James twisted around and saw High Priest Hycranus shuffling down the aisle in shackles.

He gave his father an incredulous look. "Chains?"

"Hasmond is a bit dramatic."

"John Hycranus is the High Priest of Israel."

"This isn't my doing."

Ankles swelled like ripe melons, John Hycranus hobbled to a stop in front of the royal dais.

Hate marring his rat-shaped face, Hasmond stood and pointed. "Behold the wicked viper who killed my father and brother, the ravenous wolf who chased me from my home and country, the vile buzzard who picked the bones of Jerusalem after displacing me from my throne."

The charges were beyond laughable. Rome had executed Hasmond's father and brother after they repeatedly conspired to start wars. Flabby and old, John Hycranus couldn't have looked more harmless or lost. When it came to pillaging, Hasmond and the Parthians made the Romans look like schoolboys.

Hasmond paced the dais. "I'm through with your treachery, Uncle. I hereby strip you of the title of High Priest and banish you to Parthia."

Tears streamed down John Hycranus's fat cheeks. "I'll go willingly. Remove the shackles and I will go quietly to Parthia."

"Willingly?" Hasmond shouted,. Then he jumped from the dais, grabbed a dagger from a startled guardsman, and charged at John Hycranus.

The portly man raised his arms over his head.

"Hold his arms down," Hasmond raged at his personal guard.

James cringed, sure Hasmond was deranged. Shocked exclamations ricocheted around the chamber.

Two guardsmen wrestled Hycranus's arm to his stout sides. Hasmond pinched his uncle's earlobe. James's nightmares played out before his eyes as Hasmond dragged the knife across John Hycranus's head, slicing off the High Priest's entire ear. Hycranus screamed pitifully. Blood gushed.

The room spun. The terror James had experienced at the hand of the bandits returned in suffocating force.

A man across the aisle vomited. Dismayed cries echoed through the chamber.

Hasmond gave the knife to a guard. "Take the other ear off."

The grim-faced, guard nodded.

Red blood oozing onto his white tunic, John Hycranus blubbered like a baby.

Men jumped to their feet. Shouts of protest filled the chamber. Armor-clad soldiers spilled through the doorways.

James covered his ears, but couldn't block out the sound of John Hycranus's next high-pitched howl. Soldiers dragged Hycranus out of the chamber.

Hasmond righted his red-splotched tunic, settled back on his throne, and conferred with his aides.

"Take deep breaths," Gabriel said.

"What just happened?" James choked out.

A ghost of the vibrant man he'd been a few short days ago, Gabriel shook his head. "I never thought to witness such evil in Jerusalem. The nations will heap disdain and judgment on our people and our family when they learn of the disgraceful treatment of the Lord's anointed High Priest."

The family would bear the great shame his father had brought down on their heads for generations. All for the sake of his father's selfish desire.

James looked between Hasmond and his father. "You formed an alliance with that vile creature?"

"Send your sour looks elsewhere. I had nothing to do with this."

"But you're pleased. I can see it."

His father shrugged. "Hycranus now belongs to the ranks of the marred. That only leaves Hasmond standing between me and the office of High Priest"

Hostile stares came from all quarters. The scar on James's face pulsed to the heavy thumps of his heart. He wanted to curl up into a ball and disappear, but he kept his chin up and cursed his father under his breath.

Chapter 35

Off the Coast of Rhodes - *One Month Later*

Forced to set sail during the most treacherous time of the year, the small ship carrying Herod's delegation listed perilously to one side. A powerful storm raging around him, Kadar struggled to keep his footing on the heaving deck. A cold slap of sea water mixed with torrential rain hit Kadar in the face, soaking him further. He shifted the sack of grain to his left shoulder, shuffled over the slick planks, grabbed hold of the handrail, and heaved the sack overboard.

He turned around and caught Herod's sleeve, keeping the exhausted man from falling on his backside. Together, they hoisted a barrel of pickled fish up onto the rail and pushed it over the side.

They clung to side of the ship and peered at the strip of land appearing and disappearing behind the waves.

"That's all of it," Herod said breathing heavily. They'd tossed away every item the captain had said was expendable. Conditions had deteriorated to the point where it was necessary to toss overboard everything they could lay their hands on. "Now all we can do is pray the ship holds together until we reach shore."

"I haven't stopped praying." Praying to Lydia and Herod's God. Kadar touched his father's amulet. "Not long ago I would have said the gods were against us, but I don't believe it any longer."

"We will survive," Herod uttered with grim determination. "We must. Who will avenge my father and brother's murders if I don't?" Herod turned his onyx eyes on Kadar. "We will live. You will see Lydia again."

Kadar squeezed Herod's shoulder. "I'm ready to follow you to Hades and back if it means keeping Lydia safe."

The boat rushed forward on the wings of a white-capped wave. Kadar and Herod gripped the railing and braced their feet on the deck. A wall of seawater washed over them. Kadar spit, wiped his eyes, and gasped at the sight of the rocky shore looming large. The next wave drove the ship onto a stone-strewn spit of land, knocking them off their feet.

Kadar rolled to a sudden stop against the wooden mast, cracking his head hard. He sat up and rubbed his skull. "I didn't break anything. How about you?"

Herod lay close by, stretched out flat on his back. "I've landed harder after getting thrown from a horse."

Sailors and soldiers swarmed the rail, giddy with relief now the ship was beached.

Kadar stood and gave Herod a hand up. They climbed over the rail and dropped to the beach. The leaden sky continued to send torrents of rain down on their heads.

"Will she float again?" Herod asked the group of sailors inspecting the damaged vessel.

"Our old tub looks finished," one of them yelled above the pounding rush of the sea. "Ships are in short supply. You'll probably have to have one built."

Kadar frowned at Herod. "Do you have the funds for a new boat?"

"No." He laughed and shook the rain from his wooly head. "But I do have friends in Rhodes."

Kadar grinned. "Of course you do."

"Finding a boat builder and supplies for a ship might slow us down."

"Leave it to me," Kadar said.

Herod nodded. "This detour will add months to our journey."

The euphoria of survival quickly faded. Kadar stared out

at the sea separating him from Lydia. "I was almost convinced Cleopatra would lend us help. Our time was wasted. We should have left sooner for Rome."

Herod clapped Kadar on the back. "Cleopatra has toyed with better men than us. Get me a ship, and I will get you back to Lydia before she forgets who you are."

"Will Mark Antony be as slippery to deal with as Cleopatra?"

"Antony's a different breed. He either loves you, or hates you, but at least you know where you stand. The problem will come if we catch him in the middle of a drinking, gambling, whoring streak."

"You're not helping my doubts."

Herod's lips pursed. "Don't worry about Antony. I'm not."

Except Kadar could see Herod wasn't at ease about the matter.

Chapter 36

Masada

Lydia stood between Avda and Old John, peering into the depths of the stone cistern. A cool draft rushed over her hot, dry brow. "How much longer will the water last?" she asked. The food stores were plentiful, but the winter rains were late in coming.

"A few weeks at most," Avda said.

Arm missing from just below the elbow, Old John rubbed his healed stump. "I heard the men talking this morning. Joseph wants to take two hundred of his men and try to fight his way through the small army camped at the foot of the Snake Path."

Lydia wasn't overly fond of Joseph, who was much rougher in manner than Herod, but the two brothers were made from the same brave, hard-charging material. "What will Joseph do if he's able to escape?"

Old John's cackle echoed around the cistern. "Half the men think he should go to Petra to ask for help, the other half think they won't be going anywhere because they'll be dead."

Lydia frowned. "I don't understand what you find so amusing."

The old man continued to smile. "The naysayers...the soldiers who say Joseph is undertaking a suicidal mission...most of them volunteered for the expedition themselves."

Lydia swiped away the stray wisps of hair dancing over her face. "Why would they do that?"

Old John drummed his fingers on the rim of the cistern. "They're bored to death. Hate being cooped up. I'd have been first in line to volunteer."

Fond of the grizzled soldier, who had been acting as her protector since recovering from his injury, Lydia cringed. "Truly?"

Old John sobered. "Soldiers would rather die with a sword in their hand than perish from thirst."

"Two hundred fewer men to parse the water out to will buy the rest of us a few more days, at least," Avda said.

Dry-throated for days now, Lydia swallowed, only to feel thirstier than ever. "You are both disgustingly practical." She turned away from the cistern, walked to the low wall edging the plateau, and stared across the vast, empty plain. Why hadn't Kadar returned?

Like guardian angels ready to assist her if she tripped or fell, Avda and Old John took up positions on either side of her.

She twisted her hands together. "What's keeping them? They've been gone for over two months." There. She'd said it. Voiced the unease chafing her bones.

Old John patted her back. "Kadar and Herod will come back. Building an army is slow work, that's all, nothing more."

Twelve hours later Lydia woke to the sound of rain pounding on the mud roof. The young women sleeping around her stirred, jumped up, embraced, and laughed.

Lydia rose and gazed upward. *Thank you, Lord, for granting our prayers.*

Kitra's tinkling giggle filled Lydia's ear. Thin arms wrapped around her. "I'm so happy I think I might burst from joy."

Finding a bit of empathy for the trying girl, Lydia hugged her back. "The jars we placed outside should be full of water."

Kitra gave her a smacking kiss. "Let's go dance in the

rain and drink jugs and jugs of water."

Lydia smiled. "Go. Hurry before it stops raining."

Kitra and the other girls squealed with delight and raced outside.

Sheets of water sliced across the open doorway. A refreshing, clean scent swirled through the stale chamber. The small mountain fastness rang with glad shouts.

Lydia stepped outside, lifted her face to the rain. A reprieve. Thank the Lord, they'd received a few months' reprieve. Drenched to the skin, she shivered, but it wasn't wholly due to the wintery cold. *Wherever Kadar is, keep him safe and well*, she prayed.

Chapter 37

Rome - *Two Month Later*

After months of delay, spent harassing the shipbuilders to hurry with the construction of the three-tier trireme, the last thing Kadar wanted was to watch a bunch of actors prance about a stage, but Mark Antony had insisted. Arriving in Rome less than an hour earlier, Herod's delegation had gone straight to Antony's home and found him leaving for the Theatre of Pompey.

They plunged back into the bustle of Romans going about their daily business. A string of twenty oxen carts rattled down the street going the opposite direction. Loaded down with oversize wine jars, Kadar grit his teeth against the clinking and clanking of the jars and the mournful bellows of the oxen.

They round a corner and the street grew wider, and the columned facade of the Theatre loomed ahead. Smoke from vendors selling roasted pigeons enveloped them. A troupe of dwarfs jugglers drew laughs and coins in appreciation of their hilarious antics and off-colorful jests.

Kadar and Obodas brought up the rear as they joined the jostling crowd climbing the white-marble to the theatre. Excited as a child on feast day, Mark Antony herded Herod and Pheroras to a private seating area at the front of a massive open-air amphitheatre abuzz with merriment. Antony, the second man of the current Triumvirate ruling Rome, snatched a large silver goblet from a pretty slave girl, drained the contents, and exchanged the empty cup for a full one.

Taking a seat on a stone bench behind Herod and Antony, Kadar and Obodas exchanged dubious looks.

Antony elbowed Herod. "What do you think of the place? I remember you used to drool over grand palaces and fortresses and aqueducts."

"We are in for a treat, if the actors are half as dramatic as the theatre," Herod said.

A slave boy offered Kadar a cup of wine. He refused and stared up at the impressive stage, admiring a multi-storied, columned backdrop worthy of the gods. Romans took their entertainments seriously.

Herod hitched his thumb over his shoulder. "This is my friend Kadar's first visit to a theatre."

Antony saluted Kadar with his silver cup. Ten years older than Herod, Antony had the papery, faded complexion of a man who didn't get enough sleep and who drank and ate too much. "The actors are staging one of my favorite comedies. The play is in Latin, but you should be able to follow the story easily."

Impatient with the small talk, Kadar wanted answers. Would Mark Antony provide the assistance they needed? Were they wasting their time?

Herod shot Kadar a keep-your-mouth-shut look, then turned to Antony. "I told my father Jerusalem needs a theatre. Traveling actors came to our home in Idumea a few times, but my father said Jerusalemites would never stand for a theatre in their midst."

"Please accept my condolences," Antony said. "Your father and brother were good men. Two of the best soldiers I've had the privilege of marching beside."

Sadness shadowed Herod's face. He cleared his throat. "You helped my father oust Hasmond from Jerusalem. I've come to ask you to do the same for me."

Antony slugged back another cup of wine. "I wish I'd been there to stop Parthia. Though it pains me to speak ill of my dead wife, I had no choice but to return to Rome when I learned of Fulvia's plot against Octavian. I planned to wring her conniving neck, but she died before I reached Rome."

"I'm sorry for your loss," Herod said.

Antony slumped forward. "I had to marry Octavian's

mousy sister to smooth matters." A sheepish look crossed his rugged face. "Did Cleopatra say anything to you about my marriage to Octavia?"

"Cleopatra poured her venom upon Octavian's head," Herod said soothingly. "But she is convinced you will get the best of him yet."

Kadar blew out an impatient breath. If this lovesick drunk was their best hope, they were in deep trouble.

Antony straightened. "Thank you for this excellent news. I plan to return to the east once I have secured my standing in Rome, and turn my attention to driving Parthia out of my provinces. I need men I can trust ruling in places like Judea and Syria."

Though his whole future was at stake, Herod remained outwardly calm. "If you give me funds to raise an army, I will repay your trust very generously. We've fought side by side on the battlefield. You know I won't run in the face of trouble."

"You always were a brash pup," Antony said. "I like boldness in a man. I'll arrange for you to meet with Octavian." His smile faded. "The haughty weakling is a weight tied around my leg. I can't make a move without consulting my *dear* brother-in-law."

For the first time in months, Herod smiled a real smile. "Take me to see Octavian, and I'll do the rest."

"Is tomorrow soon enough?"

"I see you haven't changed either. Charge in and get the job done."

The actors took the stage and the hum coming from the tiered seats behind them died out.

Satisfied they'd done all they could that day, Kadar relaxed in his seat.

A man wearing a brown mask rode a donkey to the middle of the stage. Painted tears flowed down the lifelike mask. Behind him a white-masked woman and a purple-robed rich man appeared on a second story balcony. The rich man pulled the woman close and tried to kiss her. She resisted, but her ardent admirer refused to give up. The man in the brown mask beat on his chest, clearly tortured by what he observed.

Obodas leaned toward Kadar. "The women's parts are all played by men. After seeing my first play, I wanted to kill Herod for not telling me the sweet virgin I'd been lusting after was actually a pimple-faced boy."

"I thought this was supposed to be comedy," Kadar whispered.

"Wait, it gets better," Obodas assured him.

"I can think of better ways to spend my time," Kadar said pushing off the stone bench. "I'll meet you back at the rented rooms." Ignoring the unhappy look Obodas gave him, Kadar slipped into the aisle, walked briskly to a side door, and stepped out into the large garden complex abutting the theatre.

Enclosed on three sides by long, columned porches, the airy forum contained lavish fountains and marble sculptures of famed actors. Normally he went out of his way to befriend the local merchants. Today he avoided the eyes of the vendors selling food and goods from the stalls skirting the garden, and made his way toward an impressive temple complex.

He stopped in front of the first temple. White marble stairs rose to tall, slender pillars framing a massive statue of a god. He pulled the hammer-shaped amulet out from under his tunic, and ran his thumb over the embossed silver surface. Pondering the notion of giving up his gods while tucked up in his bed was one thing. He thought he might feel differently standing among the homes of the gods.

He felt nothing. The gods of Gaul and Rome held no appeal. The opposite was true—the farther he went from Lydia and Jerusalem, the more certain he became his destiny was with her, and with her people, and with her God.

He moved on to the circular, columned temple dedicated to the goddess Fortuna, wrapped his fingers around the bit of precious metal—the last link to the past, to his fellow Northmen, to his father—and dragged the leather tie over his head.

Looping the tie around the amulet, he set the small bundle on the temple steps. An all-encompassing peace took hold. He turned for the nearest gate and headed toward his next stop.

A Jewish house of prayer.

Several blocks up the smooth-paved road, he turned down a narrow alley, and stopped in front of a two-storied, crumbling plaster building with a picture of a seven-branched candelabra painted above the plain wooden door.

He lifted his hand to knock. *Thundering Thor!* Was he actually presenting himself at a synagogue as a convert to the house of Israel? Would they laugh in his face? Would he have to find new swear words? He banged again on the worn oak panel before his courage dwindled away.

A moment later the door swung inward and a bearded man, similar in age to Kadar, stared back, wide-eyed. "How may I help you?"

Kadar forced his lips into a smile, hoping it helped him appear somewhat friendly. "I would like to sit and watch you study and pray. I promise not to interfere."

The man's brows rose, but he waved Kadar in. "Come. Come. We welcome strangers among us. My name is Enoch."

"I'm one of you...recently, a new convert." Kadar felt his face heat. "I'm Kadar the Nor—Ah...Just Kadar."

Enoch studied him carefully. "This is your first visit to synagogue, I think?"

Kadar lifted his hand to his chest, vulnerable and unsure without the familiar weight of the amulet anchoring him. Coming here wasn't the best idea he'd ever had. "I've visited our Lord's Temple in Jerusalem, but I've never attended..." Bone tired, he scrubbed his face. "Maybe I should leave."

"Stay. Stay," Enoch opened the door wider. "You've been to Jerusalem. Seen the Temple? I hope to visit the Holy City one day." Awe and jubilation showed on the man's bearded face. "Come and fellowship with us, my relations and brethren will be as anxious and delighted as I am to hear the details of your pilgrimage and conversion."

Kadar ducked under the lintel and breathed in the cinnamon and balsam-scented air filling the small anteroom. "I'll try not to do anything that offends you. But this is all new to me."

Enoch walked to one of three doors and pulled it open. "First you will need to cleanse yourself in our ritual bath."

Kadar's joints tightened. "I am...ah...circumcised. Do you need proof? Or—"

"We are not going to inspect you. Your word is enough." Enoch smiled to himself. "You might have noticed we are a very modest people."

In the past Kadar had mocked and laughed at the typical Jew's shyness over nudity, but today he gained a new appreciation for it. He stepped into a dank, closet-sized chamber consisting of small landing area with enough room for a bench and niches holding towels and clean tunics, and a rough-walled pool partitioned down the middle, with a set of stairs on both sides. He looked back at the bearded man. "Tell me how to do this properly."

"It's simple, really. You walk down one side of the stairs unclean, immerse yourself in the water, and emerge out of the pool up the other side of the stairs symbolically clean, fit to say prayers and read the words of the Law and the prophets."

"I can't read," Kadar confessed with regret. "And I don't know how to pray."

"I will count it an honor to read in your place and to teach you to pray."

The tightness in Kadar's shoulders eased. "Do you have a tunic large enough to fit me?"

Good-natured laughter echoed off plastered walls. "I doubt it. The ones here aren't used often. Almost everyone brings a second set of clothes."

"I'll make do." Kadar sat on the bench and began unlacing his sandals. The door clicked shut. Dim light cast by a trio of wall sconces bounced over the dark water. He stood, peeled off his tunic and descended the stairs on the right. Cool water engulfed his knees, then his thighs, then his chest, and finally his neck.

Not sure what to do next, he recalled one of Lydia's stories, one to do with a captain of the Syrian army who, after he was healed from the scourge of leprosy, gave his allegiance to the God of Israel. Kadar bowed his head. "I confess before the heavens...there is no other God in the world, but in Israel. From this day forward, your servant will offer neither burnt offering nor sacrifice unto other gods, but unto the Lord God."

He dipped under the water, floated in place, then burst free. Climbing up the other stairs, water cascading off his body, he rose a new man.

Chapter 38

Two Days Later

The whole mission and future hanging in the balance, Kadar watched Herod pace in front of a chest-high marble fireplace framed by four Corinthian columns.

He wasn't used to seeing Herod rattled, but today's meeting with Octavian had Herod on edge. Kadar, Pheroras, and Obodas stood clustered in the middle of the lavishly decorated reception chamber sharing an uneasy silence.

Carved double doors at the back of the chamber swung open, and the heir to Julius Caesar's wealth, Octavian, a young man about twenty-five years old made a stately entrance. The curly headed, soft-cheek lad walked with pomp to a blue-cushioned reclining chair perched on a small raised dais. The regal youth sat on his faux throne, and pointed at the gold-cushioned couches arranged around the low marble platform. "Herod of Idumea, I have heard much about you. Come and share your story with me."

Kadar sat off to the side, half listening to Herod recite the events of the last few months.

"He looks like a spoiled, pampered fool," Obodas whispered in Kadar's ear.

Kadar nodded, but quickly changed his mind, thanks to the young man's perceptive questions, and clever eyes that missed nothing. Mark Antony had good cause to worry about Octavian, who had already trounced him on the battlefield.

Kadar sat forward when Herod finished his story, convinced Octavian's judgment would ultimately decide matters.

Octavian's eyes brightened. "My adopted father, Caesar,

shared stories with me about the wars you and your father helped him win. He spoke of your great hospitality and what great friends you were to Rome. Your brave actions in the face of grave danger from Hasmond and Parthia prove you, like your father, are a man of merit."

Herod flashed his white smile. "Your father excelled at all he put his hand to. His praise means much to me, as does yours."

Octavian clapped for an aide. "I will call the senate together tomorrow and present your case to them." He turned from them to confer with his secretary.

Herod spoke behind his hand to Kadar and Obodas. "With the weight of Antony and Octavian's full support behind us, the senate is sure to fall in line."

"Don't allow Antony and Octavian to drag this out with meeting after meeting," Kadar said, dreading the possibility of long, drawn-out sessions where the issue would be talked to death.

"Take my place if you think you can do better," Herod growled.

Obodas interceded. "You have more patience for negotiations, Herod."

"I won't breathe easy until we rescue our loved ones from Masada," Kadar said by way of an apology.

Obodas squeezed Kadar's shoulder. "Be patient, my friend."

Herod winked. "And try smiling. You look about as personable as a charging bear."

Kadar scrubbed his face. "I'll take a battlefield over reception chambers and banquet halls any time."

Two Days Later

The Roman senate assembled with due pageantry to hear Herod's case. Kadar stood at the back of the chamber between Pheroras and Obodas, watching the solemn proceedings with his heart in his throat. Herod was seated between Antony and

Octavian. Two experienced orators took turns singing Herod's praises and decrying Hasmond's actions.

When the second orator left the podium, Mark Antony rose. "My fellow senators, after hearing of Herod's loyal service to Rome, I think you will agree with me we should throw our full support behind him."

"Aye, aye," the initial murmurs of support grew and grew until the chamber reverberated with the senate's full approval.

Herod inclined his head, acknowledging the tremendous honor.

The room quieted, and Antony placed his hand on Herod's shoulder. "I propose we reward our friend, Herod of Idumea, with the title King of Judea."

"Aye, aye," the chorus of approval was louder this time.

Herod looked stunned, although Kadar doubted the honor came as a shock. Antony and Herod had holed up in private the previous evening. A meeting Herod had remained cagey about.

The commotion died down. A vote was called for. The result, a foregone conclusion, Herod was named king.

"Good luck! The gods' speed!" the toga-clad men at the back of the hall yelled.

Herod's wide smile lit up the chamber.

Kadar bumped his elbows into Pheroras and Obodas's sides. "That couldn't have gone better."

The two men frowned.

Which put a hitch in Kadar's jubilation. "What?"

Pheroras shrugged and glanced away, then looked back at Kadar. "Almost all of Judea and Galilee will decry Rome's decision to name an Idumean half-breed king. And the zealots, who already hate Rome and Herod, will fight against us with renewed zest."

A veteran of many wars, Obodas stared ahead blankly, no doubt envisioning past combat or battles yet to come. "If you thought our backs were against the wall before, just wait till word of this spreads. Recruiting an army will be that much more difficult. Our friends will be few and far between. I'd rather have seen Herod made king after the war was won, but he's not the kind to wait for what he wants."

Kadar watched Mark Antony and Octavian honor Herod by escorting him to the head of a long procession. A golden crown was brought forward, and Antony placed the thin circlet over Herod's rough black curls. "When did this ambition to be king form?"

"Herod would never admit it," Obodas said wryly, "but he came out of the womb wanting to wear a crown."

Pheroras smiled. "My father would laugh and laugh, recalling Herod in his swaddling clothes, ordering us boys around like he was a general and we were his foot soldiers." If Pheroras begrudged his younger brother for seeking the honor and responsibility normally reserved for an elder son, he hid it well.

Head held high, Herod walked up the aisle ensconced in the place of honor between Antony and Octavian. Toga-clad senators came next in line, followed by lesser dignitaries.

Kadar nodded a salute at *King* Herod. Yes, more trouble waited them. But Herod intended to leave Rome for the journey back to Judea in two or three days. Which was enough for now.

Chapter 39

Joppa - *Two Months Later*

Working nonstop since their return home, Herod had raised an impressive army comprised of Jewish soldiers and gentile mercenaries. As the army moved south through Galilee, almost everyone threw their support behind Herod, reflecting their displeasure with the wartime atrocities committed by Hasmond and the Parthians.

Pockets of resistance still existed, however. The anti-Herod forces occupying the coastal city of Joppa were the last stronghold standing between Herod and Idumea and Masada. The Roman army dispatched to rescue Herod's family from Masada had loitered outside of Jerusalem instead, thanks to Hasmond's bribes. Stern orders from Rome had convinced the commander to march to Herod's assistance.

The forward scouts had alerted them the moment the anti-Herod forces had left the confines of Joppa to harass the Roman army. The midday sun beating down of their heads, Herod's untested army hunkered down next to a rutted road, waiting for the enemy to appear.

Kadar's blood thrummed through his limbs. He gripped and re-gripped his sword and stared through a screen of green palm fronds, waiting for the anti-Herod forces pursuing the Roman army to draw closer, waiting for Obodas to give the signal to launch the ambush, anxious for the fight to be over so he was that much closer to a reunion with Lydia.

Hunched over at an uncomfortable angle, Herod trotted up on foot and stopped beside Kadar. "The devils are almost where we want them."

"A surprise attack ought to get us off to a good start."

"What do you think...will my newly forged army hold together?"

Occupied the last two months gathering arms and armor rather than the training of the army, Kadar glanced about at the boiling mass of soldiers braced to charge onto the road below. "Obodas is a first-rate commander. His handpicked troops won't let you down."

"They aren't as oversized as you...or as ugly, but they'll do," Herod said smiling.

"This is the thanks I get for risking my hide so you can have your throne?"

Herod wagged his black brows. "Your reward awaits you in Masada."

Kadar tightened his sword grip as Obodas rose from the shelter of the long grass and gestured for them to move out.

Swords hissed from sheaths. Herod stepped out in front of the line and lifted his curved blade skyward. Stomach roiling with a strange mix of dread and anticipation, Kadar hefted his shield and his sword.

Herod slashed his weapon through the air, gave a bloodcurdling yell, and charged down the hill.

The ululating war cry of his fellow soldiers rang in his ears. Kadar pounded after Herod. Thighs burning, he burst through the leafy palms one step behind Obodas and Herod, and right into the heart of the anti-Herod forces nipping at the heels of the Roman army.

Surprised and shocked, the enemy rounded and came at them in a chaotic, undisciplined mass. Kadar blocked a blow from a sword, swung his blade under his shield, and cut his opponent's legs out from under him. He leaped over the jerking body and faced down two snarling combatants. Repelling both slashing blades with his shield, he rammed ahead, knocking one of the men off his feet. He held his shield in a defensive position and stabbed his sword into the fallen soldier's chest. Blood welled around the blade.

Another loud war cry filled the air.

Kadar looked up, and saw the Roman army was throwing their weight into the battle. The soldier he was facing down glanced about like a trapped animal.

Breathing heavily, Kadar pointed his sword at the ground. "Get down on your belly." Pinched between two pulverizing forces, they both knew the Herod-hating Jews were already defeated.

The frightened man dropped to one knee. A sword sliced through the air, taking the man's head off his shoulders.

Kadar flinched.

Face flecked with blood, Herod stepped over the dead man's crumpled body and squeezed Kadar's arm. "No one lives."

"They're Jews...one of us."

Herod's black eyes iced over. "No one lives."

A wild-eyed soldier charged at Herod. Kadar pushed Herod aside and raised his shield, blocking a blow from a bloody sword. He backed up, bracing for the next strike, and tripped over the man Herod had cut down. Kadar landed hard on his back. His sword flew from his hand.

The wild-eyed man gripped his sword with two hands and hacked downward.

One hand still locked on his shield, Kadar hefted it over his head. The heavy blade skittered over the side of the tilted leather oval, and struck below Kadar's elbow, burying bone-deep. Kadar cried out and reached for his arm. The wild-eyed man yanked the weapon free. Blood welled. Kadar's vision darkened and loud roaring filled his ears. The next thing he knew, a lifeless body collapsed onto his chest.

Someone dragged the corpse away. Herod's stark face loomed overhead. "We won't let you die." He tied a leather thong around Kadar's upper arm.

Obodas pressed a large brown cloth to the bloody wound. "Saul Gamala, get the bucket of hot coals!"

"Put a tunic on if you're cold," Kadar said, slurring his words like a drunk.

"I used my tunic to wrap your wound, you overgrown fool," Obodas said, his voice strained. "We have to sear the wound shut before you bleed to death."

Fear cut through the thick stupor. "It's bad, isn't it?"

"I'm surprised the fiend didn't take your arm clear off."

"It hurts like Hades...that's a good sign, right?"

Obodas's gaze slid away. "If you don't get the rot, you'll be back on your feet in no time."

Kadar pushed himself to a half-sitting position. "I'm not done. I'm going to Masada with you."

Obodas put his brawny hand on Kadar's torso and shoved him flat. "Stay still."

Kadar struggled upward. "I promised Lydia. I won't stop until I get back to her."

Obodas pushed him down again. "I'll sit on your chest if I have to."

Another wave of dizziness hit, accompanied by nausea. An image of Lydia's laughing smile danced through Kadar's mind's eye. He had to get back to her. Everything would be put right once he held her. If he still had two arms. "Promise me you won't feed me a sleeping concoction and march on without me."

Nothing. Silence.

Kadar gritted teeth. "Obodas, swear it."

"Damnation," Obodas growled. "You have my word."

Saul Gamala raced up with a copper bucket bristling with daggers—an immediate remedy for the plentiful gashes incurred during battle.

Obodas pulled a dagger free and inspected the grayish, flat blade.

"Thundering Thor!" Kadar yelled sucking in his breath. "Do it. Get it over with."

Obodas plunged the blade back into the red-hot coals. "Hold him down."

Herod knelt on Kadar's chest and held out a wide strap for Kadar to bite down on. "We crushed the local fighters. We'll start for Masada as soon as you can mount your horse."

Calling up the image of Lydia's beautiful face, Kadar crushed the tangy leather between his teeth, and squeezed his eyes shut. Searing pain followed by the stench of burnt flesh sent him spiraling into a deep, black void.

Chapter 40

Masada – *Three Days Later*

Lydia strolled past the young girls building playhouses and pretend towns out of shiny stones. The brilliant blue sky and sharp, clean breeze almost compensated for the unending monotony of the daily tasks of mending clothes, grinding grain, and hours of small talk.

Sweet-tempered Hannah spotted Lydia. The six-year-old girl bounced to her feet and rushed over. "Will you come and tell us a story or play a game?"

Lydia smiled. "You've heard all my tales."

The other girls crowded around. "Please, please," they begged.

"Make up a new one," Hannah suggested.

Lydia crossed her arms, tapping her chin, pretending to think and think, then made a silly face. They girls giggled.

Excited shouts came from the watchmen manning the gate tower.

Lydia sobered.

Hannah pressed up against her. "I wish the bad soldiers would go away."

Lydia forced a smile and patted the girl's soft curls. "We've nothing to fear. Joseph will chase them away again." Nonetheless, the mood atop the remote wilderness outpost turned gloomier every time Hasmond's troops tested the fortress' defenses.

But this time the guards' shouts were different. Jubilant. "Herod has returned!" men shouted.

Lydia's pulse quickened. She hiked up her tunic, raced to the low wall overlooking the Snake Path, and leaned out over the crumbling balustrade.

Herod came around a rocky corner and grinned up at his followers, who now lined the entire wall.

Armored men trudged over the last crest. She searched for Kadar's golden-blond head. Her breath backed up in her lungs. Where was he? More soldiers came, but Kadar wasn't among them. A few stragglers came over the knoll. She waited and waited for Kadar to appear. Her gut twisted. Something horrible had happened.

Then two men lumbered into view. A dark head and a blond head. "Praise the Lord," she said on a sob, sagging against the stone wall. But all was not well—Kadar's broad shoulders were stooped. His sword hung from his left hand. His right arm was in a sling.

Obodas spotted her and pointed.

Kadar lilted his chin. Although his face was dangerously pale and lined with pain, he smiled brilliantly when he spotted her.

Crying and laughing, she waved, dabbed her eyes, and waved again with both hands. Unable to stand still a moment longer, she raced to the gate, pushed through a flood of soldiers, rushed down the incline, and threw herself at Kadar. He staggered backward.

She gasped and clutched his tunic—not that she had a hope in heaven of keeping his massive body from toppling over. "I'm sorry. Did I hurt you?"

He pulled her against his wide chest. His warm, guttural voice filled her ear. "I missed you too, my *valkyrie*."

Obodas wrestled Kadar's sword away, nodded a greeting to Lydia, and hurried on to the fortress.

She pressed her face into his muscled neck. He smelled of sweat and horse and health. *Praise God!* "What happened? How are you?"

His large hand stroked her back. "The wound is healing well, but I lost a lot of blood. I guess that tortuous climb more work than I was ready for. Herod and Obodas told me to wait at the base of the mountain." His rumbling laugh reverberated through her. "I won't repeat the names they called me when I refused."

She wrapped one arm around his back. "Lean on me. I want Avda to look at the wound."

Kadar exhaled a heavy breath. "How is Hama?"

"He is a wonderful physician and a kind friend. He will take good care of you."

"I'll let him poke at me, if it will make you happy."

"Kadar!" Old John trotted toward them.

A dark shadow crossed Kadar's face. "John, I see the mountain air agrees with you."

The one-armed man halted. Wheezing heavily, he grimaced. "Obodas said you got winged a good one."

Kadar flapped his bandaged arm. "I should have use of it again soon."

Old John massaged his stump. "Herod did well for himself. I hear he is gathering quite the army."

Kadar smiled. "Herod's victory in Joppa impressed his doubters, so people are flocking to him, hoping to gain his good favor when he overthrows Hasmond. Parthia's abominable actions throughout the region have helped Herod's cause. The people blame Hasmond for not restraining the Parthian army."

The one-armed man's shoulders sagged. "I hate that I missed the battle. I don't think I'll ever get used to sitting at home while my friends are marching to war."

Kadar leaned more heavily on Lydia. "Don't put away your sword yet. I need you to keep watching over Lydia."

Old John gave her a shy smile. "I count it an honor, if your good woman doesn't mind continuing to put up with a gimpy old dog like me."

"I found your company very pleasant," Lydia assured him. Kadar was worried about how she'd fare living at a fortress surrounded by untamed, coarse warriors, but these last months at Masada in the company of Old John and Joseph's band of crude-mouthed men had soothed her mind on the matter.

Obodas returned with Avda in tow. "Stop your gabbing. Physician Hama wants to examine my handiwork. Make sure your wound isn't curdling."

"I hope Obodas didn't drag you away from something important," Kadar said. "The big brute worries over me like an old woman."

Lydia patted Kadar's back. "Thank you for coming, Avda."

Avda didn't meet her eyes. "It's no trouble."

Kadar pulled her closer. "The sooner I get rid of this sling the better."

"Come to the sick room and I'll take a look at it."

They proceeded toward the fortress gate. "Obodas said the sword struck your arm below your elbow?" Avda asked.

Kadar flexed his fingers and rolled his shoulder. "My hand feels weak, but the arm works fine."

Avda nodded, then glanced at Lydia. The troubled look in his eyes sent a chill through her.

Kadar winced, but the bandage came off painlessly.

Lydia's hands paused on his shoulders, then resumed their soothing massage.

Physician Hama bent to inspect the dagger-shaped scar. "I see Obodas used maggots to clean the wound. Good, good. There's no sign of rot, and no putrid odor. You won't lose your arm."

Lydia blew out her breath. "Praise the Lord."

Kadar patted her hand and wrinkled his nose. "They plastered my arm twice with the devilish white worms."

Hama straightened. "I call them miracle workers. Can you lift your arm over your head?"

Kadar raised his arm, twisted it one way, then the other. "Works fine."

Hama held out his hand. "Squeeze my fingers."

"Talk like that could get you in trouble," Kadar quipped, clasping Hama's hand.

"Tighter," Hama instructed.

Kadar stared at his stubborn fingers and willed them to curl "It's only been two weeks."

Hama's fingers pressed against Kadar's hand, then slid free. "I've seen a few injuries like yours. And..." Hama's frown grew grimmer. "And, the weakness might be permanent."

Kadar winced. "Might be?"

"Using a spoon and lifting a cup and such, you should manage fine, but you will never wield a sword again."

Lydia moaned softly and her forehead pressed against his shoulder.

"But I'm a warrior," Kadar said through numbed lips.

The physician's eyes softened. "There are soldiers whose tasks don't include fighting."

"That's not for me."

"Kadar has many talents," Lydia said jumping to his defense, every bit his fierce *valkyrie*.

Hama backed toward the door. "I'll leave you two alone to discuss matters."

"Thank you for your honesty, Avda Hama," Kadar said paying the physician the respect he'd give a fellow soldier.

Hama slipped from the room. Kadar drew Lydia forward.

She came and stood between his legs and laid her hands on his chest. "I hate them for hurting you."

He ran his hands over her lithe back and slim waist. "I can live just fine without my sword. What would have killed me was not being able to hold you and touch you."

"I don't care how we live, as long as we are together."

"You trust me completely, don't you?" he asked, humbled and amazed.

Eyes shimmering with unshed tears, she smiled. "From always and forever, my heart knew your heart."

Throat thick with emotion, he swallowed. "I can't remember not loving you. When you called on me to spirit you away from Egypt, I had to come."

A lone tear rolled down her dusty-rose cheek. "And now you can't be a soldier."

Not too long ago the blow would have devastated him, but not now. "I was born a Northman. And I thought I'd always be a warrior, but my desires have changed. I can see a different life for myself, and I want it." He covered her soft hand and held it over to the spot where the amulet used to rest. "Wherever you are is home to me. Your people are now my people. Your God is now my God."

"You don't have to. Not for me."

"I wanted to give up my idols."

She released a shuddering breath. "Do you know the story of Ruth the Moabite, the great grandmother of our King David?"

Distracted by the luminescent beauty of her smooth brown skin, he traced his finger over her jaw. "I missed the sound of your voice."

Her quiver echoed through him. "Do you want to hear Ruth's story?" she asked in a feather-soft whisper.

He tilted her chin up and skimmed his mouth over her soft, warm lips. "Stop talking and kiss me."

Her husky laugh speared through him. He buried his fingers in her silky brown hair and devoured her mouth. Her whimpering moans made his loins burn.

Someone knocked at door.

They broke off the kiss. "Come in," he hissed.

Obodas threw open the door, and strode into the sick room. "Herod wants everyone ready to leave at first light tomorrow."

Lydia sighed, then nipped his lower lip. "You better hurry up and marry me."

"Do you want me to leave?" Obodas asked, wearing a big, fat smile.

Kadar steered Lydia to his side. "You can help Lydia ready for the journey to Jerusalem."

Lydia's doe eyes widened. "Jerusalem?"

"I intend to pay your father a visit. I don't expect him to give his blessing on our marriage; nonetheless I must put the question to him."

Chapter 41

Jerusalem - *Three Days Later*

James clutched Lydia and Kadar's letter in his sweaty palms and entered Cousin Nehonya's dining chamber, where he'd learned his father would take his evening meal. James planned to wholeheartedly champion Lydia and Kadar's cause, collect his father's refusal, then leave Jerusalem to join Herod in hopes of finding a way to be useful to *King* Herod.

The first face he saw was Elizabeth's. Distracted by her pretty, long-lashed eyes and pink-blushed cheeks, he tugged on the neckline of his tunic.

"Have you finally come to your senses?" a sour voice demanded from nearby.

James directed a cold look at his so-called father. "I'm curious. The palace gossips say Hasmond did not sleep well last night. I hope you fared better?"

Herod's impressive army had arrived and set up camp outside the city the day before, leaving Jerusalemites humming with either speculation and excitement or dread and tension, depending on their loyalties.

His father smiled smugly. "Alliances can always be bought and sold. The generous bribes Hasmond has given Venditius and Silo ought to convince the Roman commanders to abandon Herod."

Though it wasn't the time or place to confront his father, James couldn't help himself. "What have your bribes bought you? I thought Hasmond was going to make you Captain of the Temple. And shouldn't Cousin Nehonya be the Temple Overseer and Gabriel be the Temple Treasurer by now? "

Cousin Nehonya shifted in his seat. Elizabeth looked

embarrassed. Locked in their own grief, Gabriel and Chloe remained insensible to the ugly exchange.

"That's because my family is no help to me," his father raged. "A rebellious son who shames me. Harlots for daughters."

"You're too harsh," Cousin Nehonya said.

Simeon rounded on his cousin. "You're no help, either."

"Why do you have to be so vicious?" Elizabeth accused.

"Shut your mouth, woman," Simeon commanded, then, pointing at his ex-wife, he narrowed his eyes at Cousin Nehonya. "Why is *she* still in Jerusalem?"

Nehonya paled. "She...what I mean...we—"

Gabriel came alive. "Don't speak to my sister in that manner!"

"Leave Elizabeth alone. She's innocent." James said, angry and sickened on Elizabeth's behalf.

His father's perpetual scowl deepened. "She's a disgrace to this family. Send her away, Nehonya, do you hear me?"

"I need time to arrange matters," Cousin Nehonya choked out.

The color drained from Elizabeth's face.

Gabriel rose, stood over Simeon and pointed at the door. "Go!" he bellowed.

Wilted as a plucked rose, Chloe reached for Elizabeth's hand. "Tell all of Jerusalem of my husband's sins. But don't take my daughter from me."

Cousin Nehonya exhaled heavily, and directed his gaze to Simeon. "I refuse to send Elizabeth away. Do what you must."

"I will do what I must." Simeon's voice dripped with sarcasm. "Cooperate or I will make sure your Samaritan mistress is stoned to death for adultery. Then I'll have you declared an unfit judge and see you stripped of your wealth and property."

Ashen-faced, Cousin Nehonya sagged in his seat.

Adorned in courage and strength, Elizabeth's back stiffened. "I'll leave Jerusalem by the end of the week."

James felt something snap. He went and stood behind

Elizabeth, laid his hand on her shoulder, and stared defiantly at his father. "Enough victims have been sacrificed on the altar of your ambition."

Elizabeth flinched. "What? Why are you—?"

"Don't touch her," his father scolded. "She's unclean."

"Not in my eyes."

"The witch has beguiled you, has she?" His father shook his head in disgust. "Your own stepmother."

Desperate to spare Elizabeth from suffering more of his father's hatefulness, James took a deep breath and did the unthinkable. "I will become the obedient son you've always wished for, but only if you allow Elizabeth to remain in Jerusalem."

He felt a tremble go through Elizabeth. "James, you don't have to do this."

But he did. He couldn't make amends for his father's many sins, for the plundering of Jerusalem, for Talitha's death, for the evil done John Hycranus, but he could stop this wrong. "Do we have a deal, *Father?*"

A grotesque smile spread across his father's face. "I will expect unquestioning loyalty from you, or I'll send the unclean witch to Outer Gaul."

Elizabeth grabbed James's hand. "What can I do to repay you?"

He stared into sad, lovely eyes. "When all of Jerusalem comes to hate me, promise me you will still think kindly of me."

"I promise," she whispered.

"Son, come and swear your fealty."

James pulled his hand free and circled the table. Hate poisoning every bone in his body, he fell on one knee before Simeon Onias.

Chapter 42

One Day Later

The midday sun beamed down on the quiet camp spread over the hillsides west of Jerusalem. After several weeks spent on the march, the soldiers were taking advantage of the lull to rest, repair equipment, sharpen weapons. Herod had sent his family to Samaria and set his sights on the arduous task of besieging a walled city.

Obodas and Herod marched toward the tent with grim-faced James Onias walking close behind. Kadar and Lydia stood. Kadar hated subjecting Lydia to the depravity and deprivations of an active army camp, but she hadn't blinked an eye at any of it. Full of amusing observations, keen questions, and ready laughter, she seemed to be thoroughly enjoying herself. Aside from wanting to punch every man in the camp for lusting after her, Kadar couldn't be prouder.

Herod and Obodas hung back.

After many long talks about their future, Kadar and Lydia had formed plans contingent upon what they learned from James.

Lydia gave her brother a quick hug. "James, you don't look well. Are you ill?"

James's lips pursed. "Speaking with father always sickens me."

"Forgive me for burdening you with my problems," Lydia said. "Was father overly angry with you when you presented my request?"

"He turned an interesting shade of purple," James remarked, a little too flippantly. "I agreed to move back home. I—"

Lydia gasped. "What's happened?"

James waved a dismissive hand. "I badgered the man for half the night, pleading your cause. I'll spare you the foul invectives and accusations we are both thoroughly acquainted with, but the gist of the matter...our loving father will have you killed before he sees you marry a barbarian, circumcised or not."

Kadar swallowed the crude oath on the tip of his tongue.

The color drained from Lydia's face. "Father threatened to kill me?"

Kadar touched his hand to the small of her back. "We don't need to hear more. Your sister and I wanted to give your father the opportunity to make things right between us."

Dark hate burned in James's eyes. "Are you going to kill him?"

Kadar shook his head. "I no longer have any desire to slay the man. I'll admit, if your father was standing in front of me now, flapping his evil lips, I might need someone to restrain me." Kadar pulled Lydia closer. "The Law of Moses says you shall not kill. Tell your father I will abide by the Lord's commandments. He'd be well advised to do the same. And tell him he should be ashamed that a converted heathen needs to remind of his own Laws."

James's shoulders sagged. "He will find a way to justify murdering both of you."

"We don't plan to give him the opportunity," Kadar said.

Lydia stood taller. "We are leaving. We are going to live far, far from here."

"You're running away?" James looked incredulous.

Kadar felt no shame. Northmen didn't walk away from an insult or a threat. Men like his half brother Jokul would call him a coward. Let them. Turning his back on blatant offenses would prove to himself and the world he was, at heart, a Jew. The tension in Kadar's bunched muscles eased. "We choose to go. Though we didn't hold much hope of receiving your father's blessing, we had to try."

Smiling a smile that would send a pack of ferocious dogs scurrying for safety, James said, "So you won't kill my father, but you will steal my sister from him. At least I'll have the immense satisfaction of regularly reminding my father of his barbarian son-in-law."

"James," Lydia said, sounding more sad than annoyed. "Promise me you won't antagonize father. I'd rather have him forget I exist than have him hate me for the rest of his life."

Kadar wasn't insulted. There was enough of the Northman left in him to rob from the weak and unworthy. His conscience was clear—a father who inspired a daughter to say such things deserved what he got. "You may never see Lydia again. Are these the last words you have to say to her?"

James sobered. "Forgive me, Sister. Anything to do with Father has a way of bringing out the worst in me."

Lydia broke away from Kadar and gave James a quick hug. "I know there's goodness and love in you. Promise you will work at heeding your better side instead of lashing out. Try to find some happiness."

Her brother's gaze slid away. "Joyful James. That will be my new name." He smoothed his hands over his black robe, making him look the image of Simeon Onias.

Lydia frowned. "Why are you clothed like a Pharisee?"

The color drained from James's face. He shoved his hand into his robe, pulled out a furled parchment secured with a scarlet cord, and handed it to Lydia. "My wedding gift."

"Wedding gift?" Lydia asked.

"Open it," James said.

Lydia untied the red bow and unrolled the scroll. Her brows arched. "A marriage contract signed by Father. But I thought—"

James looked over his shoulder, then back at them. "Don't ask any questions."

Kadar scanned the black marks on parchment. The only area in which he envied Simeon and James Onias was their ability to read and write. "There had better not be any trickery hidden in the words, forged or not."

"I'm not my father," James said through clenched teeth.

Lydia studied the document. A beautiful smile lit her face. "The dowry and *mohar* and espousal period have been set aside." She kissed Kadar on the cheek. "Once you add your mark, we will be husband and wife." Lydia hugged James again, crushing the parchment between them. "Bless you. How can I ever repay you?"

James's lips curved upward, and he set his sister at arm's length. "Don't get too excited. The document won't do you any good in this part of the world."

Kadar nodded. "We understand, and are prepared to do what we must."

The light in Lydia's eyes dimmed. "I hope this is not our last farewell. But if it is, know that wherever I am, dear James, you will be in my thoughts and prayers."

James stared past them toward Jerusalem. "The knowledge you and Alexandra are safe and happy will be consolation enough for me."

Kadar squeezed James's surprisingly sturdy shoulder. "I promise to take good care of your sister."

"Of course you will, Brother-in-Law." James met Kadar's eyes and held out his arm. "Our tradition calls for me to kiss you."

Kadar hesitated, not sure if he was being mocked.

James stepped forward, cupped Kadar's face, and kissed one cheek, and then the other. "Welcome into the family, Kadar the Righteous Proselyte."

Moved by the realization he belonged to a family, even one including Simeon Onias, Kadar slapped James on the back.

James winced. "Go careful there, Goliath."

Lydia's affectionate laugh swirled around them.

Herod and Obodas grinned from a distance.

Kadar waved his friends over. "Come, give your best wishes to my wife."

Herod wagged his bushy brows. "Wife?"

Kadar shared a smile with Lydia. "James obtained a wedding contract."

Herod charged over, grasped Kadar's head, and planted a robust kiss on each side of his face. Obodas repeated the gesture.

Resisting the urge to wipe his cheeks—the whole kissing thing would take some getting used to—Kadar slapped each of them on the back.

Herod turned his attention to James Onias. "We need to talk. I hope to procure your help."

James made sour face. "There's no need to tiptoe. You want me to spy for you. Correct?"

"Keep your voice down," Herod said.

James hitched his shoulders. "It will be our little secret."

"I'll pay you well."

"Money," James scoffed. "Kill my father. That will be payment enough."

"James," Lydia begged.

Herod shot James an impatient look. "Meet me at my tent, and we'll talk in private."

Looking sad enough for ten men, James turned and tramped off.

"James," Lydia called out. "Be sure to come say farewell before you return to the city."

Heedless, he trudged on.

Feeling protective of James, while also wanting to strangle his reckless-mouthed brother-in-law, Kadar narrowed his eyes at Herod. "Leave James out of your dangerous games."

"The boy is already up to his hips in danger. Besides, he'll have you watching over him if he steps into trouble."

Kadar pulled Lydia close. "No he won't. Lydia and I are leaving the country."

Herod crossed his arms and widened his stance. "I told you I'd find a role for you. Obodas wants to put you in charge of provisioning us and the Romans."

Kadar hated the thought of not seeing the war through, but it would kill him if Herod and Obodas were in a battle and he was sitting off to the side. His soldiering days were behind him. Amazingly, it wasn't the scary, unfathomable prospect he'd imagined. "I'm not staying, but I might be able to help from a distance. If you will lend the trireme to me."

"My ship?" Herod grinned. "Don't tell me you plan to

become a pirate."

Kadar smiled and shook his head. "There's money to be made trading and shipping goods. Your share of the profit will help fill your depleted coffers, and if you become desperate for supplies I can bring what you need from abroad."

"A merchant?" Obodas asked, clearly astounded.

Lydia patted Kadar's back, but he didn't need consoling. He was ready to move on, and would do so gladly with her at his side.

Herod studied him for a long moment. "The boat's yours."

"You'll earn your money back the first year," Kadar promised.

White teeth flashing, Herod gave Kadar's arm a friendly punch. "Let's see if we can scrounge up a proper wedding feast before sending you off to your bride's tent."

Kadar swallowed. "An army camp is hardly the place for—"

"I don't want to wait," Lydia said, her voice adamant.

His loins tightened. "But—"

She stared up at him with those irresistible doe eyes. Long lashes swept over rose-colored cheeks. "We will marry tonight."

Obodas and Herod's rumbling laughter barely registered past the blood roaring through his ears.

Soft lamplight danced over the tent walls. Air infused with the fragrance of sandalwood stroked Lydia's bare skin. Standing belly-to-belly with her beautiful warrior husband, his light blue eyes drinking her in, as they had all through the wedding feast, Lydia reached around Kadar's muscled neck and loosed the leather tie binding his golden-blond hair. Silky strands brushed her over her collarbone, sending a shiver spiraling down her spine.

"Kiss me," he whispered.

She skimmed her lips over his wide, firm mouth. A wave of heat spread through her. She pressed her lips more firmly to his, and nipped at his lower lip, pulling a groan from him.

A ravenous hunger gripped her. "Touch me," she urged.

Roughened fingers slid over the curve of her hips and along her sides. Prickles of pleasure danced over sensitive flesh. "More," she demanded, wanting his hands everywhere.

He kissed her back, but remained frustratingly gentle. His powerful muscles quaked beneath her hands. She'd experienced tastes of his keen desire. She wanted to be swept up in a whirlwind of his full, manly strength.

"I don't want to hurt you," he said his voice raspy.

"You won't."

"You deserve to be worshipped."

She nipped his lip. "I'd prefer to be ravaged."

He laughed, then groaned. "I don't know how a highborn woman should be treated."

"I'm not a delicate flower, or a frightened virgin."

"I'm a barbarian. Whores have been my only partners. I will hate myself if I use you like I want to."

Her insides contracted. She had suffered at the grasping hands of a deranged bandit and cringed at the touch of her uncle's pudgy pawing. Kadar's touch would never be ugly to her. "You are more lovely than a thousand sunsets, your touch is more precious than rare gemstones, your mouth is sweeter than golden honeycomb. Make me forget the misery of too many dark days and lonely nights. Fill all my senses until I am empty of everything except your exquisiteness."

His eyes became liquid blue pools. "I tried, but I never could deny what was between us. It was always there, wasn't it?"

"Our love for each other?"

"You felt it too?"

"From the very first."

"You deserve—"

She fisted his blond hair and yanked. "Are you going to talk all night or make me your woman?"

A gloriously untamed look flashed across his face. He crushed his lips to hers.

Feeling wholly alive for the first time, she drank of his open-mouthed kisses.

Chapter 43

Upper Galilee - *Three Days Later*

Lydia sat behind Kadar, resting her head on his back, as his noble brown steed, Valiant, crested the rock-strewn hill overlooking Nathan and Elizabeth's olive farm.

He gave Lydia's knee a light squeeze. "I've been thinking about where we should live."

"You're afraid I won't be happy with what you're about to propose?"

Amazed how well she could read him, he pulled Valiant to a stop, dismounted, and caught Lydia as she slid off the horse's back. "That's my *valkyrie*, not a cautious bone in your body."

She laughed and kissed his cheek. "Tell me."

He exhaled heavily. "If Nathan and his olive grower friends give the selling of their olive oil over to me, I'll be spending most of my time in Rome."

"You hate Rome."

"It's too large and crowded for my liking, but it is the ideal place to trade and sell goods." He traced her dusky-rose cheek. "I'll pay for a Roman marriage contract. Our union will be legal in the eyes of Rome."

"I doubt my father will give us a single thought," sadness underpinned her voice.

Jokul and Gerta had probably long since forgotten him, if they were even still alive. These days he viewed their betrayal in a new light. If the pair hadn't dealt treacherously with him, he'd never have met Lydia. Likewise, her father's failings were his gain. He drew Lydia into his arms. "The pain will ease."

"I feel sorry for my father, not myself. He'll never know what an honorable, *good* man I married."

He kissed her forehead. "We should go. Alexandra and Brynhild won't stop worrying until we arrive." He'd sent Old John ahead a few days ago to tell Nathan and Alexandria to expect them.

"I can't wait to see Bryn," Lydia said.

Kadar had paid to free Brynhild. The sturdy woman's broken arm had mended quickly. He had sent her on to Galilee before leaving Egypt, as her greatest wish was to be reunited with her *darling kitten.*

Lydia pulled back. "Will we have enough money to bring Brynhild and John to Rome too?"

"No, but I'll work something out. We will have to live simply."

"I am a good seamstress. And Bryn can take in mending." She reached over and patted the brown steed's long nose. "And Valiant, we have to take him with us too."

The brown steed whinnied. Kadar smiled, then smoothed his hand over Lydia's flat stomach, anticipating the day when she would cradle their child. *Their child.* He hadn't known this much happiness existed. "You will have enough to do watching over our babes. And I promise to see you are always provided for."

"Of course you will."

Her utter trust in him was a gift he would cherish until he breathed his last breath. "Your sister and Nathan might not look so kindly on our marriage."

"Alexandra and Nathan defied Father's wishes. We will have their sympathies. Rest assured they will welcome you to the family with glad hearts."

At peace with their chosen path, despite what others might say, he nodded. "Your sister and Brynhild will be very glad to see you."

Lydia smiled wide. "I plan to hug them till the sun goes down."

Chapter 44

Happy but tired after the second wedding feast of the week, Lydia smiled, watching Brynhild bustle across the yard, straw-colored braids bouncing with each firm step. Alexandra and Brynhild were getting along wonderfully as they conspired to fuss over Lydia.

Bryn arrived by the stone fire pit huffing for breath. "I've packed the pitifully small saddlebags with as many provisions as I could stuff into them for the trip."

"We were supposed to do the packing together, later," Lydia said. "Sit and visit now, please."

Kadar and Old John made a space for Bryn.

Bryn swiped her hand. "I'll sit when I awake in Paradise. Until then, I need to keep these old bones moving, or they'll grow stiff."

Old John's eyes twinkled with mischief. "She'll get her rest on the ship."

"Trust me," Bryn said, "floating in a wooden box upon a great body of water harboring giant serpents will not be restful."

"You don't have to come, Bryn," Lydia repeated for the hundredth time. "You're a freewoman, able to do as you please. Nathan and Alexandra would love for you to stay here."

Bryn batted away the suggestion, and pointed at Old John. "This one keeps assuring me the sea serpents are dead and gone."

The one-armed man climbed to his feet. "Come on, Old Girl, I'll help you carry the saddlebags to the barn."

"Don't *Old Girl* me," the pear-shaped woman chided, her ruddy complexion not quite hiding her blooming blush.

"Do you want my help or not?" Old John countered.

"Do you think I walked over here for my health?" Bryn said.

The pair hobbled off, exchanging their version of pleasantries.

Alexandra and Nathan invited the wedding guests to walk with them through the flowering olive grove.

Sharing a smile, Kadar helped Lydia to her feet.

The children raced ahead, little James with them. Her heart twisted. He'd grown a head taller over the past year. She longed to spend more time getting to know her sweet son, but didn't have the heart to interrupt the fun he was having with his cousins.

When they reached the edge of the orchard, Nathan and Kadar put their heads together to talk about the coming harvest and plans for shipping premium olive oil to Rome. A few of the neighboring olive farmers were also interested in having Kadar sell and transport their oil.

Alexandra looped her arm through Lydia's. "My emotions are so mixed. I'm thrilled you and Kadar married, but I'm sad you won't be near to see little James grow."

They passed through a screen of white blooms. Lydia stopped to sniff the sweet blossoms. She hated to lie to her dear sister, but it couldn't be helped. "You promised to read my letters to him." Judith's family had refused to give little James to her, leaving Lydia and Kadar no option but to steal him away from Judith.

Alexandra sighed. "I will make sure James writes to you."

Lydia plucked a waxy white petal from a low-hanging branch. "Your boys will soon be big enough to help Nathan."

Alexandra laughed. "They *help* now. Nathan is incredibly patient with them."

Little James came running toward them, his small legs and arms pumping hard. "Lydia! Come see the nest I found."

Hearing her son call her Lydia made her heart ache. Kadar told her to be patient, to give little James time to grow used to the idea she was his mother. She held out her hand. "I would love to see the nest."

Small, sticky fingers clasped her hand. Her son reversed direction and tugged her along. "There's three blue eggs in the nest."

"Blue is my favorite color."

"They're the same color as Kadar's eyes," little James added excitedly, halting beside a sapling bristling with green shoots. He smiled up at her. "Kadar promised to teach me how to ride his horse. I asked him if he would wait until next week, because my uncle is getting married on Wednesday. He rolled his large brown eyes. "Weddings. My grandmother needs my help, you know." He shrugged his small shoulders. "My cousins and I get to beat the rugs with sticks. That's fun. Will you be at the wedding, Lydia?"

She shook her head. "We are leaving tomorrow."

"I wish you could stay. My grandmother makes good almond cake, better than anyone else in the whole world." His love for his grandmother shone through every word.

Lydia's throat closed. "Where is the nest hiding, sweet James?"

His face screwed up. "I'm Judas. Did you forget?" He broke away from her, parted the leafy branches. "See?" he crowed proudly.

Baby James had been hers, but this tousle-haired boy wasn't her darling baby. He was Judas of Rumah. Eyes blinded by tears, she leaned in to look over his shoulder. "How lovely."

He reached for the nest. "The eggs are small, small."

She touched her hand to his slight back. "Don't disturb them." Wasn't it exactly what she was about to do—disrupt her son's happy life? Once they were a half day's ride from the ship, Kadar would double back and sneak into Judith's house in the middle of the night and take little James. Discussing it with Kadar and old John and Bryn, Lydia could only think of the risks involved. She hadn't thought about how frightening and upsetting it would be for her boy.

He turned disappointed brown eyes on her. "I'll be gentle. I promise."

"You wouldn't mean to hurt them, but might anyway." The knife in her heart twisted deeper.

He backed into her, and his little warm body melded with hers. "Do you think they will hatch soon?"

How would she live with herself if she gave him up? How could she live with herself if she wrenched him away from everything he knew and loved? "I'm not sure."

His cousins raced by, shouting for little James to come along.

He pushed away from her and ran after his friends. "I'll come check on them every day," he called over his shoulder.

She hid her face in her hands and gave into the tears.

Large, strong arms encircled her. "What's wrong, my *valkyrie*?"

She turned and tucked her face against Kadar's wide chest. "Taking little James away from his happy life would be terribly selfish of me, wouldn't it?"

Comforting hands stroked over her back. "Are you hoping I will disagree?"

She was. "What if he thinks I didn't care? Didn't love him?"

"Your sister won't allow it to happen. And the hundreds of letters you will write to your little James will be saturated with love."

She released a shuddering breath. "I can't do it. I can't take him from everything he knows."

"We could stay in Galilee, move deep into the back country to avoid the hounds trying to collect on your father's reward."

Memories of the dank caves and Judas the Zealot's somber face arose. If it was just her, she'd brave the wilds and her fears. Could she ask it of Kadar? She knew, without question, he would protect her and find a way to provide for her and their children. But was it the life she wanted for them—always looking over their shoulders, sneaking into Rumah for furtive visits with James?

She pressed closer to Kadar. "We will go to Rome."

He hugged her tighter. "Have faith. Someday little James

will seek you out on his own."

"Do you think so?"

"I know it. Though many years passed after I rescued you, my heart didn't forget. Little James won't forget either. He will remember his mother as kind, fun, and loving. He will want to spend time with his mother."

She grabbed onto this hope. "And we will have a happy home waiting for him when the day arrives."

Kadar's blue eyes beamed. "You are certain we will be happy?"

She wrapped her arms around his neck. "I believe it with my whole heart."

Epilogue

Napoli, Italy - *Ten Years Later*

Lydia stood at the white marble rail edging the veranda of their sprawling seaside villa, watching the newest of their three-tiered triremes glide across the harbor. Peace reigned in Rome, and more riches than ever flowed into the city. Kadar's one hundred-ship fleet plied all the waters of the Great Sea, carrying goods and passengers to and from cities large and small.

Her heart rejoiced seeing their sandy-haired children—two boys and two girls—sitting at Kadar's knees. Though they'd acquired riches aplenty, Kadar never boasted of his wealth.

She smiled, hearing the love in his deep voice as he read to their children. Of the many accomplishments her talented husband could boast about, the one he was most proud of was his ability to read and write. They had been welcomed with open arms into a nearby synagogue, where a young, brilliant teacher had offered to school Kadar. The two were now the best of friends.

Young James's presence made her joy complete. Kadar had assured her repeatedly her first-born son would seek her out. Six months ago his grandmother Judith had died, and young James had sent a note saying he wanted to visit Lydia. The biggest difficulty they'd had to overcome was her initial habit of calling her precious boy James instead of Judas. Today, he sat next to Kadar sketching pictures of palaces. Like his uncle, young Judas hoped to become a master builder.

Concern for her brother James was the only blight on her

happiness. Still shocked at the drastic steps James taken to spite their father, she prayed constantly for her brother's redemption.

Alexandra and Nathan loved each other more than ever, and their orchards continued to thrive and prosper, thanks to Kadar negotiating top prices for their premium olive oil. Kadar and Lydia planned to take their children to Jerusalem next year to visit their cousins, aunts, and uncles, and to worship at the Temple.

Much had changed in Jerusalem, but much had stayed the same. Herod ruled as king, although his penchant for ruling with an iron fist made for an uncomfortable peace. Lydia no longer had to worry about her father. He was dead, murdered two years after she left the country. His death had been a relief. These days she hardly ever thought of him.

She sighed. Kadar heard and sent their noisy, boisterous, wonderful children off to play. Then her broad-shouldered, blue-eyed, magnificent husband stood and strode toward her.

Her breath caught.

A glorious smile spread across his rugged face.

Lydia held out her arms, overjoyed and ever grateful she'd followed her heart's desire.

Historical Note

I wanted the heart of book two of **The Herod Chronicles** to be centered around Kadar and Lydia's story, starting from the low period of Herod's flight from Jerusalem and ending when Herod is named king.

The problem was, Herod's life was far from quiet during the years Kadar was in the copper mine. Some of the highlights include: Julius Caesar's murder, the execution of Herod's ally and friend Sextus Caesar, civil war erupting in both Rome and Jerusalem, John Hycranus's double crossing of Herod and Phasael. But the two most important events, by far, were Antipater's death by poison (along with Malichus's subsequent execution), and Herod's engagement to Mariamne. Wrestling with how to include pivotal events stretching over many years, yet keep the focus on Kadar and Lydia, I compressed the events and moved Antipater's death and Herod's engagement to Mariamne to the time of Kadar's release from slavery.

Those interested in a full account of Herod's activities in their proper chronology should look to the writings of the Jewish historian Josephus.

As in book one of the series, I use the name Hasmond instead of Antigonus to avoid confusion, as I felt Antigonus was too similar to Antipater.

For the sake of the story, I heightened the drama surrounding Herod's escape from Jerusalem. Though a bold man who comes across larger than life, Herod did not fight his way out of the city. Josephus reports Herod departed quietly in the middle of the night *'without the enemy's privity.'*

Herod did, however, make a valiant desert stand against the army pursuing him through the wilderness. And keeping his vow to construct a monument to that great victory, Herod *'some time afterwards built a most excellent palace, and a city round about, and called it Herodium'*.

Lastly, Herod met his brother Joseph in Thressa, not in En Gedi. I made the change in order to use the majesty of Masada as the backdrop to the moment Lydia and Kadar openly declare their love to each other.

I hope you enjoyed reading this book as much as I enjoyed writing about this fascinating episode in Herod's life, wrapped around Kadar and Lydia's sad yet lovely story.

Sign up for **The Herod Chronicles Newsletter**
to receive updates on new book release dates, cover
reveals, and free excerpts.

http://mad.ly/signups/117768/join

I would love to hear from you.
wathomas723@gmail.com

Visit me online:
www.WandaAnnThomas.com

www.facebook.com/wandaann.thomas

Author Bio

My interest in first century history was sparked by reading the works of the Jewish historian, Josephus. The inspiration for the HEROD CHRONICLES came about while I was doing research for another project and I discovered the particulars of Herod the Great's career. Herod was a fascinating, complicated man who left behind a lasting legacy during one of the great turning points in history.

I am a lifelong resident of southern Maine and have been married for thirty-three years to a wonderful man who supports and encourages me in all my endeavors. I've spent the last twenty years brightening smiles in my career as a Dental Hygienist. I start each day bright and early at my computer drinking coffee and writing. When the weather allows my husband and I golf, averaging three to four rounds a week. We have three lovely children who are out of the nest and building interesting, happy lives of their own. I confess to being overly fond of chocolate chips cookies, winter vacations spent in sunny Florida, and my large boisterous family.

Made in the USA
Middletown, DE
04 March 2017